North by Polaris

North by Polaris

Book One

The Michael North Series

Michael Oliver

Copyright © 2015 Michael Oliver

ISBN 1505447542

ISBN 978-1505447545

All rights reserved. No part of this publication may be reproduced or transmitted in any form or by any means, electronic or mechanical, including photocopying, recording, or any information storage system with either prior permission in writing from the author.

The right of Michael Oliver to be identified as the author of this work has been asserted by him in accordance with the Copyright, Designs and Patents Act, 1983.

This is a work of fiction.

www.sailingshipsatwar.com
@sailingships42

Edited by Catherine Hanley
www.catherinehanley.co.uk

Cover Design by Good Wives and Warriors
www.goodwivesandwarriors.co.uk

For his encouragement and support this book is dedicated to Raqib Shaw.

Chapter 1

<u>Thursday 7th November, 1799</u>

Cluney Ryan cursed as he tripped over the outstretched feet of another corpse. The stench, the dripping damp and the overwhelming presence of death on the gloomy orlop deck of the captured French ship was causing three of the other five sailors to throw up, hardened though they were to life on board ship. The French surgeon and his loblolly boys were caught in the glimmer of a few dim, smoky lanterns at one end of the deck, ghoulish scarlet hands plunging into writhing bodies, blood smearing and splattering their clothes as they worked on half-dead men. The desperate sounds of pain stabbed Ryan's ears; the awful smell grabbed and squeezed his bowels. Why was he in this hellhole?

A gruff voice sounded. 'Cluney, yer bald-headed son of Satan! Fetch Mister North, I got a live officer 'ere.'

Muttering obscenities about Bosun Giles, Cluney Ryan made his way through the torn shambles of the captured frigate's deck and peered up through the gathering darkness. The fire-red clouds on the horizon were reluctantly releasing the setting sun and filling his mind with more images of blood. Faint with exhaustion like all the prize crew, he staggered on to the deck on stiff and painful legs. He pressed his hands to his back to squeeze out the constant ache and turned away from thoughts of sleep that the night should bring. He moved forward as he saw the tall lieutenant on the foredeck, hands on hips, staring up at the pathetic rags of sails that hung from the shattered yards above.

Knuckling his forehead he coughed to draw the officer's attention.

Michael Orrick North looked down at the stocky Irishman and frowned. 'Speak up, Ryan the Rogue, I can't hear you.'

Cluney Ryan gritted his teeth at the epithet Rogue, with which he had been saddled by North who spoke the Gaelic as well as Cluney did and knew the true meaning of his given name. Recalling that the 1st lieutenant's hearing had been affected by an exploding musket fired by a marine beside him during a raid on the French batteries at Dieppe a few years back, he raised his voice and bellowed: 'Sir, the bosun wants to see you on the orlop, he's found a live officer, so he has.'

North grunted and walked along the gun deck, shouting to hurrying men as he passed. 'Get that mess cleared away, if we don't get underway soon we'll be on the rocks before we know it!' 'Leary! Get those prisoners pumping faster!' 'Costello! I want the forecourse aloft *now*, not next week.' The cacophony of mallets, the screeching of stays and blocks and the angry shouting of men was tremendous as they strived to get the damaged ship moving. There was no rest for the prize-crew as the ship drifted dangerously towards the Portuguese shore. The noise diminished as North reached the lower parts of the ship.

Hengist Giles, Shropshire giant and bosun of His Majesty's frigate *Phoenix*, of 36 guns, was crouched beside the supine figure of a red-haired man whose faded blue coat was blackened by his life's blood. 'I don't think he's got long, sir.'

North stooped. 'You're right, Giles. Can he hear us?'

'I can hear you, Devil's spawn!' The words were strained from the lips of the half-dead 2nd lieutenant of the *Epée d'Or*, his English spoken with an Irish accent.

'Your name, sir!' said North, dreading the answer he already knew.

'You ask, Michael North, you that shared my laughter in days gone by in Connemara? Am I so raddled by the years that you know me not?'

North jerked his head back. 'Colm Kennedy! So, you are here now, traitor.'

Kennedy's face streamed sweat. His voice labouring, he gasped, 'Traitor, say you? Traitor to whom?'

He tried to lift his head as he gasped. 'An English Protestant king? Some absentee Lord starving his people to fill his purse?

He sank back again his voice becoming weaker as he tried to form his words. 'No, Michael, 'tis you and your like that betray Ireland. You lick the shoes of the English like whimpering curs.' His anger seemed to give him more strength. 'Damn you for taking your forty pieces of silver from our oppressors. Well, I am going to die now, so hear my last curse....'

But the curse never came. Malcolm Kennedy, exiled from his native Ireland and serving a regicide regime in France, was dead. Never again would North's boyhood companion walk the springy peat turf of his Connemara home; never again would they skip flat grey stones over the wide waters of Galway Bay or suck the sweetness of tiny wild strawberries from under the hedgerow as they walked the Burran together.

North shook his head in sadness and reached down to close

3

the dead man's eyes. Midshipman Lang, looking over his shoulder, asked, 'You knew him, sir?'

'Yes, James' murmured North, 'he was a wild one but true to his own self. At least he will not be hanged as a rebel.'

North returned to the quarterdeck. Cast in the darkness of the night, the moon had been hidden by clouds that seemed to mock the crippled ship by rushing away from her. He saw that a sail had been rigged and set on the foremast yard. Despite the ominous groaning that spoke of a split in the mast, her sail was drawing well enough to bring the prize in a slow curve away from the shore and towards the distant *Phoenix*. That ship had her own troubles: her injuries were similar to those of her opponent and all three of her masts were stumps. He could see a spar being raised vertically on the forecastle to serve as a jury mast.

As the moon cast cold light through a break in the clouds a cry came from forward of the mast, 'Deck there! Sail bearing due west, away beyond *Phoenix*!'

North rubbed his unshaven chin. He walked forward but even with a telescope could barely distinguish more of that ship than had the lookout. The strange ship could be of any nation, as likely English as French, but he feared the worst. 'Can you give me more sail, Philips?' he called to the master's mate.

'Aye, sir, we'll have the main-course and main stays'l set this minute!' He did better. Ten minutes later as the frigate got underway the foremast also carried a topsail. Then, desperately tired and cursing the two dozen prisoners forced to work alongside them, the crew had the spanker set which made the steering a little easier.

Having lent his own weight to the process of heaving the huge canvas aloft, North rubbed his hands together to warm them. 'Then let us get those prisoners below and clear for action, Mister Lang. Mister Philips, lay a course for the *Phoenix.*'

....

Lawrence Chandler had reached the rank of post captain without spectacular success in the matter of combat, though he had some prize money from the capture of a French privateer and two brace of merchantmen to show for his year in command of the *Phoenix.* Being posted into *Phoenix* was more a result of influence than merit and he was humble enough to recognise the difference. Right now he wished that he had followed his father into parliament and sailed a desk rather than a ship of war, though some men combined both occupations. He scanned the gundeck and was unhappy with what he saw.

A week ago he had sent off to Gibraltar his senior midshipman and 46 men with two captured ships - a privateer and a trading brig. With 50 men and his First away on the latest prize, wallowing a league nearer the shore, 15 dead and nine more unlikely to see sunrise, his reduced and battered crew had done their best to clear away the damage of battle but there was still too much to do. A further reduction in manpower resulted from the 18 sailors and marines needed to guard the prisoners below who had been taken from the second French prize, a lugger which had capsized an hour ago.

The strange ship working its way towards them, tack-on-tack, was a large Frenchman; that much he had been able to discern in the gloom of approaching night. *Phoenix* had seven guns out of action on the leeward side and three on the starboard. The gunner had opined that there were two more he could not answer for due to a probable split barrel on one and a suspect carriage under the other. Chandler ordered two of the 18-pounder starboard guns to be heaved across to even up his broadsides.

His 2nd lieutenant, Joseph Spall, was beyond this world, his mind gone as he stared out of a broken gun port, spittle dribbling from a corner of his mouth as he hummed to himself. Chandler leaned over him and adjusted the bandage around his head, gently wiping away the blood that had trickled down his face.

His 3rd lieutenant's cold remains were being sown into a hammock as he stood there. Where was North? His brilliant second-in-command had few career prospects owing to his upbringing and unjustified suspicions by their lords and masters of having Catholic leanings – even if his father had been a baronet.

Chandler felt frustrated for him, though North never complained. At least nobody could deny he was an outstanding officer with the courage of a tiger. Chandler had no doubt that he was moving mountains to get his ship underway, but would he arrive in time to help?

Chandler clenched his hands behind his back and walked over to the wheel to speak to the master. 'How much longer before the Frog reaches us, Fred?'

'I would say half an hour to be in range, sir, but I think Mr North should arrive about the same time; he is definitely underway. With luck he may have some of his guns ready.' Frederick Bishop was a short, broad-shouldered man and with his hat removed to reveal the white fringe of hair that circled an otherwise bald head, he resembled more a parson than a ship's master.

'With fifty men to sail the barky, guard the prisoners and keep the pumps going there will be precious few to work those guns.'

'Sir, give me 25 hands and I will row out to meet Mr North; that way we should be able to man more guns on the prize.'

Chandler was suddenly energised. 'Do that, Bishop, and ask Kersey to come aft and act as sailing master in your place.'

Bishop had the 16-foot cutter pulled alongside the ship from where it had been bobbing on its painter at the stern. It would be a tight fit but he had to get 25 men into it; it was the only boat left to the ship.

The prize they had taken at such great cost was the *Epée d'Or*, which carried 38 guns; though both ships were similarly armed with 18-pounders on the gun deck, the French had an extra gun each side. *Phoenix* had shipped eight 32-pound carronades in her upper works which had proved decisive in close engagement in response to *Epée d'Or's* six 24-pound carronades and six long nines.

The French sail came closer and it became clear, even in the fickle moonlight playing hide and seek in the clouds, that it was a larger ship than *Phoenix*. The approaching ship was a 64-gun liner.

Five days ago, though it seemed to them like years, *Phoenix* had 271 men aboard. Now Chandler calculated in his head: they were reduced by the prize crews and the reinforcements and by 15 dead and more than 40 wounded. Now there were but 100 men and boys to fight a French 64, the floating home to more than 500. Even if North could bring *Epée d'Or* to the game, there was precious little chance of either crippled ship surviving the might of a 64.

The waiting was nearly over. The 64 fired off a bow chaser to test their quarry's nerves; the shot cleaved the waves a cable's length short. Looking over his shoulder Chandler could see *Epée d'Or* now much closer, her prize-master urging her on with a waved sword from the forecastle as Bishop and his men scrambled up the side. Four cables; about half a mile, yes, she should be in time.

A shout from aloft; they had way, *Phoenix*'s jury-rigged foremast was holding and the canvas creaking as it filled. 'Now at least we have some chance,' Chandler murmured to himself.

As if by some preconceived plan *Epée d'Or* was ranging steadily out to larboard to try to meet the enemy on the opposite side to that which *Phoenix* should reach if the wind stayed easterly. It seemed that the captain of the 64 was so contemptuous of the two smaller, badly damaged ships as to maintain a course which would place him between two fires.

With the arrival of the master on board *Epée d'Or* Michael North now had 49 men spare to serve the guns and a dozen to trim sails. With nip and tuck he could crew a shortened broadside. He chose to place four men on two of the carronades and the rest to work eight of the 18 pounders. The only strategy he could think of was to get as close to the Frenchman as possible and batter his hull; he ordered quoins to be placed under the rear wheels of the gun-carriages to depress the muzzles for the first broadside. He had no sharpshooters. There were with him ten marines but they were deployed below with swivel guns and muskets covering 95 Frenchmen, many of them wounded, the remaining 130 surviving crew having been thrust into the prize's boats. They were now abandoned, floating without oars in the hope that they could be picked up later for the head money.

The lookout called down again, 'Sir, to larboard, another ship. She looks like an Indiaman, she's under all sail!'

An Indiaman – one of ours or Dutch? North's thoughts were racing. If the newcomer was an HEIC ship, she could just about add equality to the battle. But would she fight?

What if she was VOC? Would she back the Frenchman? Either way the newcomer would have no reason to risk herself, even less if she was Dutch. Although she would be able to see the fix the British ships were in, the desperate efforts of the Batavian Republic's government to stay out of the war should keep her apart despite the Hollanders' nominal allegiance to France.

If she was an English Indiaman it was likely, even in the time of war, that she would have most of her guns either dismantled, and buried under tons of cargo or impossible to use through more cargo piled around them on the decks.

The flush deck of the approaching ship distinguished her from a navy 64, though in length and rigging she looked similar. 'Come on, I need to know,' these questions were distracting North from the approaching battle but the answers were crucial.

As if to answer his question the newcomer fired off a signal gun to larboard and started to turn towards the enemy 64. Now as the moon threw a more powerful beam he could see when she showed her skirts that she carried the Company ensign on her mainmast, thirteen horizontal stripes, red and white alternating, and although distance made it less certain, the Union Flag canton in the corner. It was after all remarkably like the flag of an American neutral in the dim moonlight but surely, that country would be unlikely to have a ship of this size in these waters. She fired off another single shot and the flag dipped and rose again. The gun! She is with us!

The French 64 seemed to hesitate and swing wildly to her starboard after a single hasty broadside aimed at *Phoenix*. But too late to cut and run. Her three opponents were surrounding her. First *Phoenix* fired, then *Epée d'Or* and a few minutes later as she shortened the distance, the Indiaman, also began firing every gun she could bring to bear.

Bright flame suddenly burst from the Frenchman, springing from every gunport; fire that clearly defined the battle for half a mile. Then an explosion that had every hand pressed to an ear with the shock. And she was gone as if she had never entered that troubled sea.

The awed silence that followed was disturbed by an almost reverential sigh from a grizzled waister, 'Oh Holy Christ.'

There was some debris, even a sail which was afire, its flames quickly quenched by the waves. All that remained was just scraps and shards; little more to hint at the existence of a 900-ton ship. North found himself speaking calmly as if they were spending the evening fishing with long lines for black bream off Portland Bill, 'Mister Lang, Mister Bishop, take the boats if you please, see if there are any survivors.'

Chapter 2

Friday 8th November, 1799

Finding himself at table for dinner on the Indiaman was a new experience for North. The ship was the *Alfred* of 1400 tons launched from Northfleet on the Thames in 1790 and owned and captained by James Farquharson. She was well-founded but the usual practice of the Company was to replace their ships much sooner than in the Royal Navy, so this would probably be her last voyage. Her commander and owner, being somewhat more intelligent than some of his confreres, had replaced most of her cannonades with the more effective carronades and had mounted 24 long 18-pounders. This had contributed to her effectiveness in the short battle as well as assuring a safer passage through the Indian Ocean.

North raised his glass of claret to the captain. 'Sir, once more, our grateful thanks for your timely intervention.'

Farquharson replied in kind. 'To the Royal Navy, Lieutenant. Tell me, have you discovered anything concerning the French 64, even her name?'

'There were but two survivors, both private soldiers; however, we know her now to have been the *Proteus* out of Toulon last week.'

Farquharson nodded. 'I suppose this habit the French have of carrying almost as many soldiers as crew is to compensate for lack of sailors?'

'Well, they don't have marines, in the sense that their soldiers serve more temporarily. They have a low percentage of trained sailors. Making up shortages by simply posting soldiers and calling them sailors makes their crews weak, I believe. Our ships may carry smaller crews but we have a higher percentage of able seamen and specialists.'

One of the two ladies present in the cuddy, the Honourable Emily Paget, laid down her knife. 'Lieutenant, is it true that your captain fell moments before the French ship exploded?'

He looked at her; she was fair-haired and lovely. Her complexion had darkened under the Indian sun and this emphasised that she was a little older than the rest of her manner and her body would have had one believe. *Alfred* had sailed from Bombay fifteen weeks ago, North had learned, bound for the Thames; she carried a mixed cargo of tea, spices and timber but also six passengers including Emily Paget. The other lady was Mrs Margaret Somers, who sat alongside her husband Francis.

'Alas, Miss Paget, he took a stray splinter of oak in his vitals. The surgeon has hopes for a recovery but he is very low at present.'

'In that case I will have my maid look out some beef cubes for a good broth. Served with sherry that will fortify him.'

North was probably ten years her junior but he was very much attracted to her; however, his temporary command of *Phoenix* and the *Epée d'Or* made it unlikely that he would met her again. He had found out from a cheerful officer that the lady was on her way home to marry the effete scion of a minor but rich barony.

The conversation turned to the Company's ships and the ladies discreetly withdrew. Due to the events of the day, the meal had been more substantial instead of the usual supper of cold cuts, but as was customary on Company ships the port was only passed once rather than several times as during the two o'clock meal. *Alfred* had replenished in Madeira and the food was excellent. It was supplemented by fresh salads grown in tubs of earth on the ship's forecastle; a common enough practice on Indiamen where passengers expected far better food than that available to crew. It gave North something to think about. It would be impracticable to grow green-stuff on a large scale in a man-of-war but perhaps for the sickbay it could be accomplished.

As Farquharson saw North to the ship's side, cigar in hand, he said, 'Ever thought of taking a commission from the Company, North? Though not excessive the pay is adequate, particularly in time of war, and most of the captains carry personal ventures which can be very lucrative. On this voyage I have several hundred pieces of excellent porcelain, a hundred-weight of fine spices and bolts of silk for my own trading. Furthermore our crews are all volunteers and we can afford to select the best of them. I have a new ship, the *Hannibal,* fitting out on the Tyne. She should prove a fast sailor and needs a good captain.'

North chuckled, 'Tempt me not, sir. I see how you feed yourself and the size of your officers' quarters alone would be worth it but I am bound to seek my future with the King's navy.'

'Aye, well, forgive me for mentioning this but I believe you are from Ireland, though your accent shows little trace. That reduces your chances of equal treatment I'm sorry to say. Excuse my bluntness.'

'It's true I was born in Ireland of an English family. My father was protestant, land rich and cash poor and the baronetcy too obscure. Some might say he was also far too kind to his tenants and thus shared their poverty. I certainly love Ireland and cannot deny it just to advance my career, though I have nothing but loyalty for the king. Although I expect I will need luck to progress, I will settle for his navy.'

Back on board *Phoenix*, as North's grateful stomach noisily recalled his splendid meal, he brought himself back to the grim present and the state of the ship. Captain Chandler was supine in his sleeping place. North had command, though none of his 'officers' except the 4th lieutenant, who now commanded the prize, were commissioned. One acting lieutenant was barely sixteen. Farquharson had offered to slow his passage to allow some mutual protection as far as the Channel and since *Phoenix* was in worse repair than her prize, her masts being particularly weakened, North had decided she would be towed by *Epée d'Or*. Farquharson had been good enough to send over some spars and canvas which was of great assistance. Earlier North had sent all available waisters and the carpenter's crew from *Phoenix* to the prize to rig as much canvas as possible, with the result that *Epée d'Or's* courses and topsails on all three masts were now filling; with two jib sails, both sprit sails, all three staysails and the driver it meant that she was well enough rigged.

He went below to the cabin. In the captain's bed-place two men hovered anxiously, Samuel Brice, the captain's clerk, and George Naylor, his steward. Lawrence Chandler was in considerable pain but attended by a competent surgeon who had been travelling in *Alfred*; his wound had been treated and now his anxious steward checked hourly for the signs of infection that often arose from splintered oak.

Chandler forced a smile. 'Well, Michael, how fare our rich cousins?'

'They do well for themselves, sir, though in view of their welcome help I begrudge them not. We are underway now, *Epée d'Or* towing us, we should see Plymouth Sound in four or five days. I am sorry to have to report that I decided to send 200 of the French crew to the shore under a cartel, so we will lose the head money. I believe having so many prisoners on the ships would be too dangerous.'

'A good decision. Have the master enter it in the log and make an entry in my journal for me to sign. Michael, there is a walnut box under my desk. Bring it to me, please.'

Chandler's desk was well worn and adorned with such random carvings as to rival any school desk. The box in question retrieved, North took it to Chandler's bedside and opened it at his request with a small brass key from a ribbon about the captain's neck.

'If I should die, Michael, I wish you would make sure that the contents reach my sister, Isobel. She is my only living close relative and my heir.'

Samuel Brice patted his captain's shoulder gently. 'You will heal, sir, I am sure.'

'The surgeon agrees with Brice, sir,' added North.

'I never heard a lie from your lips to this moment, my friend, but you must see that the fever is already upon me and before long no doubt I will rave. I have had Brice write down my last will and testament. So, with Naylor and Brice here to witness, I appoint you my executor in this matter. In the box you will find a grey envelope which contains my two shares in the North West Company of Montreal. These I give you in my will in thanks for your friendship and loyalty and as a small reward for seeing that Isobel is protected against scavengers. It is not much but I feel that these shares may have a considerable value some day.'

Little did North know it, but the two certificates in his hand were to have a momentous impact on his life.

Chapter 3

Tuesday 3rd December, 1799

It had been raining all morning, but it stopped about an hour before Captain Lawrence Chandler was laid to rest in the walled graveyard in Dulwich village. The funeral party had walked from Christ's Chapel of God's Gift along the well-graded village street, local people standing bareheaded and silent outside the two hostelries, the Greyhound and the Crown.

North looked about him.

Chandler's younger sister had been a surprise to him; she was quiet but no mouse. When he had first entered her house she had him almost unbalanced for a moment. Perhaps his heart did not exactly beat faster but she was very attractive to him.

Over the previous week Isobel Keen had found herself looking forward to his daily visits as he joined her in dealing with the various visitors that had business involving her brother's estate. Ever since her husband had died she had shied away from involving herself with another man, but Michael North was disturbing her peace of mind in a very nice way. When he had been alone with her she had a feeling of warmth inside her that she thought she had forgotten.

Her marriage had been one that had suited her family and like many women of her class she had accepted the match dutifully and perhaps too romantically. Her husband had been a handsome and athletic man but her experience of what passed for love with her had been disappointing. It had been a miserable and painful three years that she had now firmly consigned to the past. She had consoled herself by believing that such a state was normal and was her lot in life. The circumstances of his death had radically changed all that. Shot to death in a duel over another man's wife, she had shocked herself by feeling more relief than grief.

It had been two years ago when she was just 25, that her husband had met his end in the nearby Sydenham Woods. Her brother Lawrence had brought her into his house since not only had her husband frittered away his patrimony in gambling and high-living but had also wasted her dowry.

Unable to settle with his creditors she had lost her home and practically everything except the clothes on her back. Her own parents dead, Lawrence had been her only close relative and alternative to going into service as a governess or companion. So she had become his housekeeper and also looked after his property interests in the area.

North had witnessed the capable way she dealt with her brother's man of business, quizzing him over each and every disbursement and finally sending him off with a very red face after securing every penny entrusted to him. She had written to Chandler's prize agents to such effect that they had come rushing to Dulwich Village to assure her that legal redress would not be necessary; indeed, they had advanced her a respectable sum of money in cash on the spot.

North looked across at her as she stood beside the chaplain. She was straight-backed and even in thick black mourning with a heavy bonnet shielding her from the elements her fine figure and pretty face would have attracted the appreciative stares of any man she passed in the street. She tucked back a loose strand of brown hair under her hood, stooped and cast a handful of soil on to the lid of the coffin just lowered into the ground. A neighbour, Edmond Rossiter, had been walking very close to her side and offering unnecessary assistance along the street; he now slipped a hand under her elbow to assist her rising and North saw her grimace in distaste.

Looking around the company there assembled, North saw about a dozen village notables among the distant family members. There was also a rear admiral and several cloaked naval captains and lieutenants, a red-coated infantry major and some friends of Chandler's who had made the journey from Town to be here.

There was also a large contingent of villagers, respectfully to the rear of their betters along with those of Chandler's crew whom North had brought with him to the village as a guard of honour. Another man, a stranger, stood out from others, not merely because he was very well dressed in black with a fur hat, but because he stood well to the back of the crowd. He was also very tall: several inches taller than North who was a six-footer himself. He stood alone and in watchful silence, speaking to no one and intently scanning the mourners rather than the priest and coffin.

The party began to withdraw towards the village and some refreshment at the Greyhound inn. North was a little surprised but happy when Isobel Keen walked quickly to his side and slipped an arm under his. 'I hope you don't mind, Mr North; but I wish to take advantage of you. I'm afraid Mr Rossiter is a little too attentive for my present mood.'

'My pleasure, Mrs Keen.'

'Michael, please won't you call me Isobel? You have been in the village for more than a week now and I suspect Lawrence charged you with watching over me, which you have. So we must already be friends, yes?'

North felt warmth despite the weather. 'Why, yes, Isobel, I am very happy to be your friend.' Inwardly he baulked a little at some mildly lewd thoughts he had about her.

Ranging up in full sail on his starboard side was the comfortably round form of Edmond Rossiter. Before North could continue the conversation, that worthy luffed up and crossed North's stern to come alongside Isobel's larboard.

'Ahem, Isobel, my dear, if you have a moment later in the afternoon I would like to conclude our discussion concerning the mill? Sorry, sorry, not appropriate, forgive me.'

Isobel settled her arm more firmly under North's. 'I might as well tell you now, Edmond, that I will not be making any decisions soon about the property. I have no pressing need to sell and I have to think about the tenants.'

'Of course, of course. Well if you will excuse me...the chaplain... ah.' He bustled off.

Isobel let out pent-up breath. 'They hover over me, Michael, the crows for their pickings. Edmond is not as bad as some, mind you. Would you believe a coven of the village hens came to me and seriously suggested I need to marry soon because they feared I would fall prey to an adventurer, intent on my sudden wealth! Not that it is anybody's business. Being Lawrence's executor you know that I will be comfortable for life but hardly a wealthy prize.'

'Wealthy? Perhaps not, Isobel, but a great prize as a woman, certainly,' said North, startled that he had put his thoughts into words so unguardedly.

'Hmm. You and I will have to have a serious conversation I think, Michael!' she said, looking up into his eyes with the broadest smile he had seen on her face since he had brought her brother home ten days past. She could not resist impulsively squeezing his arm before leaving him to talk to her cook.

As North was contemplating the content of that serious conversation he was slightly startled as a quiet voice said, 'I wonder if I might have a word, Lieutenant?'

He turned to see the man in the fur hat, who had approached unobserved. 'You have the advantage of me, sir?'

'Forgive me, my name is William Thompson. This is neither the time nor place to talk. May I suggest we meet at the Crown; I have a room there as you do? I think what I have to tell you will be well worth your while and may I say I have the approval of the Admiralty to talk to you. Say, dinner at seven?'

North looked at him carefully, the mention of the approval of the Admiralty intriguing him. This approach was obviously not official or he would have received orders to that effect. 'Very well, Mr Thompson, I will join you for dinner.'

Thompson had reserved a private dining room overlooking the cricket pitch behind the Crown. North always thought that cricket pitches in winter gave a mixed impression of helpless gloom and the hope that comes for the sublime laziness of a summer afternoon.

He was able to get a better look at the man without his cap

22

and coat.

Thompson was six years older than North, in his mid-30s, and over six and a quarter feet tall; not a man who could rely on being inconspicuous. His face was darkly handsome and although elegant in his bearing he had the build of an athlete. He returned North's gaze with equal interest.

He reached over to fill North's glass. 'What I am about to discuss with you comes about through several strange coincidences. You are, I believe, a shareholder in a certain Canadian company?'

North blinked. 'Well, I don't know how...'

'Forgive me, Mr North, it will save time if I tell you that my information is from an innocent source that has your interests at heart. At this stage I would prefer not to elaborate. If it was not for the unfortunate demise of Captain Chandler it would be him I would be talking to but as you are now the owner of those shares, here we are. I realise that the shares came so recently to you that it is unlikely that you have any deep knowledge of the North West Company?'

With slight asperity, North said, 'Enlighten me.' He was more than a little displaced in his temper with the thought that others had been discussing his personal affairs behind his back.

Thompson elaborated on the history of the North West Company of Montreal.

'To start with I must take you back to the rival company, the renowned and wealthy Hudson's Bay Company ...'

The Hudson's Bay Company had been in existent for more

than two hundred years but it was only fifteen years ago that the North West Company was formed. A group of traders in furs had set it up with 16 shares, firstly in a Montreal Coffee House, then moving to their own premises in Vaudreuil Street. The company was effectively a smaller but important rival of the Hudson's Bay Company. More recently it merged two years ago in 1787 with Gregory, McLeod & Co, now with 20 shares. Though these shares were sub-divided over and again to trappers and agents, the primary or voting share gave the holder the right to sit on the Board and vote.

Some of these voting shares were held by Montreal agents and some by wintering partners – those that oversaw trade in the field with the native people.

Thompson explained that the two shares now owned by North had most likely been the property of Capt Chandler's late uncle, an American called Peter Pond, one of the original partners. By the end of 1787 two men had formed a company called McTavish, Frobisher & Company that controlled 11 shares and therefore the North West Company. It was important to point out that the partners did not form or control policy in the company without restraint. This privilege was reserved to those that held voting shares – the Board.

In the intervening years there had been a loosening of Frobisher's control in favour of Simon McTavish and some of the voting shares had been sold to a few of the other partners so that previous control was lessened. Frobisher, who had married the daughter of a French Canadian surgeon, had begun to spend much of his time after 1792 as a member of the Lower Canada Parliament for Montreal East and as Seigneur of Champlain. He had held one particular voting share which he sold to Patrick Small, another investor and partner. This share was gifted by Small to the girl child, Charlotte that he had with a Cree woman. Charlotte had recently married William Thompson's brother, David.

North interjected. 'Just a moment, can I just make sure I understand this? I now own two of the 20 voting shares and your sister-in-law owns one share? Is that correct?'

Thompson nodded, 'Bear with me; I know it sounds complicated but you will see the significance in a moment.'

While with the Hudson's Bay Company David Thompson had made a name for himself as a great explorer, being called by the native people *Koo-Koo Sint* – Stargazer – having followed in the footsteps of the company's surveyor, Peter Turner. It seemed, however, that he was much inclined to throw in his lot with the North West Company, having become involved through his relationship with Charlotte Small and also being unhappy with the Bay Company's policies. So two years ago he had left the larger company and joined the North West as its senior surveyor.

Relationships between the two fur trading companies had always been poor. The Bay had the best fur trapping lands – they owned all the country around the Hudson Bay and every river than ran into it, stretching over more than a quarter of the land area of Canada and reaching down into the American republic to the west of the Great Lakes. The North West had substantial lands but the quality of the furs was inferior to that of the Bay.

Thompson came to the present day. Looking around him, he rose and checked that the door was closed and that there were no eavesdroppers.

'The British government sent me out to Montreal last year where I met with my brother. He had walked 80 miles to Montreal to be there and he introduced me to several partners of the North West Company. What they told me matched the suspicions of the Foreign Office.

'The French would like nothing more than that the United States of America should join them in their war against us. Causing trouble on the borders of Canada and the United States would suit France well, not to mention their obvious longstanding designs on retrieving Canada itself. On the other hand the Americans are rightly suspicious that France will ally with Spain to the extent of re-asserting their links with Louisiana and Florida.

'Spain's weakness has meant that the United States has had virtually the freedom to run the port of New Orleans to their great advantage. If France is in a position to control New Orleans, we believe this might drive the Americans into *our* camp. But if France can pre-empt that and in some way have America also at war with us, it would be to *France's* advantage.

'For our part the war with France means we have few troops to spare to defend such a long frontier to the north of the United States so any degree of common interest with the Americans would be welcome. We still maintain a naval and military force in Halifax, though actual troop numbers are quite small. In fact the military presence is barely adequate.'

North nodded. 'I would say *in*adequate. It seems to me that having lost the colonies, the government does not consider America to be very important.'

Thompson agreed. He leaned over to refill North's glass and

went on to explain that spies in Paris had discovered details of a plan which involved a turncoat in the North West Company who was planning, in league with a counterpart in the Hudson's Bay Company, to bring about a major escalation of the so-far minor but significant armed skirmishes between the two rival fur companies. This could lead to widespread disruption and conflict throughout the areas controlled by the companies.

At the same time several companies of Spanish mercenaries, joined with two regiments of French regular infantry, were preparing to leave France and invade Canada, using the desolate Sandwich Bay on the coast of Labrador as a point of entry.

Then, under the pretence of all being mercenaries, paid to support the Hudson's Bay Company's troops, they would push south and take Halifax, which would also be attacked from the sea by a French squadron. Thompson emphasised that there was no suggestion that the majority of the Directors in Canada of the Hudson's Bay Company or the North West Company were in any way complicit or even aware of this expedition.

The squadron included four ships of the line and several heavy frigates under Rear Admiral Étienne Eustache Bruix accompanied by troopships. Once they were in control of Halifax more troops would be sent from France to push the invasion south and west to regain the lands that had been ceded to the British following the Seven Years War and add the rest of the British territories in subsequent campaigns. Unrealistic, perhaps; but to counter these moves Britain's thinly stretched forces would be placed under even more pressure.

Admiral Vandeput, who commanded the naval forces in Halifax, had just three 64s – the *America*, the *Asia* and the *St Albans* – two 32s, *Andromache* and *Cleopatra*, and two sloops of war. These ships were needed for defence but also to patrol the whole eastern coast down to the Caribbean. On Newfoundland Station was posted at present just one 20-gun brig, the *Camilla*, with two smaller vessels. The station commander and governor in St John's Newfoundland, Rear Admiral Pole, was still in England, his 64-gun *Agincourt* being refitted. The 18-gun brig *Voltigeur* was being advertised as about to take passage for Newfoundland in a few days.

There was a further complication in the form of divided national loyalties of the two main shareholders in the North West Company which was causing conflict on the board and could be resolved only by the two people holding the balance of the shares – Thompson's sister-in-law and North. If this failed then the North West could find itself funding and backing the French invasion.

Thompson reached into his jacket and pulled out a folded, sealed paper, handing it to North, who read it.

To Lieutenant, the Hon. M. North, RN, by hand of Mr W. Thompson,

Evan Nepean, Esq., Secretary to the Navy, 30ᵗʰ November, 1799.

Lieutenant, I am directed to request that you present yourself at 64,St.James Street, London, on Thursday the 5ᵗʰ day December, at 10.30 in the forenoon precisely, dressed in civilian clothing. You will introduce yourself by the name Mr Jones of Addington to Mr William Newton, the proprietor. He will conduct you further; no conversation should take place.

You will exercise full discretion in your comings and goings so that none shall be aware of these instructions, excepting the bearer of this note.

I have the honour to be, your obedient servant,

Nepean.

North stared at Thompson in amazement. 'What on earth is this about?'

'I am sorry I cannot explain further, the person you are to meet will be known to you, at least by name and reputation. I assure you that there is nothing to cause you concern. Now, shall we not take a final glass of port wine?'

Chapter 4

Thursday 5th December, 1799

As he walked up through St James' Park, North turned his thoughts back to the previous afternoon.

He had called upon Isobel and sat with her in her drawing room. She had out on the large side table a pile of papers, deeds and plans. As the executor of her brother's estate he had looked through these documents as they talked, glancing as discreetly as possible at her profile and happily absorbing what he saw.

'It seems,' said Isobel, 'that the estate is unencumbered due to Lawrence's prudence. This house is on leasehold land, of course, but there are 53 years to run. The maximum lease is 63 years, though there is some dispute, since the College Statutes say 29 years. In any event the 29-year rule seems to apply to the nine cottages I now own in the village – therefore these leases expire in 18 or 16 years' time. I understand renewal of the leases is fairly automatic. There are also six small freehold properties in Kennington near Westminster and a harbour house in Weymouth. All these except the Weymouth house are rented out and I have the leases and sub-leases.

'Then there is the mill on the County Brook at Beckenham with a large parcel of freehold land. I have had my legal advisors write to each tenant, maintaining the present rentals and other terms and requesting that next quarter day the rents be paid directly to my account with Featherstone's Bank in Fleet Street.'

She paused for breath before continuing. She frowned. Michael North's presence was having that same slightly disturbing effect on her.

'I have settled sundry small debts from the funds with Hammersley's Banking House and the account now stands at £15,567, twelve shillings and four pence with interest due on the next quarter day. I intend that half of the Hammersley deposits be transferred to my Featherstone account. There is £2,989 with Henry Hoares' bank and the prize agent's account shows currently £3,002. Concerning the matter of the realisation of the other prizes, you are aware that this is proceeding slowly.'

North had been listening attentively. It was his duty as Chandler's executor to know these details but he found himself wishing the conversation was more intimate.

Isobel added, 'the mill at Beckenham and 30 acres of land thereabouts is rented out to Mr Leonard Springer and his son and I intend that, despite two offers to buy, I will keep that arrangement in place at present.'

North smiled broadly, somewhat bemused by her attitude of determination and command. 'You have no need of me, Isobel; you are the finest executor one could wish for.'

She dropped the papers on to the desk and looked directly at him. She made up her mind. Moving gracefully, she stood directly in front of him, her face turned up to his. 'Do you want to kiss me, Michael?' she asked.

Since this was indeed the thought in his own mind he was not surprised by this sudden question, he smiled and said, 'I do indeed!' and proceeded by enfolding her in his arms and devouring her lips for over a minute.

'Um, well,' she gasped as she broke away. 'That was anything but half-hearted!'

'S-sorry, I'm afraid I was taken with the moment.'

'Be taken again, dear sir, and know that I enjoyed it very much!'

For a blissful five minutes he demonstrated that his passion for her was extremely sincere. Her hair tumbled down from its pleat, she gasped and said, 'Stop, I beseech you, I am enjoying this *too* much!'

Releasing her, he walked over and opened a window to dispel the warmth threatening to engulf him.

'Do you love me, sir?' she asked anxiously to his turned back. She was almost shaking with horror at her own temerity.

He turned back to her and took her in his arms once more. Actually, he thought, that is exactly how I feel.

'With all my heart, Isobel.'

She laughed, 'I thought people had to know each other well before falling in love but now, for the first time in my life I am sure what love is. I love you, Michael, and if I may be so bold, I want you. However I have no intention of spoiling what should be a beautiful courtship by allowing you to bed me so soon. Patience may be difficult for both of us but I entreat you to suffer with me in denying that pleasure for a while.'

'With difficulty, dear Isobel.'

'Now where were we ... oh yes, the estate.'

They both laughed. She pinned up her hair and took his hand as they discussed the few necessary things needed to finalise her inheritance. He asked her to speak to his own trusted family solicitor and man of business since she was clearly unsure of the probity of the man who had handled Captain Chandler's affairs. Unlike their late father, his brother Sir James was a shrewd manager of financial matters and if North was absent at sea and she needed help, North was sure he would be there for her.

....

North had left Dulwich from the Crown at three, taking the mail-coach to London and walking to his brother's house in Panton Street to spend the night. The house at No. 30, three doors from where the end of the street joined Haymarket, had been built nearly a hundred years before but was well-appointed and had a small but lavishly cultivated garden which had been the great love of his late mother.

His elder brother was at the estate near Blackheath that had come to him by his marriage but their old retainer John Brennan received him with obvious pleasure. Despite his brother's own acuity there had been debts against their inheritance that had taken some years to clear. Due to North's good fortune in prize money in recent years, a portion of which had been devoted to clearing those debts, the whole family was now financially secure and their servants had mostly been with them for many years.

St James' Park was quiet this morning; passing over the canal by the Chinese bridge North saw little human life, though in the distance troops were parading in the tented encampment in the park. Cold breezes of early winter were beginning to disperse the browned fallen leaves of autumn and a sleek young fox was nosing through the carpet in the hope of a worm or the delight of a small vole.

As he crossed the Mall and came alongside St James' Palace he had to jump quickly to avoid being spattered with mud by a passing diligence. He looked down at the borrowed breeches and boots from his brother's wardrobe, tugging at the dark green coat that was a little narrow across the shoulders, even if the waistband of the breeches left some room to be filled. He had not found a hat that fit him so had tied up his old-fashioned length of hair in a black ribbon and walked bareheaded.

He turned right into Cleveland Row on the north side of the palace and walked up St James' Street. His destination, 64 St James' Street, was home to the Cocoa Tree Club which had moved into the building the previous year after leaving nearby Pall Mall. Her new proprietors had decorated the premises with fresh paint and furnishings, perhaps to try to dispel its previous reputation. As 'the Club at Weltje's' it had a dire history for excess of all description. Weltje's amalgamation with the Cocoa Tree, which itself had a somewhat racy reputation for gaming, lifted the premises into a slightly higher level of Tory respectability.

North stood for a moment looking at the building. It was on three storeys with a garret above. There was an iron balcony on the first floor and a band-course along the line of the windowsills on the second floor. The bottom storey was oddly shaped on one side with a square-headed entrance door placed beside the passage leading into Blue Ball Yard, while on the nearer side as he approached there was a three-light sash window. In the centre of the street wall, below the

second-floor band-course he could see an inscription –
Universal Literary Cabinet.

North ducked his head to enter the Club, which at that time
was sparsely lit since members were not about in any
numbers at this time of the day. He heard feet shuffle and
turned as a rotund, completely bald man dressed in a long
claret-coloured waistcoat approached.

'I am Mr Jones of Addington.' North said, 'Are you Mr
William Newton?'

'Indeed I am, sir,' responded Newton in a cultured though
somewhat husky voice.

Without another word he indicated with his arm that North
should follow him through a large interior room which was
distinguished by a tall golden tree set in its centre.

He opened a door and led North out through a courtyard
stacked with bottles and barrels and pervaded by the sour
smell of ullage. On the far side of the straw-strewn yard was a
stable block against the wall. Newton walked in front of him
up a short wide staircase to a door opening into a long room
above the horses, and showed him in before retiring.

Here was indeed a wonder. The room was well carpeted with
exotic rugs that appeared to be of the highest quality and a
dozen or more deep sofas and chairs. The walls were lined
with shelves of books except for the longest wall at the rear
which had several dozen oil paintings of excellent quality. At
each end of the room was a writing desk. There was a marble
fireplace against each end wall, the logs snapping and
crackling as the welcome heat filled the room.

The only person in the room a heavily built man, past fifty years of age by his appearance, was dressed in black with a large white neck-cloth. He rose from one of the armchairs near the fire and advanced towards North.

North was again surprised. The man in front of him was none other than the Duke of Bridgwater, the wealthiest man in England, reported to be worth more than £2 million. Having been introduced briefly to him at Michael Bryan's art gallery in Pall Mall earlier in the year, North recognised him by his roman nose and well-filled cheeks, his sparse head of hair was covered with a light brown wig. In appearance though taller he was not dissimilar to the king himself.

'Mr North! Do come and sit with me and share this cheering fire. Not too early for a glass of Madeira, is it?'

'I will take a glass and thank you, your grace.'

'Do me the kindness of calling me Egerton, at least while we are alone. Now, let me look at you, Lieutenant North. Held by quite a few of your contemporaries as sometimes a mite too courageous but not lacking in intelligence. Given the laudatory name "Tiger" North by your crews, it seems. 29 years old, unmarried, middle son of the inestimable and much lamented Sir Richard North, lucky in prize-money but born the wrong side of the Irish Sea for some tastes. How would you like to be promoted to captain and made post by midnight tonight, huh?'

Almost reeling from this rapid fire litany and the final amazing question, North could only nod for a moment. Then pulling himself together he said, 'While I am aware you move in very high circles, your gr... sir, I can't see you persuading their Lordships to promote me that quickly.'

'On the contrary, North, it is a done deed. Even without the machinations of certain interests I represent – patriotic and honourable interests, I must add – your promotion was assured some days ago. I was merely adding theatrical zest to my comments. It would appear that the First Lord was much impressed by your conduct in the matter of the frigate *Epée d'Or* and your subsequent actions in bringing your prize and the *Phoenix* home, not to mention your career which has been crowned with considerable success on a number of occasions.

'I have to caution you his decision was not unopposed but, damn it, a lot of voices were against Arthur Wellesley for the same stupid reason. It matters not where you were born. Our country needs heroes, *don't blush* like some schoolboy being handed a book prize! Whether you like it or not with those damned good looks and derring-do, you fit the bill perfectly. More so, I might add than that philandering shrimp Nelson!

'Now, for reasons I shall explain in a moment, it don't suit us to have you too publicly on display, no it don't. We would prefer you stay slightly below the horizon so as not to attract the attention of Paris for a while. Let me refill that glass.'

North felt he ought to refuse more drink but, still stunned by the possibility he was made post, he simply nodded.

'Lord Egerton, how are you so connected with the Admiralty?'

'Good question. It so happens that opportunities in life and in business attach themselves to the well-prepared. I ached to do something for my country but, as you see before you, soldiering or sailing are not best suited to my figure – fine though it is, of course. A few years back I made the acquaintance with a quite remarkable man, the Westminster Magistrate, Dr Patrick Colquhoun. Another member of my little circle is my friend Michael Bryan, the art dealer, who also did well in business in Holland and Belgium. These friends and others are all joined in aiding the war-effort

'But to turn to more pressing matters. Thompson has already told you something of the Frenchies' plans to invade Canada, using the disputes between The Bay and North West as a diversion and a cover?'

North replied, 'An alarming plan, my Lord.'

'It grieves me to say this but Whitehall leaks information to the Frogs like a bottomless barrel, therefore much of what we are doing has to be kept very close -*very* close North. On the other hand sometimes those leaks can be used for some sleight of hand.

'You are probably aware that ships are normally only at St John's for about ten weeks of the year but they were kept back this year. Traditionally the two North American stations have had different functions – Newfoundland to guard the St Lawrence and thereby Canada, while Halifax is supposed to concern itself since the Rebellion with defending Nova Scotia and reaching down the American coast to discourage trade with the enemy.

'In my view we have repeatedly underestimated the importance of the Americas – hence the success of the Rebellion and the parlous state of our arrangements to defend Canada. Nevertheless, the powers-that-be are now beginning to realise that these deficiencies need to be addressed. In the meantime we need to keep Paris off balance and half-hearted in re-invading Canada.'

He shook his head and reached over to refill North's glass.

'Now what I am about to tell you is so secret that the only people at the Admiralty who know anything about it are Lord Spencer, Lord Arden and Secretary Nepean and only then since William Pitt thought it essential that working members of the Admiralty knew.'

North interrupted, 'Excuse me. Should you really be telling me this? After all, I am just a junior naval officer.'

His Lordship nodded and crossed his arms. 'Well, of course if there was a choice no doubt that would be so, but the part we wish you to play makes it necessary.'

He went on to describe secret intelligence obtained from Patrick Colquhoun's most trusted spy in Paris; a man who had the closest possible access to the plans of the Directory and Major General Bonaparte in particular. It seemed that Bonaparte had drawn up a number of plans for what could only be described as a madman's scheme to dominate the entire world. After the fiasco in Egypt it appeared his ambitions were aimed elsewhere, although he had not abandoned his dream of an Asian empire.

These plans included clandestine negotiations with the Spanish to help re-acquire New Orleans and use that place as a bridgehead to invade the United States – a scheme of which the Americans themselves were not entirely unaware. In that country their biggest fear was that the French would free the slaves in New Orleans and that this would lead to uprisings of slaves elsewhere.

Of course Napoleon had no wish for the Americans to know about their dealings with Spain since they might themselves pre-empt the re-colonisation before the French could take possession again. The French were desperately short of ships of the line. To this end Bonaparte was also trying to buy or bully from the Spanish six ships of the line. Similar designs to acquire Florida from the Spanish were being more forcibly rejected by them.

The duke continued, 'Some Americans are, of course, anti-British and even considered for a while joining a League of Armed Neutrality – which would have favoured France. The Congress in Philadelphia on the other hand seems determined to stay out of the war.

North had heard informed friends expressing the view that Bonaparte might try to regain possession of New France and drive the British out of Canada. On the other hand this would reduce his military resources nearer home.

Holding the territories of Louisiana and regaining New France would give France an area of land much bigger than the United States. To counter this, on behalf of their government, Mr Jefferson seemed to be negotiating to buy Louisiana from the Spanish or the French. The Americans' rights to use New Orleans and the Mississippi had been granted and withdrawn several times and no doubt they wanted a permanent solution.

'But back to Canada. It is true to say that we are in a strange position regarding its defences. We enjoy the goodwill of many of those people that are of French descent, since they have little liking for the Revolution. Furthermore the Act guaranteeing their religious freedoms means we don't upset the Catholics too much.

'Then there are the American Loyalists. Many thousands of loyal colonists came north after the surrender at Yorktown and settled permanently in Canada. An invasion from the United States is possible but the people themselves would resist and I am sure that the Americans remember full well the advantage of a local population resisting invasion and the invader having stretched supply lines.

'Lower Canada would be a tough nut for the Americans or the French to crack but Newfoundland and the Labrador coast are more open to invasion. Rather than their old harbour at Louisbourg which is now virtually defunct, Halifax would be a perfect place for the French to use as a base.

'To defend it there are some soldiers locally raised, the Fencibles, but the only regulars we have to spare to them are under-strength battalions of the 7th and 66th regiments and two companies of the Royal Sappers and Miners. These also need to be available for the rest of the eastern coast of Canada.

'Things are not good in Newfoundland. There is a small garrison which includes a high proportion of Irishmen. With the present discontent in Ireland it would not take much for a mutiny to take hold.'

'Not exactly a heavy defence force, Lord Egerton.' North observed.

'Indeed. Of course Admiral Vandeput has his marines but even then, still not enough. I have explained at some length because it is important that you know all the facts.'

'This afternoon you will receive a note to attend on Lord Charlie Arden at the Admiralty. He will know that I have discussed the matter with you but officially he has to pretend no knowledge. You will be offered your own command, which I trust you will find acceptable. He will give you two sets of orders, one officially recorded and the other known only to him, the First Lord, to Evan Nepean and to me. The official orders you will disregard. I assure you that you are thoroughly protected or I would have refused to be involved, you have my word on it.

'You will be given command of a suitable ship of adequate power and will be free of superior authority excepting the Admiralty itself. Secret orders will have you proceed as covertly as possible to English Bay, a small fishing village on the island of Anticosti in the Gulf of St Lawrence where you will anchor under a French flag and go on board the brig *Voltigeur* commanded by Isaac Thompson, a cousin of your acquaintance William Thompson.

'That ship, contrary to published information is already in the St Lawrence Estuary. *Voltigeur* will carry you into the St Lawrence to meet David Thompson. There you will learn more of our plans.'

North's head with spinning with all these facts and the promise of promotion and his own command.

After a few more brief words Bridgwater bid him a good day. 'On your return from the New World, whenever that should be, leave word here, and we will meet again. Good luck.'

On his arrival at his brother's house North found a summons awaiting him. At two o'clock he stepped out of the house again, this time in his best uniform, head properly covered and walked down to Whitehall to the Admiralty building, entering the black-painted door from the cobbled yard.

On receiving his name a clerk took him directly up the staircase to the Board Room past groups of waiting officers, much to their annoyance. Lord Arden was ensconced in a leather-backed chair on one side of the long mahogany table in the middle of the room, paper and ink in front of him. Charles George Perceval, 2nd Baron Arden, Member of Parliament for Totnes, was in his early forties, a lean but open-faced man with a broad smile. He rose to his feet and extended his hand.

'Well now, Mr North, the noble lord you met earlier let the cat out of the bag, no doubt, but I have pleasure in appointing you captain with immediate seniority and post, and handing you your new commission, which is to go on board and take command of His Majesty's ship *Aboukir*.'

North frowned, 'Excuse me, sir, but to the best of my knowledge the only *Aboukir* on the list is a 74, the French *Aquilon* renamed. She was taken at the Battle of the Nile last year but I thought she was too badly damaged to rebuild and lies at Plymouth waiting to be broken up. I have never heard of a first posting to a 74!'

'In fact she was officially towed out to sea and sank on her way to Chatham,' Arden said, smiling.

'But obviously she was not?' asked North.

'Correct. You are to command a ghost ship, young man. I trust you are not superstitious? The truth is that it suited us to let it be known she was beyond repair when in fact she was worked round to Buckler's Hard in March this year. Reports of her being in Plymouth at all have been exaggerated. I saw her but ten days ago. She is a fine ship, only six years old and the shipwrights at Buckler's Hard have worked feverishly but splendidly bringing her up to full fitness.'

His eyes gleamed with enthusiasm as he continued. 'She now carries twenty-eight 36-pounders on the lower gundeck, twelve 24-pounders, and eighteen 18-pounders on the upper deck, with eight 24-pound carronades and twelve 9-pounders on the quarter deck and forecastle. She is a mite heavier than the French designed her to be but I am assured she will swim and fight just as well. Of course she will carry a hundred or so less crew than the French are wont to use but in any case one of our jacks is worth either five Frogs, ten Spaniards, two Americans or one and one half Dutchmen and your ship is a match for an 80-gun ship. As to the unusual step to promote you into a 74, necessity drives our decision from several different directions, as you will discover.

'The dire shortage of a ship of the line in the area to which you are being sent is the reason for your being given this 74. By which I mean the Pacific coast of South America, of course,' he said with firm emphasis and a straight face.

'I am still puzzled by this command, sir, surely unusual for a newly promoted captain even if the reasons be sufficient?'

'But fitting for your official mission, which is to cruise the Pacific coast of South America and bring terror to French intentions there. We have information they have designs on Mexico from that side.' He again looked at North with the same straight face and North nodded.

'Indeed, sir, and being that the ship does not exist, a great advantage of surprise.'

'Inwardly he was exulting. His own ship and a 74 – it was unbelievable!

'Your orders, in fact *an authority* from their lordships, will give you complete independence and therefore temporarily the seniority of a commodore, though this must be used judiciously, of course. Yes, that is almost unheard of but it is necessary.

'Now, as to the matter of crew; you brought with you to Dulwich two midshipmen, The Honourable James Lang and Mr Keith Boswell, also the boatswain of the *Phoenix,* the cox'n and eight seamen as an honour guard for Captain Chandler; all of whom you keep.

'Mr Lang, having satisfied their lordships as to his skills by examination, is promoted to lieutenant; I had the pleasure of seeing him this morning and giving him his commission. At this moment he and the rest of your men are travelling down to Plymouth where a merchantman has been chartered to collect the Master and most of the warrant officers from the *Phoenix,* with 50 prime hands chosen by Lieutenant Lang.'

North listened attentively to the briefing.

'You will also have the followers that would normally be transferred with the ship's late captain. The rear admiral there has orders to produce a further 150 seamen from the ships at anchor in the Sound. The whole party will then be carried to Buckler's Hard where you will join the ship and read yourself in. You will note the ship has once more been renamed, and is now the *Prince Rupert.*

'The dockyard commissioner at Chatham, Captain Coffin, has been ordered to personally select 100 prime seamen, which with 200 from Portsmouth and a company of marines from Dover will provide you with most of the crew you need.

'You need not fear being palmed off with gaol birds, the sweepings of the Press and raw landsmen. Admiral Bridport will visit Buckler's Hard on the 20th December and if he finds

45

any that are below his own standards he will replace them from the Channel Fleet

'As to officers, I am obliged to Sir Sidney Smith for releasing one of his most valued lieutenants, Mr Spicker, as your Second, an older man but I am assured of the highest intelligence and ability. As your Third, I am sending you Lieutenant Lewis Shepheard, of whom I personally have great hopes. Lieutenant Lang will be your Fourth. I have not selected your First or your Fifth – who will also need to be a newly commissioned lieutenant. When I have found the right men I will send them down to you. Spicker and Shepheard, excellent though they are, are too junior in appointment to serve as First. I trust you will also have no objection to a suggestion of Lord Spencer that you find space for a family friend's 22-year-old son, the Hon. Charles Boyle, as servant or midshipman. Any questions so far?'

'I am still somewhat taken aback by my promotion, let alone the commission of such a large ship, my Lord!'

'Believe me in this, Captain North. If Lawrence Chandler had been alive he would have captained the ship but in my opinion we could not have chosen a more worthy substitute.'

After another half hour of discussion he left the Admiralty with two sets of orders, one for public use and a second secret set which he was enjoined to guard with his last drop of blood and only open 24 hours west of Ireland. He had at least ascertained that his crew would not arrive for another three days and that journeying down to arrive at the same time would be acceptable. Once there he would have less than three weeks to get the ship fully fit for sea and depart on Christmas Day.

From the Admiralty North walked through Haymarket to reach his tailor, Henry Hawkes at 14, Piccadilly. In the well-appointed shop he shook hands with Hawkes, who had an assistant produce two cups of excellent whole-leaf tea. When being told of his requirements Hawkes congratulated him heartily and, looking him over with a critical eye, nodded and said, 'the last time I measured you was about 18 months ago; hmm, I would say perhaps a little broader about the waist.' He flicked out his tape then consulted his record book, 'No, I am in error, in fact a half inch less.'

He assured North that he could have a dress uniform and an undress working uniform made up and sent down to Buckler's Hard to arrive by Tuesday next week at the latest. In the meantime the captain could take a coat from the rack which would be a reasonable fit. He selected one which was about the right size, and, producing a bright new epaulette, he sewed it in place on North's right shoulder where it would remain until joined in three years' time by a second epaulette on the left shoulder.

North knew that the coat was second-hand but it was in good condition. Hawkes would sometimes buy clothing from the relatives of deceased officers, often giving almost as much as he had originally been paid. In this way, without doing it ostentatiously, he was able to do something for a wife or child who might be on hard times.

After selecting a pair of white kerseymere breeches, several pairs of silk and woollen stockings and two white waistcoats, all of which were packed into a parcel by Hawkes' assistant, he left the shop and walked to his brother's house to collect his baggage.

As he was about to leave the house a man arrived and was admitted by a maidservant. He was in footman's livery and carried a package wrapped in brown paper. He handed North a note from the Duke of Bridgwater in which after greeting him, Bridgwater asked him to accept the gift carried by his servant and wished him well in his enterprise and joy of his command.

In the package was a rosewood case containing a pair of beautifully made pistols. North wrote a note thanking the duke for his kindness and assuring him he would take good care of the pistols. He smiled and shrugged his shoulders. This probably meant he would need to leave the pistols securely in the box! In fact, like many of his contemporaries, he favoured a heavy sea-pistol in battle for the fact that after discharging it, it was normal to use it as a cudgel.

His next priority was in the village of Dulwich but before hiring a chaise he made his way to the shop of Francis Thurkle of New Street Square where he purchased a new sword with a fine 28-inch Solingen blade. The hilt was of the five-knot design. The sword's balance was perfect and the simple black leather scabbard was of the highest quality.

He hastened through the late evening to Dulwich, arriving at the Crown at ten o'clock. He could barely stop himself from hurrying to call upon Isobel at that hour but restrained himself until morning.

The following morning at nine he walked to Ashtree House only to find that Isobel was not there, having left not more than half an hour since. However her maid handed him a letter with a smirk, which he opened impatiently in the lane outside the garden gate.

Dearest Michael,

I feel sure that you will come to see me but unfortunately a crisis has occurred at the Weymouth house which urgently needs my personal attention, I will not bore you with the details.

My dear, dear, man, how can I put into words how I feel about my gallant sailor? To say I love you seems bare and without force but I can only say how truly my happiness has been awakened by your coming into my life. For a few short years that seemed much longer I was wife to a man not worthy to polish your boots. Saying this is not disloyalty, simply fact that I can now look in the eye. Now, I believe, Heaven has given me a real chance of joy.

Leave word for me, darling, and an address where my letters can reach you and be assured I am yours and yours alone though the fulfilment of my awakened desires will sit heavily on me until I come to your arms once more.

I am, eternally, Your Isobel.

He was a little taken aback by the strength of her expressed feelings but since he was of the same mind, he was jubilant at the same time. Back at the Crown he penned a reply. Being unsure of where he would be when she wrote, he gave his brother's address and that of the master shipwright at Buckler's Hard.

Chapter 5

Friday 6th December to Sunday, 8th December 1799

North had taken a post chaise from Dulwich 12 miles to the Bear in Ewell where he was able to join the noon mail coach to Portsmouth. He was set down at the inn at Chandler's Ford later that evening. The following day at 8.30am he took a hired four-horse chaise to Weymouth reaching the George on the Melcombe side of the town. Though the distance was less than 65 miles it took until six in the evening as the horses staggered and strained through sodden and mud-filled highways.

When it finally arrived the yellow painted sides of the chaise could hardly be seen under the mud. Tired from the journey he was tempted to rest up at the George inn where he left his baggage but being mindful of the last time he decided to delay visiting Isobel, he left immediately. He was a nodding acquaintance of John Keys the landlord who welcomed him keenly and took care of his baggage. But North forced his tired footsteps onward the short distance to East Street where with some slight hesitation he knocked upon the door of No. 17, a double-fronted house built less than 20 years ago.

Isobel opened the door herself and threw her hands up in surprise before taking him in both arms and hugging him tightly. Though their feelings had been clearly exchanged in Dulwich he was taken back by what happened next. Pulling him by the arm without a word, she took him up the staircase to a large comfortable bedroom where she proceeded to tear her clothes from her body and urge him please to lie with her.

Half an hour later, as they were both still gasping for breath, she said, 'that disposes of my immediate problem, Michael, but why are you here?'

'My love, I have a ship and a promotion and I am bound for distant waters so I had to see you before I left, there was no alternative.' He went on to explain more fully.

She smiled and ran her fingers through his hair. 'I wish you joy of your promotion, Captain North, and of course joy of your command. This secret mission, should you have told me the details?'

'Isobel, I see no reason for lack of candour with you of all people. I love you very much. Besides through Lawrence I am come into possession of the North West shares and therefore you are involved as his sister.'

'When must you leave me?'

'I shall have a day and two nights with you, if you will have me? And shall I marry you before Christmas?'

She laughed, 'I did not expect such a proposal; really there is no need. I am happy to be your mistress or your wife for I have a certainty in me that you will be as true to me as I surely will be to you, such is my instinct for the depth of our love. You may marry me when you return, if you wish, but I hold you to no promise.'

'You mistake me, darling, I am eager to make our union official but the choice is yours. If I am to be away for months, which is likely, I simply wanted what was best for you.'

'We shall take care that I am not with child by tomorrow night but it is unlikely despite the fact that you will surely take your fill of me as I will of you. So let us have a happy plan to treasure while we are apart and you shall surely make of me an honest woman on your return.'

With those words they slept blissfully until morning.

....

After a day and two nights of happy closeness to Isobel the next part of North's journey to Buckler's Hard in Hampshire was in a hired carriage and due to the dreadful state of the road it took nearly three hours to cover 20 miles, but got him there by 11.30am. He looked out from the broad expanse of the dockyards to the Beaulieu River. There was only one fully rigged 74 at anchor and she was a delight to see. In the bright December sunlight she floated on the still waters like a powerful black and buff-yellow swan, her French paint being maintained and indeed not greatly different from the British pattern that had been common in the past seven or eight years. Her gun-port lids were open to the chill but fresh air and showed scarlet against the black. Her yards were rigged and set but bare of canvas and one of her cutters was being rowed slowly about her. He recognised the slim form and elegant head of his new 4th lieutenant, James Lang, as he checked the trim of the vessel.

He had not heard the approach of a man behind him who discreetly cleared his throat. He turned to the man in the uniform of a lieutenant who removed his hat. 'Good day, sir, Captain North, I presume.' He had a noticeable German accent.

'Yes, I am he and you must be Lieutenant Spicker, good day to you.'

52

'I must report that Lieutenants Shepheard and Lang have arrived but we still await the other lieutenants, sir. We have six midshipmen including four from *Phoenix* and one whom Mr Lang brought with him from being on shore at Plymouth. The other man is an older midshipman, the Hon Charles Boyle who is the younger brother of Captain Courtenay Boyle, captain of the *Saturn* 74.'

North said, 'I knew Captain Boyle when he commanded *Hyaena* in the Mediterranean; I know nothing of his brother.' He almost missed the slight frown on Spicker's face as he mentioned Boyle's name. If there was something worrying Spicker he was not so indiscreet as to mention it.

'Your steward arrived this morning with your trunk and two large kitbags from *Phoenix*. If you have any more baggage I will have it attended to, sir.'

North had memorised some details of his new officers. 'Your given names are Gustavus Joachim, I believe? How do your friends address you?'

Spicker smiled, 'In England, usually as Spick, sir. I have no objection to that.'

'Well, Mr Spicker, I think it bad for discipline should the common jacks hear you being addressed thus on board so, with your leave I will call you Gustavus.'

He took a good look at the man. He was a pleasant man, in his early thirties, his deep voice suiting his broad frame and solid face. He stood a little under five feet and five inches but his lack of height was more than compensated for by a natural air of confidence and if he was a favourite of Sir Sidney Smith it would be for his abilities as an officer, not from any connection of influence.

'Have you lived in England long, Gustavus?'

'My parents sent me to England in my tenth year to expand my education and through our English cousins the Spickers and Branders of Christchurch to obtain a berth as captain's servant. My father was killed two years ago by Russian bandits and my mother and sister joined us in England. I served on *Resolution* from 1780 to 1786 when I was advanced to midshipman. I passed my examination in '89 and was appointed lieutenant in '96 and posted to the frigate. For the past year or so I have been with Sir Sidney Smith on *Tigre* as 3rd lieutenant after he escaped from Paris. I returned to London as prize-master for three of his captures in Biscay in August.'

North knew that Spicker's posting to *Prince Rupert* was due to the glowing letter of recommendation by Smith, who was inclined to be somewhat vain and disliked any officer of talent being with him for too long. On the other hand Spicker's progress over the past almost 20 years had not been fast and North suspected his 'foreignness' might have held him back. In fact though his own seniority as a lieutenant was longer than Spicker's he was several years younger and had joined the navy twelve years after him.

'Well, Gustavus, I am sure we will suit each other well enough. Be so kind as to join me in the great cabin for dinner tomorrow evening as I will wish to get to know you and the rest of the officers better. Now shall we make our way to the ship?'

Lang had spotted his captain on the shore and had already sent the launch with alacrity. North was greeted at the quayside by the grinning faces of Cluney Ryan, and his Jamaican inkle-weaver, Reuben Hibbert as well as half a dozen other old *Phoenixes.* It transpired that fully half of *Phoenix* crew had fiddled, wheedled and tricked their way into the party sent from Plymouth.

'Rogue Ryan! I mean to advance you to second cox'n. Report to my cabin at six bells; I will give you some silver to rig yourself properly for the rank. Have somebody pick up my dunnage from the shipwright's office and bring it on board, *lively.* The rest of you stop your gawping and lean to your oars. Why, I have never seen such a crowd of beetle-headed, giggling old women in my life! You, Jubal Higgins! The moment we come on board get that filthy shirt off your back and a clean one on before I have the bosun take a cane to your backside!'

They stilled their chuckles but whispered, 'he's back all right.'

At the entry port he removed his hat to the ensign and watched as his red swallow-tailed pennant was hoisted to the main topgallant masthead to signify that the captain was on board. He would fly the red ensign as he was under direct Admiralty orders. Bosun Giles and two of his mates had shrilled three pipes in greeting and every man on deck except marines removed his headgear. Lang stood beside another lieutenant. The older man had a shock of red hair and a gangly frame with a height barely an inch below that of North, and he had a very young face: he was barely 23. This was Lewis Shepheard, the 3rd lieutenant, and North took an instant liking to him. After shaking hands with the two lieutenants he moved on to his sailing master, greeting him with especial warmth, quietly addressing him as Frederick. Most of his other warrant officers were mostly known to him except that there was not yet a surgeon or a cooper on board. There was, however, a chaplain. North frowned, quickly clearing his face as he reached the man. He was not in favour of Rooks on ships, from his childhood being himself lukewarm towards organised churches, but since the *Prince Rupert* was a 3rd rate, with 600 and more souls to her complement when filled, he felt he had little choice in the matter.

The marine captain – by courtesy addressed as Major – was Jolyon Bracewell, a bluff Yorkshire man who owed nothing to influence and everything to courage – a qualification of which North completely approved. Bracewell was newly joined with half his men; the rest were marching from Dover with his lieutenant to join the ship.

Turning to Lieutenant Spicker, he ordered the crew to muster for the usual address. In rows and ranks, smartly dressed seamen and bandbox-bright marines filled the spar deck and flowed over on to the foredeck. The pale sun emerged from thin clouds and shed cold light on the ship in the chill air.

North walked briskly to the quarterdeck, took station in front of his officers and senior warrant officers, took a parchment from a sealskin pouch under the tail of his coat and holding his commission in front of him, read himself in.

By the Commissioners for executing the Office of the Lord High Admiral of Great Britain and Ireland &c and of all His Majesty's Plantations &c.

To Capt the Hon. Michael Orrick North hereby appointed Command of His Majesty's Ship, the Prince Rupert.

By Virtue of the Power and Authority to us given We do hereby constitute and appoint you to His Majesty's Ship, Prince Rupert, willing and requiring you forthwith to go on board and take upon you the Charge and Command of Captain in her accordingly. Strictly Charging and Commanding all the Officers and Company belonging to the said ship subordinate to you to behave themselves jointly and severally in their respective Employments with all the Respect and Obedience unto you their said Captain; And you likewise to observe and execute as well the General printed Instructions as to what Orders and Directions you shall from time to time receive from The Lords of Admiralty or any other your superior Officers for His Majesty's service. Hereof nor you nor any of you may fail as you will answer the contrary at your peril. And for so doing this shall be your Warrant. Given under our hands and the Seal of the Office of Admiralty, this 4th day of December, 1799, in the 40th Year of His Majesty's Reign.

By Command of their Lordships

(Seniority, 19th day of November, 1799.)

The Commission had three signatures appended as required by the regulations: those of Lord Spencer, Lord Arden and Evan Nepean, the secretary.

Some captains on this occasion would go on to read aloud the Articles of War, a requirement many of them simply deferred to the nearest Sunday. Others had prepared speeches. North spoke for a few minutes directly and without notes.

'Men, most of us are new to this ship. Some of you have sailed with me before and others have not. We still await drafts from Chatham and Dover but for now we must make do with what we have. We are bound for foreign parts and there is little time before we must leave, so with no time to spare, we must all look to our duties and work hard to see that this ship is the best in the fleet. There will be practice at the guns once we are at sea but for now I want the officers, warrants and petty officers to get to know you and you to know them. So I will be watching keenly and I am sure you won't let me down.

'We have a fine ship, good friends and bright prospects, so let us with a cheerful heart and alacrity carry out our allotted tasks and be about our business.'

....

'So, what's he like, our lord and master, Cocker?' asked one of the hands transferred from the *Scipio* in Plymouth.

'Bit too bleedin' daring for my tastes! Savage he is, like a tiger,' grumbled Joe Cocker of the forecastle watch.

'Shut your yap, Cocker, you moaning slob! Captin North is the best officer I've ever sailed with, that's a fac',' a beefy topman said, cuffing the rat-like Cocker around the ear. 'There's many a man what knows 'im would rather sail with 'im than Nelson 'imself. What's more 'e may be strict but 'e's fair and don't like the lash. Play the game with 'im and 'e'll look after you; but cross him and run for cover quick.'

Cluney Ryan had been sewing a button onto to his best shirt so that when he went to the cabin to receive his promotion he would be more presentable.

Ryan's father had been a skilled gardener who travelled the island working in the houses of the landed gentry and even the Catholic bishops – though himself a vociferous protestant. Eventually he had become head gardener on the Earl of

Morne's estate. Cluney Ryan had been brought up to follow his father's trade.

When he was eighteen and in his third year apprenticed to his uncle Lewis Ryan, Cluney had been working in the gardens of an absentee English landlord in County Cork. He had gone for a Sunday afternoon walk by the sea when he saw the 32-gun frigate *HMS Heroine* bathed in sunlight a mile off shore.

As if entranced by the beauty of the ship he had walked ten miles to Cork Harbour and signed up as a volunteer that day. At times he had regretted his choice but for the most part his years at sea had been good ones; no more so than the years serving with North. He had watched the brilliant young lieutenant rise to command the 74-gun *Prince Rupert.* Now he was being appointed second-cox'n. It may not mean much in the way of pay but it was something to be proud of!

In the nearby wardroom Lieutenant Shepheard watched as the new senior midshipman the Hon. Charles Boyle, son of the Earl of Cork, poured himself a second glass of sherry and looked around him with barely concealed contempt. He coughed loudly and stared into the glass.

'Problem, Boyle?' he asked calmly. The officers present watched the two men. Lucius Bright, gunner's mate, hesitated in the doorway, having brought a report on the repair of a carronade slide for Lieutenant Spicker. The tall, bony Shepheard looked down at the equally slim, elegant 20-year-old whose uniform had not just been tailored but crafted.

Boyle said, 'this sherry is abysmal, old boy, not fit for the pigs of the lower deck. And by the way, I prefer that you address me by my title, Lord Boyle.'

'Do you now, laddie!' Shepheard rumbled.

The sailing master, having just stepped into the room, jerked his head at the gunner's mate to clear off before he witnessed something he shouldn't, and closed the door. The stuck-up young toff had been getting up everybody's nose since the moment he had flounced on board three days ago.

Boyle set his glass down and looked Shepheard in the eye. 'You may be senior to me on deck *Mister* Shepheard but in the wardroom I will be addressed with courtesy.'

'So you think courtesy is the same as respect, do you?' replied Shepheard. 'Respect and form require you to call me sir, until you pass me by on your way to being Lord High Admiral. Courtesy is secondary to discipline and on this ship, while I am senior to you, your nobility is irrelevant. If you are worth your lordly title you should know that. If you act properly you will automatically receive respect but until now I have seen nothing but improper conduct and arrogance.'

Lieutenant Spicker nodded behind Shepheard. 'Not only that, Boyle, but as senior midshipman you will act in every way to give a good example to the younger gentlemen. That includes less sherry. You are dismissed!'

After Boyle had left, his sherry now untouched, Fred Bishop shook his head. 'He's trouble.'

'Aye, Master, I think he is,' said Spicker, 'he's on board because the First Lord has foisted him on the captain and Boyle knows that means he might be able to take advantage – up to a point. I think he'll push his luck until he is slapped down. It's up to us to see that the captain doesn't have to crush him and thereby upset Lord Spencer.'

Shepheard asked, 'Where did he serve before, sir?'

'He was with Admiral Keith for a couple of years, then with Captain Louis on *Minotaur* who sent him off with a prize six weeks after he joined, probably to get rid of him. He's failed his examination twice and has been at the Admiralty fetching and carrying for two years. Let's see how he performs but I hold out no hopes.'

'A wonder they haven't just pushed him through to keep his pa happy?' asked the marine captain who up to that point had been quietly watching with interest.

Spicker shook his head. 'I expect it will happen sometime but even the Admiralty must know you can't just pass somebody who has the navigation skills of a blind, one-winged duck and not one single recommendation from a commanding officer.'

Harris, the wardroom servant, arrived with a steaming tray of boiled chicken joints and bowls of potatoes and peas and the company set about their meal with much fervour.

For the first time in his service separated permanently from other officers by the convention of command, North looked around him at the trappings of his quarters. He had no opportunity to imprint his own personality upon it with furnishings but he was pleased with the efforts of the person who had preceded him in permanent command. Despite the levelling effects of the revolution the French captain had equipped the great cabin and the other spaces with excellent furniture in walnut, chestnut and exotic woods; the walls were of panels of lighter elm, birch and paler woods that could be quickly removed when the ship was cleared for action. The apple wood bookcase held but ten books, all he had in his chest. In most British naval ships the captain eschewed any indulgence in his quarters as being 'Persian ' and a sign of moral turpitude but North would at least make himself comfortable – after all, this was his home.

He ran a hand along the ornate carvings on the edge of the walnut desk, closed the birds-eye walnut case that held his pair of chronometers, touched the rosewood of his pistol case and then walked through to the bed space in which hung a roomy box-bed and a small armoire cupboard that could be lifted up by two men to be carried below.

He reflected once more on his sudden and seemingly miraculous advancement. Each time he entered the ship he would be met with silence and bare heads; no man would dare speak one word to him unless bidden. His officers would move to the leeward side of the deck as soon as he set foot upon it and as if in the presence of God Himself, would remove their hats. He was a judge from whom there was no appeal. He would take no direct part in the running of the ship unless he deemed it necessary. On the other hand, every action the crew and ship took was his responsibility and failure would bring punishment down upon him and no other. All this, so suddenly.

Normally when a captain moved from ship to ship he would be allowed to take his personal followers, cox'n and crew, some warrant officers, clerk and purser and depending on the rate of his previous command, a number of able seamen. In his case he had with him what the Admiralty had deemed a courtesy, the followers of Captain Chandler.

He sat at his desk and carefully re-shaped a quill pen before making an entry in his journal. He raised the pen but paused as he listened to the noises outside the cabin and the gentle creak and groan of the anchored ship as it was touched by the incoming tide.

In all his years at sea he had never lost his fascination for ships and particularly one on which he was carried. Every hour of every day could bring a new challenge or indeed a new delight. Like most successful officers he had developed a sense or feeling that was exclusive to the ship. Now he would need to get used to the new peculiarities and foibles of this huge vessel. He smiled and dipped the pen. Then he moved the lantern closer – a necessary extra light even during the daytime in his cabin.

He was fortunate in his steward and clerk, both of whom had not only previously served on *Phoenix* with Captain Chandler but looked upon him with respect and loyalty. His steward entered from the half-deck.

'Ah, Naylor. What do you have for me?'

'Vegetable soup, then boiled chicken, potatoes and cabbage, sir. I made sure the cabbage was only boiled for one minute, the way you like it. If I remember, sir, you do not take coffee, so I took the liberty of obtaining some best quality teas and getting the purser to pay the account.'

'Excellent. Here, Naylor, in celebration of our new commission, take a glass of this burgundy wine with me. The landlord of the George in Weymouth supplied me with a half dozen, probably under the nose of the Revenue, I assume. I believe it is better than the clarets we usually get. I will have you go into Hythe town and buy some supplies for the cabin tomorrow, though be sure to use the lawful suppliers; the purser will arrange a cart for you at the New Inn.'

After eating he wrote a letter to Isobel before the opening the hefty pile of ship's books, forms and his new spotlessly empty journal. He took up his pen again with a sigh. Being in command was not a sinecure.

The provisioning of the ship was proceeding apace. Lighters were being towed up the river from Portsmouth filled with barrels of salt beef and pork, flour, dried peas, rum, biscuit, gunpowder, oats, nails and beer, boxes of sweet-smelling black tobacco and all the other hundreds of tons of items needed for the floating city. Water and wooding parties were plying back and forth. Other supplies were arriving overland together with twenty bullocks and a dozen pigs for the slaughter, several goats and sheep and three coops of hens for the officers; these besides fresh meat and vegetables being purchased for the crew while they were in port. From a trading brig from Xante came one hundred nets of oranges and four hessian sacks of currants through the shrewdness of the purser.

North checked every pistol and musket, rejecting several that were unserviceable, but while it was his responsibility, such was his trust in his purser that much of the other work was delegated to him. The purser at the peak of his exertions too often went without sleep but, unusual in those of his profession, North had noticed that he applied honest and meticulous principles to his work. Ledger rested across one forearm he listed each item, inspecting the contents of barrels, causing canvas and cable to be laid out and checked, berating a man for spilling flour.

The master too had responsibilities which included inspection of the ballast, stowing it to best advantage, seeing to the coal and firewood, ensuring that older stores were set on top of those newly arrived. He attended to the cable tier and the sail-rooms and kept the key to the spirits store. He also had a duty to inspect the carpenter's and bosun's accounts.

Shot came down to the shot locker via a long chain of men from the deck, working rhythmically, a fiddler lightening the work somewhat.

The bustle and noise was incessant but not unpleasant. Many long days were spent at such strenuous work, at the end of which North sometimes gave the welcome order for double issue of rum in appreciation of the crew's hard work.

As North was eating his evening meal in solitary comfort, the seamen of Mess 10, having the starboard watch this evening, were at supper with the rest of the watch but also had an hour's stretch until the second dog watch, starting at six in the evening. Then, two hours later, 'down all hammocks' and seven or eight hours of glorious sleep until the morning watch at four the next day.

Second Cox'n Ryan, having finished eating, was talking to Long Tom Leary, a seaman with an unfortunate pair of crossed eyes. 'Now, Tom, I'll give thee sippers of me next two tots if you write a letter for me to me Mam. I wanna tell her as how I've been promoted to second cox'n, bless the dear captain.' He was wearing his new bum-freezer jacket with gold-plated buttons to boast his status.

Leary, who wrote most of the Irish lads' letters for them, replied scornfully, 'Be gone y' cafler!'

'Póg mo thóin!'

'Up *your* arse too, Cluney, I ain't doing it for less than two gulpers!'

Several of the hands joined in, judiciously weighing the value of a page or two of writing against recognised measures of rum such as sippers and gulpers. Two of the younger midshipmen were hunting millers nearby and stopped to listen. They were soon distracted as a particularly fine rat scuttled by, its flour-whitened coat from raiding the bread room reflecting its nickname. In port the trade in rat-flesh was slow but, fattened up on weevilly biscuit, two or three months out and well away from the nearest port, each rat was worth three pence skinned and ready for the pot.

At the mess table, Len Cramp, topman, who was mess cook, returned from the galley with a steaming currant duff, much to the delight of those present; this effectively ended the highly technical debate about payment for writing a letter.

Chapter 6

<u>Wednesday 18th to Friday 20th December 1799</u>

This morning, having come on shore for the first time in days, North stood with arms folded looking with satisfaction at *Prince Rupert*. Beside him stood the lean figure of Henry Adams, master shipwright and, at 86, almost as spry as he had been 30 years before, probably the most respected shipbuilder and timber merchant in Britain. His secret of success had much to do with his open and agile mind. If he saw an innovation he liked he worked it over, tried to improve upon it and applied it and was not ashamed to say he had learned much from his French counterparts. Unlike some of his peers he refused to use green wood on his ships and the repairs to the *Prince Rupert* were therefore of much better quality than in most British ships, particularly since the French shipbuilder had also been a perfectionist. In the short time he had been here Michael North had become firm friends with the big-hearted Hampshire man, who, with respect to his age and skills, he always addressed as 'sir.'

'I am well pleased, sir. I am fortunate in my crew and must also thank you for your prompt and expert help.'

The thin-faced man nodded. 'She'll do, Michael. She is one of the best of her class and though one of the shorter length 74s she has an unusually low centre of balance, perhaps because of the extra elbows in the hold and more pig iron than we would load. That said, I recommend you have a boat or two sent off Chesil Beach or Selsey to tow my big lighter and dredge another ton or two of shingle. In any case I don't think the extra weight of armament above is any problem at all. When you try her next week my chief assistant would appreciate being carried upon her to see how she swims and report back to me – just out of curiosity. I have a mind in future to use that French idea of more ballast to counter heavier guns. You know they tried replacing *all* the 18s with 32-pounders, I think that was a step too far.'

'Your assistant will be welcome, sir.'

'I enjoy a challenge, Michael. I had this idea to copy some designs from Gabriel Snodgrass, the Honourable Company's chief surveyor who retired a year or two back. It's always a problem finding the right timber for compass timbers like knees and Snodgrass has got the builders to put iron knees and other fittings in the ships built for the Trade. I've been a shipwright man and boy but the fact is the navy designs are old-fashioned and expensive. Of course there's not much I can do to change a design once it is put in the contract.'

North chuckled. 'Especially with the Admiralty overseer watching your every move?'

'Oh, they're not so bad. James Williams was here for fifteen years and the new man Joseph Seaton who started last year is a fair man. In any case I can hardly complain about overseers since that is how I came to be at Buckler's Hard in the first place.'

Aboukir's original boats had been reduced to a 32-foot pinnace and two cutters between being captured and reaching Buckler's Hard. The full seven boat complement for a 74 was a 33- or 36-foot launch or barge, two 32-foot pinnaces, a 28-foot pinnace, two 25-foot cutters and one 16-foot, 4-oar cutter, which was usually called the gig.

North had decided to dispense with the third pinnace which

was always difficult to stow considering the amount of space needed for all the boats. In the past ten years or so it had become commonplace to stow two boats on davits which were set on both sides of the ship towards the stern. These were generally referred to as the quarter-boats and in *Prince Rupert's* case two new 28-foot pinnaces hung there.

The new launch sitting between the cutters was stowed on the deck with spare spars beneath when not in the water, as it was today, and the 16-foot gig would be lashed to its own cradle in line behind the three larger boats. It was the lack of the gig that was exercising North's mind this morning.

'How are your apprentices getting on with building the gig, Mr Adams?' he asked.

Adams pointed his pipe to the rope-walk. 'It should be finished by tomorrow. The lads decided to carvel-build it as opposed to clinker, so apart from *Agamemnon* you'll have the only carvel gig in the fleet.'

North replied, 'Personally I have no preference for either style though some argue the carvel is smarter and swifter in the water.'

The master shipwright looked around as a noise which North had not heard attracted his attention. A neat new two-horse carriage had stopped at the entry to the wide expanse of grass that led down to the slipways. From the carriage stepped a supple and obviously young woman dressed in a maroon-coloured cloak and bonnet. She looked down the slope at them and waved.

'I think you have a visitor, Michael,' Adams said with a grin.

Isobel ran to him and he swept her up in happy surprise. 'This is wonderful, darling,' he cried. 'I am so pleased to see you.'

She was breathless. 'I wasn't sure; you must have so much to do...'

Henry Adams withdrew discreetly. He and his wife had been more than pleased to entertain North in the Master's House at the top end of the small village and he had grown fond of the young captain. His own sons, Balthazar and Edward, were away. Balthazar was in London negotiating a contract with the navy to build another 74 and two sloops, and Edward was learning fresh ideas from a commercial shipbuilder in Aberdeen. Balthazar had taken over most of the business in 1795 when Henry had reached his 82nd birthday, though Henry was still very much involved. In fact Henry was a little wary that after he had gone to the great sail-loft in the sky and the war was over his boys would not have enough business sense to keep the yard going when peace came.

Without making his views known, North was aware and worried that Balthazar Adams was a man who had high ambition and a tendency to live above his means. He dressed elegantly and affected manners which, on his visits to Town had allowed him admission to Almacks and other places where the good and the great tended to gravitate. Edward was just as bad; he had built a yacht for his own use and was often seen cruising the Solent.

North took both Isobel's hands in his and smiled widely. She returned that delight and said,' I am on my way back to Dulwich but I had to see you for a day or two before you sailed, Michael. I hope I don't come at a bad time?'

North was thinking how much she seemed to have changed

70

since he met her. From what he thought had been a quiet, rather solitary person to what she was now, a warm, loving part of his life. 'Not at all, dear one. For propriety I must find a room for you with Mr and Mrs Wort at the New Inn but I would be pleased if you will come on board and approve the ship?'

'Very well, let us do that this afternoon after I have rested from the journey. Do you like my new carriage?' The carriage was lacquered black; her handsome matched geldings were grey.

'It is splendid, the horses particularly.'

....

Three hours later they talked about everything and nothing as they walked to the shore. Lieutenant Lang, having been warned that a lady was setting out to come on board, had arranged a bosun's chair for her. North climbed the man-ropes alongside her as she was drawn aloft.

There were 'wives' aboard though being a somewhat quiet and unusual port for commissioning such a large ship they were few in number. By 'wives' it has to be understood that the word was applied very loosely; loosely not being an inappropriate description of the ladies themselves, in course. Isobel, if she was aware of the didos being cut below, showed no sign of noticing. Life on one of His Majesty's ships of the line was in some respects not dissimilar to life in the bowels of most cities – ruffians and saints, sinners and evangelists, demons and angels.

Like a vast beehive the ship hummed with subdued noise below decks during daylight hours, sometimes a contented buzz; more rarely a disturbed roar. Men on watch did their work determinedly or reluctantly, depending on their inclinations, except that all was busy unanimity when 'He Next to God' strode the spotless decks.

Working with a will, all the upper works and spar deck were as alive as a busy market street. Lieutenant Spicker, his muscular torso in shirtsleeves, was adding his considerable strength to shifting a carronade on the forecastle with the quarter-gunner's team, not disdaining to work alongside them. Henry Adams, at 13 years old the youngest midshipman, newly joined, was the grandson of master shipwright Henry Adams. Lieutenant Shepheard was impressed by his already compendious knowledge of the quadrant and of navigation.

Parson Rumbold, his schoolmaster's slates under his arm, was wont to sort sheep from goats at every opportunity and as he approached the lady who had arrived with the captain he was mentally and visually assessing her. Too pretty by far but apparently modest enough; clearly not an innocent woman though. He scanned the fingers of her hand for a wedding band but was frustrated in this test by her dove-grey gloves. Her bonnet was large but not too fancy; her cloak covered her discretely but something... ah, yes, the look in the captain's eye... SIN! Oh, how he was beset by SINNERS on board this nest of evil men and harlots! Why did his captain not follow the example of Nelson and refuse to carry women? No, that was a bad example, Nelson was the arch–SINNER; a man who had abandoned his lawful wife to spend his life in a sordid relationship with a painted whore whose husband was so deeply in thrall to Satan that he allowed his wife's adultery under his own roof! Oh Lord, how long, oh Lord?

He extended a hypocritical hand to greet the woman and smiled so falsely that even the circling gulls cackled in laughter.

The courtesy of introducing Isobel to the unwanted cleric over, North turned to introduce Mrs Keller, the wife of the carpenter, who with her nine-year-old twin boys and a huge basket on her arm was about to go on shore to walk up to the market. The large, cheerful, young German woman dipped a knee to the lady and greeted her with kind words. Maria Keller, in common with most of the hands and all the women, liked their captain. Three years ago on *Phoenix* Maria had seen him as a young lieutenant, wounded in battle, urging the surgeon to look after her husband who had a bad head wound that to this day still troubled him. Clear to her that this was the captain's woman she showed her happiness and approval in her ready smile.

The carpenter, the gunner and the purser were all married. Because of a relaxed interpretation of Admiralty rules, as the senior warrant officers they had wives and several children living aboard but the lovely Isobel was a welcome sight and to the crew it was somewhat satisfying to realise that their captain had a human weakness after all.

Having spent ten minutes showing Isobel around the main deck he ushered her into his quarters and, in the privacy of his day cabin, took her in his arms and feasted on her lips. Hand-in-hand they stood inside the gallery looking out through the stern lights at a line of swans and cygnets as they made their stately progress across the Beaulieu River.

'Shall you come over to the New Inn for supper, beloved?' asked Isobel, 'I am on the menu.'

He grinned, 'Splendid idea, darling. What do you think of the ship?'

'I think I have a rival for your love, Michael. She is a great beauty and like all Frenchwomen she is very alluring. Your quarters need some softer touches. Perhaps I should sail with you and work on it. My distant cousin Admiral Cotter told me that captains are forbidden to carry their wives on board but if they wish to carry a mistress, a blind eye is often turned. May I be your mistress, please?'

He laughed. 'If this was peacetime and the dangers of my mission not so real, I would delight to have you on board, if only to scandalise that thin-lipped bible-hugging Rook I am saddled with. That you are so precious to me makes me resist with utmost difficulty that temptation; not because of any sense of propriety.'

He had a light lunch served then saw her to the side. Much as he wished he could spend every minute with her, the ship, his other mistress, leeched most every waking moment from him.

Captains rarely slept out of their ships and North was no exception, though for two evenings returning to the ship shortly before eight bells in the First Watch was a slight intrusion on the night.

It was on the second evening, as he reached the deck, trying to free his mind for the moment from thoughts of his energetic and loving Isobel, that he witnessed something that made him explode in anger. Midshipman Boyle was in the act of laying a rope's end across the shoulders of a ship's boy; the lad's cries muffled by his hands which were clasped to his face, tears streaming over his white-knuckled fingers. Three grim-faced seamen were nearby, one of whom pulled a belaying pin from its place under the rail and advanced towards Boyle with obvious intent to strike him.

North's shout could be heard all over the ship. '*Cease* Boyle! My cabin, *now!* Officer of the watch!'

Lieutenant Lang came swiftly from the deck below at the sound of the disturbance. His captain was fuming with anger. 'Lang! What is the meaning of this? Where were you while this boy was being beaten?'

Lang stuttered. 'S-sir, I was summoned to the lower gundeck where one of the hands had collapsed; it seems likely a heart attack. I left Midshipman Boyle in charge.'

'The man; how is he now?' North asked, making the welfare of his crewman a new priority.

'It's Hobson of the afterguard, sir. The surgeon's mate is with him, luckily he knows his craft. He says he thinks it will pass but he will need rest. I would like him to be carried to the cockpit?'

'Make it so! Then come at once to the great cabin. Have this boy taken to the gunner's wife.'

He turned to the seamen who were watching anxiously. He pointed at the man who had just surreptitiously replaced the belaying pin, beckoned him over and spoke softly to him.

'Dove, I know you were just tidying the pin away but it is as well there was not an accident involving Mr Boyle's head. Do I make myself clear?'

Derek Dove knuckled his forehead and as his captain turned away let out pent-up breath. Con Riley tapped him on the shoulder, 'thank God it was our captain that saw you, you daft looby.'

North's temper was up again as he slammed the cabin door behind him, causing the marine sentry, who was still stiffly at attention, to wince at the noise. He then pulled himself up to the door so that he could hear better the explosion that was about to happen. He was pulled back by his chalky cross belts by Lieutenant Lang and almost dropped his drawn sword in surprise. 'Now then, Baxter, no good comes of eavesdroppers,' said Lang.

Lang knocked and entered after a shout from North that could probably be heard as far away as Pompey.

'*Mister* Lang! I found this midshipman using a rope's end on a child when I came on board! You know my views on corporal punishment. I will tolerate the warrant officers' and their mates' rattans if applied judiciously and sparingly but no man, hear me, NO MAN carries a rope's end on my ship and NO OFFICER applies corporal punishment! Was this gentleman aware of my wishes in this respect?'

Lang was a young man of strong character and he never dissembled, especially where his captain was concerned. 'I made your standards clear to all the young gentlemen, sir, as did Lieutenant Spicker.'

North turned to Boyle, 'Your explanation, Boyle?'

If North had been aware of the deep rage Boyle was feeling by the humiliation he felt and his difficulty he would have been astonished.

'The idiot boy ruined my best breeches! The ship's boys were skylarking and pulled down the washing line that my servant had fixed, causing my breeches to fall into the sheep-pen and thence were dragged around by the sheep. They are not fit for rags now.'

'Your *servant*, am I going mad? Did I understand you to say you have a *personal servant* on this ship?' North asked in amazement. The oldsters were served by a mess-boy who cooked their food and once a week washed the 'linen' – though this consisted simply of the filthy hammock spread upon the midshipmen's table. For a quarter bottle of unwatered rum each Saturday night one or two of the hammock-men would consent to lash and stow their hammocks and possibly wash a shirt or two for a chaw of tobacco. But although a personal servant was not unheard of North had made it clear that none of the midshipmen were to have one. Many of the midshipmen could barely afford the basic uniform let alone have a servant or more than one pair of knee breeches and North would not countenance an elite amongst them, making life even more unbearable for the less well-heeled.

'Lorimer. Came on board with me. I employ him,' replied Boyle, casually.

North turned to Lang in amazement, momentarily lost for words.

Lang said, 'Lorimer is a landsman sir, volunteer, previously employed at the Admiralty as a junior clerk.'

North sat down in his chair suddenly. 'I am living in some mental asylum! Midshipmen on my ship do not have personal servants; I have made that abundantly clear. Lorimer is paid to work for the ship, not you personally. This will cease immediately. Mr Lang, have Lorimer report to the Gunner to be permanently employed by the aft quarter-gunners and if I hear one rumour that he is engaged otherwise there will be trouble. You will see that the watch-bill is marked accordingly. Now, Mr Boyle, what the hell do you mean by beating the boy? This is outrageous and I will not have it. You will go to the masthead now and stay there until I allow you down. Be thankful I don't have the cat put to your back. *Go!'*

Boyle rushed from the room. He was furious and silently vowing revenge but too terrified to defy the monster captain.

Lang shuffled his feet.

'Very well, James. The incident is closed but I am making you responsible for keeping a close watch on that hooligan. I will not have brutality on this ship! Now, regarding Hobson, the man who is sick. The surgeon posted to us is due to arrive momentarily and I will have you make sure he examines the patient minutely. If there is any doubt as to his fitness you will see that he is sent to Haslar at my expense for the carriage and properly cared for. Please ask Mr Spicker to come aft now.'

While he waited for Spicker, North cast his mind back to his own days as a midshipman. He had joined the *Albion* 74 a few days after his 14th birthday, having spent the previous two years at the Naval Academy in Gosport and therefore being made midshipman on entering the ship. The following year he had passed his master's mate examination and had passed for lieutenant at the age of 18, though like other talented lads had two years fictionally added to his age to satisfy the qualifying age rule.

He remembered well life in the gun room and then when he

reached 15, berthing with the oldsters and master's mates in the stinking bedlam of the berth on the orlop deck. The memory of the smell of the bilges and the stink of rancid cheese and butter from the nearby purser's store room had stuck with him these many years and had determined him that the lower berth on any ship he commanded would be ventilated for two hours a day regardless of weather and season unless in a storm. The ballast in the hold would be flooded at least twice a week, the filthy water pumped out and gunpowder burnt in pans to cleanse the air. Although Royal Navy ships were remarkably clean compared to most other ships including those of the Honourable Company, some dirt and smell was inevitable. With a population the size of a large village in a space 184 feet long and 49 feet wide, cleanliness and order were difficult.

He remembered a poem shown to him by a very young midshipman, Jack Mitford, when North served for a short time as acting lieutenant on *Zealous*. Mitford was composing it with a view to selling it. Having heard Mitford repeat it over and again to commit it to memory as he walked the quarterdeck during North's watch one particular stuck verse stuck in North's mind:

"'Twas folly trying
To read i' th' Berth~ for what with shying
Hats about—and playing flutes,
Backgammon—Boxing—Cleaning Boots,
And other such polite pursuits.
Skylarking—Eating—Singing—Swigging,
And Arguments about the Rigging,
'This Mast how taut!
'That sail how square,'

All Study had been fruitless there."

Spicker entered the cabin and stood with his hat under his arm.

'Gustavus take a seat will you? No doubt it is all over the ship but are you aware of what has just occurred?'

'Yes, sir, I am sorry that I only found out after the event.'

'No matter, you were not on watch and Mr Lang was quite rightly not on deck having been called to a serious incident. We have to trust our midshipmen, even more the senior mid., which is why I want to speak to you. I am far from happy with Mr Boyle and if there is any recurrence of this unacceptable behaviour I will set him on shore or put him before the mast. Even if he is well connected I will not be blackmailed into keeping a bad apple on my ship. I want you to see that he stays at the masthead for 18 hours of the next three days. He will have water with him and be allowed to relieve himself but take food and exercise only once during the day.

'When he returns to his duties you will, assisted by Mr Lang, see that he reports to the officer of watch, properly and cleanly dressed, every four hours day and night until further notice. The punishment may seem harsh but it is lenient compared to what I really want to impose. Perhaps there is a slight chance he will mend his ways. That is all.'

The morning of Friday 20th December had been hectic. It had seen the departure of Isobel for Dulwich; North had managed to snatch a few precious minutes with her as she boarded her carriage. He had handed her a plain gold ring attached to a ribbon. It had been his grandmother's wedding ring and he asked her to keep it as a token of his constancy. In turn she had taken a small gold brooch from her dress and presented it to him with a kiss. It had a cornelian intaglio of a woman's head. Her father had it made for her mother on Isobel's 18th birthday; the portrait was of her.

As the carriage was driven away, Isobel waving once from the window, a diligence arrived carrying three men with a fourth, clearly a servant, on the box. The first of the men out of the coach was Surgeon Weller. Knowing that he had been one of Admiral Keith's surgeons North was sure he could not have been posted to *Prince Rupert,* but he had. North was struck by his good fortune. Weller had studied under James Lind who had revolutionised the treatment of scurvy and led to the carrying of lime juice and lemons on all ships.

The second man was his new 1st lieutenant, a dark, slim man who said little but had quick observant eyes. His name was Erskine Rockwell and he was an American by birth. As soon as he was on board he changed into a working coat and set about his work with expert vigour.

The third man was not expected. A civilian, he was another silent man and probably the oldest on board. Jeremiah Wolfson was above 60 years of age. He was slightly stooped and wore old-fashioned but scrupulously clean clothing. He had with him a manservant who confided to the captain's steward that Mr Wolfson had 16 linen shirts in his baggage and changed them twice a day.

Wolfson handed him a letter. It was from Lord Arden.

Captain Michael North on board His Majesty's ship Prince Rupert,

Sir, this note comes by the hand of Mr Jeremiah Wolfson who will explain in private his position in the matter upon which you shall be shortly engaged. I request that you treat him with courtesy as a valued friend of this Office. You will show him on the ship's books simply as a passenger. He brings with him one servant.

I am, sir etc,

Arden.

North tucked the note into the tail of his coat, shook Wolfson by the hand and arranged that he be settled into the clerk's cabin next to the great cabin, the clerk to berth in the cubby next to the steward's pantry. He explained that he was expecting a visit from Lord Bridport and apologised that he would have to speak to him later.

As four bells were sounded marking two o'clock in the Afternoon Watch, the lookout called that a barge had entered Fiddler's Reach from seaward and was pulling for the ship. North stood easily nearby the entry port, his officers in their best uniforms except Midshipman Boyle; he was confined to his quarters. North's first inclination was to keep the rascal at the masthead but relented so that he would not bring shame on the ship during admiral's inspection.

He nodded his approval to the immaculately dressed bosun, resplendent in short blue jacket with gilt buttons as were all the ship's warrant officers today except for the master, who wore a long coat. The bosun had five pipes ready. North had standing orders that all the seamen of the crew were issued from the purser's stores with white duck trousers and blue shirts, black silk neckerchiefs and blue pea jackets, to wear as their best uniforms each with a black japanned straw hat. The shirts needed to be purchased especially in Portsmouth, the cost of which he subsidised from his own purse to the extent of £30. Each had at least two purser's check shirts, a tarred jacket for wet weather and a pair of blue trousers for everyday wear since white trousers would not be white for long. North was also insistent on an inspection being made weekly of every man's shoes to be sure they were in good repair. Other clothing would be tolerated on make do and mend days provided it was clean.

The admiral's barge was the epitome of elegance with much gold leaf and scarlet figuring, her rope-work pristine white and displayed in fine Turk's head and other examples of the coxswain's skill. In the stern next to a chubby midshipman sat the admiral. Alexander Hood, KB, Baron Bridport of the Irish Peerage, was a sharp-eyed, white haired man, now eighteen days past his 73rd birthday. He cut an impressive figure and had a distinguished record but he was known as a humane man, trusted by ordinary seamen.

As the first of 17 guns were fired at exactly even intervals, North noticed that admiral's barge was followed by a second boat, the flagship's 36-foot launch, wherein was carried Captain John Purvis, commander of the *London 98*, along with the Second Captain. Slowly handing himself up the white man-ropes, held away from the ship's side by felt-slippered boys, the admiral arrived on deck, removing his hat to the ensign as the five pipes shrilled a salute.

North saluted but Bridport extended his hand to be shaken. He was then introduced along the line of smartly turned-out officers. Bridport stopped at the sailing master and greeted him warmly; it transpired Fred Bishop had been a master's mate on one of Bridport's ships.

Lieutenant Rockwell greeted Captain Purvis and the other officers who were also introduced to the officers of *Prince Rupert*.

The inspection was slow and thorough and the crew mustered on the main deck were scanned and approved by the admiral and also by Captain Purvis. They spoke briefly to about one man in ten. The whole process, including walking the upper gundeck, lasted about an hour. Nodding to himself Bridport allowed North to lead him and his party to the main cabin.

'Well, Captain North, a splendid turnout. The ship does you credit, sir,' he said, twirling a glass of excellent wine from the Margaux area. 'I cannot think but you seem to have an excellent crew. How many do you lack of your complement?'

'Sir, I have 503 officers, men and boys including 68 marines. I am expecting 30 volunteers to arrive tomorrow from Deal having been transferred from *Romney* courtesy of Sir Home Popham and 20 marines from Chatham in a few days.'

'So, still about 40 seamen short from what I would expect myself and your marines by about a dozen. I'll see what I can do. *Eagle* is carrying some extra marines, taken off a wreck a few weeks back. Officers?'

'Full complement, sir, except for my Fifth.'

'Now, the First Lord entrusted me with finding you a 5th lieutenant, North. I am well aware that this often means you getting either an admiral's favourite or an idiot but I have a very good young man that may suit you very well. He is the son of a sailing master who was with me some years ago and has been serving as senior midshipman on *Colossus*. Lockyer was given his commission two days ago. I will have him report to you later today.' He paused, 'Ah, you would oblige me by taking a midshipman? Wouldn't normally ask but you know how it is, too many female cousins with too many snivelling brats. Though this lad should be all right. Er-hmm, well known to my brother Samuel through a friendship with a certain lady, if you take my meaning. I've had him with me for half-a-year and he seems less dim than most.'

'Pleasure, sir,' replied North, hoping he didn't sound too insincere and sincerely hoping the lad would be different from Boyle.

As if reading his thoughts, Bridport added, 'You've got the Boyle boy, haven't you? I know the earl, his father, well. A word to the wise; don't show him any favour and work him hard – his father would certainly not object to him being knocked into shape, get my drift? What about warrant officers?'

'I lack sailmakers and a cooper, sir?' asked North, hopefully.

Bridport turned to his flag captain and raised his eyebrows. That worthy rubbed his chin and said, 'The *Colossus* has a good team of sailmakers and I dare say will spare you an experienced sailmaker's mate. As to a cooper, don't mind a Frenchman do you, North? It so happens we picked up a boat full of Royalists last month including a man who was in the wine trade making barrels. I've already got a good man, so you would be welcome to him. He's a bit strange though; came on board with a barrel of books and every time I see him off duty he's got his nose in one.'

'I would be grateful, Captain,' replied North.

Bridport rumbled, 'Good, good, stores all right? Wine...?'

North took the hint and refilled the large glass he had given the admiral.

'Hmm, good stuff, this,' said admiral, appreciatively.

'A gift from my fiancée, sir,' said North, making a mental note to get his steward to put half a dozen of the bottles in the admiral's barge before he left.

Half an hour later the admiral and his entourage left the *Prince Rupert* and things returned to a semblance of normality. Three hours later with unexpected celerity five boat-loads of men with their trappings came alongside sent by the admiral. 33 first rate seamen, 16 marines and the promised lieutenant, midshipman, sailmaker and cooper. North wondered if the gift of fine red wine had anything to with it but was very grateful in any event.

The midshipman looked about him curiously. By his rank he was second to come on board after Lieutenant Peter Lockyer and was received by the monkish-looking 1st lieutenant. He produced his papers. Lieutenant Rockwell waved them away, 'Go to the cabin and show them to the captain, after he has seen Mr Lockyer. When he has finished with you report to Lieutenant Lang and he will see you are settled in. Welcome aboard.' He turned to a nearby hand, 'you there, Crosswell. Take the young gentleman's chest to the midshipmen's berth and ask the acting senior, er let me think, Mr Boswell, isn't it, to make sure Mr Dunne is shown the ropes.'

The immaculate marine at the captain's door came to attention and Dunne gave his name. The marine knocked on the door and announced him in a hoarse bellow. The unknown person in the cabin, who could be an ogre or not, called 'Enter!' and Dunne marched in as smartly as possible, doffing his hat as he did so.

The tall captain stood up, dabbing spilt ink from the fingers of his right hand with a scrap of linen. He was muscular, though not excessively so, and from the base of the thumb to high on the wrist he had a long scar on the back of the hand he was mopping. Dunne was struck by his eyes. They were distinctly green in colour, almost as dark as emeralds. His dark hair was tied at the nape of his neck with a length of black ribbon. Many younger officers were now in the habit of having their hair cut short but apparently the captain was more traditional in that respect.

Dunne realised that he had been silent too long as the captain looked at him curiously. He cleared his throat and held out his papers. 'Samuel Clover Dunne, sir, come on board by orders of Admiral Bridport.'

Not looking at the papers, North placed them on his desk and said, 'Indeed. Well, Mr Dunne, this is a newly commissioned ship but I already have seven midshipmen, now eight, and I am still getting to know most of them so at least you won't be the only new face. There are four oldsters, including yourself, and two more youngsters will be coming to join us sometimes soon. I will expect you to stand watch of course. How are you with the signal book?'

'I am competent, sir,' he said shortly.

'Good, then that shall be your position in battle or when otherwise essential. My rules are simple. Keep yourself clean, act in all respects as a gentleman, be assiduous in your schooling and learn to be the best officer you can be. I will not countenance bullying or using foul language to the jacks. They are not in a position to defend themselves against oppression so it is the duty of every officer to behave fairly and with compassion. On the other hand I expect you to be disciplined and to require utmost discipline from those you command. To gain their respect you must needs be aloof from their petty concerns and conflicts but have an ear and eye ever open to their health and well-being. You must lead by good example but ever be mindful that from your men will often come wisdom that you should be grateful to receive.

'From the admiral I have the tongue of good report in your favour, so you are off to a good start. Serve me and the ship well and you will enjoy my confidence and approval. Fall below the standards you will quickly see about you and I will be displeased. You will please join me and the second lieutenant for breakfast here tomorrow. Bring with you your journal that I might see how you are progressing.

'I trust this has the makings of a happy ship, Mr Dunne, but to promote that happiness it must receive contributions of good conduct and friendship, leavened by discipline and leadership from all officers and midshipmen.'

He extended his hand, the heavy scar like a magnet for Dunne's eyes. 'Welcome on board, Samuel Dunne, I hope you will be very happy here.'

After he left North recalled his friend Captain Cuthbert Collingwood's dictum that he would have the men salute a broomstick if it supported a midshipman's coat, but in Dunne's case North sensed that the serious young man would have little difficulty in gaining respect without force.

Later that day when inspecting the main gun deck North met the new cooper, who was berthed next to the senior gunner's mate. He was an odd-looking man. He was rail-thin with long legs, a crook back and a completely bald head with penetrating eyes that looked incongruously through steel-rimmed glasses perched on the end of a very long nose. Relieving this rather sinister collection of features were china blue eyes that by their surrounding wrinkles were seemingly those of a man who was no stranger to laughter. His ready smile added to this congenial air. His movements were slow and peaceful but deliberate. Very soon he attracted the inevitable nickname, the Heron.

He quickly produced his warrant for North to inspect; it was but newly written and signed an hour or two back. He had a book open on the small drop-down table in his cabin and in French North enquired as to its nature, *'Je comprends que vous êtes lecteur studieux. Quel est le livre?'*

Georges Lascaux peered up at him and extended the book, replying in good English, 'The first time I am reading this, sir; Bernard Le Bovier de Fontenelle, *Entretiens sur la pluralité des mondes.'*

North took the book, 'I remember reading Fontenelle; he was a favourite of my tutor.' He opened the book and read from it aloud, *'Voici un univers tellement immense que je suis perdu en elle. Je ne sais plus où je suis. Je suis rien du tout.'* He translated. '"Behold a universe so immense that I am lost in it. I no longer know where I am. I am nothing at all." Profound thoughts, Lascaux. Welcome aboard.'

He moved on.

Chapter 7

Tuesday 24th to Wednesday 25th December, 1799

All was ready for *Prince Rupert* to leave the Beaulieu River at four bells in the Morning Watch on Christmas Day – 6am on the height of the tide, two hours before a winter's dismal dawn, slipping out in darkness past Needs Ore Point and Gull Island through Bulls Run and into the western Solent.
In the lower parts of the ship the crew had hung fresh green boughs to celebrate the festival and tots had been hoarded for many days against the following morning, though likely the captain would see that they had double rations. Having finished their rehearsals a group of Sussex men were ready to perform a mummer's play and many of the crew would happily join in the singing of favourite songs. The mess-cooks were making duff with raisins, obliged to whistle while stoning the raisins lest their messmates suspect them of eating the fruit.

James Lang was writing a letter to his father. Baron Lang of Sevenoaks was a retired General and had expressed a wish that James, his youngest of three sons go into the Church. His mother had thought otherwise, having been the daughter of a bishop and knowing her son well realised that his personality and temperament would lead him to a frustrating and unfulfilling life in a pulpit.

Although James Lang was newly promoted to lieutenant he was mature beyond his years. He had joined *Phoenix* at the age of 14, having already been carried on her books for two years. He had been a quick learner and had an outgoing but even temperament that had gained his respect from officers and crew alike. He was able to match the skills of those around him and show leadership and courage in a number of clashes with the enemy. He admired Michael North and counted himself lucky to have followed him into *Prince Rupert.*

His only problem, like many midshipmen had been luck of ready cash. Midshipmen were unpaid servants of the captain and relied on allowance from home for anything beyond bed and board.

Since his elevation to lieutenant had been quite sudden and unexpected, Lang was even more bereft of tin than usual. He pursed his lips as he dipped the quill and tried to frame a request for a remittance that did not sound too grovelling. He could visualise the *paterfamilias,* silver tankard of champagne in hand, his heavy red cheeks puffed out in indignation. 'What does the boy think? Do I walk on a carpet of bank-notes? Sink me, I have barely enough to put bread on the damned table!'

Then he would line up his six younger children and deliver a homily on profligacy in the young and the burden of absent ingrates. Retiring to his den once more he would write a note to his banker to send some cash to the reprobate James. Then he would probably chuckle to himself and refill his tankard.

The younger midshipmen's berth in the gun room was also decorated for the season but most of the occupants were too dispirited to think about any happiness the following day. In the absence of the gunner and his wife, who were spending the evening with the bosun and his wife, Midshipman Boyle had pushed aside the curtain and entered. He was drunk and this could only mean trouble for all, especially Midshipman Poole, a 13 year-old waif of a lad, who was made to perch awkwardly on a stool in front of Boyle.

He bit back a rising sob. The rest of the youngsters held their breath and tried not to look at Poole's white face.

'Again, you little shit! Who is the swine in the great cabin?'

'The, the, captain, my Lord.' The sob escaped his lips and a tear fell to his cheek.

'Why is he a swine?'

'I ... I won't! He is *not* a swine!'

Boyle kicked the chair from under him and as he fell, kicked the boy in the chest. 'I'm going to check the spirit room, if anybody wants me.' Then he laughed and left the cabin to find Halsey, the gunner's mate who kept him supplied with rum and incidentally had fashioned an illicit key to the spirit room door.

As he left the berth, a man who had been sitting nearby, listening with disgust, came to his feet and followed Boyle.

Boyle weaved unsteadily across the orlop deck. There was a heavy step behind him and strong hands gripped him from behind and swung him over the companionway leading to the hold below. He fell, scrabbling at the air, and landed hard on his side in the three inches of slimy green water covering smelly shingle, an arm and a leg broken in several places. His assailant leapt down after him, pulled him on his front and knelt on his back, thrusting his face hard into the water. In agony Boyle struggled but drowned within half a minute. To be sure, the man on his back returned to the deck above and dropped a heavy hessian-covered box taken from the steward's storeroom. The box contained a set of pewter plate and some cutlery.

There was somebody else watching the murderer. That person was Lieutenant Lockyer, who stood in the shadows near the rudder. Lockyer had been on the ship for just a few days but that was long enough to realise that the senior midshipman was terrorising the younger middies. Having only a week ago been a midshipman himself, Lockyer knew well that something had to be done. Well aware of Boyle's tyranny and his own experience with another bully on the *Ville de Paris* four years ago, Lockyer paused and then stepped further back. Despite his lack of years and experience as an officer, he firmly believed that he would have done exactly the same thing himself. As far as he was concerned, the incident never happened.

Another recent arrival, the surgeon, had not witnessed the incident but had heard the sound of something falling heavily. He looked out from his open cabin door and saw the 5th lieutenant walking away but thought nothing of it at the time.

Boyle's body was found by the carpenter as he routinely checked the depth of water in the well of the ship late on the afternoon of Christmas Day, uncharacteristically not having made his first inspection before the forenoon watch due to the morning service on deck. The day's celebrations had gone on without anyone noticing the demise of the senior midshipman. Only the midshipmen's berth had missed him, thinking hopefully that he had gone off somewhere with a bottle and was sleeping off a monumental drunk.

The captain, the surgeon and the 1st lieutenant, with Lieutenant Lang a few paces away, looked down at the lifeless body.

North addressed Surgeon Weller. 'Well, Doctor, what has happened?'

'I can only suppose he fell from the ladder, possibly while carrying the box on his shoulder, broke his neck, left arm and leg and was unable to lift himself. He definitely drowned, I'm afraid.'

Rockwell said, 'So, a tragic accident?'

'Ah well, to that I cannot be sure. I have no reason to say if it was by the hand of another or if by accident.'

He's not telling the truth, thought North, how interesting. 'Very well; have the body sewn in a hammock and we will bury him at sea in the morning, Mr Rockwell. Have Mr Boswell come to see me at 6 o'clock, will you; he is now Senior Midshipman. Mr Weller, join me in the cabin for a moment.'

....

North handed the surgeon a glass of wine and sat in the green leather armchair opposite him, while Weller sat on the similarly upholstered bench. North waited a moment or two before speaking and studied his surgeon carefully.

'Mr Weller, apart from the surprise and indeed the honour of having you posted to *Prince Rupert*, I am impressed by with reports I have received of your active care of the crew's health. However, this incident with Charles Boyle has me puzzled as to your hesitance in coming to a conclusion since while I have no medical training I find the death very suspicious. As my old tutor would say, "let us observe carefully, interpret and come to a conclusion".'

He sipped his wine and continued. 'In this case we find that

Midshipman Boyle fell not a great distance, some eight feet from the orlop companionway, into a part of the hold where is found the spirit room. This seems the only place he could have reasonably wanted to visit in the hold, bearing in mind the testimony of the midshipmen's berth that he had expressed that intention. Why would he be carrying a box of my personal stores on his shoulder? Was he stealing it? He seems to be well provided with funds; surely he did not need to do that?

'There are three berths in that area, yours, the purser's and my steward's cabins each of which with doors open have an unrestricted view of the companionway. The purser is nursing a torn muscle in his shoulder, as you are aware and my steward, though he berths there, was in my quarters most of the time and besides is physically incapable of the degree of violence equal to killing a man with his bare hands.'

Weller drew in his breath, 'Am I being accused, sir?'

'Hear me out, Mr Weller. I am not accusing you. I observed that Mr Boyle's left arm was broken at the wrist and elbow. This could mean he landed on that side of his body. He was found face down and drowned in a mere inch or two of water. However the most interesting thing was that the whole area for several feet around the body was disturbed and crushed down as if caused by a struggle or excessive movement of the deceased before death. Now if we accept that his leg was broken below the knee it would be difficult enough to explain such movement but we also find he has a broken neck. It seems to me that the disturbed area could have also been caused by somebody pulling him on to his stomach and attacking him. If it was an accident, what are the chances of such flaying around by a man in that state of injury? An eight foot drop and him drunk, no less. Drunks relax their bodies which is why often they come to less harm when falling. Furthermore around the neck it seems to me that there was distinct bruising or am I in error about that?'

'It is possible.'

'Probable, I would say. I am sure that you were not his assailant but why you were uncertain that his death was by the hand of another? Did you see anything from your cabin?'

Weller shook his head but said nothing. North wondered why he was so reluctant to speak: had he seen something? Someone? If so, whom? North was still sure he was concealing something but decided to change the subject.

'Very well, I will let it rest for now but mark my words, murder cannot be justified by reference to the bad character of the victim. I intend to find out the exact cause of Midshipman Boyle's death but for now I will record it in my journal as by means unknown.'

Weller wanted to clear up another matter. He leaned forward. 'Sir, you expressed puzzlement as to why I was sent to your ship. I would like to explain – for your ears only, please.

Weller's story was told hesitantly.

He had experienced a difficult time over the past two years. He had involved himself with a much younger woman and as a result had foolishly adopted a lifestyle completely alien to him. He had spent all his money in high-living and gambling. As a result he had been hiding in the sanctuary of the Savoy, where the spongers could not arrest him for debt.

'I am sorry, this is difficult for me, sir. You see before you a man reduced to shameful penury and desperation entirely through his own stupidity. Even my chest of instruments came to me as a generous gift from Lord Arden, a friend from better times who rescued my from my plight. Having retired from the fleet, I had built a thriving practice on shore, now thrown away. I am deeply ashamed.

'Since coming on board I have felt drawn back to some of the happier times of my life again and I am more than content to be on the ship. If I knew the true reason for the young man's death, sir, I would tell you. I value my good fortune in being here and would not jeopardise it. My reticence is due simply to uncertainty.'

North rose and crossed to the emotionally distressed man and patted his shoulder.

'Thank you for confiding in me. Have no fear: your secret is safe.'

After Weller had left the cabin North frowned. He accepted the surgeon's innocence but he was still puzzled as to why he had not come to a more firm conclusion about the death. While he pondered the matter he opened the chronometer case, drew out the left-hand piece and wound it, as was his custom in this half of the day. He checked the watch in his waistcoat pocket against the chronometer and then slipped his fingers into the other pocket to touch Isobel's locket – an almost unconscious routine.

Isobel being in his life was a great joy to him. In the early morning when he habitually walked the deck, he often thought about her, the miles separating them, and the months they would be apart. It may be that some people would have thought that the progress of their love had been far too swift but he could honestly say that he regretted not one moment.

He sent for Lieutenant Lang.

'James, I want you to make a point of finding out all you can about Boyle's death. In view of the man's conduct whilst on *Prince Rupert*, I fear he has made more than one enemy, so your task will not be easy. On the other hand it is an unfortunate fact that being so well connected a great deal of interest may be shown in his death. I suspect strongly that he was murdered, so we must do our very best to solve this.

Lang nodded. He knew as much as North and there was no need for discussion at that moment, so he left the cabin.

North sat looked down at the blank sheet of paper in front of him trying to think how to phrase the news to Boyle's father. His thoughts were interrupted by the sentry announcing Jeremiah Wolfson, another man of mystery.

Wolfson's presence on *Prince Rupert* had something to do with North's mission but as yet he had not had a chance to talk to him. This meeting had been arranged and rearranged several times due to other pressing matters. He indicated the stern bench recently occupied by the surgeon and poured a glass for his visitor.

'So, Mr Wolfson, why are you come on board my ship?'

Wolfson smiled, 'I was told you were a man that preferred directness, captain, and it seems that is true so let me be equally direct. I am here because a mutual acquaintance does not totally trust certain people at the Admiralty and to make sure that you are not made the victim of a conspiracy to shift blame if all goes wrong in Canada.'

Having rolled this bomb along the deck Wolfson sipped his wine and sat back.

North said thoughtfully, 'Apart from me, you are the only person on board that knows our true destination. That means that the person you refer to knows also – you are connected to a certain peer. I suspected that you were not simply here as a passenger.'

'On the contrary, the best interests of my friends and indeed our king and country will be served if I can in any way help while at the same time accurately recording the events which will proceed once we have reached Canada. Since my presence is to a degree unofficial I will stay firmly in the background. I am, so as to speak, your insurance policy – a walking record of your actions.'

North was fascinated. 'This is intriguing. You will oblige me by telling me exactly what is happening, since I would be very resentful if I am being used for unworthy purposes.'

Wolfson explained. It had probably not escaped the captain's notice that he was a Jew, and the fact of his religion meant he was barred from public office. Most of his life had been spent as a schoolteacher and tutor to his own community, adding to his modest income by authenticating and valuing paintings by mainly Italian masters. A few years ago he had been able to be of service to the Duke of Bridgwater over a distinctly embarrassing matter concerning a stolen painting of which provenance the duke had been completely unaware. In gratitude the duke had taken him on as his private secretary, a position which entailed complete trust and access to momentous secrets, including the secret war that the duke and others were waging on behalf of the government.

There had always been a somewhat ambivalent relationship between British and French men of substance. Even at the height of the war between their countries contact had been kept alive by various open means. This also served as a useful channel for espionage and its bedfellow treason. It was well known that there were spies in both capital cities assiduously gathering intelligence, much of which came from loose tongues and slipshod security. Alongside this were those who had no loyalty to their country and for either monetary or idealistic reason would betray secrets to the enemy.

Where there are spies and traitors there are also those who would weed out these poisonous creatures and the duke and a number of other people were heavily involved in indentifying spies and traitors. Of course it was not always easy to prove a case against these people especially those that might be in high office.

Wolfson paused and, lowering his voice, continued to explain.

'Captain, what I am about to tell you is known to very few and must remain so. There are three people working at the Admiralty that are involved in deepest treachery, one of whom is so highly placed as to be virtually above reach and final proof being lacking, cannot be touched. This is the main reason why Lord Spencer and Lord Arden, with Secretary Nepean's support, have involved the duke and his friends in order to keep strictly secret your true mission.'

The two lesser traitors, once identified, had been contained and fed useless information. One of them had been vulnerable to pressure from Lord Arden and had been turned back to the British side. He had been the main traitor's conduit for passing information to the French. As a result they had found that information concerning the resurrection of *Aboukir* and its alleged mission to South America had been passed to Paris and although there was every reason to believe they knew nothing about Canada, this could not be taken for granted.

It was suspected that the French were keenly interested in North and his ship. This led to the decision to send Wolfson on the mission with North but just as importantly, to warn him of something that would happen in a few days' time which they could not openly tell him because it would disclose that they had turned the traitor.

Wolfson's instructions were not to disclose this to North until *Prince Rupert* was out of sight of land. North could see the sense of this but wished he had known sooner.

The French considered that the mission to South America was not a big threat to their ambitions but saw an opportunity to score a victory by recapturing their ship. They planned to have a number of small vessels keep track of *Prince Rupert's* movements but their main trap was two third-rates which had been detached from Admiral Breux's squadron and were sailing west of Cork intent on taking the English ship.

'So, forewarned, we must alter course to avoid them,' said North.

'Forgive me, no. That could expose our man. Lord Arden has a more elegant plan. Your ship will be a Judas Goat, if you allow it. Knowing fairly accurately the location of the French ships, our 80-gun ship *Caesar,* accompanied by *Lion* 74 is cruising to the north of Cork; warned by one of three schooners, she will close with the French 74s at the same time you arrive, thereby turning the trap around upon them.'

'A plan which could be open to mischance.'

'This is why, having told you, my instructions were that the decision must be yours alone. Of course the Admiralty also consider a Royal Navy 74 equal to two French 74s but to at least give you eyes, the schooners *Juniper* and *Crow* of eight guns each will join you off Plymouth and permanently act under your command.'

'None of this was put into my orders.'

Wolfson smiled. 'Have you opened your second set of orders yet, sir? If not, why don't you look at them now?'

North went to his desk and returned with the sealed packet which had been in the lead-weighted bag. He opened it to find that there were two very short documents. The first paper said that he should be assured that he had the full confidence of their lordships and that he was required to follow the verbal orders of which he was aware. The second document was quite extraordinary.

To Whom it May Concern,

By the Commissioners for executing the Office of the Lord High Admiral of Great Britain and Ireland &c and of all His Majesty's Plantations &c.

Be it known that Captain the Hon. Michael Orrick North of His Majesty's Royal Navy is acting under explicit command of this Office. In consequence of being the receptacle of our utmost confidence Captain North is empowered to request and require all subjects of His Majesty of whatsoever Rank and Station to follow such directions and commands that shall to the said Captain North seem fit to give in pursuance of the satisfactory fulfilment of

Instructions given by their Lordships. In this you shall not fail at your peril.

Given under our hand...' etc, etc.

North turned to Wolfson. 'This is incredible, it literally gives me authority over generals and admirals, ambassadors and prelates, does it not?'

Wolfson laughed, 'You will recall that the triumphant Caesars were bound to carry on their chariots an attendant who would whisper in their ear as they drove through the exultant crowds, *"Te sunt humanum; te sunt humanum."* You are human. You are human. So perhaps I am the quiet voice in your ear.'

North joined him in laughter, 'Just as well, Mr Wolfson, for I am hardly a likely Deity.'

'Of course you will use this authority with discretion and although this document, having been penned by Evan Nepean himself is unlikely to be known to the French, even so, by its very tone, should the French become aware of the contents you will become a target of even more extreme interest. As you say such an authority is practically unheard of. It is designed to free you from the control of others as much as anything.'

North said, pensively. 'It also supposes that I have the judgement and skill to use that power to produce the desired result – qualities which I fear I may not have. I will do my best, but it is a heavy responsibility.'

Chapter 8

Tuesday 31st December, 1799

The southern tip of Ireland was out of sight and the only land between Europe and the Americas was a small island called Rockall. *Prince Rupert* had hugged the Irish coast as far north as Eagle Island off Belmullet.

Three days ago North had anchored in Plymouth Sound where his schooners joined him. He was looking for a certain ship that he had good reason to believe would be nearby. Remembering the gallantry of her owner and captain, James Farquharson, of the Indiaman *Alfred*, North had an idea which he wanted to discuss. Farquharson received his note and was carried over to *Prince Rupert* on North's launch. Ensconced in North's cabin, he took a glass of sherry and listened while North outlined his plan.

Having seen the unique written authority possessed of Captain North, Farquharson agreed that his ship and crew should be hired by the Admiralty and, since she was an armed ship, to be placed temporarily but officially under command of Lieutenant Gustavus Spicker. It was customary for a navy lieutenant to command a hired merchantman if armed and since Farquharson quickly came to the conclusion that Spicker knew his business he was content with the arrangement.

So it was that the two ships met in darkness off the west coast of Ireland in the channel between the mainland and the remote Eagle Island and both crews set too with a will. *Alfred*, at 1200 tons, was roughly the same length but three quarters the weight of *Prince Rupert*. She was within a hundred tons of a two-decker 64 and with some embellishments could be made to look like a larger ship, though her armament was much lighter. Having taken on board her a large quantity of paint and extra canvas in Plymouth, *Alfred's* black and white hull was transformed to buff and black. They painted sham gun ports and false extensions were raised on from her sides constructed from spars and canvas like a higher poop and forecastle.

At a distance she could pass for a 74, which was the intention.

At the same time an opposite disguise was being perpetrated on *Prince Rupert* which made her look like an Indiaman of far less power.

Before turning west, fully aware of his trackers, North had led them out to sea having sent on ahead the schooner *Crow* to make contact with *Caesar* and to advise Commodore Williamson that North intended to spring the trap west of but in sight of Rockall. He had an alternative plan should *Caesar* and her consorts fail to arrive but their absence would make the plan far more risky.

It lacked but a few minutes to the end of the second dog watch when lights were seen due south of *Prince Rupert*. North's orders had included advice to him that *Caesar* would carry two white lights to the stern and one at the forepeak if they met at night, *Prince Rupert* the same. The stranger bore two lanterns at the stern but a single white light to starboard and a red light to larboard. North ordered the topsails furled and slowed his progress, calling all hands to action stations. *Alfred* followed suit. A night action between two ships was one thing but co-ordinating an attack by two ships upon two others was more difficult and North guessed that his opponents would try to keep him in sight until daybreak before pouncing. He was acutely aware that the French plan to retake his ship if it succeeded would not only embarrass the Admiralty but would confirm in some minds the sheer stupidity in giving such a powerful ship to a newly commissioned captain. If he made a mess of this he could say goodbye to his future naval career.

The ships moved on with *Prince Rupert* and *Alfred* giving no sign that they were aware of the French ship, which had speedily doused all her lights a few minutes after she had been spotted.

At this time of the year, New Year's Day, the first day of a new century, the first light was at 8 o'clock – eight bells in the morning watch.

It was still gloomy and the sun, weak though it was, would not be seen for another half hour. Midshipman Miles-Trevor, a 17-year-old that North knew to have nerves of steel but a slight deficiency in grey-matter, was ordered to keep a running note of everything that happened during the coming encounter. He stood conscientiously, journal in hand, under the poop deck overhang a few feet behind the helmsmen.

He noted that at 7.55am the two French 74s were about a league due south.

As the gloom lightened North saw their masts blossom with extra canvas, royals and studding-sails filling. As he halted the watch, which was about to change over, North looked across at the *Alfred*. With alacrity she had matched the French and crowded on all the canvas she could carry. *Alfred* fired off a quarter-gun as if to attract *Prince Rupert's* attention to the danger then surged forward and away to the north.

106

8.03 am. All hands had been called on *Prince Rupert* but an appearance was given of panic. Like many merchant vessels at night she had reduced her sails to mizzen and foremast mainsails and was not alive enough to have set more canvas at dawn. Now sails were loosed and appeared to be frantically managed by the usual Indiaman's inadequate size of crew. The result was a picture of utter confusion not helped by the wheel being turned to bring her to the north too quickly and the ship being suddenly taken aback. The result was that *Prince Rupert* was now within a mile and a half of the leading Frenchman and sailing due west while the false 74, *Alfred,* was making off at top speed increasing the gap between them and headed away at 90 degrees to her merchantman companion.

8.10am. Continuing the ruse of being a ship in complete panic, *Prince Rupert* turned south, heading straight into trouble, then east as if to escape to the shore.

Having thoroughly rehearsed the manoeuvres North watched and grunted with satisfaction as one of the French 74s greedily turned to snatch up what she thought to be a hapless Indiaman, while the other pressed on after *Alfred* supposing her to be the 74.

8.28am. The watery sun was through the light covering of clouds. When both French ships were well and truly committed North gave the signal that his crew eagerly awaited. 'At them, lads!' The Company's duster was run down and replaced by the Union flag.

In what must have seemed an instant, *Prince Rupert* luffed up less than two cables length from the French 74 – was this another blunder? Clearly not; as her guns came to bear, *Prince Rupert* hurled shot after shot into the Frenchman's prow. Her gunnery was not perfect for three days' practice could hardly suffice but it was good enough. She luffed up again and the distance was now less than one cable's length; about 200 yards. The Frenchman veered to starboard in order to bring her larboard broadside to bear but *Prince Rupert* continued her turn, matching her opponent.

'Now, Mr Rockwell!' shouted North.

8.36am. Each of *Prince Rupert's* three starboard carronades bellowed out in turn as the gunner himself ordered shots that were trained with considerable accuracy on the French ship's mainmast. The huge balls flew true. One moment the French ship was sailing free and fast, the next her mainmast collapsed with a huge groan over her starboard side effectively slowing her to a crawl.

8.39am. North ran to the wheel to help the four helmsmen. *Prince Rupert* crossed the stern of the French ship. Her name, *Dieppe,* was blown into a thousand pieces from her transom as *Prince Rupert's* every larboard gun found its mark, chain-shot and grape driving hell through the length of both gun decks.

Now for the other ship. North urged his ship northwards. It was remarkable that barely two French shot had struck *Prince Rupert* and just one man had been wounded, though his injuries were severe. Damage was trivial. He signalled to the schooner *Juniper,* a mile or so west, to stand away from the stricken Frenchman but keep a watchful eye upon her.

Nearer the horizon the other French 74, the *Stella Provencie,* had been in pursuit of the *Alfred* but now began to turn southwards to assist her consort. This was more than North had expected and meant he would not have to chase his enemy's stern worrying that perhaps she was faster than

Alfred, though that was unlikely.

8.56am. The two ships approached each other though North had the weather gauge. In a classic manoeuvre the French captain began to tack his ship, an unnecessary move that simply tired his crew because if he hove-to *Prince Rupert* would have come to him.

Now fully aware that what had been believed to be an Indiaman was in fact the 74 he had been seeking, Commodore Lascelles was prepared for the contest.

Closer came the convergence and Lascelles could now see the English captain's swallow-tailed pennant at the main masthead. He was confident that his own experience far outweighed that of the young, newly promoted Captain North. Perhaps he forgot that he had risen like cork through the ranks due to the murderous effect of the Terror on many senior naval officers of the old regime.

The exchange of shot began at precisely 9.15 in the morning. North had urged his officers to ensure that no gun was fired until within pistol shot, regardless of the enemy's effect on the ship. The French captain, as did many of his contemporaries, set about destroying his opponent's rigging, sparing the hull in case she sank and he was deprived of a prize. This greedy practice was in contrast with the English way of sending as much shot as possible into the enemy's hull. It also, paradoxically, spared more of the English sailors. The Frenchman would fire his guns well into the up-roll; while the Englishman's custom was to fire as the ship *began* to roll up. Thus for the English gunner if the hull was missed there was still a good chance of damaging the enemy's rigging.

There was a furious exchange of musketry from the tops as

Prince Rupert, battered but not bowed, ranged close to the Frenchman. Then the order came to fire and *Prince Rupert's* broadside roared out to hellish effect on the enemy. By now the *Stella* had seven of her cannon smashed or thrown from their carriages and a stray shot from a quarter deck 9-pounder clean took off the commodore's head and the right arm of the ship's 2nd captain. All was confusion. The *Prince* had forged ahead with the intent of crossing the stern of *Stella* but an unlucky musket ball from a French marksman had smashed her fore-topmast fid, causing the topmast to collapse, swing forward and check her way.

With all her senior officers injured or dead, the French 1st lieutenant decided that he must now withdraw from a fight he could not win. It took 18 vital minutes for *Prince Rupert's* damaged foremast to be temporarily repaired by which time the *Stella Provencie* was more than a mile distant; every scrap of canvas she could carry was aloft. North decided not to pursue and had the ship turned south again.

There was time to check on the state of *Prince Rupert's* sickbay and he went below to the noisome, cramped cockpit. In the barely adequate light of tallow candles on the table and ensconced in heavy lanterns on the bulkheads, the surgeon and his two assistants, their shirtsleeves rolled up to the shoulders, were sawing and cutting to a dire chorus of screaming and whimpering casualties. The wounded lay side by side on a bloodstained spare sail on the deck waiting their turn. The purser, the chaplain and the captain's clerk moved amongst them with watered limejuice and sometimes raw rum, to comfort them. At least the cessation of the bombardment spared them from the awesome crash and rumble of the guns above.

Over his shoulder as he worked Surgeon Weller said quietly, 'Six dead here, sir, and three will not see another sunrise.'

North patted him on the shoulder and moved on, offering a word of comfort or listening to a man who felt nearer to death than he really was, earnestly pleading that his wife was told how well he died. After ten minutes North returned to the quarterdeck. The total loss was 11 dead and now 21 wounded.

Miles-Trevor, his hand shaking after the horror and tension of the battle, picked up his pencil and continued to note down the events. The duel had ceased at 9.59 am. In the meantime *Alfred*, completely unscathed, had come about and was ranging a cable's length from *Prince Rupert's* larboard side.

10.23am. As they came in sight of the damaged *Dieppe* her injuries were only too clear. Her mainmast had gone by the board taking with it most of the mizzen. Although her crew were furiously hacking at the wreckage which had the ship listing heavily to port, it was clear they were not going anywhere soon. Her captain had evidently not realised his mistake about *Alfred* until he had lowered his ensign in surrender. Pleased by the opportunity to spare the effusion of more blood, North had Lieutenant Shepheard take command of the *Dieppe* as prize-master with a midshipman, a master's mate, 50 seamen and 40 marines. He had her officers brought over to *Prince Rupert* and 120 of the *Dieppe's* crew put into her boats to be towed so as to lessen the number of prisoners to be guarded. Her warrant officers were put on board *Juniper*.

The other welcome surprise was another British ship, the 32-gun frigate *Glasgow*, which arrived on the scene and exchanged signals with *Juniper* shortly after *Dieppe* had struck her colours.

Her commander was Captain Longhurst. He saluted smartly as he reached the deck of the *Prince Rupert*. He was a short man, barely topping five feet, with an engaging smile and the ironic nickname "Lengthy Longhurst". North invited him to the cabin and sat him down.

'You arrive here at an opportune moment, Captain. My mission means that I can spare few of my men as a prize crew so I wish you to escort *Dieppe* south to the Cove of Cork taking on board *Glasgow* as many of the prisoners as you can carry. *Alfred* will also carry a number of prisoners and you will oblige me by lending them a dozen or so of your marines. The officers will stay with me on *Prince Rupert* for the time being. Lieutenant Shepheard will carry with him my report to Admiral Kingsmill where he is with *Polyphemus* and then carry a private despatch to London. I would be obliged if you will see that the rest of my prize crew is placed on board *Juniper*, which will follow me to my destination.

'In order to make sure you are not censured for assisting me and neglecting your own orders I will put my orders in writing. For your own eyes this is my authority from the Admiralty and I would be obliged if you will only use your knowledge of this unusual document if it is essential and that after doing so you communicate the circumstances of that usage to Lord Arden at the Admiralty.' He passed the document to Longhurst to read with raised eyebrows.

After Longhurst had left the ship North recalled Lewis Shepheard from *Dieppe* to give him his orders.

'After you have reported to Admiral Kingsmill, and handed him this sealed despatch, you will make the best of your way to Whitehall where you will hand this other package to Lord

Arden or Secretary Nepean personally and to nobody else except Lord Spencer. As it is the custom to promote the bringer of news of a victory I trust that you will receive your step, at least as commander and your own ship. Good luck, Lewis, and God speed.'

Six hours later as the weak sun dipped into the sea in the west, North and Lieutenant Rockwell stood on the quarterdeck watching *Juniper* lead and *Glasgow* follow as *Dieppe* set off for the naval base at Cork with *Alfred* on the leeward side of the three ships after having received North's grateful thanks. At her forepeak *Dieppe* carried a Union flag over the Tricolour and *Prince Rupert's* number 921, indicating that she was prize to the latest 74 on the Fleet List.

The plan was that North and *Juniper* would rendezvous at Fox Bay, at the eastern end of Anticosti Island. North knew that *Voltigeur* would be waiting for *Prince Rupert* at English Bay, 130 miles away at the western end of the island. Both ships, being French-built, were supposed to fly French flags for the benefit of local people who, though nominally loyal to England, could well harbour French spies. On the other hand North felt there could be a benefit from keeping the presence of *Juniper* secret for the time being.

Hoping that he was now free of deliberate French interference North looked up into the moonless sky and identified Polaris, the North Star. 'That's your guide, Mr Rockwell, and you will oblige me by setting course due north by Polaris for the next three days before turning north-west.'

Chapter 9

Saturday 1st to Sunday 2nd March, 1800

James Lang had spent eight weeks trying to solve the mystery of the death of Midshipman Boyle without success.
He prided himself on having the respect of the crew but whether anybody knew the murderer or not, there was considerable reticence in discussing the affair but no information was forthcoming. It seemed nobody had seen what had happened and the killer had not confided in anybody who would speak out. Lang had spent many hours asked the same fruitless questions and felt like giving up but knew that he could not

In fact the killer, though he felt little conscience in what he had done, had not said a single word to anybody. However, in the darkness of the First Watch, he felt bad about the reputation of the ship and its captain. Even more important, he had thought about the future. He was realistic enough to know that like everybody else here he could fall in battle or die of some disease. So at least he could write a confession and hide it in his possessions. That might just ease his way past St Peter.

Prince Rupert had entered Fox Bay on 28th February and anchored in nine fathoms close to the northern shore. The voyage across the North Atlantic had been uneventful and although there were a number of ice flows and bergs in the past hundred miles or so, the Estuary of the St Lawrence was ice-free, which was very unusual this early in the year and set North ahead of his schedule.

The two surviving officers of the *Dieppe,* Captain Le Blond and his 3rd lieutenant, Giles Chabat had given their parole and were therefore allowed a degree of freedom on board ship. Le Blond, a realistic man, had spent several evenings with North playing chess and as far as his circumstances could admit, enjoying his company. Though reliant on a crutch he had recovered somewhat from his wounds and North had promised that he would land him in Quebec City if possible, where he had relatives.

North wrote a letter to Isobel that took the form of a serial of events. He hoped to be able to post it off in Montreal. In the letter he took care not to include any information that might be useful to the enemy if it was intercepted but shared his thoughts on most of the everyday events of any note. Though to be sure the murder was not an everyday event. North found Isobel in his thoughts in many moments of solitude in his cabin. To say that he adored her was less than adequate to express his feelings. He was lifted by joy when he thought about her.

Clearing his mind with some effort, North came on deck at the hail of 'Land ho!'

North's information was that the whole island except for a permanent small community in English Bay was uninhabited during the winter, the trappers and fishermen going to the mainland. Once at Fox Bay North had immediately sent off the red cutter with Lieutenant Lang to visit the small cluster of buildings to the west and find fresh water. In fact as the shore party walked up the slipway they found that the bay was not uninhabited. Two men left the doorway of one of the buildings and walked down to meet them.

None of the boat's crew had ever seen a native American before and they stared with interest. Both men were wearing heavy buckskin jackets fringed with strands of the same skin and fur leggings. There were designs in red ochre on their clothing which had a long time ago resulted in them being called Red Indians from the great reverence they had for that colour. That name was now commonly given to describe all the native peoples hereabouts. These men were of the Miawpukek Mi'kmaq nation and it transpired some distance from their home in Labrador. They greeted the landing party by laying down their muskets and holding open palms upwards.

Lieutenant Lang looked them over. They smelled of animal grease and pine needles. Both men were tall and slim and though their features may have been misleading, he guessed they were in their early forties.

One of them, the shorter of the two, spoke in French, a language in which Lang could easily converse. 'Greetings, sir, our canoe was wrecked here and we seek to be taken to mainland, can you help us?'

Lang replied, 'Are there any more people here?'

He said there were not.

'You must come to the ship and speak to my captain.'

Both men nodded agreement. Leaving a small party to investigate the area, Lang took them back to *Prince Rupert*. Like their comrades on the shore, the sailors in the ship gawked at the athletic men, their black hair tied in leather braids on each side of their heads. They in turn noticed that many of the ordinary sailors wore a single pigtail on the back of their heads.

North's cabin was a place of great curiosity to the Mi'kmaq men. The captain himself was impressive even to the taller of the men. The taller Indian it was that spoke first, his French showing signs of some education.

'Greetings, sir, we are loyal subjects of King George. We were hunting for seals in the mouth of the Great River when a storm forced us into the river and cast us up in this bay, wrecking our canoe.'

Replying in the same language, North asked, 'Are you hungry?'

'Not so much, sir, there is plenty of caribou on the island.'

North made a mental note to send out hunting parties to get fresh meat for the ship. 'Do you know the waters of the great river further inland?'

The two men spoke to each other in their own language and the shorter man, translated by his companion, told him he had once been as far as Montreal with his father having been carried on a trading brig. He had spent two months there but did not know the river well.

North asked their names. Pointing at his friend the taller man said, 'Patrick Membertou. I am Joseph Sanipass, sir; we are good Christians - hallelujah.'

If the Mi'kmaq were capable of irony, North felt there was a slight laughter in Joseph's voice. 'Well, I will call you Patrick and Joseph and you are welcome on my ship. We are staying in the bay for a while but I can have you taken in the launch to the north shore if you wish?'

'Thank you, sir, if we can get across the river we can go home to our families,' said Joseph. Patrick tugged at his friend's jacket and said something urgently in Mikmwer. Joseph turned to North and said, 'Excuse us, sir. Patrick says we must tell you about the French ship that passed by the Bay two days ago. He says she had many cannon.'

North spoke to Patrick in French which his friend translated. 'This ship; was she a big ship, like this one or a smaller one?'

'Maybe as big, I think bigger than the other one.'

'The *other* one?'

'Four days ago a smaller ship passed by. She had the same flag of yours, a British ship. She was travelling the same way,' said Joseph. He pointed west.

North called for the coxswain to carry the two men over the channel to the mainland and gave each of them some salt, a bag of oatmeal and another of dried peas with a 2lb bag of fine-mealed gunpowder and several handfuls of musket balls as being the most practical gifts he could make.

After the Indians had left to be sailed across to the north shore of the mainland, North called in his lieutenants.

'Gentlemen, it seems that there is a large French ship loose in the area and possibly it will mean danger for the crew of *Voltigeur* who are probably unaware. *Voltigeur* should be at English Bay and I am going to sail *Prince Rupert* there to make sure she is safe. I do not anticipate the arrival of *Juniper* for at least five or six days but I will leave a shore party here to make sure they know where we have gone. Mr Lang, you will be in charge here and I will leave you the gig and 20 marines.

118

You will also have the cox'n and the crew of the red cutter when they return from their present mission. When *Juniper* arrives she is to stay here for a further five days. If we do not return or you receive word, the whole party shall make their way to Quebec City and report to the senior army or navy officer there.'

So they weighed anchor an hour later and set off westwards. Sped partly by an incoming tide and strong currents, eighteen hours later *Prince Rupert* hove-to half a mile short of English Bay and North set off in the launch in company with the green cutter to probe into the bay itself.

North cursedly inwardly as he looked towards the shore; what had been a small cluster of houses and warehouses was now a mess of smoking ruins. He could clearly see bodies on the shoreline, including several red-coated marines. In the high ground behind the town more smoke rose but there was a strange regularity to cloudlike puffs. It seemed there must be people there, possibly sending a signal.

He brought the boats in at the eastern arm of the bay, in direct line with the smoke from the hill and leapt out on to the shingle. There were two small gigs and an empty cutter drawn up on the beach, their clinker-built design indicating that they had been made in Deal, therefore that they were most likely English. The marine lieutenant Hodge deployed his men in a screen which preceded the rest of the party.

'Mr Hodge,' said North, 'You will take ten men to the top of that hill and find out who is there. I suspect it is an Englishman who has been able to see *Prince Rupert* from that point. Whoever they are, have him or them brought down. Ryan, take the launch back to *Prince Rupert* and give the 1st lieutenant my compliments, he is to bring her round into the bay.'

North walked into the ruined hamlet counting at least a dozen corpses including five marines. He was alerted by an anxious marine, pointing at a dead comrade, 'Sir, I know this man, name of Kirby, one of *Voltigeur's* marines.'

North was seething. If only he had sailed straight to English Bay! But he would probably have still been too late even considering the state of the fires. They could only have started less than 18 hours ago but not within the past six hours.

They searched for half an hour. North said wearily, 'What is the count, Mr Hobbs?' The pale-faced midshipman replied, 'Nine dead marines and twelve civilians including two women, one of them naked and burnt but there are also two sailors that I think are probably French, sir.'

'Very well, organise the burials in the area inland of the houses, please.' He beckoned a master's mate, Joss Toller. 'Take six men and supplies for three days and follow that track leading inland, see if you can find any trace of survivors but be back here in 36 hours.' He sent a message to *Prince Rupert* to fire three guns in case this might attract the attention of Commander Thompson's party if they had not gone too far.

Lieutenant Hodge returned as Toller's party disappeared into the woods. With him he had two men, shivering from the cold, dressed only in blue trousers and blue and white checked shirts. As they came along the pathway, a sailor from *Prince Rupert* came from one of the few buildings that had not fully caught fire. He had two bear fur robes which he draped over their shoulders.

North looked at the men. He did not know either of them. 'Report!'

The older man knuckled his forehead. 'John Moseley and Peter Franks; able of the fo'c's'le of *HMS Voltigeur*, Captain.'

The story they told had a sad inevitability about it.

Twelve hours ago, apart from a small party of seamen and marines sent off to cut wood, with the surgeon's mate to see that they did not drink unfit water or eat suspicious berries. *Voltigeur* had been swinging at her anchor in the bay. Both her cutters had been drawn up on the shingle, awaiting the cut timber. Moseley recounted that he had looked out over the bay to see a 74-gun ship rounding the point. He realised that she was flying the tricolour but had been told that *Prince Rupert* would likely be flying that flag as a *ruse de guerre*. As the ship was French-built, no doubt Commander Thompson was of the same thought which is why he did not clear for action, coupled with the fact that there was no reason to believe a French 74 would be on the St Lawrence. By the time he realised his mistake it was too late.

As the French ship opened fire Moseley had seen the much smaller *Voltigeur* disintegrate before his eyes; her masts were sheared off and she listed dangerously within minutes. He saw men diving over the side of the ship and an attempt being made to launch the two boats still on the deck, successfully with the gig, but the ship itself was doomed. He and all those ashore ran to the water's edge and into the water to help their mates who were struggling ashore. Around half the brig's crew made it to dry land.

Commander Thompson was seen to leap from the stern of the ship as it started to slide beneath the water. At first they thought he had drowned but he came up near a floating spar and caught hold. The four-oared gig, which was almost on shore, turned and rowed hard to bring him back; despite a heavy bombardment of muskets from the French ship they made it safely to land.

The captain immediately ordered a withdrawal inland since the only weapons they had, apart from those of the marines already on the landing, were a few dirks and one or two soaked pistols. He left nine marines as a rearguard and urged the trappers and fishermen to leave for safety immediately. Armed with their own hunting pieces, those loyal men decided to stay. It had transpired they were all French Canadians who had sworn allegiance to the English king, having been Royalists and not in any way in favour of the Revolution. Their womenfolk insisted on staying with them but two young children were sent away with the sailors. There were two Cree Indians who volunteered to guide Commander Thompson and his survivors to Fox Bay though it would probably take a week to ten days.

By this time the French ship had launched her boats which were fast approaching the shore.

Pausing only to order Moseley and Franks to take up lookout on the hill in order to tell *Prince Rupert* what had happened if she arrived here, the party moved as quickly as they could along the trail leading east. Most of the sailors were dressed in wet shirts or pea jackets and despite stripping the houses of all the food they could find had barely enough to last them for three or four days.

North sat on an upturned barrel as he listened to him his teeth gritted. His anger suppressed for now, he heard the details of the tragedy.

Once ashore the French had made short work of the marines and settlers and had then set fire to all the buildings presumably to deny to the fugitives any chance of using them. On the hill-top the two English sailors shrank down and waited for *Prince Rupert.* Franks sobbed as his mate described to North what had followed. There were two trappers and five women who had survived and been taken prisoners. As they watched from the hill, the trappers were hacked into pieces by the French soldiers while a short officer wearing a sea captain's coat watched. The women were dragged into a long shed and they could hear their screams for more than twenty minutes as some of the enemy soldiers crowded in and out of the building. Two of the French sailors appeared to be arguing with the officer. He drew his sword and stabbed one of them and shot the second with his pistol. Then, with the women still inside, the captain had waved an arm and dozens of flaming brands were thrown in through the door. One woman managed to get out, naked and with her hair afire, and the captain took a musket and shot her dead.

As they spoke the hardened Englishmen around them gasped in horror.

The French ship had left the bay about four hours ago and made off westwards upriver.

North ordered that the two men be fed and then that all hands return to the ship as soon as Toller's party had returned.

Almost as soon as North was back aboard *Prince Rupert* a lookout reported that Toller was back on the shoreline with a large number of men, survivors of the brig; most of them were far gone with the cold. As these men were brought on board they were taken below by the crew and fed steaming bowls of soup, swaddled in blankets and tied into hammocks.

Commander Thompson, blanket about him and dressed in spare dry clothes from the wardroom, sat in a green leather armchair in North's cabin swallowing beef and pea soup, while North waited patiently for him to restore himself. Thompson had tears in his eyes. 'We stood no chance, sir. I blame myself. If only I had posted a lookout on the point earlier at least I would have had the guns run out.'

'Calm yourself, Thompson, there is no shame in being sunk by a ship more than three times your size. You did well to keep so many of your crew from being taken by the Frenchman. The important thing now is to catch up with them, wherever they are, and deal with them. I have ordered the ship west. Now, here is what I think will be the best chance of finding them.

'Even though there is no naval presence in Quebec City, I cannot see that they will risk travelling that far. This is the chart of the river. I believe that they will make for an anchorage either here, on the south bank in the area of Cap-au-Renard, where I am advised there is a sizeable Acadian settlement, though poor ground to anchor, or more likely on the north bank in one of these sheltered bays near the Sept-Isles. I will cover both possibilities by sending a pinnace south and taking *Prince Rupert* north.'

'Sir, forgive me, but what makes you so sure she will go upriver? As you say, she has little to gain it seems?'

North nodded, 'It is a good question. Your orders were to carry me upriver to meet your cousin David, correct?'

'Yes, sir. He will be in a hired lugger off the small island of Isle-au-Basques for the next few days, and after that at the settlement on the Saguenay River.'

'I believe those orders may be known to the French, hence the presence of the 74. It follows that all our secret precautions may have been in vain, but I could be wrong. There are other possibilities; a chance meeting between the 74 and a smaller vessel which may have seen us at the mouth of the river, for example. Although we now occupy the islands of St Pierre and Miquelon some of the French fishermen are still there and on the Newfoundland shore nearby. They could have warned the French that this ship passed south of the islands. In any case with *Voltigeur* sunk he may assume that *Prince Rupert* will head up river to keep the rendezvous.

'I intend not to disappoint him but we will proceed with stealth, with the launch under sail ahead of us to look into the bays. Perhaps this time it will be his turn to be taken by surprise.'

....

Early the following afternoon, North's best guess was proved correct. The launch tacked back to the ship to report that the French 74 was in a large bay formed at the mouth of the River Moisie.

At the dining table in the great cabin North pointed to the diagram he had drawn. 'Gentlemen, we have some advantages, apart from surprise. We have 70 officers and men from *Voltigeur* which brings our own strength back to its normal level and a total of eight boats for our use. I intend to cut out the Frenchman.' He paused, listening to the release of pent-up breath as his officers took in the audacity of the idea.

125

'Here is the plan.'

By the time the moon rose, all eight boats were being rowed with muffled oarlocks along the west side of the hook-like bay. The French 74-gun ship, the *Ailes de Mercure* (the Wings of Mercury) was anchored fore and aft half a mile into the bay on the west side.

North had brought with him 260 men in the boats. The launch had its 18-pound carronade mounted on the slide that ran the length of the boat; both of *Prince Rupert's* pinnaces had 12-pound carronades. None of these guns would be used unless the French ship became aware of their attack before they reached her.

The crew of the French ship were mostly asleep, with the watch only casually looking about them as they had been indulged by their captain in an overgenerous reward of wine in celebration of their victory at English Bay and to suppress murmurs of disquiet concerning the heinous actions of the soldiery. Therefore the shock of bodies clambering over the rails of the *Ailes de Mercure* was the first indication that some dreadful calamity was about the befall them. Completely unprepared, the 700 men on the ship were overwhelmed by one third of their number, their captain being hauled by the night-shirt from his bed space by Lieutenant Brazier, late of the *Voltigeur* brig.

The French were hampered by lack of ready weapons and many were so wretched drunk that they could hardly stand. Even so for a time the conflict was severe.

Cluney Ryan, boarding pike in hand, considered it his duty to act like a shadow to his captain and where North was during a fight, he was never far away. The quarterdeck had been cleared quickly and North hurried below to the most likely area of resistance – the officer's quarters.

Incautiously, Ryan rushed forward almost having his bald head cleaved open by a sword wielded by a young *aspirante.* North's left hand shot out and snatched him back a hair's breadth from his death blow. North's sword was swung upwards only to be broken in two by the force of the descending sword of his opponent. Ryan, gasping out breath in relief saw the antagonists pause for a moment, as if puzzled by both having a broken sword in their hands. Then North struck. Ten inches of steel thrust deep into the young Frenchman's chest. The sword locked deep in the dying man's wound. The eyes were wide, the mouth open in a silent scream. He fell.

From the corner of his eye Ryan saw another danger in the semi-darkness. A seaman, dressed only in dirty trousers had a pistol in his shaking hand pointing at his captain. Ryan hurled the boarding pike without aiming it. He almost vomited as he saw the Frenchman's face open like a split papaya, broken teeth and gushing gore projected almost to Ryan's feet.

As Ryan and North stared at each other, speechless with relief, the sounds of fighting died down and were replaced by the only too familiar screams of horribly wounded men.

Eighteen Frenchmen, seven British sailors and one marine were killed. There were also over 40 injured Frenchmen, including many who had been subjected to the rage of the *Voltigeurs* of the cutting-out party. Nine English sailors and three marines from *Voltigeur's* crew had been held prisoner chained in the noisome stench and misery of the bilges.

Capitaine de Vaisseau Louis Parmentier was ignominiously thrown at the feet of Captain North who looked down at him and addressed him harshly in French. 'Stand up. I want to look into the face of the man who ordered the rape and massacre of innocent civilians in English Bay.'

Parmentier was shaking with fear. He stayed on his knees, clasping his hands together. 'No sir, no, I did not give such orders, what the men did I had no part of – I never left the ship – my first lieutenant it was who went on shore.'

Another voice cried, 'Liar!'

An English officer staggered into the cabin, supported by one of the released *Voltigeurs*. His face was filthy and bearded and he was dressed in a torn tailcoat and ragged breeches. North barely recognised Lieutenant Crosby, the second-in-command of the missing schooner *Crow*.

Crosby pointed a shaking finger at Parmentier. 'This villain led his men ashore. Although I was chained in the hold I could hear what his men were saying. He killed one woman and allowed the soldiers to rape the others; most of his crew are outraged!'

North helped him to a chair. 'Crosby! My God, this I could not have expected, you here?'

Crosby gratefully accepted a mug of wine handed him by Captain Thompson. He looked up at North. '*Crow* was seized by a French privateer a few hours after we parted company with you, sir. Captain Rice and I were being held in their wardroom and being treated decently. The following morning, somewhere south of Cork, the privateer met up with this ship. This man, Captain Parmentier, came on board the privateer and found us there. The privateer captain told him who we were and Parmentier demanded we be handed over to him. The privateer captain, who I believe to be a decent man, refused him. Parmentier then threatened him that if he did not hand us over he would sink his ship.

'Of course he had no choice. As soon as we were on the *Ailes de Mercure,* Parmentier demanded our parole, which Captain Rice and I refused. We were then beaten and put in irons. Two hours later Captain Rice was taken to the cabin; he never returned. One of the crewmen, a Dutchman, told me that Parmentier had got two men to hold Captain Rice down while he tortured him with a red-hot poker until he told Parmentier where *Prince Rupert* was headed.'

Crosby stopped and wiped the back of his hand across his face, his eyes red. 'Then, I am told, Parmentier stabbed Captain Rice through the eye with the poker, killing him.'

'No, no, this is not true, Captain North, not true!' cried Parmentier.

'So, if it is not true, what happened to Captain Rice?' asked North.

'He tried to escape, he fell overboard.'

'Nonsense! How could he believe he could possibly escape leagues from the nearest land or even swim with his legs in irons! How did you know to pursue us here?'

Parmentier hesitated and answered with an obvious lie. 'Orders were passed to me when I rendezvoused with the captain of the *Dieppe,* shortly before taking these two officers aboard.'

'Really? What day was that?'

Parmentier said promptly, 'The 3rd of January, I remember it well because it is my wife's birthday.'

'You are absolutely sure of the date, the 3rd of January?'

'Absolutely!' Parmentier breathed easier.

North folded his arms. 'How interesting. Lieutenant Rockwell, bring our French guests on *Prince Rupert* over in the launch, if you please. In the meantime take Captain Parmentier to the wardroom and have him dress in slop clothing – he is not fit to wear the uniform of an officer.'

Twenty minutes later Rockwell returned. He was accompanied by Captain Le Blond and Lieutenant Chabat, late of the *Dieppe,* who, having given their parole had been on *Prince Rupert* since *Dieppe* had been captured.

North asked Le Blond, in French, 'Captain Le Blond, do you know this man?' He indicated Parmentier. 'He is captain of the *Ailes de Mercure.'*

Le Blond looked at the cringing man in duck trousers and a tattered shirt. North held up his captain's jacket and threw it on the floor in front of Parmentier. Le Blond said, 'Sir, I don't believe I have ever seen this man before. We were supposed to look out for this ship but we never saw her.'

'He tells me that his ship rendezvoused with yours on the 3rd day of January this year. Can you tell us where you and your ship, the *Dieppe,* were on that day, sir?'

Le Blond looked at him with a puzzled expression. 'Why, Captain North, you know full well I was on your ship, two days after you took the *Dieppe*. As far as I am aware *Dieppe* was probably under escort or in Cork Harbour.' He raised his hands and turned to Lieutenant Chabat for support. Chabat nodded, equally puzzled.

'Anything to say, Parmentier? I thought not. So we know you are a liar. Now, concerning what happened at English Bay. You went ashore and it was you who put the settlement to the torch and oversaw the raping and murder of the womenfolk, *was it not*?'

Parmentier almost sobbed. 'You have to believe me, on my honour, none of this is true. The crew – my officers – they all hate me, they lie!'

North went to the door of the cabin and beckoned to a man standing next to the marine. He entered the cabin but those inside could not see him clearly behind North.

North moved aside to reveal a short bearded man dressing in elk skin clothing, his head bandaged. 'This is Marcel Piedmont, one of the trappers in English Harbour. He was shot but luckily the ball knocked him out and he was left for dead. Tell us again what you saw when you woke up, Monsieur Piedmont.'

Piedmont spat on the French captain's feet before speaking in French. 'Sir, I was lying twenty feet from the boat shed. As I came to my senses I realised there were dozens of French soldiers and sailors standing around so I pretended death. I saw this man, this scum, he was there. He ordered my friend Louis Rimmel and his brother Jacques to be cut into pieces. The brothers pleaded with him, saying they were French – to save their lives.

'This animal said, "True Frenchmen would have died before allowing the English to stay in the settlement without trying to kill as many as they could. You are traitors to France!" Then he slashed both of them across the eyes with his sword and the soldiers joined in, it was terrible. I could barely hold myself still for trembling – I believed I had moments to live if they discovered I was not dead.

'Then his soldiers dragged the women into the shed, tearing their clothes from them, the wife and daughter of Jacques Rimmel, Madame Gaspard and two of the Fragonard sisters. The third sister was already dead. Even those sailors with him were protesting and I believe two of them would have mutinied but this man stabbed one to death and shot the other man in the mouth; he took a long time to die. I knew that all I could do was to bear witness but I wish I could have died a thousand deaths instead of what followed.'

He choked and fell silent.

Captain Le Blanc and Lieutenant Chabat were clearly horrified. Chabat shouted, 'You, *you*, did this? You *swine*, you are a disgrace to France!'

North said gently to Piedmont, 'Do you know which of the women attempted to escape the flames?'

The trapper straightened himself, anguish disfiguring his face. 'Louise Gaspard, she was barely twenty, married but six months and carrying her husband's child. This offal from hell shot her to death!' Before anybody could stop him he lunged forward with a huge knife in his hand and stabbed at the Frenchman's chest. Captain Parmentier fell on his side with a scream; nobody went to his aid.

North, shaken as was every witness, said, 'Enough, Piedmont, enough! I want him alive to hang. Conway, fetch the surgeon.'

A dozen or more crewmen of both English ships, hovering outside the cabin, some of them able to understand the substance of Piedmont's report from the French to the English, aghast at the revelations, quietly slipped away. Five minutes later Midshipman Dunne ran into the cabin where North was sorting through the French signal book and the ship's papers.

'Sir, the men, sir! I tried to stop them. They have hanged the French first lieutenant and their bosun.'

North turned wearily and said quietly, 'Have them cut down, Mr Dunne, and their bodies thrown into the water. You witnessed nothing, is that clear?'

The young man straightened himself and returned his captain's direct stare. 'Sir, I witnessed nothing.'

There was much to do. North decided that almost 700 prisoners would place far too great a drain on his resources. Sending the remaining two French lieutenants and the *Ailes de Mercure's* master under guard to the wardroom of the *Prince Rupert,* he ordered that the whole crew be taken ashore and left with a week's rations and no weapons except six muskets for hunting. He would report their presence to the garrison commander of Quebec City and leave it to him to secure them.

While they were in the bay *Prince Rupert's* guns were run out to cover the Frenchmen on the shore.

It was a difficult choice but North felt he had no alternative but to crew the prize with 50 of his own men and the 70

Voltigeurs and send them off to Halifax with a full report for Admiral Vandeput. At least this would give the admiral a great addition to his defences. It was adding to the losses his crew was suffering but with luck *Juniper* would arrive soon carrying the men he had detached as prize crew of the *Dieppe* and those he had left in Fox Bay.

He handed Thompson his orders. 'I have decided that there is little need for further reticence regarding the presence of *Prince Rupert* in the St Lawrence. I will take her in to meet your cousin and then go to Montreal. Your orders are to go on board His Majesty's prize ship *Ailes de Mercure* and read yourself in. As senior officer on station I have written your new commission. I trust their lordships will confirm your promotion to post captain.

'You will proceed at best speed to Halifax where you will place yourself under the orders of Admiral Vandeput. No doubt he will buy her in though I expect that he will cause her to be renamed since we have a ship named *Mercury* as well as a *Hermes* in the fleet. Perhaps with a completely different name it would also help to obliterate the shame of the name she now bears. God speed and good fortune, Captain.'

'Thank you, sir, and good luck to you in your mission.'

North kept Captain Parmentier with his remaining two lieutenants on board *Prince Rupert* though in Parmentier's case his ankles were shackled at all times. He offered his parole but North declined it in front of his countrymen, since he had proved himself to be a man without honour and therefore his word meant nothing. The other French officers refused to have anything to do with him and to avoid further unpleasantness he was confined to an empty lieutenant's berth and fed there.

The captain had been remarkably fortunate in his wound. No vital organ had been damaged but he had lost a lot of blood. Surgeon Weller was confident he would face the court martial due to him. The lieutenants, having given their parole, were allowed the freedom of the ship, though North suggested they should not stray far from the wardroom or the side of a British officer for fear his crew would dispose of them, so full were they of the horrific conduct of the French soldiers.

Although he had hidden himself amongst the crew there was another French officer on board, an army lieutenant who had taken off his jacket and dressed himself as a private soldier. His name was André Creuze-Latouche. As he was about to leave the ship to go on shore with the crew one of the French sailors saw him and called out in French to his comrades, 'that bastard Latouche is trying to disguise himself!'

The trapper Piedmont, who was nearby, waved an arm in the direction of the officer and shouted to the bosun, 'hey, he was one of them with Parmentier! Don't let him get away!'

The English sailors surged forward and thrusting the Frenchmen aside reached out to grab Latouche. He moved quickly to his left and drew a concealed pistol, waving it at his attackers. North, who had come on deck to see off Captain Thompson, shouted, 'Stand fast!'

It was as if everything became frozen in time. Every British man on deck stood still. The Frenchmen who had been scattering away from Latouche also stopped in their tracks, stunned by the immobile men around them.

North walked forward and stood in front of Latouche. 'Put

down the pistol. You have one shot and then you will die.'

'Wretch! That shot is for you, *vive la France!*'

North could see that the pistol was not cocked. Before Latouche could correct this North reached out and snatched the gun by its barrel and threw it to one side. Latouche let out a scream and lunged forward, his hands reaching for North's throat. North unsportingly kicked him hard between the legs, bringing him to the deck, his scream rising several octaves.

North turned calmly to the bosun. 'Have this creature strapped to the mainmast. I will deal with him later.'

There was an audible release of pent-up breath from the crew as they realised how close they may have come to losing their captain. Some accounted his actions as foolishness on his part, others to a rush of insanity.

Following on Captain Thompson's departure Jeremiah Wolfson came to the cabin and accepted a cup of tea as the two men conferred. North believed that *Prince Rupert's* presence in the St Lawrence was known well enough to the French that further secrecy was not warranted. He laid out the chart of the St Lawrence, unconsciously reaching into his waistcoat pocket to touch Isobel's locket, a habit he had developed when he was thinking.

'David Thompson should be waiting for us here at the Isles au Basques or if we miss that rendezvous, he will take his hired lugger up the Saguenay River to the settlement at Tadoussac. I intend that you and I shall leave *Prince Rupert* to make her way to Quebec City and wait there while we take a boat into the Saguenay. '

On the lower gun deck men who were hanging their hammocks were strangely hushed. Most of them had a straw-filled mattress – a "donkey's-breakfast," – plus two blankets and sometimes a pillow all to be put into the hammock and slung in 16 inches of space – though in some ships it was a bare 14 inches. At least in *Prince Rupert* there was a sensible policy that the two watches slung their hammocks side by side so that the watch asleep had twice as much room. One man, Hector Barwell, for several instances of tardiness in leaving his bed in the morning had his hammock confiscated and locked in the bosun's store for a month. Being sick of sleeping on the damp, bare deck, he had managed to secure a couple of bearskins from the *Ailes de Mercure* and was arranging them in a space by one of the guns.

His friend, Derek Dove, swung his own hammock above the space – privileged with a double space now that he was a gun captain. He shook his head as he spoke to Hector and to Con Riley, who swung his own hammock nearby.

'I can't believe what the captain did! He could have been shot.'

Riley shook his head. 'He's the captain. Don't surprise me one bit. The Frog will get hung for that, attempting to murder the captain – articles of war, ain't it?'

Barwell said, 'I still can't get over what they did at the village. That Parmentier and Latouche will get themselves hung for that anyway, won't they?'

Dove agreed. 'I seen many things since I was pressed from the old *Henry Fletcher* merchantman, lads, and I wish that I will see better times before I die but this day has been like a taste of old Nick's parlour itself. I can see them burnt bodies now and that smell; Gawd rest the poor women!'

'Amen to that, Dovey! The only time I saw something worse was in the Baltic ten years back,' said Riley. 'There was this huge battle – strike me down if I lie – 500 ships there was – never did I see such a thing.'

In the aftermath of the battle, during which the Russians lost more than 7,500 killed, wounded or captured against the Swedes 300 dead, Con Riley with a number of seamen was sent under a Swedish officer to the small island of Baklandet at the mouth of the Gulf where some survivors of the Russian frigate *Sankt Nikolai* were believed to be stranded – they had been there for three or four days.

'Those Russians were the lowest humans I ever did meet. On the island there were just a dozen families, most of them Finns with one family of Swedes and one of Russians. When the Russians landed they cut all the men to pieces, then the women, and as we got there they was roasting a young baby over a fire.'

At this point William Lorimer, who had been persuaded by a handful of silver to come on board the ship by the late Midshipman Boyle and deeply regretted the moment he had lost his wits to do so, rushed to the nearest fire-bucket and regurgitated his last meal of beef and oatmeal. Lorimer was universally detested amongst the seamen as a useless landsman who never improved and also as one of the master-at-arms' white mice – informers, narks. As a consequence he was refused in every mess and like those of his kind forced like a rat to eat his meals in odd corners – beaten and harried by all. He spent his hoarded cash on illicit booze and tried to keep his misery at bay by being constantly half-drunk.

Drunkenness was a flogging offence for seaman and as far the ship's boys were concerned, the cane over the back lashed to a ship's gun – kissing the gunner's daughter –but drunkenness was quietly rampant, even on *Prince Rupert.* Setting sail on Christmas Day had deprived the sailors of the full vigour of their usual 'wet-Christmas' and the beastly drunkenness of that day which made every officer steer well clear of below decks life. This was as well, since even with a considerate Captain like Mr North, there could have been a dozen or more flogged at the gratings the following day.

In fact apart from Boyle's death the only untoward incident on that Christmas day was the drunkenness of Henry Golightly, ship's boy of 13 years, who had climbed to the forepeak singing Hearts of Oak so tunelessly that the marine corporal was tempted to shoot him down to spare the crew's suffering eardrums. The captain had sentenced the diabolically hung-over lad the next morning to six strokes of the cane for being drunk and one more for the dire rendition of such a patriotic song.

Michael North had the privilege of serving for a half-year as a lieutenant under Nelson's friend Captain Cuthbert Collingwood. That honourable man was a strict disciplinarian but flogged a man only for the most serious offences. Even then on average only once in every month or so the cat was let out of the bag; almost never to the extent of more than a dozen lashes. Yet he had the most disciplined, well-trained and hard-working ship in the navy. North agreed with Collingwood that flogging – which should be the last resort – made a bad man worse and broke the spirit of a good man, who would thereafter never be of much use to the ship.

Chapter 10

<u>Tuesday 4th March, 1800</u>

Lying between two rounded hills, the village of Tadoussac consisted of a community of about 70 people permanently living there in single-storey wooden cabins, their numbers increased by fur traders for part of the year. The French had been trading and trapping from this place, their first settlement on the river, for almost 200 years.

The Saguenay River itself was tidal at this point, and with spring coming early this year it was virtually ice-free. On an incoming tide it had not been difficult to negotiate but the boat's crew was thankful for the rest that a run on shore gave them. Cluney Ryan and his boys settled down in the oak-beamed tavern that would normally have been closed up for another month or more and were content to keep the rest of the cold world outside.

In a nearby cabin North and Wolfson shook hands with David Thompson, a shorter version of his brother in England. He was clearly fully adapted to his chosen country and still wearing a long fur coat; he sat on a settle near the door and left the warmth of the fire to his guests. Hot wooden mugs of rum with sugar and cloves in hand, the three got down to business.

Thompson had acquired a slight French accent and confessed to North that he rarely spoke English now, conversing with his wife and her people in the Cree language or with traders and trappers in French. Unexpectedly he started to speak of his wife before any business was mooted; he was angry and distressed.

'My wife has been kidnapped, Captain. I cannot prove it but I see the hand of Harwell, the North West's chief secretary behind it. I have received a demand from the kidnappers to exchange her for an undertaking to stay away from Montreal and the North West's business and hand over her share document.'

Wolfson frowned. 'This is very bad news, Mr Thompson. Have you any idea where she has been taken?'

'I do not know yet. News only reached me this morning – a trader brought this note.' He handed a piece of paper to North, who read it aloud:

To Mr David Thompson,

It pains me to have to tell you that we have found it necessary to detain your wife. Be assured we have no intention of harming her. Your defection to the North West Company has shown distinct disloyalty to your former employer and therefore it has been considered necessary to put a stop to your nefarious activities.

You will withdraw forthwith from the vicinity of Montreal and return to Ottawa, where you will remain for the next twelve months. Your wife will be released when you have deposited her Share certificate in the North West Company in a sealed cover at Fort Lennox by the 15th day of March, to be left in the care of Mr Peter Seaforth, without communicating the contents to him.

The note was unsigned.

Wolfson said, 'You say you believe that the chief secretary of the North West Company is behind this but the note seems to imply that the Hudson's Bay Company is involved.'

Thompson replied, 'I left the Bay Company two years ago

without giving notice because I was disgusted by the way they treated the native trappers. Most senior people in each of the companies are above reproach – at least as far as their loyalty to King George is concerned – but I am certain that a few on each side are in league with each other and with the French. Harwell is a greedy man and leads a dissolute life but he is also highly intelligent and cunning. For a number of reasons I believe him to be the lynch-pin.'

'Remind me, where is Fort Lennox?' North asked.

'To the south of Montreal on the River Richelieu sometimes called the Chambly river, lies St Jean sur Richelieu – Fort Lennox is on the Île de Noix, an island in the river south of the town, built to defend the river passage from the United States, the border being just a few miles south.'

'And the man Peter Seaforth?'

'An innocent, I believe. He runs the storehouse on the island and is known widely as an honest and very religious man. I could be wrong but I believe he is being used. This morning I sent some of my people including my wife's two brothers in the lugger to take a canoe up the Richelieu, to watch the island and the surrounding area for any signs of the kidnappers.'

North stood up and walked to the rough bench at one side of the room to refill his mug. He paused and looked at David Thompson.

'It seems to me, Mr Thompson that finding your wife and releasing her must be your priority and in this endeavour I wish to put myself, *Prince Rupert*, and the crew at your disposal. However, I am bound to ask you to tell me about the situation in Montreal. I am aware of the background to this matter and that my ownership of two of the twenty shares is a part of the plan to thwart these French sympathisers but I am unsure where our votes will make a difference. Please enlighten me.'

It appeared that the North West Company's board consisted of those who owned the twenty voting shares and in whose hands all important decisions were placed by the partners, many of whom were not voting shareholders. The members of the board and their share holdings were Simon McTavish (4), William Mackie (4) – Mackie was currently chairman– William McLaren (3), John Cecil Ross, (2) James Ross (1), Alexander Campbell (1), Father Henri Petain (1), James Livermore (1) and the share of Thompson's wife with North's two shares totalled 20.

'We can discount James Ross and Alexander Campbell and their two votes. They set out to find a river route to the Pacific in December and are not expected back until the middle of the year. The remaining fifteen are divided into two groups - Mackie, Petain, and McLaren with eight votes; and McTavish, John Cecil Ross, and Livermore with seven votes.

'Because word came that Captain Lawrence Chandler had been killed it was thought his two shares would devolve to his heirs and being in England need not be considered. Proxies are not allowed; therefore absentees do not get a vote. Even my wife's share would be immaterial to decide a final vote because if by her voting with McTavish and his side sixteen votes were cast evenly, Douglas Mackie would cast his deciding extra vote as Chairman.'

'Who are the villains in this matter?' asked North.

'Mackie and his friends. They are anxious to merge the

company with the Hudson's Bay Company. Petain was not easily persuaded that they should support a French invasion, he is after all a churchman and a Royalist but he seems now firmly in favour. McLaren is a greedy man and a close friend of the secretary Harwell; I believe a large amount of gold is his incentive.'

'Why have they not simply had a board meeting and voted things their way already?'

'They would have done but McLaren, who has interests further south, has been in Albany these past two months and is expected to return on or about the 20th of the month. So Mackie has used his privilege as chairman to delay the meeting until then. '

'Hence also, perhaps, the deadline of the 15th in the kidnappers' note?'

Wolfson spoke up. 'There is another important matter. I had not told you about this, Captain, because it had been decided that a few facts should be held back until this meeting today in order to prevent the French discovering them under torture if you were to be captured.

'A few days after you received your commission a French spy left London and set off for Montreal, via Boston, probably arriving on or about the end of January. Our own turncoat found this out after he had gone. Our man told Lord Arden that the spy had information that not only were you in lawful possession of the Chandler shares but that you were bound for Montreal and that the conspiracy to aid the French was well known in London. Mackie and the others could draw the correct conclusion. With your two votes weighed on the side of loyalty – with Mr McTavish's group – there would be nine against eight and the chairman's vote would not carry the day. It would appear that Mrs Thompson's share has therefore become crucial to Mackie's plans.'

North said, 'I take it your wife's share would need to be passed to Mackie, Mr Thompson, with at least an appearance of legality. I expect that forcible persuasion would have to be made to get her to sign away her right?'

'That must be the case,' said Thompson unhappily.

North hesitated. 'This is a problem, isn't it? I believe that if they forced her to sign they would have to make sure she was unable to testify that the transfer was under duress.'

'Yes, they would have to kill her. You see the impossibility of my position. If I hand over the share, they will kill her; if I don't hand over the share, they will kill her.'

North pulled on his boat cloak and prepared to rejoin the ship. 'Then we must get her back before they do that. This is what I suggest we do ....'

....

Midshipman Boswell stood beside the master, staring out at the bare rocks in the tortuous traverse between the shore and the Îsle d'Orléans as they approached Quebec City. Navigating this stretch of water was dangerous but it had been proved 40 years ago when the Master of the transport *Goodwill* had refused to trust captured French pilots. That was in late June of 1759 when the British had laid siege to the city and a few weeks before Wolfe and Montcalm had both died in the battle of the Heights of Abraham.

'A bad place to lose one's concentration, Master,' said Boswell.

'Killick, the Master of the *Goodwill,* was my great-uncle. Apparently he said to the French pilot, who he thought was leading the fleet into danger, "I'll convince you that an Englishman shall go where no Frenchman dares show his nose!" Then off he went and not a single British ship got into trouble.'

Boswell looked to starboard at his captain, standing silently, his gaze shifting from the foam-covered rocks to the foremast sail. Without a word North nodded and went below. No better show of confidence could he have displayed in the Master and crew.

Chapter 11

<u>Wednesday 8th to Friday 10th March, 1800</u>

The party consisted of Captain Michael North, Midshipman Keith Boswell, David Thompson and second cox'n Cluney Ryan with the ten-man crew of the captain's 32-foot launch. The launch carried spritsails of identical size on her two 18-foot spreet-poles. The carronade was not being carried.

The journey upriver from Quebec City had been without incident apart from portage to circumvent the rapids at Chambly. Since reaching St Jean they had been circumspect in showing the launch's true colours. All on board were dressed in nondescript warm clothing, their uniforms being carried in sealskin bags in one of the two long birch-bark canoes being towed behind. A Cree Indian chosen by Thompson sat in the aft end of each canoe to steer and balance her.

North had left *Prince Rupert* two days ago with the 1st lieutenant in command under orders to return to Fox Bay and bring *Juniper* with him when she arrived to anchor at Quebec City. He was then to represent the ship at the trial of the French captain and Latouche for murder. If North failed to return before 12th April, Rockwell was to sail to Halifax and report to Admiral Vandeput.

Fort Lennox was at the opposite end of the island as they approached the Île de Noix from the north. Seated in a moored heavy canoe they found Thompson's Cree brother-in-law. Thompson called him Kane, instead of the jaw breaking name Kaneonuskatew; meaning 'walks on four claws'. He was with another member of the tribe, Ahtahkakoop ('star blanket') who answered to the name Arthur.

Kane reported that he had three men on the island, two watching the gates of the fort and remembering the faces of all the fort's visitors. Thankfully this early in the year they were few and far between and since access to the island was only by boat, they could be closely monitored. The third watcher was inside the fort. He was a Scotsman, Donald McDonald, a familiar visitor who sold blankets and leather goods to the soldiers and was tolerated by the storekeeper Seaforth, who was a distant cousin of McDonald's wife.

North and Thompson went on to the island and walked as far as the fort. Their entry was checked by the sentry but his examination was cursory.

McDonald was hunched up in a fur robe on a bench outside the store. He reported that no suspicious character had been in the area in the past few days, confirming an observation by the watchers at the landing stage.

The log-built store bore the legend Seaforth Trading Company above the door. Inside the atmosphere was stuffy and smelled strongly of camphor and animal skins. There was a smoky stove in the centre of the room. Sacks of grain, salt and various boxes and bundles vied for space with bales of check cloth, neat racks of boots in various sizes and a disorderly pile of snow-shoes. Seaforth was a short, round-faced man with long black hair neatly pigtailed and tarred. North suspected a naval background but did not care to enquire too closely. At least the reputed honesty of the man seemed to shine out from his clean, neatly shaven face. The man was alone in his store.

North decided to come straight to the point. Keeping his expression neutral, he looked the man in the eye.

'Mr Seaforth? My name is Captain North of the Royal Navy; I represent His Majesty's government. I believe you are expecting my friend here, Mr David Thompson? I could introduce myself to the commanding officer but our business is with you. Do you understand?'

A puzzled note in his voice Seaforth replied, 'I was told to expect Mr Thompson who would leave a sealed document to be collected. I know nothing more.'

North nodded. 'It would appear to be as we suspected. The other party in this matter is clearly using you, Mr Seaforth. I will not beat about the bush; I must ask if you are aware that Mr Thompson's wife Charlotte has been abducted?'

Seaforth's appearance of shock could hardly have been faked. He turned and picked up a bible from the counter. 'Truly, as God is my witness, I know nothing of this – I was simply asked to hold a package to be collected. What must I do, Captain?'

'We need to know who gave you these instructions.'

'A Frenchman, Jacob Dufour, but I can't believe he is a traitor, his family was persecuted in the Terror, his father and brother guillotined.'

North said, 'It could be that he is acting for others, innocent himself.'

North and Thompson had considered the matter carefully. Today was probably the first possible day Thompson could have arrived at the fort, perhaps even a few days more would have been necessary if the share certificate had been in Montreal. Dufour or whoever was sent to collect it would likely not arrive for a day or two. It was risky but they had decided to allow the package to be collected and then follow the messenger to where the kidnappers were holding Charlotte Thompson. If the messenger met one of the kidnappers somewhere else they would have to decide at that point what to do.

Asking Peter Seaforth to hand over the packet without comment, they left the fort with McDonald still on watch and deployed their forces.

Thompson would wait with Kane and Arthur in their canoes and North would take the launch upstream where he and his men would conceal themselves in the channel that ran between the shore and the small island opposite a promontory called L'Abri-du-vent-de-Nord, the Shelter from the North Wind, which was a short distance south of the fort. North suspected that they might have carried Mrs Thompson south across the border into Vermont, which could mean that he and his crew would be crossing illegally into the United States. Although there was no war between Britain and America, he was taking a risk and if caught he could be detained. A diplomatic incident could trigger catastrophic consequences, even if American activities were sometimes just as provocative near the border.

He and his crew slept as best they could in bearskin robes and blankets under tarpaulin in the launch which at eight feet and six inches wide was roomy enough. They rose at dawn and cooked on a fire on the shore a hot meal of oatmeal and salt-pork with mugs of hot grog.

At ten in the morning the lookout waved from the shore and they made themselves ready as he ran to rejoin the boat. A big canoe was coming up river with at least eight men paddling and a man in the stern with a long sweep.

North had the launch rowed down to the south end of the channel and waited. As the canoe passed, being paddled at an easy pace, he could see that the man in the bows was dressed in a dark blue greatcoat and wearing a tarpaulin hat of the same pattern used by English warrant officers in the navy. With the exception of the helmsman the rest of the crew, who were a mixture of Europeans and natives, were dressed mainly in buckskin coats or furs. From his dress North believed the cloaked helmsman to be a French officer.

North waited until the canoe had disappeared from view round the next bend of the river before following. As the launch pulled out into the main river Cluney Ryan, who was sitting beside him, drew his attention to another canoe which was about 100 yards behind them and coming up fast, driven by four paddles. David Thompson at the prow waved his arm and pointed downstream in the direction of the other canoe. Then, by arrangement, he dropped back a little so that if their quarry looked back they would just see the launch, which not having followed them from Fort Lennox, could be a vessel on mundane business.

For an hour or so the leading canoe could be seen easily at each bend of the river then at a quiet warning from the midshipman in the bows, North gave the order quietly to avast rowing and let the launch drift to a stop against the slow downstream current, just keeping a pair of oars working to keep her in the same position.

When Thompson had come alongside, North whispered to him that the canoe they were following had pulled in to the east bank of the river.

Thompson replied, 'I have to tell you, sir, that we passed the marker a mile or so back denoting the 45th line of latitude and we are now in the United States. We are a few miles north of the town of Alburg.'

North smiled, 'Well, David, necessities of the war, I submit. Let us go on shore to see if we can find out why they stopped. 'Boswell, wait here until I return; I shall transfer to the canoe.'

Thompson, North and the Indian, Arthur, crouched hidden by a low bank in the long winter-dry grass about 30 yards inland of the river and 50 yards north of the landing point. The big canoe had been drawn up on to the bank and the occupants were lifting out back-packs and muskets ready to march off.

After a brief consultation North and Thompson returned to the shore while Arthur prepared to follow the enemy party. Once North had his men on the riverside he instructed Midshipman Boswell and two men of the launch crew to remain with McDonald and two of his companions while the rest of the party followed in pursuit of the kidnappers. He took with him David Thompson, Cluney Ryan and eight of his crew, together with Kane and three of his people. They were well armed and carried with them provisions for seven days' march.

It took about half an hour for them to catch up with Arthur, who emerged from a stand of fir trees and joined them, pointing up the track-way as it rose to a gap between two hills about half a mile away. On the other side of the gap the road ran down to a tributary of the Richelieu on the banks of which were three log huts. The kidnappers appeared to be heading for that settlement.

Wasting no time, they mounted the hill and concealed themselves in scrubby bushes each side of the road. North took a small telescope from his pocket and scanned the scene below. There was a clearly marked trail, hardly a road, leading north and south with the buildings on the east side. Two more men had emerged from one of the huts to greet the arrivals. North turned to Cluney Ryan. 'Ryan, I want you to take four men and work your way around to the rear of those huts. Wait in the trees until you hear my signal. If it is a hail you will know that all is well and you may come forward; if a shot...well, you know what to do.'

Taking the remaining men with him North proceeded cautiously taking an indirect path that swung south of the buildings through a heavily wooded area of trees. It was not certain that this was where Charlotte Thompson was being held but it had been decided they would go forward and confront the people in the settlement. They reached a point 30 feet across a meadow from the largest hut before the alarm was raised and several armed men rushed out on to the track. North called to them to lay down their arms but as he did so a shot rang out from the hut and one of the boat's crew fell, clutching at his thigh.

North gave the order to fire and all four men outside the hut were cut down, three of them dead. North called for his men to cease firing and for those in the hut to throw out their guns and surrender because they were surrounded. There was a flurry of activity as two men ran from the rear of the hut and were shot down by Ryan and his men. Then a musket was thrown from the window, followed by two pistols and from the doorway several more pistols and five muskets. Calling for them to come out with their hands raised, North and his men moved forward.

There were seven men lining up, hands above their heads .
Ordering his men to collect the weapons, North and
Thompson entered the hut. There was no sign of Charlotte
Thompson but the package containing her share certificate
was on a table near the door.

The man whom North had thought was a French officer was
clearly not the man in charge, and nor was the man who had
been in the bows of the canoe. The honour of command went
to a thin, narrow-faced man wearing a fashionable green
tailcoat, white kerseymere knee breeches and hussar boots,
and a long green cloak over one shoulder. This was the man
North took to one side first to interrogate.

North looked him up and down, 'Your name?'

'My name is Cyrus Keeble from Burlington, Vermont and
what in hell do you think you are doing! You're English aren't
you? What is this, a damned invasion of my country?'

'I don't intend to waste time on you, Mr Keeble. The man
standing over there is David Thompson.' Keeble looked
startled, and North nodded. 'Yes, that's right, you didn't
expect him to be here, did you? Now do I get answers from
you or shall I leave you to the mercies of Mr Thompson and
his Indian friends, some of whom are relatives of Charlotte
Thompson?'

The man shook his head. 'What do you want to know?'

'Where is Mrs Thompson?'

Realising that he had no cards to play, Keeble replied, 'If you
have a map of the area I can show you where she is being held

or I can take you there. None of these men have the information; they are merely paid to escort our messenger and me.'

'Even the French officer? What is his role in this?'

'I don't know. He was about to tell me why he is here when you arrived.'

'Who are you working for?'

Keeble answered without pausing, 'The man who has Mrs Thompson is called Harold Palmer. He is from Montreal and is employed by the North West Company. I do not know who he works for; he is just paying us good money to help. I have nothing against Mr Thompson and his wife.'

North called Thompson over. 'Do we have a map of this area, David?'

Thompson was a surveyor who had mapped hundreds of thousands of square miles of Canada and anything he did not have in the sealskin bag he always carried with him was in his head. 'I can draw a map in minutes. How much territory do I need to cover?'

They went back into the hut with Keeble, who described the limits of the area he wanted to be shown.

The area of land where they were at present was a peninsula into Lake Champlain. On the west the lake emptied into the Richelieu and on the east an arm of another body of water reached down from the Baie Mississquoi. At the southern end of the peninsula on the eastern side was Dillenbeck Bay, where in a fortified cabin Palmer was holding Charlotte Thompson. Keeble pointed to the place where the cabin was built. It sat on the shoreline with rising ground behind it. 'It has slits for windows and an eight-inch thick door. If you storm it he will probably kill her.'

David Thompson grabbed him by the throat. 'Not with you leading the way, you jackal! You are going to take me into the cabin.'

North restrained Thompson. He shook his head. 'I presume this man Harold Palmer knows you?'

Thompson replied, 'He is one of the secretary's creatures, a pathetic little man whose neck I could snap with two fingers.'

'Obviously you cannot go in first. I have an idea how we can get inside without Palmer suspecting. You, Keeble, how much is Palmer paying you?'

Choking after his manhandling Keeble mumbled, 'Not enough to risk my life. He advanced me 50 guineas I needed to settle some urgent bills and he is supposed to give me 50 more after he receives the package.' He nodded to the package on the table.

'I will pay you 100 guineas and allow you to go free unharmed if you throw your lot in with us. What do you say?'

'Willingly, sir,' said Keeble, extending a hand which North ignored.

'Very well, this is what we shall do...'

After laying out his plan he sent Keeble outside with Ryan to watch him since he would never trust a turncoat. He had the French officer brought in. The man removed his cloak to reveal a well-tailored pale blue uniform with the heavy gold epaulettes of a lieutenant of the French navy. North asked him in his own language who he was and what part he played in this shameful business. '*Je suis le Capitaine North de Marine de Son Majesté Britannique. Qui êtes-vous et quel est votre rôle dans cette affaire déshonorante?*'

The Frenchman replied in good English, 'My name is Lieutenant Martin Duchamp, I am attaché to the Embassy of the French Republic to the Congress in Philadelphia and I demand to be released immediately!'

'Do you indeed, Lieutenant? Well firstly, you will address me as sir, and you will remove your hat in the presence of a superior officer! Now what are you doing here?'

'I refuse to answer, *sir*.'

North said, 'I warn you, Lieutenant, I will not be trifled with. You were at large in Canada from whence I followed you. Do you wish me to treat you as a spy in time of war? I caution you that the activities of one of your countrymen in recently overseeing the rape and murder of innocent women on the St Lawrence river has put the patience of my crewmen under considerable strain and should they choose to execute you I might be unable to stop them! Now what do you know of this man Palmer's plans?'

Duchamp's jaw fell open. 'I know nothing of this! I haven't even met Palmer. My orders were to liaise with certain people who are partners of the North West Company. I was invited to come on this expedition to secure a document which would have a bearing on those people being able to control the company. Now I am told a woman has been kidnapped. On my honour, I assure you I knew nothing of this.'

157

'Very well, I accept your word but I am afraid you cannot be released. I intend to take you back to Montreal to confront these traitors. You can give me your parole that you will not try to escape or I will be forced to have you tied up, your choice.'

Duchamp said wryly, 'I suppose it is no use reminding you, sir, that you have no right to ask for my parole as we are in a neutral country – a country where your armed presence is probably a violation of that neutrality? However I will give you my word of honour as a gentleman that I will not attempt to escape. Indeed although this whole affair is extremely distasteful to me I am curious to see what happens if you return to Montreal.'

'Very well, Lieutenant Duchamp, now I have to trouble you further by removing your uniform coat and handing me your hat in exchange for mine.'

With Keeble leading the way, North, Thompson and four seamen with four of Thompson's Indians went south-east about seven miles until they left the forest and stood on a slight promontory overlooking a curved bay with a large island lying off to the east.

It was early afternoon but the sun was now low on the horizon, heavy clouds obscuring it from time to time. Above them the clouds were darker and it started to rain heavily.

As they walked towards the single-storey shingle-roofed cabin the driving rain made the turf under their feet so slippery it was difficult to maintain their footing. On the other hand visibility was reduced to a few yards which could prove an advantage. North brought them to a halt 30 yards from the cabin and whispered instructions. He had been assured by Keeble that apart from Charlotte Thompson there was another woman, the wife of a man named Gould. Gould was in the cabin as was Palmer.

'Keeble, Ryan and I will go in alone. While we are distracting them the rest of you will quietly take up position against the outside walls. After three minutes exactly you will storm the building.'

Thompson was clearly unhappy, 'It is risky, sir. In the mêlée Charlotte could be injured.'

'I have thought of that. Riley, is your powder dry?'

'Yes, sir, I've kept it wrapped in two oilskins.'

'Good. Now, Riley has a grenade which he will ignite seconds before your advance and throw it on to the ground. I believe this will be a sufficient distraction for me to grab your wife and shield her but it does mean you will have to break in immediately. Ryan will stand just inside the door when we enter, ready to open it the moment he hears the explosion. It is the best plan I can think of, David.'

Unhappy but resigned, Thompson agreed.

Keeble and North walked forward boldly with Cluney Ryan at their heels and Keeble banged his fist hard on the door. A voice called, 'Who is there?'

'It's me, Keeble, open this damned door, I am soaked through!'

The door was opened by a sallow-faced unshaven man

wearing a red checked shirt and blue trousers. He was short but muscular and showed every sign of being a heavy drinker. He jerked his head at them and stepped back as they entered. The room was very hot, with a blazing fire. Evil-smelling tallow candles set in scooped-out holes in the mud plaster of the walls threw some smoky light on the dark-coated man who stood facing them, leaning on a table in the centre of the room. Two women sat in cushioned chairs, one either side of the fire. As he threw down his sodden boat cloak to reveal his French uniform a quick glance made North certain that the younger, darker-skinned, attractive woman with her hair in two braids must be Charlotte Thompson. Her face was strained and anxious.

Without prompting, Keeble pointed at her, and started to walk over to where she was seated, thereby confirming North's assessment. 'Don't worry, Mrs Thompson, I have the share certificate, soon you will be released. Isn't that right, Mr Palmer?' he turned to the man at the table.

Palmer nodded but the three men could see that he was out of the line sight of Mrs Thompson as he smirked and said, 'Of course, all I will need is her signature.'

North moved forward to stand directly in front of Palmer, who was a darkly handsome man with black hair and dark brown eyes. In poor English he said, 'Lieutenant Duchamp, you are expecting me, m'sieur?'

Palmer started to speak, then a tick appeared at the corner of his mouth and his eyes widened. North knew he was not convinced; he moved closer as Palmer started to turn towards Charlotte Thompson, reaching out with his right hand to a pistol lying on the table. North lunged as a tremendous

160

explosion came from outside the cabin but Palmer had the cocked pistol up and as in a dream North saw it coming up to fire. As the gun was fired Keeble threw himself over Mrs Thompson.

All was confusion. There was a second explosion as Ryan fired his dag at the man Gould, who was attempting to reach a musket leaning against a trunk near the window. The door opened. There was a rush of bodies. Meanwhile North had grappled Palmer to the floor. Thompson rushed over to where his wife was pulling herself from under Keeble's limp body. Mrs Gould sat immobile, shocked into silence.

Meanwhile North and Palmer continued to struggle; Palmer freed a hand and managed to pull a knife from under his coat. North caught his hand and forced it back. Palmer was panting with exertion, his teeth bared and eyes staring. North felt himself being pushed over on to his back. As Palmer freed his hand and lifted it to plunge the knife into North another shot rang out as Con Riley fired almost point blank into Palmer's face. There was blood everywhere. Palmer's lifeless body sagged away from North and fell under the table. Riley helped his captain to his feet.

Still shaken, North called out to Thompson, 'Is she all right, David?'

'Yes, yes, thank you! Keeble saved her life!'

Keeble was dazed but otherwise almost unhurt. The bullet had struck him on the side of the head, taking away part of his left ear.

Palmer, the traitor, was buried in the mud at the water's edge. Gould was left to his wife's care, his shattered shoulder causing him considerable pain.

Keeble, still shaken but happily in possession of another 200 guineas plus the contents of Palmer's pockets amounting to 125 dollars, set off in Palmer's canoe for Burlington beside Lake Champlain. The following morning North led the party back to the launch where McDonald, Arthur and the rest of Thompson's people bid them goodbye and set off in their canoes. Still with one canoe in tow North had the launch rowed across the boundary line into Canada where the navy men dressed themselves once more in their uniform clothing.

Chapter 12

Sunday 11th to Monday 19th March, 1800

Three days had passed since the death of Palmer and the rescue of Charlotte Thompson. North was standing in the galley at the stern end of his cabin looking out on the waters of the St Lawrence as the ship swung at her anchors under the guns of Quebec City. The weather was now a little warmer and North had given leave for some of the crews to go on shore. *Juniper's* commander, Lieutenant William Fowler, had reported on board as soon as North had arrived and then sent over the men who had been detached from *Prince Rupert* to take the *Dieppe* into Cork. He had also brought with him another two dozen hands that had volunteered from a wrecked merchantman in Sligo Bay.

North had found two more British ships in the bay, the 28-gun frigate *Carysfort*, Captain Volant Vashon Ballard, and the 16-gun ship-sloop *Peterel*, captained by Commander Francis Austen. *Carysfort* and *Peterel* had been sent by the Admiralty to augment his force after finding that the secret mission was secret no longer. Ballard, who had attended upon North as soon as he had arrived, carried orders with him to the effect that after attending to the business outlined in his previous secret orders, North was to take *Prince Rupert, Carysfort, Peterel, Juniper,* and *Voltigeur* – which latter ship the Admiralty had no reason to believe had been sunk, to join Admiral Vandeput in Halifax to await the impending invasion, should it transpire.

Ballard was a smartly dressed man who displayed energy and efficiency. He was 26 years old. North gave him temporary command of the small squadron while North removed into *Juniper* to sail up to Montreal the following day.

North returned to the dining cabin as the sentry announced his guests for dinner, David Thompson and Jeremiah Wolfson. The captains of the three other ships and Lieutenant Rockwell followed shortly afterwards.

The meal was pleasant and convivial. There was fresh venison, kale and turnips followed by syllabub, a speciality of North's steward, and some excellent local cheeses. North noted with some satisfaction that none of his guests were heavy drinkers but even so four bottles of wine and the best part of a bottle of port were enjoyed and conversation flowed freely.

The sun was shining with some slight but welcome warmth on the following morning when North was piped on board *Juniper* for their journey up to Montreal. The river was turbulent on the incoming tide as they upped anchor and began to sail upstream with the swift current. The river here was still between a mile and two miles or more wide. Navigation was possible all the way to Montreal and the journey of about 160 miles took less than two days, wind being in the schooner's favour for most of the way.

David Thompson stood on the foredeck with Jeremiah Wolfson, pointing out the small settlements as they passed. North stood on the starboard side of the poop deck with Lieutenant Martin Duchamp.

'Lieutenant, I intend to take you before the board of the North West Company to give evidence concerning the kidnap of Mrs

Thompson but we both know that your masters intend to invade this country by posing as mercenaries working for the Hudson's Bay company in some manufactured armed conflict between the two companies. I am not asking you to betray your country but you must see that such a plan cannot possibly succeed. My country has a tight blockade on all the French ports and it will be impossible to supply your army, even if it gets as far as Canada.'

Duchamp gave a Gallic shrug of the shoulders. 'I am only a lieutenant, sir, but I believe that the Directory sees Britain as militarily weak in Canada. While, as you say, there can be little chance of reversing the losses France suffered forty years ago, I believe that they are hoping to draw off your ships and troops to reinforce Canada. It may be that they are also hoping that the Americans join in on the side of France.'

North grunted, 'A vain hope, I doubt that President Adams and Alexander Hamilton with their Federalist policies wish to make war on Britain, rather the opposite, even though apparently they cannot stand the sight of each other. They see their best interests as being based on friendship with Britain. In any case for the past three or four years America and France have been preying on each other's shipping and while Adams would like to make peace with Paris he will not join an alliance against Britain.'

Duchamp replied, 'There is an election in America next year and if Jefferson becomes president, he might well join France against your country. He may offer an alliance as an inducement to have the business of the Louisiana Purchase completed.'

'A lot can happen in a year, Lieutenant.'

The offices of the North West Company in Vaudreuil Street were a short walk from the harbour. North and his companions were received at a heavy wooden door set in a long grey wall. The man who responded to their knocking was a short, thin-faced Scotsman. Thompson addressed him, 'Good morning McLeod, we have an appointment with Mr McTavish.'

'Aye, Mr Thompson, he is in his office. I am pleased to see you, sir. Things are not looking good for Mr McTavish. You know how he is, he says what he thinks and he is used to getting his own way ...' He was interrupted by a booming voice, shouting from the top of a broad wooden staircase.

'McLeod! Is that young Thompson with you?'

Thompson called back, 'It is I, Mr McTavish.'

'Then come on up!'

The man they followed into the warm comfortable office was a bear of a man with long white hair and stern features. He stood with his back to a blazing fire and gestured towards a side table, 'Good scotch whisky, gentlemen, help yourselves and don't be mean with the measures. It is from Islay, a dreary place full of bigots and running noses but at least they make an honest whisky. Well now, David Thompson, who are these people with you? A naval captain – you'll be the commander of the *Prince Rupert* 74 whose praises the governor has been singing. Stole two 74 gun ships from the Frogs on your first voyage, by God! My partner in the London office, John Fraser, sent me a copy of the Gazette concerning the capture of the *Dieppe;* I doubt you have seen it yet, eh? Then this dreadful business with the *Ailes de Mercure?* The French captain was hung in Quebec last week, wasn't he? Damn good thing too!'

166

He paused for breath.

Thompson took advantage of the momentary lull in the forceful man's monologue to introduce Jeremiah Wolfson.

McTavish smiled as he pumped Jeremiah's hand. 'I received the letter from the duke, Mr Wolfson! Thank heavens we have somebody with brains in London. Now, we don't have much time.'

He went on to explain that William McLaren had returned from Albany the night before so it was providential that they had reached Montreal today. Mackie had called a Board meeting for 11 o'clock – in about half an hour– and McTavish had feared they would not be in time. After Thompson had recounted the story of his wife's kidnapping, McTavish was incandescent with rage.

'Those damned traitors! We must be thankful for your wife's safe return, Thompson!'

Thompson replied, 'We cannot prove it was at the bidding of the chairman or his people, sir. In fact I did feel it may be better not to say a word about it at the meeting and leave them uncertain as to what has happened but why don't we see what occurs. To avoid any further risk in the future I have sold my wife's share to Mr Wolfson for one guinea – he will be able to speak at the board meeting along with Captain North. If I remain outside the boardroom, out of the way for the time being, with Lieutenant Duchamp, you can send for me at the appropriate moment.'

McTavish smiled, 'That is a very good idea!' He looked curiously at Duchamp, who was dressed in full uniform, and spoke to him in accentless French. 'How are you involved in this, Lieutenant?'

'Your company secretary, Mr Harwell, met secretly with some people from our legation in Philadelphia and I was sent here as an observer. I cannot discuss with you any matter concerning my country's plans but I can confirm that I was present when Harwell instructed William Palmer to kidnap Mrs Thompson and get control of her voting share.'

McTavish's jaw dropped open. '*What!* Harwell! Palmer is his creature, I know that but *this* ... where is Palmer, I'll have him arrested!'

David Thompson said, bluntly, 'He is dead, Mr McTavish. He tried to kill my wife and stab Captain North to death. One of the captain's seamen shot him.'

'Too damned right!' said McTavish. He was shaking with rage to such an extent that his tumbler of whisky splashed over his fingers as he refilled it. 'Come along, gentlemen, let us go to a board meeting.'

The board room of the Company was long, heavily carpeted and well furnished. Its walls were covered by oak panelling on which hung a number of stern-faced portraits in oil and some scenes from the Orkney Islands. On one wall was an enormous map of eastern and central Canada and the Great Lakes. The long table was covered in a green cloth upon which were arranged carafes of water and small plates of biscuits. In front of the rotund chairman was a bowl of sweetmeats, into which his pudgy hand darted frequently.

The board members were ranged each side of the table with

Simon McTavish, as the other major share holder, at the end facing Mackie. To Mackie's right was the Secretary, Owen Harwell, a pallid man whose size was in sharp contrast to the chairman. He had a high-pitched Welsh accent and a habit of frequently wiping his nose on the cuff of his coat. He was however, very well dressed. In particular his coat seemed suspiciously expensive for a man on a clerk's salary.

'Take the minutes of the last meeting as read, Mr Chairman?' he piped.

Mackie nodded. 'Any dissenting?' After a suitable silence, he continued. 'Make it so, Mr Harwell.'

McTavish spoke up. 'Before we open the agenda, let me introduce two voting shareholders from England, Mr Chairman.' He snapped his fingers and McLeod, who had been standing behind his chair, went to the door and opened it to admit North and Wolfson.

Mackie half rose from his chair, 'What the hell is this, McTavish? I forbid this!'

Instead of answering, McTavish nodded to North who, in his dress-coat and sword, walked to the head of the table and held out a parchment. 'My name is Captain Michael Orrick North of His Majesty's Royal Navy. I have two voting shares in this Company, willed to me by my friend the late Captain Lawrence Chandler.' He produced a letter. 'Here is the notarised declaration of His Majesty's Solicitor General, confirming that ownership.'

He turned away from the Chairman and walked to the far end of the table to sit next to Simon McTavish. Mackie's mouth was still open in shock when the black-coated Wolfson, in

169

turn, followed North. 'My name is Jeremiah Wolfson, secretary and agent to the Duke of Bridgwater. I have here a duly recorded letter of authority from His Grace and one voting share certificate I purchased from Charlotte Thompson on 11th March this year.' He followed North to a seat beside him.

Uproar broke out around the table, though noticeably the majority of the noise was being made by Mackie's supporters. He hammered for silence.

His face was considerably whiter than it had been a few minutes before and the sweetmeat bowl was forgotten. 'Very well,' he said tightly, 'Let us not beat about the bush, shall we. We all know, especially you, Simon McTavish, that there has been a continuous series of provocative and dastardly attacks on our people and on our property by agents of the Hudson's Bay Company. I believe it is time to put a stop to this once and for all. We have over 2,000 associates and employees depending on us and common sense demands that we move against the Bay and teach them a lesson that will make them leave us alone in the future.'

McTavish leaned forward,' Sounds like you want to declare *war* on them, William? Well then, let's vote on it. Fellow board members, the proposition is that we attack the Hudson Bay Company and its people, all those for the proposition?'

As had been predicted Mackie, Petain and McLaren voted their eight votes in favour of aggression and McTavish, John Ross and Livermore their seven votes against. Then all six men looked at North and Wolfson and waited.

Jeremiah Wolfson voted against the proposition.

North stood up. 'Mr Chairman and gentlemen. Before I cast my vote, which I presume will decide the matter I wish to say a few words which may come as a surprise to some of you. My purpose in coming here was not simply to use my votes as I thought fit. I am sent as a special representative of His Majesty's Lords of Admiralty. It has come to their lordships' notice that France intends to send 3,500 troops, in advance of a further 17,000, to invade Canada. The ships are almost certainly at sea as I speak.'

There were shouts of astonishment and rage. Mackie looked like he was about to faint.

'Hear me out, please! The plan is for the troops to be landed on the Labrador coast and then turn south spreading the word that they are men hired by the Hudson's Bay Company to teach the North West Company a lesson for attacking the Bay Company's settlements and people. The majority of the Hudson Bay people in this country have absolutely no knowledge of this and are free from blame. The French soldiers and mercenaries are supported by a French squadron of four ships of the line and a number of frigates that will attack Halifax with the intention of capturing it or burning it to the ground. Of course, should you decide to carry the proposition of aggression into effect, you will give them that pretended justification and also further alienate your rival company.'

Father Petain stood up and shook his fist angrily at Mackie. 'You would have had us be blamed for provoking war with France, sir! You are either a fool or a scoundrel! I withdraw my vote in favour and I am now against the proposition.'

'As am I,' said North. 'I now call upon the chairman to resign and propose that Mr Simon McTavish be elected in his place.'

'*Seconded!*' shouted Petain.

The vote was carried with one abstention, McLaren, and none against. Mackie stood up and started to rush from the room in fury but he was stopped at the door as Thompson entered with the French lieutenant at his heels, having been fetched by McLeod.

Thompson called out, 'Permission to address the board!'

McTavish replied cheerfully, 'Permission granted. The chair recognises Mr Thompson.'

His hand firmly against Mackie's chest Thompson pushed him back to his chair, walked round him, and, grabbing Owen Harwell by the scruff of the neck, dragged him out of his chair and threw him across the room. 'I accuse this man of commissioning the kidnap of my wife. Lieutenant Duchamp will bear witness that Harwell instructed Harold Palmer in the matter. Palmer detained her to force me to hand over her voting share.'

Duchamp said, 'This is correct. Palmer's man Keeble told me this himself.'

Harwell shouted, 'It's not true! Bring Palmer here; let him say this to my face!'

North said, 'Palmer is dead and I was present when it happened. Mrs Thompson was being held by Palmer against her will, you have my word on that.'

Duchamp said, 'And mine. I have no reason to lie; I am an officer of the French Republic.'

McTavish pointed at the cowering Harwell, 'Leave here immediately and do not return. If you are found within twenty miles of this place after midnight tonight I will have you seized up for conspiracy to kidnap. *Go!*'

He turned to Mackie, 'Have you anything to say?'

Mackie shook his head.

'I suggest you return your shares to be sold and retire to your estates, William. You have no place here now.'

Mustering what little dignity he could, Mackie left the room.

After the meeting the other board members gathered around and expressed horror and indignation. North was convinced any talk of attacking the Hudson's Bay Company was now dead in the water.

Chapter 13

<u>Tuesday 20th to Saturday 24th March, 1800</u>

The journey back to Quebec City was without incident. North found that all was ready for the flotilla to depart and called his captains on board *Prince Rupert* being very conscious of the somewhat bizarre situation that though he was in fact senior by virtue of the Admiralty authority, most of those present had been in command of their own ship for some time. Nevertheless he acted with firmness and leadership as required for good order.

'Gentlemen, a situation in Montreal which would have seriously complicated matters has been resolved and need no longer be a consideration. My orders are now to proceed with the flotilla to Halifax and place it at the disposal of Admiral Vandeput. However we will delay our departure for two days. In discussion with the authorities in Montreal and here in Quebec, I have obtained a commitment for local militia to augment the garrison at Halifax. The city has chartered a merchantman sufficient for 350 men, but we will have to distribute 420 men amongst our ships together with their baggage and extra powder and shot. They should start to arrive within a few hours. In any case we will set sail on Thursday morning.'

Prince Rupert had 50 extra hammocks squeezed into the crowded upper gun deck and 100 more in spaces below. The sailors looked curiously upon the mixture of townsmen and farmers, trappers and hunters and a contingent of 40 Iroquois Indians from the shore of Lake Superior. The Iroquois, who would sleep at the stern under the poop overhang, hated the

French for allying themselves many years previously with the Huron. During most of the voyage they sat silent and watchful on their piled animal skins.

Used as they were to their own kind, with the stink and dampness of life below decks, the crew took no heed of the smell of damp leather and sweat which bore the odour of the fresh meat diet to which their guests were accustomed. Their white guests were like the sailors in their customary consumption of rum and chewing tobacco; though there were a few tense moments when shouts of alarm and warning rang out as one or two of the colonials lit up pipes of tobacco. After being told in no uncertain terms that smoking was only permitted in the galley, one of the first lessons of the hazards of fire on ships was taken to heart.

There was some annoyance as to state of poor personal cleanliness of some of the trappers, since the British sailors were used to regular washing and clean clothing but with customary superiority when it came to non-sailors, they tolerated these shortcomings.

More ugly and potentially a cause for great concern was an incident that occurred on the fourth day of the voyage as the ships moved through the channel south of Anticosti Island. One of the Montreal men, a clerk who had been conscripted with the promise of a £10 bounty, had left his satchel unattended beside one of the guns. Warned by a friend, he had found a trapper delving into the bag and a fight had broken out.

Armed with a wicked-looking skinning knife the trapper had bared his teeth and lunged repeatedly at the clerk, who produced a pocket pistol and was fumbling with it as he dodged his opponent.

One of the master-at-arms' corporals, pushing his way through the crowd, blew his whistle and ordered the two men to lay down their weapons. The clerk panicked and fired the pistol. Thankfully nobody was hurt. Several seamen threw themselves on to the two men and they were shackled to the mainmast strap. The 1st lieutenant brought them before the captain at 11 o'clock in the morning as was customary.

North listened to the master-at-arms' account of the incident and asked if anybody had been injured.

'Thomas Davies the Second, sir, quarter-gunner. He was stabbed in the leg but the surgeon says he will be all right in a few days.'

North addressed the Montreal man. 'Was anything stolen from your bag?'

The clerk was a short, stocky man in his early twenties with a large nose and thinning hair. 'A picture of me wife in a silver frame, sir. The sailors took it out of his jacket and give it me back.'

'In the circumstances your actions were provoked,' said North, 'but when you came on board you and all the passengers were instructed to hand over your firearms to the gunner for safe keeping. You understood that order, did you not?'

'Yes, sir.'

'In spite of that order you kept a loaded pistol in your coat. That cannot be tolerated on a crowded ship and you are fortunate that when you fired it nobody was injured or worse.

While you are on this ship and indeed while you are in service with the militia you are subject to naval and military discipline, wherein you have clearly offended by disobeying a direct order. Six lashes. Take him away!'

He turned to look at the trapper, a bald-headed man in his late forties wearing a filthy buckskin jacket and felt boots. He was broad shouldered and had a large belly. He returned North's gaze with sullen defiance.

'You were caught stealing and to compound the offence you stabbed another man. Have you anything to say?'

The trapper shrugged his shoulders. 'I ain't part of your navy, mister Captain, and I ain't gonna be whipped like some fuckin' Indian.' He spat on the deck. The master-at-arms growled and moved forward with fist upraised.

North snapped, 'Leave it, Anderson!' He looked at the trapper with open contempt. 'You stole from a fellow passenger and you don't even have the decency to show contrition. You are clearly worthless to the militia and I see no point in having you on board this ship. I sentence you to a dozen lashes for stealing and a further dozen for assault and wounding. You will then be taken on shore and left there. Get him out of my sight.'

After the men had been sentenced, North decreed that their punishment should be carried out immediately. As seven bells rang to mark 11.30, all hands were piped to witness punishment, including the passengers.

The deck was considerably more crowded than usual and there was some jostling and an undercurrent of noise from the passengers, despite being urgently shushed by the sailors.

North came to the quarterdeck where his officers in dress uniforms and wearing swords and a line of marines with fixed bayonets were already standing. The militia officers stood with them. As he reached the forward end of the deck and rested a hand on the rail, all the naval men removed their hats to their captain and stood motionless. In the silence that followed, the passengers, seemingly struck with the sudden realisation that they were involved in a situation far outside of their experience, fumbled their hats from their heads. They shuffled uneasily as the captain looked down at the assembled crowd.

Lieutenant Rockwell, standing half a pace behind him, was about to read out the charges and sentence when North raised his hand to stop him. Pausing to allow his gaze to scan the whole crowd, he started to speak.

None present, including the French speakers and the native Indians were in any doubt as to what was being said since after speaking in English he repeated the salient points in French.

'We are together on this ship in conditions alien to many of you militiamen and I make allowances for that. However the safety and well-being of this ship and every man on board can only be served by strict discipline and obedience to orders. One man amongst you has committed one of the most shameful and offensive crimes that can occur on board ship – stealing from another. Were he one of my crew the punishment would be severe, as each and every one of them are aware. Moreover that punishment would be compounded by the treatment he would receive from his messmates. Another man has risked the safety of the ship by deliberately disobeying my order that all firearms brought on board must be held by the gunner unless otherwise directed.

'The crew of one of His Majesty's ships depend on each other for their lives as well as their personal security and stealing is rightly considered an offence against all, not just the loser.

'Hear me well! Every person on this ship, crew or passenger, is equally bound by the Articles of War and *will* be dealt with severely if he defies my commands. You have all been warned. Mr Rockwell, read the charges!'

Some of the passengers were a little startled as the officer read out the charges in an accent that was more familiar to them than that of the captain and most of the crew. When he finished speaking, the American-born Lieutenant Rockwell called out, 'Bring forward the prisoners for punishment.' The Montreal clerk was first to be brought forward.

North ordered him to be seized up.

As the bosun's mates tied his arms to the grating, the man began to whimper. One of the embarrassed sailors muttered, 'shut your mouth and act like a man!' This seemed to settle him a little but as the captain gave the order 'Do your duty!' he moaned aloud. Another bosun's mate came forward with the baize bag and brought forth the cat, handing it to a wiry colleague who, despite appearances, laid on the first stroke with considerable strength. The clerk howled.

'Stop that man's noise,' North shouted, hating the fact that the man had to be flogged but convinced that it was essential at this point in the voyage and in these circumstances. The bosun thrust a fid, covered in a cloth, into the man's mouth and tied it around his head with a short length of cord.

The other five blows were equally hard as the master-at-arms called out the number and turned a quarter minute glass with each stroke. When the man was cut down the deep red cuts in his back were bleeding freely. He was carried below, having fainted.

The hefty trapper was in his shirtsleeves. The bosun reached forward and ripped the shirt from his back. Two of the bosun's mates lashed his wrists to the grating that had been lifted into place against the starboard rail. The trapper yelled out, 'Fuck you! You English bastard, you won't break me!' He struggled but had met his match and suffered rougher handling than might otherwise had been the case.

North waved his hand at the bosun. The bosun's mate with the bag produced a fresh cat. Each of the thongs had been knotted nine times reflecting the seriousness of the offence of theft.

As the first strokes were laid across his back the man laughed. His back was already bloody by the fourth stroke. The bosun's mate ran the nine tails through his fingers to clean off the blood and skin. On the fifth stroke the man fell silent; on the seventh stroke he uttered a loud gasp through tightly clenched lips. On the tenth stroke he screamed. Another bosun's mate came forward to administer the second twelve with a fresh cat. By the time the master-at-arms had called eighteen the trapper was screaming in agony. At twenty strokes he was sobbing and begging for mercy.

He collapsed at the next stroke and North called, 'Enough, cut him down.'

He turned to Rockwell, the disgust on his face reflected by Rockwell's own expression. 'At six bells in the morning watch have the creature taken to the nearest shore and left there. Dismiss the men and then join me in the cabin, please.'

On reaching his cabin North unclipped his sword-belt and dropped it on to the stern couch. His steward was standing by him with a glass of brandy and lime juice in his hand which North took with a nod of thanks. 'One for Mr Rockwell, Naylor,' he said as the lieutenant was announced.

'Bad business, Erskine,' North said.

There was a minute of silence as both men reflected upon the events of the morning. 'Erskine, these militiamen need to be occupied in something since idleness sows the seeds of trouble. I want you to organise regular arms drill, with empty muskets, that being an exercise which will prove useful on land for them, and have their corporals carry out any other schemes which may occur to you. You will also oblige me by gathering together their petty officers and impressing upon them that they are in no way being singled out for punishment but their men must obey the orders.'

....

Cluney Ryan looked back without pity at the trapper as he sat on the north shore of the estuary of the St Jean River, his head in his hands, a broken man. He had at least been given his musket, satchel, a blanket and seven days' supplies, something which neither Cluney nor the rest of the crew of the launch would have given him.

The previous evening three of the militiamen had spoken to Cluney as they put up their hammocks. One of them, a corporal called Smith, had served as a regular soldier in the American army and Cluney suspected he had deserted. He offered Cluney a handful of walnuts.

'I seen floggings before. Once saw a man get 50 for insolence to a young shit of a cornet. Them bosun's mates of yours sure know how to lay it on though. I guess about a dozen from them is about equal to three dozen from a soldier. Anyhow, I guess your captain must have been in a good mood just to give him two dozen, specially letting him off the last three.'

Cluney cracked a walnut on the nearby bulkhead. 'The captain is strong on discipline but he only flogs when there's no other way. I've served with captains that flogged half the crew in the first six months out at sea and I saw a man flogged round the fleet. He died after about the first hundred. That trapper was lucky. Most captains make thieves run the gauntlet, that's worse than a flogging.'

'How's that?' asked one of the other men.

Cluney explained that the thief was sat on a tub and dragged round the deck with the crew belting him with three-tailed knotted ropes after the man had received a dozen at the grating. The men are lined up either side of him and if they didn't lay on with a will, their mates thought they were involved in the crime. Then once the punishment was over the man would lose his mess and be forced into eating alone in some corner of the ship, shunned by the whole crew.

Chapter 14

Sunday 29th March, 1800

The view across the wooden houses of the town and the broad bay from the governor of Canada's headquarters in Halifax on this early spring day was pleasant but Captain Robert Murray was impatient to get back to his own domain. As waited in the hallway of the building to be conducted into the governor's presence he frowned in irritation. With everything else that needed his attention he would rather not be here, but in any case he was rarely pleased to be in this building.

Although Murray was commanding on the American station, in the absence of Admiral Vandeput, the military governor of Canada was Prince Edward, Duke of Kent. By choice the prince resided in Government House in Halifax rather than Quebec City. Naturally both were too polite to display it openly but the prince and Murray did not get on with each other. Murray was a straightforward man with something of a temper and strict views on morality. Although he had a strong sense of discipline and required the same from those who served under him, he was not a brutal man and never acted beyond the necessities of good order and justice.

Like Chief Justice Strange, a long-term Halifax inhabitant who had left a few years ago, he refused to attend social functions at Government House if the duke's mistress Julie de St Laurent was present. However it was in the matter of discipline and military ability that the captain found he had no use for his nominal master. He was singularly unimpressed with the duke's treatment of mutineers in Quebec. Like others he believed that inflicting punishments of 500 lashes on a man served no purpose but to bestialise the whole process of military discipline; better that the man be hung or shot, for his sake as much as that of justice.

As Murray waited he brought to mind an image of the duke? He was very tall, well over six feet in height, had dark receding hair that he made no effort to disguise with a peruque, and with his round face and heavy lips strongly resembled his father. He never been known to be drunk; his own self-esteem forbade that, but through his early mentor, the Baron Wangenheim, had a love of food and delicacies and good wine. One of his passions that provided him with relief from military rigours was his love of freemasonry and in this he was uncharacteristically democratic. There were sergeants and sergeant-majors in the lodges he had sponsored from Gibraltar to Quebec City – but even he drew the line at private soldiers.

The duke was an inveterate spendthrift and spent his whole life continuously in debt. On the other hand he had been responsible for turning Halifax into a splendid well-developed naval base with excellent defences and had masterminded the successful transformation of a small town into a modern well-appointed though tiny city. Much of this had been due to his conviction that Halifax was far better fitted for a military headquarters and place of government than Quebec. He was thoroughly unpopular in the army; in direct contrast to his reputation as a 'hail fellow well met' by his social set.

Murray had the same opinion of Kent's brother William, Duke of Clarence, who in his view was a God-awful sailor and martinet of the worst kind.

The Duke of Kent's grasp of naval matters was woolly to say

the least but he had the good sense to allow Vandeput and Murray a free rein. Admiral Vandeput was cruising in his flagship the *Asia* 64 south along the American coast, having left his flag captain in charge at Halifax.

It was with these thoughts in his mind that Murray looked up as a flunky announced him to the King's son and he walked into the sanctum sanctorum. The duke, elegant in exaggerated military finery as always, stood with one hand on his hip looking out through a long window at the anchored ships in the vast harbour. Beyond the harbour the coast was fog-bound, as it often was, and a small trading ship emerged like a ghost and moved slowly into the Sound.

'Ah, Captain, a good morning to you! I see that Captain North has arrived. Damn me the harbour is beginning to look like a fleet of Frenchies! What a splendid fellow. A stroke of genius, North persuading the Montreal and Quebec people to send along the militiamen. I intend to hold them in reserve but we may have to send them into Labrador with the regulars if the crapauds land. I have invited North to a reception this evening, hope you'll be there too, Murray?'

Grudgingly, since he could hardly absent himself when Captain North was being received, Murray agreed. In fact he was not only happy to see North with his flotilla of reinforcements but exceptionally pleased with the man himself. He found himself in a strange position in a way. Despatches from the Admiralty carried aboard the Post Office packet had made it clear that this newly made captain had their utmost approbation. Not only that but he had made given unprecedented powers in the Montreal business and their lordships had courteously advised Vandeput that it might be in his best interests to give North a great deal of slack in any operations in which he felt North could be employed.

North had, so as to speak, been an answer to a prayer in ways not even envisaged by their lordships. Unaware until December that there was a strong possibility of an invasion supported by a flotilla of French ships, Vandeput had also given his two senior frigate captains a cruise south as far as the Caribbean. Israel Pellew had the *Cleopatra* 32 and Robert Laurie the *Andromache* 32. Laurie was among the best captains in the fleet and although Pellew was far from equal to his famed brother Edward he had an excellent ship and crew.

Unfortunately their absence robbed Murray of all his smaller ships except for two brigs, the 18-gun *Pheasant* under Commander Henry Carew and the *Lilly* 16 under Joseph Spear. His two 64s left in harbour were ageing. *St Albans*, Captain John Oakes Hardy's command, had been launched in 1764 and was to all intents and purposes fit only to be used as a prison hulk – though if needs be, she would have to stand in the line of battle. The 23-year-old *America*, his temporary pennant-ship, was in better condition and thanks to her captain, Joseph Bingham, would acquit herself well enough, though hardly with great success, he feared, against four French 74s.

It was with considerable surprise and relief that he had seen the red ensign over the French tricolour as *Ailes de Mercure* was sailed into the harbour a few weeks ago. Now with the other French 74, the *Aboukir* – or as he must get used to calling her, *Prince Rupert* – he had a far better chance of facing the French squadron, especially since he had a third 74 that he had not expected.

The other welcome addition, though it had been made clear this was on a temporary basis, was the *Dieppe* 74. He had smilingly called the three French ships North's fleet! On behalf of the absent admiral, Murray had bought in the *Ailes de Mercure,* which had needed very little attention from the dockyard, and renamed her *Polaris* as a subtle compliment to her captor.

More problematical was the absence of Vandeput's deputy, Rear Admiral Charles Morice Pole, and his flagship *Agincourt* 64. He was away from the Newfoundland station, still refitting in England. The naval force at that base was at present under the command of Captain Robert Larken of the *Camilla* 20 who, with a single brig *Pluto* 14 and the 6-gun schooner *Trespassey,* was all that stood guard over the St Lawrence estuary from a northerly approach by the French. Furthermore there were worrying signs of rebellious discontent amongst the Irish soldiers in St John's which might necessitate Murray sailing there to reinforce Larken.

Murray was duty-bound to tell the prince of his decision in disposing his ships, which was the reason for this visit.

'Your Highness, as you are aware we have a dearth of ships in Newfoundland especially since the loss of *Voltigeur* and if, as we suspect, the French decide to land troops on the Labrador coast, I feel we should have a stronger presence at St John's. The garrison is far from perfectly disciplined and I feel it needs a ship of the line in harbour with her guns run out to dissuade any unrest.

'At the same time we must be prepared for the French Squadron. Extending the cruise area to cover the sea from here to Labrador, I intend to keep a squadron at sea under my command, consisting of the three 74s and the smaller vessels Captain North brought with him – *Carysfort, Peterel* and *Juniper.*

'*America* with *Pheasant* in company will proceed to Newfoundland under Captain Joseph Bingham, who will take command there. I have every confidence that all of the naval officers, including Commander Carew of the *Lilly*, will acquit themselves to great satisfaction. As you will recall Carew was promoted to commander because of his exemplary conduct during the Nore mutiny, when he was first lieutenant of *Repulse.*

'I will shift my pennant to *Polaris.* It transpires that North is in fact the senior of the three captains. Isaac Thompson has *Polaris* and their lordships promoted Lewis Shepheard and gave him *Dieppe.* My deputy will therefore be Michael North and in my absence he will take temporary command of the squadron.'

'Heavens, Murray! Rapid advancement for one so young and newly commissioned, what? But you are absolutely right; he has proved himself the man for the job – Horatio Nelson, watch out!'

'Indeed, sir, and I believe their lordships will not be too surprised by my decision. I shall, of course, be in command but should I fall, I have made it clear that North assumes command.'

The prince rubbed his chin, 'I notice you didn't mention John Hardy?'

'He is senior to North, of course, made post in 1790, but *St Albans* is virtually unfit for sea and I believe would be better here as a supplement to the forts, should there be a direct attack from the sea. Besides, the exceptional authority given to North by their lordships actually makes him senior even to me, though he would not exercise it in that way.' He carefully ignored the grey area that the document did not actually specify any extension of the authority beyond settling the Montreal business.

The prince seemed sceptical. Murray knew he was more than satisfied with the fortifications, but he did not seem happy with the disposition of the ships. However, that was the navy's business.

Murray had no wish to move Hardy into one of the 74s and if he could have managed it he would have sent the man packing. Hardy was an inveterate drunk and a tyrant. His ship was the most unhappy that it had been Murray's misfortune to visit; an opinion which Vandeput supported. It had been so bad that shot had been rolled across the deck in the night watch – a clear warning of impending mutiny. Although Vandeput was reluctantly stuck with the man he had devised a way of diffusing the situation. He had sent Hardy into the shipyard as acting dockyard superintendent where several frigates were under construction. These ships would not be completed for at least two years but Hardy had been given the task of ensuring that all possible progress was being made. In fact the dockyard people had simply supplied Hardy with an office, an almost murderous amount of paperwork and a similarly murderous amount of alcohol and had done their best to ignore his presence – which suited Murray extremely well.

Murray was content that with North and his fellow young captains in the 74s he had the best possible advantage of good commanders. He also had the advantage of surprise. The French may or may not have been aware of the destination of *Prince Rupert* but unless he missed his guess, the presence of *Dieppe* and *Polaris* would come as a considerable shock to them.

At that moment Michael North was deep in thought on board *Dieppe*. With a glass of Lewis Shepheard's best Madeira in his hand he was only half listening to his ex-second lieutenant, who for the second time was expressing his gratitude to him for his present situation. Absentmindedly he reached into the pocket of his waistcoat to stroke Isobel's brooch.

'Lewis,' he said, 'you thoroughly deserve your promotion and the lordships clearly saw, as I did, that you are not only worthy of it but it was a very good decision to give you the *Dieppe*. I am a little concerned that you are so short of marines, however. You say that the men promised from the Cork garrison failed to come on board when you presented the orders to the garrison commander?'

'Yes, sir, a sticky moment, actually. It seems that the Admiralty should have got Horseguards to put the orders into writing rather than promise to send a message. As you may be aware His Royal Highness the Duke of York is not on the best terms with the Admiralty at the moment and the promised note was not received before I arrived at Cork. The port admiral did his best but could not insist. Colonel Fincham, the garrison commander, decided that we had no authority to take army men on board as marines and refused to release them. In the circumstances I sailed with just a sergeant and 20 marines who should have been discharged ashore from a brig that had been condemned in the harbour. I was also glad to have the best of the seamen – 39 of them. They would have been dispersed amongst the rest of the ships in the harbour.'

'So, you have 530 seamen, boys and marines? You shall have a corporal and a dozen of *Prince Rupert's* marines. I believe you should also have at least another 20 or 30 seamen which I suggest you recruit from any suitable merchantmen that are in the harbour – starting with the *Cornflower,* which brought in the rest of the militia this morning. Do not send a press gang on shore; it is forbidden by the governor here and in St John's, and while not unlawful it is better to restrict your efforts of impressments to merchantmen and fishing boats. If a fisherman is able to produce a partly completed contract you must release him. If you decide to keep a man and he accepts the chance to volunteer, you must see that any money owed to him by his employer is paid to him.

'The popular view here as in England is that the press-gangs are vicious thugs that will sweep up any man that can walk on two legs whether he be a seaman or not. We both know this is not true but be judicious. Men who have seagoing experience may be pressed but I will only accept landsmen who are fit enough to work and who volunteer. No dealings with crimps and no fugitives from the law.

'I shall discuss your shortages with the commodore and no doubt we can come up with a way to augment your lobsters, I cannot see that less than 80 in total would be sufficient for your needs. Apart from that, you have a taut ship and a good crew. I am sure Admiral Vandeput will be as pleased as I am.'

As he left *Dieppe* North had his launch rowed around the ship once more and was well satisfied. He then proceeded to *Polaris* to continue the inspection ordered by acting Commodore Murray.

He was piped on board by three pipes and the officers, lined up to be presented, were full of smiles. Captain Thompson, his commission to command the ship confirmed by Murray, was pleased to see the man he considered to be not only his benefactor but, by virtue of the rescue of his cousin's wife, a good friend in time of need. Most of the crew he needed were on board. Murray had shrewdly reduced the crew of the *St Albans* by more than half on the basis that if the ship was to be employed as a floating battery, the bulk of the topmen and many of the others were superfluous. Thompson had therefore been able to add a further 340 men, 50 marines and two dozen boys to his 117 original crew and a further 50 seamen had been drafted from the *America*. He had also scoured the shoreline and sent impressments parties into more than 20 merchantmen to bring another 63 aboard. Unlike the experience of Isaac Thompson in Cork, he had the blessing of the colonel of the 66th to recruit 12 of his men and a further nine volunteers from the engineer company to add to his marines. He was therefore within 30 or 40 of full strength.

The sailors from the *St Albans,* relieved no doubt that should Captain Hardy return they would be long gone, had settled in well and he had the makings of a good crew.

North was as impressed with *Polaris* as he had been with *Dieppe*. Thompson had explained to him the commodore's touch of whimsy in re-naming the ship after the North Star, and North, slightly embarrassed, had dismissed it with a shrug. In any case the Admiralty might decide on a different name.

North's report to the commodore was concise but accurate.

Murray looked across his desk in the office he used

overlooking the bay. As North placed the three captain's journals on his desk, Murray could see the long purple-red scar on North's right hand; an honourable scar, as he recollected from his own days six years ago as a supernumerary on the *Audacious* when North had been a valued and very promising lieutenant on that ship.

'I remember the day you got that scar, Michael,' he said, pouring them both some reasonable French wine taken off *Polaris* when he bought her in. 'I have no doubt Andy Langdon remembers it too.'

North had boarded a supposedly surrendered French privateer to take possession but the crew had run up her colours again and tried to make off with the boarding party in an attempt to escape *Audacious* and hold the Englishmen as hostages against Captain Parker firing at them. A fight had broken out between the 80 French crewmen and North and his 35 outnumbered men. Midshipman Andrew Purcell Langdon had fallen at the feet of a French officer with whom he had been fighting at close quarters. Seeing the Frenchman start to lunge at Langdon with his sword, North leapt forward. He had dropped his sword in his own fight but he took the cutting edge of the blade on his upraised hand and forearm as one of his marines fired a pistol into the Frenchman's head.

'It seems an age ago, sir,' North replied. He raised his hand and made a fist. In cold weather he could still feel a stinging sensation reminding him of the agony of that moment.

'Aye, so it does,' said Murray reflectively. 'Now here we are again, me an acting commodore and you a post captain and in effect also acting commodore. Can't say how pleased I am that their Lordships came to their senses after such a long time.

Still, you aren't that old, even now, and there's plenty got posted older than you. Larken was made post when he was forty – that was four years ago.'

Murray brought himself back to the present with a quick swallow of wine. 'Now that you are satisfied with the state of the ships, apart from *Polaris* and *Dieppe's* marines, to which I will give some thought, I want the squadron ready for sea in 24 hours. I intend that we shall stand out to sea and send out our scouts to try to anticipate the French. Our target is mainly their transports, though no doubt we shall have to deal with the 74s first.

'The Admiralty has given the admiral their best informed opinion and the vital information that the French managed to slip out of Toulon and past our ships off Gibraltar on the first of February. At best speed they would reach here in a few days from now but it could be weeks, of course. We believe they intend to land the troops at Sandwich Bay, before the warships turn south to Halifax; therefore we will cruise to the south-east of that area. If the admiral returns in time he may amend those orders, of course.

'Now, to another matter. I have the unpleasant duty of convening a court martial and you, Thompson, Shepheard, Larken and Ballard are the captains I want to try the matter. It is a nasty one, I'm afraid. You will have noticed that the frigate *Galatea* arrived yesterday and is now at anchor in the harbour; she flies the red ensign since she is under the direct command of their lordships. Shortly after *Galatea* came into Halifax, her captain brought his second lieutenant, Thomas Fry, to me in irons. He is accused of murder, desertion and stealing a large sum of gold, the property of the British Treasury.

'In view of the secrecy of his mission the captain thought it best to have the matter tried here, especially since the vicinity in which the alleged offences occurred was within the command area of this station. A court martial needs be convened urgently since *Galatea* is under orders to proceed to England with all possible speed. Normally for an enquiry of this gravity flag officers would be a part of the court but in their absence his grace, the governor, has obliged me by providing a letter of approval as to the constitution of the court.'

The background was that *Galatea*, under secret Admiralty orders, was sent to rendezvous with a merchantman a hundred miles west of the port of New York. The captain of the merchantman was supposedly in possession of vital information concerning French intentions in Guadeloupe and San Dominique which he would only hand over to a Royal Navy captain in exchange for the sum of 4,000 guineas. The Admiralty had sight of enough of some of the information to be reasonably sure that it was genuine.

Murray continued. 'A few days before the rendezvous was due to take place *Galatea* fell in with a French trading brig, the *Auguste Renard* of 800 tons, who surrendered to her after a brief chase. Lieutenant Fry was sent to take possession of her. What followed is a matter for the court martial to hear and it would be improper of me to elaborate further.'

....

The court martial was held aboard *Prince Rupert* the following morning. North had been appointed president of the court over four other captains: Thompson, Shepheard, Larken and the youngest, the 26-year-old Volant Ballard of the *Carysfort*.

195

The minutes were taken by the admiral's clerk, Robert Peace. Prosecuting was Commander Tyson King, at present unattached being on shore with the admiral's headquarters, and the accused was represented by Lieutenant Elias Mugford of the *St Albans*.

At 11 o'clock a bow gun was fired off to mark the commencement of the court martial. Lieutenant Fry was escorted to the cabin which had been cleared and extended. On the benches facing the captains' table sat a dozen or more junior officers and marine officers, as well as the duke's aide-de-camp and officers from the Halifax garrison. Also present were fifteen prominent citizens, both men and women. They watched the proceedings with keen interest.

Fry's sword was placed on the table and Robert Peace, acting judge advocate, read the warrant and charges. North had checked and rechecked the accuracy of the document before the court sat. He listened to Peace wishing things could move on more quickly but realising that the correct form must be observed.

'Pursuant to an order made by Commodore Robert Murray, 2nd Naval Officer in Command, Halifax, dated the 28th day of March instant and directed to the President, he shall inquire into the Cause and Circumstances of the Theft of the sum of four thousand guineas, the property of His Majesty's Treasury. Further that he shall inquire into the Death of Jason Herring, Captain's Servant. Further that he shall inquire into an act of Desertion in Time of War, those matters having been said to have occurred on the 20th day of March in this year of Our Lord, 1800, and in all these matters to Try Lieutenant Thomas Edward Fry of His Majesty's ship Galatea. All manner of persons having anything to do with this Court draw near and give your attendance. God save the King and this Honourable Board.'

The acting judge advocate read out the list of captains comprising the court. The surgeon of *St Albans* certified the usual fiction that Captain Hardy was ill and the court noted and excused him.

With Peace reading aloud and North feeling the burden of making sure that all the correct procedures were being followed, the process commenced.

The members of the court and the acting judge advocate then in open court and before they began their duty, respectably took the "several oaths, enjoined and directed in and by an Act of Parliament made and passed in the 22nd year of the reign of his late Majesty King George II entitled 'An Act for amending explaining and reducing into one Act of Parliament, the Laws relating to the Government of His Majesty's Ships, Vessels and Forces by Sea.'"

The captains sat down. All other witnesses being required to leave the court, the first witness to give evidence was Captain Leary of the *Galatea*. Having taken the oath he began to outline the reasons for the presence of his ship in the North Atlantic. At this point North ruled for the minutes that particular circumstances of *Galatea's* mission were secret and had no bearing on the case, to which the defence assented.

Leary went on to describe the events of 21st March. At 7.45am a lookout had spotted the French trading brig *Auguste Renard* half a league inshore of *Galatea* running towards the safety of the nearby neutral coast. Crowding on royals and stuns'ls *Galatea* had come up with her and she surrendered after a single shot had been fired from the British ship's forward gun.

The captain ordered Lieutenant Armstrong, his 3rd lieutenant, to take possession of the prize and had her captain brought on board. He decided that the prize should be sent into Halifax while he continued to wait for the ship he had been sent to meet. Lieutenant Fry had come to him and asked to be allowed to take command of the prize since he had relatives in Halifax and would appreciate the opportunity to visit them. Accordingly Armstrong was recalled to *Galatea* and Fry was given command. He took a midshipman, Peter Jackson, the ship's purser and eight men; the mate and twelve-man crew of the prize having been carried over to *Galatea*.

Half an hour after the prize had disappeared northwards the master-at-arms came to the captain in a state of alarm to report that he had found the murdered body of Jason Herring, the captain's clerk, in the hold. As he was about to leave the cabin the captain noticed something untoward concerning his desk. A locked drawer had been forced and a leather bag which had contained 4,000 guineas was missing. Immediately suspecting the worst he gave orders to overhaul the prize, which by this time had disappeared over the horizon.

Two hours later *Galatea* came across a boat being rowed towards the ship, the men in her shouting and waving. In the boat were Midshipman Jackson and four seamen. Jackson had been shot in the shoulder and was in a bad way. Of the prize there was no sign.

The court asked, 'Given the nature of the contents of the desk drawer, how many sentinels were assigned to the cabin door?'

Answer, 'One man with drawn sword.'

The court, 'Was this man present when the theft and murder took place?'

Answer, 'He was not.'

The court, 'Why?'

Answer, 'It seemed there was some confusion about the man being relieved and he took it upon himself to leave his post. He was disciplined by being issued with ten lashes the following morning.'

What happened on the prize was later told to the court by Midshipman Jackson and two of the prize crew, seamen Samuels and Lefroy. Jackson recalled little of what happened since he was barely conscious at the time.

The sailors said that having shot Mr Jackson, Lieutenant Fry had given them a choice: either join him or be cast adrift. Since Fry and the purser and two of the other seamen had pistols pointing at them, they could not fight them. As a result they were bundled aboard a boat and set adrift.

In his own evidence the captain had explained that having determined from Samuels and Lefroy that the last they had seen of *Auguste Renard* was of her tacking southwest towards the fog-bound shore he followed that direction and after a further hour saw the prize about a mile off shore apparently abandoned and drifting. Nearer to shore was a cutter under six oars making heavy going against an ebbing tide.

Taking *Galatea* alongside the prize and commanding the launch himself, her oars double-banked, he set out to catch the cutter.

His quarry reached the shore less than two minutes before he arrived and he immediately leapt into the shallows and fired a pistol over the heads of six men running up the beach. Three of them, the purser and two of the seamen, turned and fired back but were all cut down by his own men. The purser was fatally wounded, the two men dead.

Fry was found crouching in a gully, frantically digging a hole in the sand to hide a small trunk. The trunk was found to contain the stolen guineas. Of the other two deserters there was no sign – they had managed to disappear inland.

Fry was bound and he and the purser were brought back to *Galatea*. On the *Auguste Renard* the bodies of the two other seamen were found. They had both been shot. The purser was not long for this world and made a dying declaration that Fry had approached him shortly after the *Auguste Renard* had been taken and put to him that they could be rich men living in the United States if they could steal the gold and take the prize into a neutral port. He had two sailors he could trust and he was sure that with the prospect of freedom and several hundred guineas apiece the rest of the prize crew would fall in with their plan.

The purser's dying declaration continued: shortly before leaving *Galatea* Fry had come to him, his face ashen, to say that the captain's clerk had disturbed him while breaking into the captain's desk and that he had to stab him to death. The two seamen who had been with him had carried the body to the hold wrapped in a hammock.

The signed declaration was entered into the court martial's records of evidence.

Galatea had kept her rendezvous and secured the documents they had been sent to buy and then made her way with the prize to Halifax.

200

That was the evidence against Fry.

The court asked Captain Leary, 'The sentinel having been punished, have you any objection or complaint to make against any other member of your crew?'

Captain Leary, considering as he did that all other persons that carried off the prize were now either dead or run, had no other complaints.

Lieutenant Fry appeared calm and in control of his emotions. His counsel stated that Lieutenant Fry pleaded guilty to all charges and threw himself on the mercy of the court.

North asked him, 'Have you nothing to say to us concerning your reasons and your conduct?'

Fry opened his mouth and closed it again, simply shaking his head.

North persisted. 'You are aware of the peril in which you place yourself? In considering our verdict we may take into account any explanation you can give. An expression of remorse even?'

Fry said bluntly, 'I am sorry for the death of the captain's clerk, it was unfortunate but on seeing him I knew I had to silence him. As for the rest of the charges, I gambled and lost.'

The court was cleared and the captains discussed the case while eating lunch. At 2.30pm the court was reconvened and North ordered that the prisoner be produced. In the 45 minutes of adjournment a remarkable change had seized Fry. His face was drawn, his eyes desperately wide and staring, his very limbs trembling. On the table he saw his sword, point towards him and he sagged and almost fell. Since he had pleaded guilty the symbolism of the sword point was of little moment but it magnified in him the peril of his situation.

North banged a carpenter's mallet on the table to hush the murmurs of those on the benches opposite him and read out the judgement.

'This court having heard evidence and considered the several charges against Lieutenant Thomas Fry, is of the opinion that on the 21st day of March, 1800, the said Lieutenant Fry did murder Jason Elliott Herring, captain's clerk on His Majesty's Ship *Galatea* and that having been given command of His Majesty's prize ship, *Auguste Renard*, did desert His Majesty's service in time of war and that he stole from His Majesty's Treasury the sum of 4,000 guineas.'

Anticipation reduced the whole court into absolute silence.

North addressed Fry in a calm but firm voice. 'Having pleaded guilty to all these heinous crimes, the court, having enquired into all the circumstances finds no reason to dealt with you leniently. It is therefore the judgement of this court that you be reduced to the rank of seaman and that you will be taken from this place and hanged by the neck until you are dead, and may God have mercy on your soul. Remove the prisoner.'

Although the sentence could not have been unexpected, the audience let out a collective sigh of breath. Fry fainted away and had to be carried from the cabin. North, with his fellow captains in complete concurrence, could not close the proceedings without dealing with another matter.

'Captain Leary, step forward please. This court, having considered the matter we were asked to deal with, cannot retire until we have placed on record your zeal in apprehending the deserter Fry. However we also wish it to be noted that we admonish you for the lax manner in which you carried His Majesty's property. It is clear to us that no blame can be attached to you for Fry's actions but the casual and insecure way in which you stored the coin led to the unfortunate death of your clerk and the subsequent heinous occurrences.

'When you were asked you could not give a satisfactory explanation as to how Lieutenant Fry was aware that you were actually carrying such a large sum of money. It would appear from this that there was a serious lack of judgement on your part. No doubt if he had not been aware there is a strong chance this wretched affair could have been avoided.

'Therefore your conduct fell short of good sense and attention to duty. You failed to ensure that an armed sentry was on duty at the door of the cabin at all times the coin was in your desk and indeed if such a guard had been present, the body of Mr Herring might not have been taken from your cabin. You may leave.'

The duke of Kent read the minutes of the court martial while Commodore Murray sat opposite him, his thoughtful gaze watching the harbour as *Galatea* set off for England. She had on board the secret documents purchased from the spy on board the Danish merchantman with whom she had rendezvoused on the 23rd March but she also had a copy of the minutes of the court martial of Lieutenant Thomas Fry and a sealed full report by Captain North as well as a covering despatch from himself.

There were three further sets of these papers, one lodged in the admiral's office and two to be sent off on each of the next two Post Office packet boats.

He doubted that Captain Leary's future career would prosper but ironically, as a post captain, even if he stayed on the beach and lived long enough he was likely to end up a Yellow Admiral. He would probably also not suffer financially, even on half-pay, as the *Auguste Renard* had been brought in with her cargo of sugar and rum

The prince broke in on his thoughts. 'Awful business, Murray, though if I had been president I would have had him flogged severely before he was hung.'

'Yes, Your Highness.' No doubt you would, thought Murray but at least with a man like North as president the matter had been dealt with swiftly and decisively and with some humanity even if it was hard to see that such mercy was appropriate.

He had his launch rowed out at noon and came on board *Polaris* with all formality to witness the execution, inwardly wincing as the execution gun rang out and the yellow flag was run up. On every ship in the harbour the crew was mustered on deck and faced towards *Polaris*. Normally the hanging would take place on the miscreant's own ship and by the hand of his own crew but the urgency of having *Galatea* resume her voyage meant it was the ill-luck of *Polaris* to draw the short straw. He noticed with private frustration that the duke had his own ornate barge rowed out and anchored; with him was a party of sycophants, glasses in hand, in an almost festive mood to watch the proceedings from the water nearby.

Dressed in seaman's clothing the prisoner had been brought to the forecastle, hands bound behind his back, preceded by the black-clad chaplain.

He was made to stand while a 26-pound shot in a net was attached to his ankles and the noose placed about his neck. He was calm and resigned and said nothing. Eight seamen caught hold of the rope, ran the length of the deck and hoisted him aloft. Unfortunately the noose had slipped up under his chin and Thomas Fry struggled grotesquely for more than eight minutes before he finally expired. It was not unusual for a man to take that long to die but the nervous tension of worrying that the damned rope might slip from his head altogether seemed to make matters worse.

Chapter 15

Friday 4th to Wednesday 9th April, 1800

Prince Rupert was the rear ship with *Dieppe* next in front and *Polaris* leading under the commodore's broad pennant; three heavy ships taken from the French and now probably destined to fight ships built in the same shipyards. The seas were still grey-cold and the wind chilled quickly as soon as North left the shelter of his cabin. This year the winter had retreated abnormally early. It was not unusual for there to be ice and snow right through March into April and even early May in these latitudes. The coast was notorious for fog and barely submerged rocks. The Atlantic crossing itself was still hazardous and a voyage time of six or seven weeks could be considered less than average. So when would the French arrive? Many days could be spent at sea and each day the cold dawn would be met by these three ships and their smaller companions with their crews standing with guns loaded and in every way ready for action.

The commodore's information appeared to indicate that if the French had made good time and survived the hazards of the crossing, they could be expected any day but it might be weeks before they arrived.

Aboard *Prince Rupert* Lieutenant Spicker had the watch but since they were in convoy, the 1st lieutenant was nearby. Although the wind was light, it was bitterly cold. North gestured for them to stand where they were and said, 'Cold day, gentlemen. Mr Rockwell, have the cook make an extra brew of chocolate for the watch as they go below, will you. Mr Spicker, when you are relieved, I would like you to check the tackles on the first three forward lee guns. I noticed several slack ropes. Hawkins is the quarter-gunner we received from the *St Albans*. If he is not up to the task, I want to know.'

North was about to make a turn forward along the spar deck when Midshipman Dunne called out, 'Sir, signal from *Polaris*. Enemy in sight, close on the flag.'

North snapped, 'Is *Polaris* making more sail, Mr Rockwell?'

Looking away from his telescope Rockwell replied, 'Aye sir, she's setting royals.'

Calmly North said, 'Have our own shaken out, please, Mr Rockwell. I will be in my cabin if you need me. Use your judgement when to douse the galley fire, that chocolate may be the last hot drink the men get for a while.'

An hour later North was called back to the poop.

He could see ships sailing on a parallel course to leeward about 15 miles distant. Through his glass he picked out two large ships that appeared to be 74s, though hull down it was difficult to distinguish between 74s and heavy frigates, the sail plans being practically identical. Beyond these two ships were several others. He could not see clearly. The extra height above the deck of the mainmast crosstrees would present a better view.

'I am going aloft, Mr Rockwell.'

He climbed the mainmast shrouds swiftly and skilfully despite this being the first time he had been aloft this year. Straddling the crosstrees alongside the lookout he focused the telescope on the enemy ships. They were a little closer now; possibly unaware of their pursuers, they did not appear to be sailing fast.

Now he could see most of the enemy flotilla. There were two ragged columns, each led by a larger warship and with another large ship at the rear of the columns. There was a single smaller vessel, a sloop or corvette, a little to the north-east of the seaward column and two other ships, frigates by the look of them, about halfway along the length of the inshore column and close into the shore of Labrador.

Between the 74s in the columns were 14 big transports most of them straggling and wandering about like silly sheep between four collies.

North smiled. The French had split up their 74s it seemed; a mistake for which they could pay a heavy price. It was such a basic error that it was tempting to assume that the senior officer in command was incompetent. As he watched he saw a puff of smoke and then another from the rearmost seaward 74. They had at last seen the British ships.

Although it had been planned that the expedition would be under the command of Rear Admiral Étienne Eustache Bruix, at the last moment he had been sent hurriedly elsewhere and acting Chief of Division (acting Commodore) Julien Marie Cosmao-Kerjulien had been given the unenviable command. It was not just the British that believed he was not up to the task. The lack of confidence emanating from the officers under his command was weakening his position even further.

Called to the quarterdeck of the 80-gun *Tonnant,* he slapped his thigh in annoyance as he saw the three English 74s approaching about ten miles to the south east. 'Damn it!' he said to his flag captain, Horace Bethune, 'Where did they come from? The British are supposed to have just three 64s fit for sea in these waters! Very well, signal to the transports to execute Plan Rouge. Turn us into the wind and signal *Bonne Citoyenne*, *Mont Blanc* and *Ville de Mons* to close on the flag. Have those idiots in the frigates escort the transports and recall the *Rossignol* to repeat my signals.'

'Just three 74s, Commodore, we have them outnumbered and outgunned.'

'It is foolish to underestimate the British, Bethune. We have the better ships but I would rather have them each crewed by just one hundred English sailors than the rabble and scum we have.'

He stamped off the deck and went to open a bottle of Armagnac, his usual comfort in times of stress. Bethune refrained from pointing out to him that the three enemy ships were to his eye clearly *all of them* ships that had been built in France.

....

Murray had briefed his captains exhaustively. They formed their ships into a tight, even column. Murray's smaller ships *Carysfort* and *Peterel* stood in towards the land, anticipating the movement of the transports, and *Juniper* was east of the column to repeat signals. The 74s ploughed on towards the enemy liners that were, with considerable disorder, scattering in the general direction of the lead ship, distinguishable as carrying 80 guns. The sea was not heavy which boded well for a battle.

As the distance closed the French managed to bring their ships into some semblance of order. *Ville de Mons* led with the flagship following; after a gap of about half a mile came *Mont Blanc*, closely followed by the *Bonne Citoyenne* which had a nasty habit of yawing to lee.

The first exchange of shot rang out as *Polaris* fired off her bow-chasers in answer to an unsynchronised and half-hearted broadside wasted by *Bonne Citoyenne*. Forging ahead, *Polaris* came up on *Mont Blanc* and let rip with a perfectly timed broadside, causing the loss of her opponent's main topmast. Almost at the same time *Dieppe* came alongside *Bonne Citoyenne* and emptied her own broadside mainly into her stern as she swung to larboard. Then followed a disaster for the two rearmost French 74s as *Mont Blanc*, suddenly slowed by the weight of her dragging top-hamper, fell afoul of *Bonne Citoyenne's* jib. The two ships came to a crashing mess of rigging as they locked together.

On *Polaris*, not believing his luck, the commodore signalled to *Dieppe* and *Prince Rupert* to close with the two leading ships while his own guns pounded the luckless duo.

Now with the odds somewhat evened, Commodore Cosmao had a sudden vision of doom. He shook his head to clear it of the vision and of the somewhat over-indulged brandy.

'Turn the ship, Bethune. We must support the fools!'

Sending up extra sail-trimmers meant losing some of his best gun crews but Bethune gave the order. The whole situation was becoming farcical. As *Tonnant* lost way and began her turn Cosmao noticed to his front that the *Ville de Mons* was blissfully sailing on and he remembered that he had not signalled his intentions to her. Incompetence was rapidly leading to doom. Desperate measures were needed and the nerve to implement them was lacking. Cosmao was seething with frustration.

Before he could rectify the situation it seemed to him that the two 74s that had bypassed the mêlée to the south were on him like wolves, attacking from each quarter. His determination was undiminished but from whence would come the support he needed?

The fight intensified. All three ships fired off their broadsides, though *Tonnant* was much hampered by having to shoot from both sides of the ship at once and that with guns manned by poorly trained men. A lucky shot cut the tiller ropes on *Dieppe* and she fell away. *Prince Rupert* came closer to *Tonnant* and both ships fired hellish tons of metal into each other, the thick yellow smoke making things as dark as night.

On *Prince Rupert*, Michael North, surrounded by the overwhelming roar and stink of battle, stood on the quarterdeck looking grimly at the *Tonnant*. He was close enough to be able to pick out the senior officers. As he watched the younger of the two men, who appeared nevertheless to be in command, fell backwards clutching his face. Those around bent to succour him.

North looked forward. His ship was taking some heavy punishment but all but one of his starboard guns was still firing. As he watched a voice called to him to 'Look out, Captain!' He looked upwards as the mizzen mast broke with a harsh crack that he could hear clearly above the din of battle. Ponderously but decisively the topmast collapsed throwing its sails and rigging over the starboard side. Luckily nobody was injured by the falling debris, though North pulled himself from under a heroic but unnecessary marine before regaining his feet. Immediately *Tonnant* started to pull ahead and North feared she was about to rake the prow of his ship. It was not so. Captain Bethune, his commodore having been carried below unconscious, decided that he had had enough. Within a quarter hour *Tonnant* was well clear and headed due east away from land.

Urging his men to clear away the wreckage, North cursed his luck in losing the mast. At that moment the *Ville de Mons* arrived on his port side but simply raked *Prince Rupert* in passing and forged onwards, though unlike the flagship she was sailing west towards the foggy shore.

North took stock. Further south lay the two French ships *Mont Blanc* and *Bonne Citoyenne,* still locked together and being battered at close range by *Polaris*. Nearing the three ships was *Dieppe* her rudder jury-rigged but preparing to join the battle. As she closed on the scene the two French ships, as if with one accord, lowered their flags in surrender. *Polaris* steered close to *Dieppe* and gave her captain instructions. Then she turned towards *Prince Rupert* where North already had men working hard to bring the collapsed mizzen topmast back on board. When she was almost alongside, the commodore hailed North with a speaking trumpet.

'Captain North, my compliments! Is your ship fit to pursue the Frenchie that is heading west–south–west?'

'Aye, aye, sir, within the next five minutes.'

'Very well. I am going in after the transports. *Dieppe* will take the prizes into Halifax with *Juniper* to assist. Good luck, Captain!'

North's crew had performed wonders. The mizzen topmast

was completely sheared off but he could carry the mizzen main sail and spanker. Though his speed was diminished a little there was a good chance he could come up on the *Ville de Mons*. The French ship was barely in sight like a ghost ship being received into the tendrils of fog about her.

There was time to send the men to a quick meal in groups of fifty or so and he ordered the galley fired up. The rest of the crew were employed in clearing away the damage and debris of battle. He had lost 18 dead and about the same number badly wounded with perhaps 50 less severely injured. With considerable exertion the overturned gun had been righted and though *Prince Rupert* had more than a third of her superstructure and hull damaged to a greater or lesser extent he was confident that she was fit enough for the task ahead.

As they entered the fog bank the wind failed completely. As they neared the coast he called for silence. He had two men with leads sounding from the bows and their reports were swiftly carried back to him in whispers by a chain of seamen. The pinnaces were hauled from their position towed behind the ship, crewed and set to tow her forward through the windless fog. The French captain was clearly underestimating how sound carried in the still air. Voices were heard and North could tell they had closed the gap. Evidently he had been helped by the *Ville de Mons'* captain dithering and turning south so sharply but predictably that *Prince Rupert* had 'cut the corner'.

The ships were about fifteen miles west of Styles Harbour and it seemed clear that the French 74 was making for the St Lawrence Estuary though whether there was some plan involved, North knew not. Now and again the fog cleared and on two occasions *Ville de Mons* could be seen under topsails only and being towed by her boats through the still fog, as was *Prince Rupert*. The chase had taken most of the day and darkness was not far off when the fog lifted completely. As the breeze strengthened a little, the *Ville de Mons* suddenly cut loose her boats and unfurled fore-mainsail and mizzen. Moving slowly in the water, she waited for *Prince Rupert* with her guns run out. She was off shore of a barren, rocky island directly east of a bay called Wild Cove.

Loosing his towing pinnaces North approached warily. The master had advised him that the waters here were treacherous with numerous rocky outcrops just below the surface.

The wind stronger now, *Ville de Mons* let fall her main sail without warning and swung quickly due east, aiming no doubt to cross *Prince Rupert's* bows. It would seem that her master did not have the skills of *Prince Rupert's* paragon. The French ship stopped dead in the water so suddenly that all three of her masts went by the board at almost the same moment. The horrendous crash as her hull split on the rocks could be heard from half a mile away.

North ordered *Prince Rupert* to be turned into the wind, backed his fore and mainsail, then had all sails furled, bringing the ship to a stop. He set out a sea anchor against the steady inshore current. He ordered his towing boats to go to the Frenchman's assistance. The launch, cutters and gig were lowered to join the searching pinnaces and despite the antipathy of war, the British sailors pulled as hard as they could to reach the stricken ship. *Ville de Mons* was already listing wickedly and men were diving over her side into the freezing waters. By the time *Prince Rupert's* boats had reached her there were barely a hundred men to rescue, half of them being on the French cutters. Nearly six hundred had perished as the ship turned turtle and sank.

The only officer that survived was the 1st lieutenant Pierre Delacroix, who was barely able to speak, so badly was he affected by the tragedy.

Having taken all possible steps to be certain that there were no more survivors, North turned his ship north-eastwards to find *Polaris* and the transports. He found them the following morning a few miles south of Sandwich Bay at North Harbour. The only ship he had seen was a French schooner which had emerged from a fog bank less than a cable's length from *Prince Rupert*. After a half-hearted attempt to escape she had let fall her pavillon and surrendered. She was the 8-gun *Rossignol* that had stood clear of the battle and had been tasked with repeating signals.

Polaris, assisted by *Carysfort* and *Peterel*, had caught up with 11 of the 14 transport ships within sight of Sandwich Bay. The two French frigates had taken a different course to the south with the other three transports and would not been seen again in these waters. North repaired on board *Polaris* and after the usual salutations was conducted to the commodore's cabin, where he made his report.

Murray looked tired but elated. Isaac Thompson, who had arrived earlier, and North sat in comfortable armchairs opposite the desk.

'Thank you, Michael. The sinking of the *Ville de Mons* was a satisfactory result - one more ship lost to the French. For our part *Polaris* came upon *Carysfort* and *Peterel* in time to drive off the two French frigates. The transports quite rightly lowered their colours immediately, except for three that were furthest from us which went off with the frigates. We find that of these

215

eleven ships six are troop carriers carrying 2,400 men, more than half of them Spanish or Dutch and five stores ships. We also captured 150 hussars and their horses. We believe of the three that made off, two carry troops, around 450 men all told and there is one ship carrying army cannon and powder as well as other supplies.

'I intend to convoy our captives into Halifax but I want you to search south again for those that escaped me. There are a number of possibilities, the most likely being that they will abandon their mission and return to France. However Newfoundland is vulnerable to attack right now. Even if Major Skinner had his Fencibles they would be heavily outnumbered but they have been sent into Halifax. Although *America* is in St John's she could be taken by surprise by the frigates which are both of 44 guns.'

North agreed. 'I will set sail straight away, sir. I wish you joy of your prizes.'

'Prizes of the squadron, North. 'All my ships have performed so gallantly that I believe share and share alike should be the watchword.'

Chapter 16

Friday 18ᵗʰ April, 1800

Despite a thorough search lasting three days North found no trace of the missing frigates and transports. It would seem that they had departed to return to France, provided as they were with stores he assumed that they had only gone towards the shore to take on fresh water and wood and perhaps steal or hunt fresh meat.

As *Prince Rupert* came to anchor in Halifax harbour a signal gun was fired from the quayside and North saw that the flags summoned him to repair on shore and wait upon the Flag forthwith.

As he stepped inside Murray's office North knew that something was wrong. Murray looked tired and drawn. He leaned back in his chair, away from the papers he had been reading.

'Michael, I am glad to see you. Bad news I'm afraid. Admiral Vandeput is dead. He died of natural causes aboard *Asia* in the Caribbean on the 14ᵗʰ of March. I was informed on my return here two days ago when I found that Israel Pellew had returned with the news in *Cleopatra*. The admiral's body has been taken into Jamaica to be carried home. It being so recent I have no news from London of his replacement but I shall continue in his stead until relieved. It seems also that bad news likes to travel in company. As you are aware I sent Joseph Bingham in *America* to bolster the presence at St John's, but it seems she did not arrive. In a sudden squall she was driven ashore and only with great difficulty was she warped off. Having serious damage beneath the waterline, Bingham took her into Glace Bay where she is being repaired.

'Yesterday news came from St John's that the Irishmen in the garrison have mutinied in support of the uprisings in Ireland stoked up by the French. I understand order has been restored and the vice-governor is sending some of the mutineers here for trial. I have arranged for four companies of the 66th to be carried on *Cleopatra* and a hired lugger to quell the mutiny if it reignites and keep order.'

North frowned. 'Difficult times indeed, sir!'

'Just so. However I am conscious that London knows nothing of these matters and must be informed as soon as possible. At the same time your mission here is completed and your original orders were to return to Portsmouth when all was accomplished, therefore carrying news of the mutiny shall be conveniently by your hand.

'I am bound to say, Michael, that you have behaved with the utmost satisfaction to me and dare I say to the Admiralty. Indeed your conduct throughout, commencing with the capture of *Dieppe*, the subsequent capture of the *Ailes de Mercure*, your mission in Montreal and your actions here under my command deserve the highest possible approbation.

'The present danger of invasion being averted I must reluctantly dispense with the services of those ships you brought with you and here are your orders to sail as soon as convenient as acting commodore on *Prince Rupert*. You will take with you subject to your broad pennant, *Polaris, Dieppe, Carysfort, Peterel* and *Juniper*. I have sent the schooner *Rossignol* away ahead of you with one set of despatches. Tomorrow the Post Office packet *Princess Augusta* will leave carrying duplicates.

'I also hand you my despatches. You will not be surprised that I cannot provide you with a flag captain, commodore. I have seen fit to report upon your conduct and that of your fellow captains and crews in such a manner that I trust will please their lordships and reflect my sincere respect.

'This evening the duke plans to hold a reception for all captains and first lieutenants. I trust you will be able to accept; I am sure any delay to your departure will be justified since the duke's hospitality is not to be missed.'

North was stunned. So recent was his commission as post captain that being advanced, albeit temporarily and without extra pay, to commodore was almost unbelievable.

Murray continued, 'I should like a note of your prize agent's details, Michael. We have a considerable sum building to your credit as well as to your crews. Being under Admiralty orders at the time you captured the two 74s, the whole award is thereby exclusively to your ship including the remnant of the crew of *Voltigeur* in the case of *Ailes de Mercure* and of course *Juniper* for *Dieppe*. Your ship's share of our captives including head money for the 100 you took off *Ville de Mons* as well as that for *Bonne Citoyenne* and *Mont Blanc*, the transports and the schooner, will be a fair sum too. Let us take a glass together to celebrate our good fortune, despite the bad news of Admiral Vandeput's demise and the mutiny.'

....

Government House had been furnished without thought as to the cost, as was Prince Edward's customary profligacy. This evening, a cool April day, great fires of Cape Breton coal burned fiercely and hundreds of beeswax candles added to the warmth and brightness. The wealthier burgesses and dignitaries of the town strolled with happy smiles and full glasses amongst the army and naval officers, decked in red, green or blue immaculate uniforms – and none so fine as that of the prince himself.

Madame Julie de St Laurent was discreetly at a distance from her protector and surrounded by young male admirers though it was common knowledge that she had committed her heart to the prince many years ago.

North found himself accosted by Judge William Cottnam Tonge, who was with his rather plain daughter Griselda. Tonge was an important member of the Nova Scotia Assembly and renowned for his continuous quarrelling with the Lieutenant Governor Sir John Wentworth, who was also present in the room. Tonge was an irascible though well-respected man. He had obviously imbibed well but not wisely.

'That right, Murray made you up to commodore? Most irregular of course but then the navy were always a law to themselves, what?'

North threw Tonge off balance by saying, 'You are right, of course, Mr Tonge. We are a law unto ourselves in many matters that landsmen perhaps resent but then His Majesty would have it that way. Just imagine the problems that would arise if I was unable to keelhaul at least one sailor a month. Discipline would go to pieces all over the fleet.'

Tonge allowed himself to be led away by his daughter.

'That was very naughty, Captain,' said somebody standing behind him. He turned to find himself looking into the

220

laughing eyes of Lady Wentworth, her husband grinning over her shoulder.

'The man is a pain in the arse,' said Wentworth. 'Still that is the nature of democracy and he does not bother me as much as I seem to bother him. Would you mind stepping this way, Captain North?'

The Duke of Kent had mounted the orchestra platform at the end of the ballroom and stopping the music, clapped his hands for attention. As the Wentworths brought North forward, the orchestra struck up and a voluptuous soprano and a diminutive bass sang Handel's 'See the Conquering Hero Comes' much to North's embarrassment.

'Oh Lord spare me,' he muttered under his breath, much to the amusement of his escorts who had each taken him by an arm.

Feeling even more heated in the close atmosphere of the room, North arrived in front of the King's fourth son, Edward, Duke of Kent and Strathearn and Earl of Dublin.

'Captain North. It is a great pleasure to receive you and on behalf of the people of Canada to thank you for the part you have played in averting an invasion by the French. Throughout your time in Canada you have acted in an exemplary manner and I have sent despatches communicating my sincere admiration to my royal father.

'The people of Lower and Eastern Canada through their assemblies in Montreal, Quebec City and here in Nova Scotia, have charged me to present you with this sword of 300 guineas, which though wrought in the city of Quebec, we judge to be as fine as any in London. May you wear it in affectionate memory of this country, which will always fondly consider you a friend and a hero.'

All present applauded loudly and the prince, taking him by the arm, led him to a line of waiting dignitaries who wished to shake him by the hand.

It was with considerable relief and an unaccustomed slight list to starboard that he regained his ship two hours later, an anxious Lieutenant Rockwell coming up the side behind him ready to try to catch him if he fell.

Chapter 17

Thursday 1st May to Monday 17th May, 1800

North's flotilla had left Halifax on the 30th April, the ships well provisioned and with their powder magazines fully replenished. The naval yard had done sterling work in repairing and replacing though time being short more work would have to be carried out in England. The whole town turned out to watch the departure of one of the biggest assemblies of naval vessels seen since the abandonment of Boston in the final days of the Rebellion. The flotilla was joined by two mast-ships laden with Nova Scotia masts and spars for the English dockyards and a large merchantman that was unusually so well handled that she did not slow the flotilla's progress.

An unsavoury incident had occurred a day or two before they left. Some of the Irish mutineers from St John's, assisted by crew members of a transport in which they were being carried prisoner to Halifax, had seized the ship and run into Canso on the northern tip of Nova Scotia hard by Chedabucto Bay. Murray had sent the 16-gun sloop *Lilly* after them and brought back a number of them. They had been swiftly tried and hung at noon the previous day.

North felt sympathy for Murray. Sensing that they might possibly take advantage of the lack of an admiral in the port, a number of merchants had assailed him with notes and complaints concerning the number of men being pressed for His Majesty's ships. A typical memorandum stated that with the continual draining of men from the fishing fleet many had fled to the United States and it was becoming almost impossible to carry on that trade. The last North had seen of Murray as he left his office after bidding him farewell and handing in his final report was of Murray taking a vociferous fishing boat captain by the scruff of the neck and the seat of his breeches and throwing him down the steps of the building, to the delighted cheers of several sailors nearby.

Now, out at sea and away from politics of the town, not to mention the many temptations opened to his crews, he and his captains sat down to count the cost of desertions and the pox.

Captain Thompson lamented, 'Nine ran! Several of them had been with me for five years on the old *Voltigeur*. At least the guard boat boarded a Danish brig and brought me two back but after flogging them, they are probably no use to me anyway – just more mouths to feed.'

Captain Austen was also annoyed,' I have two deserted and sixteen, would you believe, *sixteen*, poxed up! I never had more than three or four even when we were in St Kitts with all the hands lying with the slave girls.'

Captain Shepheard said, 'It is odd, is it not, that men run – five of my own – when they have had such a successful cruise. I calculate my seamen can see the best part of £20 each from this adventure of ours, Thompson.'

North had lost two men himself, both pressed men, one of whom had been flogged twice and was, he felt, no loss. He also had a dozen with the diseases of Venus paying for their folly by having to purchase the surgeon's remedies. He lifted his empty glass and waved for his steward to make the rounds. He said, 'Desertion is the plague with have to live with and dare I say we are probably better off without those that run in any case. Sadly, however they needs be severely punished to discourage others. I remember a case in '94 back in Gibraltar. A man named Topham was taken off an American brig. He had run 20 years ago – what on earth he was still doing at sea I cannot imagine. He was full sixty years old and Admiral Bowyer gave him a lenient punishment, half a dozen lashes. The old boy was tough enough to stand the cat and the scars on his back showed that it wasn't the first time.

'Three weeks later he was in a tavern in Gibraltar, when the lieutenant that taken him off the American brig came in. Topham rushed over to him, pulled out a knife and stabbed him in the stomach. He then ran off up the Rock, chased by a number of sailors. He was laughing insanely. As those that chased him watched as he cast himself from a ledge and perished on the rocks below. The lieutenant recovered from the wound but was unable to continue in the service. They found him a billet at Greenwich. I suppose if Topham had been flogged round the fleet or hung, the lieutenant would still be hale and hearty somewhere right now on one of His Majesty's ships – who is to know?'

....

Lieutenant the Hon. James Lang moved the candle closer, re-shaped a quill and opened his log to write up his entry for the day. He dipped his pen and carefully ruled up the page with its headings in the prescribed form. On the left page, left to right, he wrote at the head of the columns, Month and Day, Date, Wind, Course, Distance, Longitude, Latitude and Bearings and distance at Noon. On the right-hand page he headed 'Movements on Board HM Ship Prince Rupert' and ruled a line straight across both pages. He consulted the notes he had made in his rough book.

He wrote in a sloping, copperplate hand, 'May/ Sunday/15th /SSE/ 54°26'/24°10' /n.i.s.l.' – meaning not in sight of land. On the right side he wrote, 'PM mod. airs and pleasant, cloudy, exercised great guns, at 5, in 2nd reef the Topsails at 12, in co. Squadrn. Polaris NNE @ 1mile. AM at 1 in 3 reef of the T.sails and then bore up and to the North at 10 spoke Juniper. 11 out all reefs and T.G.sails.'

He scattered a little sand from the sandbox to dry the ink, closed the log and leaned back. He would have to submit the log to the Admiralty Office for approval before he could receive his year's pay. He arched his back and moved his head from side to side to work the stiffness from his neck as he reached out for the glass of watered brandy the wardroom servant had placed near his hand. Jolyon Bracewell nodded to him.

'Well, James, I do believe we can look forward to another day or so of good progress with the wind from the north east? Is it much changeable in this part of the Atlantic?'

'The master has a great deal more experience of this area. He told me that the weather around here can change very quickly even at this time of the year so don't be too sure. In any case we should raise Ireland in about four days and then perhaps another three or four to Plymouth, with any luck.' He turned as a quiet cough announced able-seaman Frank Todd, a volunteer who had joined the ship in Halifax, on transfer from HMS *America*.

'Ah, yes, Todd, come in and sit down. You wanted some help with your Will?'

On the lower gun deck Con Riley and his messmates were hunched over several scruffy sheets of greyish paper trying to work out their shares in the prize money. It was all just a notion of course; it could take years for the authorities in England to sort it all out. In the warmth of that contented moment most petty quarrels were suspended but the peace nearby was being tested. Con Riley was literate and had a surprisingly large repertoire of Shakespearean sonnets that he was wont to sound off dramatically at the drop of a hat. Accordingly, he was deferred to in all matters; including the arcane art of adding-up and long-division necessary to their deliberations. The quarrel to his left was distracting him.

Bosun's mate Summerhayes was tipsy and singing tunelessly of some place called Ilkley Moor. Derek Dove was doing his best to ignore him as he struggled with a primer lent to him by Lieutenant Lang who was encouraging him to learn to read.

'Put a cork in it, Joe, I'm trying to read here.'

'Ho, yes, which I can see yer fucking lips movin' can't I.'

Dove was not easily annoyed and said gruffly, 'Come on, Joe, stow it can't you?'

Ignoring the warning signs Summerhayes raised his voice and warbled, 'Here's a health unto his fucking Majesty…'

That was as far as he got. Dove dropped the book and snatched up a freshly darned pair of Summerhayes' socks. His powerful arm around the bosun's mate's neck, he stuffed a sock into his mouth and was applauded loudly by his audience.

As he turned away Summerhayes snatched the sock from his mouth and swung a fist at the back of Dove's head, knocking him to the deck. Dove was dazed by the contact his forehead had made with the timber. Summerhayes began to kick him repeatedly as he lay there. The master-at-arms, on his rounds, pushed his way through the crowd now yelling at Summerhayes to lay off.

Summerhayes, seeing the approaching master-at-arms, completely lost his senses and, snatching up a rammer from nearby, swung it around his head in the confined space. Midshipman Poole, coming at him from astern, was struck hard and staggered to one side, caught by the hands of two seamen as he fell. The master-at-arms lashed out with his cane, catching Summerhayes across the nose. Blood spurting through the fingers clutched to his face, Summerhayes collapsed to his knees and was carried off to be put in irons on the deck and cuffed to the mainmast strap.

The following morning at 11am Summerhayes was brought to the captain's table, his eyes blackened and his broken nose causing him to wheeze. Midshipman Poole's arm was broken and Dove's head bandaged.

North slammed his fist on the table. 'Summerhayes, you drunken idiot! You were rated bosun's mate because I believed you were reliable and this is the way you justify my faith? You are disrated and fined one month's pay for drunkenness. For assaulting Seaman Dove you are sentenced to a dozen lashes but the assault on Midshipman Poole cannot be so easily dealt with. Striking an officer is a court martial offence.'

Poole interrupted, 'Sir, forgive me, may I say something?'

'You may.'

'Not excusing anything Summerhayes did to Dove, in my case I believe the blow was unintentional. I realise that when he picked up the rammer and swung it about his intention became immaterial but I would like to ask you to deal with him as leniently as possible, sir.'

North folded his arms and looked at the midshipman for a long moment.

'Your concern does you credit, Mr Poole. I suppose since you take that view as the injured party I can but deal with the matter as you suggest. Very well, Summerhayes, the punishment for striking an officer is meant to be condign because discipline above all has to be preserved in a ship of war and were we to deal with such a matter lightly it could put the whole ship at risk. You do realise you could hang, do you not?'

Summerhayes, terrified, stammered and nodded his head but could say nothing intelligible.

'On this one occasion I will take it upon myself to interpret the incident as an accident and hope that the Admiralty does not disagree. In additional to your other punishments you will be given six lashes and employed permanently as captain of the heads until we reach England. Master-at-arms, put the irons around his ankles and have this man make his own cat. Punishment at six bells in the forenoon-watch tomorrow.'

For Summerhayes the worst part of the punishment was having to clean out the latrines every day rather than being able to walk the decks as bosun's mate. The loss of pay and his degradation to the lowest rank of landsman was such an indignity as to be almost unbearable, but to be made to clean the necessary-house like some drooling half-wit was too much.

At two bells in the midnight watch, his legs in irons, he cast himself into the sea and was drowned before the lookouts could sound the alarm. For the sake of his young widow North recorded the incident as 'accidentally lost overboard' so that she might receive his pay and prize money.

There was, however, a surprising postcriptum to Summerhayes' death. In amongst his effects was a letter addressed to Captain North which revealed that Summerhayes had been the man who murdered Midshipman Boyle. He gave his reason as his anger at the brutality that Boyle had displayed in an unremitting fashion since joining the ship. North tore up the letter feeling justified in his mind in not seeing Summerhayes' family suffer through this confession.

Chapter 18

Monday 9th June, 1800

'Back on Shore and Home Again' they might be but shore leave for all was out of the question until their lordships had decided what to do with them next. Michael North was unusually of the opinion that in the normal course of events as many should be allowed on shore as possible and if they ran, he was better off without them. Very few of his crew let him down.

The ships of North's flotilla swam in a single impressive line in the Downs with *Prince Rupert* at the eastern end of the column and the brig *Peterel* at the opposite end.

It was given to the schooner *Juniper* to continue to the Thames bearing Captain North and Jeremiah Wolfson to London. Landfall at last at Westminster and North and Wolfson made their way to Whitehall through the bustling crowds. A young midshipman, who was negotiating with a somewhat older but well-dressed ankle- flashing whore, spied a fully rigged captain almost at his shoulder and scuttled away down a side street, his face cherry-red. The woman of the town threw back her head and laughed while North and Wolfson grinned at each other.

They entered the courtyard through the Nash screen but before they could reach the front door of the Admiralty it opened and a balding shirt-sleeved clerk ran out, his hands held up.

'Captain North! Not this way, follow me, please.' Apparently the telegraph stations from Deal had reported the time he was expected to arrive. The clerk led them to the smaller entrance of Admiralty House on the south side of the courtyard and to the left of Thomas Ripley's newer building. They climbed up a narrow flight of stone steps. From thence they followed him along several poorly lit corridors until they reached a small room at the rear of the building, where they were asked to wait looking out over Horse Guard's Parade and cattle grazing in St James' Park. This building was from time to time the residential part of the Admiralty and it was here, a few minutes later, that they were ushered into a comfortable sitting room where Earl Spencer and Lord Arden were standing. The weather being quite sticky, windows had been opened allowing some less-than-fragrant air into the room. The grey-haired earl was dressed splendidly in a well-cut brown coat with the blue sash and the star of the Garter while Lord Arden's black jacket and breeches struck a note of contrasting simplicity.

Both men were smiling widely.

'Give me your hand, Captain North!' said Spencer, coming forward and shaking North firmly by the hand. 'And you too Mr Wolfson.'

Arden followed suit and said, 'what a splendid adventure, eh, North? Well done.'

'I received despatches from Captain Murray and indeed from the Duke of Kent praising you to the heavens, and of course your own reports have been most interesting. Come, let us sit down and you can go over again the details of the cutting-out of the *Ailes de Mercure,* which ship I am pleased to confirm will hence forward be called *Polaris,*' said Spencer.

A little later and with full glasses in hand, Spencer toasted them both. 'Well, well, most satisfactory, Captain, well done! Now, of course your industry and ability deserve reward but we serve in a hide-bound system and you being so recently promoted to the list of post captains will need to wait quite a while to move upwards. Mr Pitt and the rest of the very small group of people that are fully aware of this matter would like us to maintain the secrecy with which we have surrounded this operation and therefore public recognition will be slight – with the notable exception of your two Gazettes concerning the capture of each of the 74s.

'On the other hand on behalf of a grateful nation, Mr Pitt has successfully petitioned His Majesty for some mark of his favour. The King has seen fit to present you with the property known as Tarring Manor, near Worthing in Sussex, with its lands, farms and perquisites.'

North was thunderstruck. 'I don't know what to say, sir.'

Arden grinned, 'No more than you deserve, Captain, though I believe the earl and I would have preferred you had your own baronetcy – though perhaps in time …'

Spencer nodded, 'Yes, well, this secrecy business has its difficulties in some respects. The point is that you may well have saved the country a huge sum of money in sending a fleet and soldiers we can hardly spare to deal with a French invasion of Canada. There is little we can do publicly for the moment as we wish to keep First Consol Bonaparte in the dark as much as possible. So, I expect you will want to go to Dulwich and give the good news to the excellent Mrs Keen?

'However, I will require you to return to this office in ten days' time at 11am. We have another task we intend to burden you with – such is the nature of war, I am afraid. Mr Bradwell the assistant clerk awaits you outside and will arrange for you to meet His Majesty's solicitor who will sign over to you the deeds of Tarring Manor.

'As for you, Mr Wolfson, what can I say? You have discharged your duties to the duke of Bridgwater in an exemplary manner and I know he is keen to welcome you home. We are not unaware of the debt of gratitude we owe you and although still hamstrung by this wretched need for secrecy it would be invidious not to recognise your valuable contribution. In consequence we have arranged for a draft in the sum of 5,000 guineas and Government Bonds to the same amount by way of a pension to be delivered to you, care of the duke.'

After they had left, the First Lord turned to Arden. 'You know, Charlie, Michael North is destined for great things, I am sure of it. Quite remarkable. I haven't seen the like of him since Nelson.'

Arden's homely face was creased in a smile. 'For our own peace of mind it is fortunate he is considerably more modest and shy of public acclaim than Nelson, your Grace. He will no doubt be much less noticeable and just as useful as the so-called Duke of Brontë.'

Spencer chuckled, 'sticks in your craw a bit, don't it? King Ferdinand gives Nelson a dukedom last year and despite being made Baron Nelson of the Nile and Burnham Thorpe a few weeks ago he stills thinks he should be a duke or an earl of this kingdom. I don't begrudge him any of it but with his love of showy pageantry, clockwork Turkish *chelengk* on his hat and other gaudy trinkets he don't make the navy look too clever, do he?'

Arden shrugged his shoulders. 'That's Nelson. The people love him and he gets away with things nobody else can do. We have had no sailor more brilliant since Hawke or Drake. This business with William Hamilton's wife is too much for me but I daresay he will be forgiven. Though His Majesty has apparently ordered that Lady Hamilton is not to be received at the palace, they say he called her a fat fishwife – a little cruel about her weight, I thought. I remember her in her youth, she was the most beautiful of woman. Ah well! No doubting Nelson's talent in action though. It's Fanny Nelson I feel sorry for.'

....

Both Wolfson, now financially independent for the rest of his life, and North, lord of the manor of Tarring by Sea, felt they were walking on a cloud as they went back to Whitehall and shook hands before going their separate ways. On impulse, North decided to hire a chaise and go to Dulwich immediately, pausing only to return to *Juniper* and collect his baggage, his steward and Cluney Ryan, newly promoted to cox'n of *Prince Rupert*. His predecessor had been given a boatswain's warrant and transferred to *Dieppe* to replace their bosun who had died at sea.

The truth was that due to the secrecy of his whereabouts he had managed to send Isobel just five long letters in the half-year he had been away, but he had only received one of hers, via *Juniper* when that vessel had joined him in Quebec.

....

Isobel's house in Court Lane, Dulwich, had a long garden at

the front and it was here in the warm sunlight that Michael North found her. She was dressed in a simple smock dress with a brown apron, her head bare except for a kerchief which kept her hair out of her eyes as she knelt on a burlap sack, weeding her daisies with great industry. As North approached her from behind, unheard, she said, 'Damn you, pernicious weed, it's the compost pile for you!'

She threw the weed over her shoulder and it handed at North's feet.

'A fine way to greet me after all this time!' he said with a laugh.

She came to her feet, her features struggling to express either shock or pleasure, then she fell into his arms sobbing.

'Oh, my dear,' said North tenderly, 'I am sorry, I did not mean to startle you.'

Her face wet but smiling broadly she said, 'Idiot! Don't you know better than to creep up on a poor woman like that?'

'Were I at sea determined on a succulent prize I might gain much by stealth.'

'Oh Lord! Look at me,' said Isobel. 'What must you think; I look like a kitchen maid.'

'You look divine,' said North. 'I am come upon the fairest prize I could ever wish.'

They kissed passionately until she pulled from his arms laughing. 'We are observed, my love, by two sailors with silly grins on their faces.'

North turned to introduce Naylor and Ryan, who had carried in the baggage from the chaise, then he handed Naylor two crown pieces to pay the driver generously for the day's hire. Isobel, having charmed the seamen greatly, sent them to the kitchen to be fed. They could stay in the loft above the stableblock and for decency's sake she had Ryan place North's trunk in a spare bedroom on the first floor of the house.

For the next few hours neither expressed the deepest desire they had at every second, being content to wait until later for that ecstatic union.

She had changed into a pretty summer dress and he noticed that, if anything, she appeared younger than he remembered her. Watching the emotions cross his face, Isobel said, 'since you have been away I have missed you so much. I awake at night feeling you near me in spirit and I take so much comfort from that but having you here now, to touch and see your adored face, is the fulfilment of my every dream. I love you so very much.'

'Enough for me to burden you with the title of lady of the manor of Tarring by the Sea?'

'How so?' she asked in puzzlement.

After he had told her of the King's special gift he said, 'Dearest, I have but ten days and so much to crowd into it because I fear their lordships would have me go to sea most quickly. Marry me this week, please?'

She laughed. 'Hmm, I am not sure that that was the best and most considerable proposal you could have made but I get your drift, shipmate. If you *could* crowd me in, I suppose I have to agree.'

As he swept her into his arms he felt that this moment of happiness could never be matched.

....

The wedding was a simple affair the following Monday afternoon in the Dulwich Chapel of God's Gift but despite the short notice, well attended. The Duke of Bridgwater, his face wreathed in smiles, sat contentedly with Jeremiah Wolfson in a back pew. The captains of the *Dieppe*, the *Polaris* and *Juniper*, with Captain Spicker and Captain Rockwell both promoted the previous week, made a group of five behind Isobel's few family members and numerous friends.

Both of North's brothers and their wives had travelled up, delighted with Michael's bride.

Two days later, a second carriage loaded with wedding gifts and items she wished to take from the Dulwich house, Isobel North travelled down to Tarring with her servants and one of North's oldest and trusted seamen, Con Riley, who was now self-consciously the holder of the office of bailiff of the manor of Tarring. In any case Isobel was perfectly capable of running the estate and Riley would work under her directions. North reluctantly returned to Whitehall to attend upon their lordships, hopeful that he would at some point have more time to enjoy his new home.

He had ridden down to Tarring with Riley on the previous Wednesday and stayed until Friday. The house was a well-built Palladian mansion with an octagonal pavilion at each end finished in the 1770s with fourteen bedrooms, very similar in style to Buckland House in Berkshire. It had been designed by John Wood the Younger, the son and successor architect of the most important buildings in Bath and the

Royal Exchange in Bristol, who here, as in many other buildings, had inserted Masonic symbols in subtle places.

The parkland around the house encompassed some 300 acres and included the home farm and mill, a 20-acre lake and trout stream, with stands of mature trees and walled gardens. The rest of the estate was in good order. It comprised some 9,000 acres which reached down to the sea and included the dwellings and lands of some 280 families, seven farms, two inns, a church and a thriving boatyard. The present steward was employed by the government since the estate had been seized by the Crown following the execution of its previous lord for high treason. After working for a few weeks to acquaint his successor with the estate, he was eager to hand over the responsibility to the new owner. It was evident from the state of the accounts and the good repair and general contentment that he had carried out an excellent job in keeping and maintaining the estate for the past eight years.

Chapter 19

Monday 23rd June, 1800

North was welcomed into the Board Room by Evan Nepean, his long, handsome face set in an uncharacteristic smile. The only other person present was Lord Arden.

Arden had North sit opposite him with Nepean at the head of the table, his knees in the space underneath with the clerk's pediments and drawers to each side.

Arden began to speak. 'Congratulations on your marriage, Captain. I am sorry to say the service requires that we tear you away from your bride for another voyage. This is not something that I would have wished for you but, frankly, our trust in you is such that you were the first and best choice.'

He lifted a part of a small sheet of cloth which had covered the chart in front of him. 'Know what this, Captain?'

North looked at the map curiously. 'Coral reefs, my lord? Indian Ocean, I would say, or possibly south of Sumatra?'

'Not bad. This is the Indian Ocean,' he moved more of the sheet and North nodded.

'Mauritius, sir, Île de Bourbon, and here, about 350 miles east, Rodrigues. So these marked must be the Chagos Islands. Not that I know anything about them.'

'Not too surprising. They are nominally British though we have not settled them whereas the French have, as on Rodrigues. In the case of the Chagos Archipelago there are very few Frenchmen, mainly on Diego Garcia, farming

240

coconuts with slaves they have brought from Africa. In fact Britain claimed the islands in 1786 but it was the French seven years later that brought in the first settlers.'

'But they belong to us, my lord?'

'Legally, yes. This is our lawful justification for part of your mission. We want a presence in the islands and a small naval base, at least for the time being. As I am sure you are aware, the never-ending complaint of the East India Company is that we don't do enough to protect their ships from the Mauritius and Île de Bourbon privateers. A base here would be of great assistance, though the facilities are not wonderful; for example, fresh water is a big problem.

'Our other difficulty is the privateers themselves. Small ships mainly, difficult to track down. Whenever we send ships into the Indian Ocean they scuttle away like rats. So at the suggestion of Captain Home Popham, we have come up with a new approach.

'What we want you to do is to take *Prince Rupert* and lead two sloops and two schooners, who will all enjoy considerable freedom to chase down and destroy any French privateers they can find. In addition you can retain *Juniper* as tender to *Prince Rupert*. In conjunction with Indian army units, you will take possession of the Chagos Islands and use it as a base for our raiders. The Honourable Company has undertaken to keep the base garrisoned and supplied with stores and ammunition. The whole exercise will be for a maximum of six months' duration or terminated at your discretion. We believe that after that time there is a real danger that France will send in a heavy flotilla with several ships of the line to evict us and destroy our ships.

'Admiral De Pleville may already be in those waters, of course, with at least three French 74s, but our judgement is that by the time word gets back to France of our operation and then orders are sent to De Pleville you can call off your hounds and return home. Whether we continue to keep a naval base there will be decided at some later stage.'

North looked down at the chart. 'It sounds like a good plan, sir, by why not Rodrigues? I doubt it is heavily garrisoned and it is nearer to the trade routes.'

'We considered that but think about this for a moment. You admitted you knew nothing of the Chagos. It has been barely noticed over the centuries *because* it is distant from the normal trade routes and because, economically, of not much use to anybody. Such a base, smaller than Rodrigues and off the beaten track, should not prove obvious. The East India Company will recommend that all of its ships take a more southerly course than usual during that period to gain more protection from your presence. They can provide a 500-man garrison and cannon for Diego Garcia Island but Rodriquez would require too many men. The main objective is to create surprise and uncertainty amongst the French privateer venturers, so that they will stay away for a very long time.

'As I have mentioned, you will have *Prince Rupert*, with *Juniper* as tender. The other ships are a 20-gun corvette, the *Sarabande*, under Commander Maurice Cartwright, captured from the French in '96, the Bermuda sloop *Fly* 18, Commander Henry Samuel Butt, and the 10-gun schooners *Garnet*, Lieutenant William Grainger and *Heron* – commander to be appointed. Your command will be independent of any senior officer in the Indian Ocean and you will be ranked as commodore for the mission – though without extra pay, I am afraid.'

North could not be but pleased. It was a sign of the trust reposed in him that the Admiralty would choose him to lead a flotilla even if they were of such small vessels. Clearly they would be ideal for the job.

His lordship continued, 'I anticipate that there will be prizes and these will be taken into Bombay where the Royal Navy representative and his prize court will decide whether they are to be bought in. Of course if it suits you, you may choose to keep any of the prizes with you that may serve your purposes. The Capetown brig *Rose Harcourt*, at present in Dover, has been chartered as a supply vessel. She will be based in Bombay and serve to convey prize crews back to Diego Garcia. She will also carry 150 seamen and a company of marines for the augmentation of your crews as and when required as replacements.

'Any other ideas you may have as to how to best prosecute your mission, you have leave to follow. In order to buy information or defray unusual expenses you will carry with you on *Prince Rupert* 1,000 guineas. If you need to spend more, I have provided you with signed bank drafts on Admiralty funds; needless to say not to be used for any profligate purpose.'

After an hour of discussion, North left the Admiralty to keep an appointment with the duke of Bridgwater. The following day he planned to travel in a hired carriage to go down to Buckler's Hard once more where *Prince Rupert* was undergoing more permanent repairs to damage received in Canadian waters. Once there, having received permission to sleep out of his ship it was barely 70 miles by post chaise to

Tarring.

North walked through the noisy and often noisome London streets in the warm sunshine. He was not a regular visitor to Town but was wise enough of her many traps for the gullible not to let down his guard as he passed the bawdy houses and bagnios near the Strand 'by craft she draws th' unwary in; and keeps a publick mart for sin.'

His destination was the Beef-Steak Society at the Covent Garden Theatre, which had a limited and invariable membership of exactly 24 comprising mainly actors, artists and men of letters such as the late Dr Johnson, but also men of considerable rank. It being Saturday and each member allowed one guest; the duke had invited him to join him with the other members, who disdained to call themselves a 'club'. In fact he was in time to sit down and eat shortly after he arrived. He noticed that the members wore buff waistcoats under blue coats and that the brass buttons on the waistcoats were embellished with a representation of a gridiron and the words 'Beef & Liberty'.

The beefsteaks which were the ostensible reason for the society's existence were justly famed as the finest in London and were consumed simply without a gravy but with horseradish or mustard, according to the diner's preference and stacked piles of roast potatoes which could be speared from huge dishes in the centre of the tables. The drink was simple, small beer or porter, but this light alcohol did not inhibit the jollity of the atmosphere.

After they had eaten, the members joined together in horseplay and raucous laughter but the duke shepherded North to a side room where a bottle of excellent port wine and a silver plate of wafers and grapes was waiting.

'A wonderful meal, your grace; had I such a cook at sea I would no doubt put on the pounds like wildfire!'

'Glad you enjoyed it, Michael. Now, I wanted to have a talk with you in this place because, noisy and disorderly though the members be after dining, it is one of the most private places in Town. You will recall that mention was made of traitors in the Admiralty. While their lordships quite rightly do not wish it to be known that they have this problem, clearly it is something of which they would like to rid themselves. We now have clear evidence that the leading light in this treason is a young rake, the Honourable Winslow Marshall.

'Marshall's father, Lord Edward Marshall of Tonbridge, was a friend of the elder Pitt. On that basis the son was firstly given a sinecure as a director of ordinance at the Tower and more recently in overseeing the contracting and purchasing of cannonballs, chain-shot and other ammunition for the Ordinance Board with offices in the Admiralty building – a job ably carried out by his staff of five with little or no need for his presence. For this paper post he is paid around £1,080 per annum – around six times as much as a frigate captain. Even so, such are his profligate habits that he is continuously in debt and therefore was an easy target for the French spymasters. Neither does it help that he keeps company with ne'er-do-wells like Lord Camelford and his coterie of buffoons – not that Tom Camelford is a traitor – far from it.

'It would be a simple matter to solve except that he has the ear of the duke of York and therefore it is desired to remove him quietly and with as little fuss as possible. This is where you come in.

'Officially this has nothing to do with their lordships, but if Marshall was to take a long, bracing cruise in foreign waters and perhaps decide to settle in the Azores, it is felt that his health would benefit enormously.'

North said bluntly, 'You want me to kidnap him and drop him off in the Azores.'

Bridgwater laughed. 'Now, nothing so crass, Michael. Marshall will receive orders to inspect the improvements to *Prince Rupert's* armament installed by the shipwrights at Buckler's Hard. This will entail a practical demonstration of the efficacy of the carronades that are in place of the long 12s, as you sail down the channel. Should you absentmindedly forget to drop him off at Plymouth, of course your next landfall will be at Ponta Delgado?'

'If it was not that he is a traitor and spy I might refuse but send him down and I will deal with the matter.'

Chapter 20

Wednesday 25[h] June to Friday 10th August, 1800

If he had any preconceived ideas as to the nature of married life they fell far short of the real thing. While at home when he was separated from Isobel by just a few yards or on the other side of his estate, he wanted to return to her side. Having finally torn himself away after a week of married happiness he found it difficult to concentrate on the business of preparing to sail halfway round the world.

The usual business proceeded with loading stores, replacing several cannon that would not serve, checking over volunteers and king's men. He made time to receive the commanders of the two sloops, *Fly* and *Sarabande,* which with *Juniper* would sail with him.

In order to preserve some secrecy, the schooners *Heron* and *Garnet* and the hired merchantman *Rose Harcourt* would proceed directly to the Azores, where he would meet them. These smaller ships would blend themselves in with the regular Capetown convoy. In the Azores all his vessels would take on wood, water and other stores, carried by two HEIC ships which would also be waiting there. One of those ships was carrying 200 of the Indian army soldiers who would garrison Diego Garcia and they would sail in convoy with the rest of the flotilla. All the ships would then stand out to sea well clear of the Cape. Thence to the Chagos about 6 degrees south of the equator, avoiding landfall as far as possible, the convoy would land and take possession, being joined by three more HEIC ships with the balance of the proposed garrison together with their stores and equipment.

In the meantime the crew of the *Prince Rupert,* urged on by their new 1st lieutenant Alan Goddington and their new 2nd lieutenant David Crosby, late of the schooner *Crow,* were working well and to North's complete satisfaction. There was another new lieutenant, the 4th luff, whose name was Henry Gibson. Gibson was quiet almost to the point of rudeness but since he carried out his duties in an efficient manner, he was simply accepted for what he was.

He called Midshipman Henry Adams to the cabin. The lad had broadened and become more quiet and mature since joining the ship in the previous December.

'Mr Adams, I would like you to take my servant and Seaman Boyce up to Chesney's Farm with my goat, Charlotte. She is beginning to dry up and needs to be put to the billy-goat, for which occasion she has been driving us all mad with her bleating these past two days. Also take Emily, the smaller goat. She may or may not stand but she will be dry before the year is out if she is not with kid. Here are two shillings for Mr Chesney. Empty the cash from Boyce's pocket before you go and don't let him anywhere near the inn, is that clear?'

Henry, being the shipwright's grandson, knew Farmer Chesney well and anticipated a pleasant outing. What he did not reckon on was Chesney's well-intentioned invitation to sample his cider. Later that afternoon, with George Naylor struggling to keep two goats in check on their chains, Midshipman Adams and Blair Boyce, giggling like girls, were making their unsteady way up the side of the ship when both fell into the green brackish water. Since this had a sobering effect and rough hands rescued them before they drowned, the incident did not *officially* reach the captain's ears. He did, however, find a reason to masthead the lad the following day,

248

seeing the sad state of his crumpled and smelly uniform.

Surgeon Weller, who had been a stalwart in the time he was on *Prince Rupert* had been poached by the hospital at Haslar. Comfortably provided for by virtue of the prize money shared between the warrant officers, he had left the ship with North's grateful thanks and letter of sincere commendation. His replacement made North uneasy. Hopefully there would be a chance to do something about it when at sea, but Doctor Richard Horrigan of Dublin showed every since of being an alcoholic. He had with him an Irish servant with whom he conversed in the Gaelic, not knowing that it was North's second language.

Overhearing their conversation it became clear that the surgeon had an arrangement with one of the crew to be supplied regularly with spirits for his own consumption. North was unable to identify the crewman from the conversation.

He called the 1st lieutenant, the master and the master-at-arms to the cabin. Addressing the master-at-arms he said, 'Andrews, it has come to my attention that somebody is either trading in spirits or stealing from the spirit locker. I am going to send my clerk into Portsmouth to buy a sturdy padlock with two keys. I want you and the gunner to see that a chain is fixed to the spirit room door. From now on those keys will only be held by the first lieutenant and the master, one of whom will be present when spirits are drawn. If I find that any other key has been improvised or manufactured I swear I will stop the rum of every man on this ship until the culprit is found. I dare say after a few days of rum-less water and lime juice someone will be discovered! Make sure everybody on the ship knows this. In the meantime get your white mice to sniff around and look yourself to see if anybody has stored spirits anywhere but in the spirits room.'

After Andrews had left the cabin the 1st lieutenant said, 'It still amazes me that on a king's ship where a reasonable amount of alcohol is freely provided some people just cannot resist selling or buying more of the stuff.'

'It is the word "reasonable" that is the problem, Goddington,' said North with a sigh. 'I recall an incident the master of the old *Bellona* 74 told me he witnessed when he was in the West Indies in '59. The captain had allowed some local women on board with three barrels of what they said was local ale. The master-at-arms discovered that two of the barrels contained pure gin so he stove them in. The gin ran into the scuppers and as the ship rolled, the gin ran out and down the side out of the scupper holes which acted like funnels. Fifteen or more went over the side and put their mouths to the holes and sucked it up. They swallowed so much that within three minutes nine of them were so drunk that they fell into the water and drowned – the others were fished out.

'So it shows how much some will risk just for alcohol. I believe that at least one third of our crew is tipsy on most days but thankfully they conceal it well enough. If I had the temerity to search their dunnage, no doubt many of them would have a secret store of a bottle or two but that is to be expected. On the other hand deliberate trading or stealing liquor to sell it cannot be countenanced.'

The arrival of the Honourable Winslow Marshall was conspicuous for the fact that he was delivered by a decked cutter which he had hired personally to carry him round from the Thames. He expected North to pay the captain of the

250

cutter who came on board to be paid. Not willing to see the skipper out of pocket, North handed him four guineas and after he had left the cabin stood up and walked over to Marshall who was lounging in an armchair near the bookcase.

'Mr Marshall, I don't expect to pay your bills for you. You will kindly remember that while you are on board my ship I will not stand for liberties to be taken, do I make myself clear?'

Marshall looked bored. 'You seem to be mistaken as to our relative positions, Captain North. I represent the First Lord on a matter of some importance. On my assessment of your ship's skills in gunnery might well depend your future as a captain of one of His Majesty's ships.'

North threw back his head and laughed. He held up the letter that Marshall had brought with him. 'You have clearly much to learn about the navy, Mr Marshall. While you are on *my* ship you are subject to my command and nothing in this letter contradicts that custom. It has been made very clear to me that you are a minor functionary at the Admiralty and something of a damned nuisance to them. I advise you to keep very quiet until you leave this ship and I will try my best to pretend you don't exist. You will take the spare lieutenant's cabin and mess with the wardroom. Think yourself lucky you are not accommodated in the hold.'

He went to the door of the cabin and told the marine to send for Lieutenant Crosby to escort the gentleman to the wardroom. Marshall left the cabin visibly shaken.

North's last task before leaving for the Indian Ocean was to visit the prize agent who served most of his crew in Portsmouth, William Le Cocque in St George's Square. Le Cocque had done well for himself having started out as a slopseller. The crew thought well of him – he advanced money to their wives against their entitlement and even paid the rents on several of their houses. He also acted as a sub-agent for North's own prize agent, William Marsh of Marsh and Creed's Bank in London. North had found him honest and reliable and begrudged him none of the 3% he charged for looking after the sailors' affairs.

Le Cocque showed North into a comfortable office and produced a leather-bound ledger from a rack near his desk.

'For your warrant officers and seamen from Marsh on the 14th May this year I have received £790.5s in respect of the *Dieppe*, and on the 20th May, £1,100.8s.6d for *Polaris*, both being bought in by the Admiralty straight away and unusually quickly paid out. I dare say this reflects the high regard that their lordships hold you in personally. So far in relation to the rest of the prizes from the Canada mission I have not received any monies in but of course that could take some time, especially in the matter of merchant ships and transports.

'From the monies already received the prize court has sent the usual 5% to Greenwich Hospital and after paying out those who have attended this office – I have a list made out for you – I have a total of £1,004.3s to disburse. I have also invested £522 in the funds for various claimants, as you will also see on the list.'

North said, 'Thank you, Mr Le Cocque, as usual an admirable report. As to the money still to be paid out, here is a list of 19 men who are deceased, and details of their next of kin. There were six deserters in Canada, and one in Plymouth, here are the names, their prize money to be remitted to Greenwich. As regards the remainder I will thank you to hold it over until I notify you as we will be leaving port again soon.'

'Well, Captain, I have to say that your successes seem to pile one upon the other, I will have my clerk count out cash money to pay out those on *Prince Rupert*. While we are waiting may I offer you some sherry so that we can toast to more prizes in the next voyage?'

North left Le Coque's place of business to deal with a more unpleasant matter. Another prize agent, Joseph Goodman, had his place of business in a tallow-chandler's shop nearby. He acted for six of *Prince Rupert's* crew who had been previously carried upon the sloop *Diligence*. In the time they were on that ship their cruise in the West Indies had been very successful and they had captured ten ships and shared in the capture of two more. Although *Diligence* had been wrecked subsequent to the taking of the prizes, all hands had been saved. Like many of his ilk, it appeared that Goodman had held on to their cash even after the transactions had been settled by the government.

On his way to Goodman's he stopped at the Benbow Tavern where Cluney Ryan and John Bradman, bosun's mate, were waiting for him. Handing Bradman the leather satchel with the crew's cash to carry, North explained what he was going to do next. They walked a few hundred yards to a narrow side street. North looked in at a dingy window of what appeared to be a closed shop. He was looking around him to decide his next move when a voice hissed at him from a nearby alleyway. 'Captin, over 'ere!'

He looked across to see a thin woman wrapped in a thick tartan shawl. He crossed and stood in front of her. She looked him up and'down and said, 'are you after that bastard

Goodman?'

'I do want to find Joseph Goodman, yes.'

'He's in there, Captin; you gotta go round the back. He won't answer the door but 'e's definitely there.'

North said, 'Thank you, I'll come back and give you something for your trouble if I find him there.'

"S'awlright, I don't need money, just screw the sod down for what he did to me daughter.'

North beckoned to his men and walked down the side alley beside the shop where he pushed open a creaky gate. The back door of the shop was slightly open and as he approached a man emerged carrying a large bag. His eyes widened and he dropped the bag, moving quickly back into the doorway but too late for North's outstretched hand which caught him by the front of his coat.

'Mr Goodman, it is not polite to avoid visitors in this way. I don't intend to take up much of your time but I will have from you what is due to six of the crew of the *Diligence*.'

Goodman blustered, 'No, sir, all monies were forwarded to Greenwich Hospital after the *Diligence* was wrecked near Havana last September.'

North shook his head. 'Nonsense, Captain Hodgson-Ross and his crew were rescued almost immediately. No report came to England to the contrary.'

'Then I shall deal only with Captain Hodgson-Ross, sir.'

'Sir, you will not. I have a power of attorney here on behalf of

Gunner's Mate Lincoln, Able Seamen Gurney and Thompsett and Seamen Long, Duvalier and Church. You will hand to me the sum of £203.8s.6d, immediately, or I shall have you taken up by the bailiff.'

'Those amounts are disputed!'

North produced another sheet of paper. 'The prize court has condemned the following; the French privateer *Fougouse* taken 13th February, 1797; the Spanish privateer *La Nativetta*, taken 3rd March, 1797; a share of the prize money for a Spanish privateer and a Spanish packet taken near Jamaica in September, 1797. Also the French ship *L'Epervier*, 27th September, 1797 and seven merchant ships, cargoes and head money.' He rested his hand on the hilt of his sword. 'Now, hand over the money.'

'Captain, captain, there is no need for this; all will be settled as soon as I receive the monies from the main prize agents, Ommanney and Druce.'

North stepped forward and again gripped his jacket. 'You snivelling little creature! Do you think I have not checked with them? I have had enough of this. Ryan, open that bag!'

Ryan obliged by tipping out the contents of the bag on to a nearby bench. Pushing away sundry items of clothing, he held up a metal cash box. 'Locked, I think, sir.'

North turned to Goodman who was pressed against a wall by the beefy Bradman. 'Give me the key.'

'I don't have it here, it is at my house.'

North nodded to Ryan who set the box down and inserted the point of his dirk into the crack beneath the lid, springing it open, before handing it to North.

North counted out £620 in Bank of England notes, £320 in notes drawn on other banks and half a hundred sovereigns, half sovereigns and silver coin. 'Very well, Ryan and Bradwell, you will witness that I am taking from this box sovereigns and other coin to the tune of £75, and Bank of England notes for £250 which includes a sum to be passed over as interest on their dues. The remainder of the money will go with us when we take Mr Goodman to Mr Snell, the clerk of the exchequer at the dockyard, and hand him into custody.'

Goodman managed to free himself from Bradwell's grasp and drop to his knees.

'No, I beg you, let me go free and I will make amends.'

North said, 'You are a scoundrel and an embezzler and deserve no mercy for defrauding innocent seaman. You and your kind sit here in comfort while those men serve their King and Country, suffering the horrors of battle and shipwreck, so that they can became prey to you. No, sir, it will not do. Come along now and face the consequences. Think yourself fortunate I don't hand you over to the press gang instead.' He pointed at a schooner riding at anchor a cable's length from the shore. 'There lies *Cambridge's* tender, the *Castor*, shall I hail her?'

....

Prince Rupert was used to sailing in the night from Buckler's Hard to avoid notice but on this occasion she sailed on the morning tide and headed directly for the Channel blockade where she exchanged signals openly with the flagship and then set off as if returning to Canada with her line of cygnets behind her. For three days she sailed due west before turning south for the journey to the Azores.

It was here at Longitude 17 and Latitude 43, before reaching the islands to the south west, that Winslow Marshall asked to see the captain.

In the three weeks since he had come on board North had avoided speaking to him but since he had kidnapped him he relented.

Marshall still seemed comfortably arrogant. 'Captain, I am aware that you intend to put me on shore at Punta Delgada. Since we are in the middle of the ocean I admit that my intentions have always been to leave England and settle in France. You must agree that being taken summarily from my home with no chance of settling my affairs I am at least entitled to a small sum of money to tide me over until I can secure passage to France.'

'Why do you think you will be set on shore?'

Marshall shrugged. 'Since you will no doubt be away from England for some time I might as well tell you. Lord Arden believes I am the only person passing information to Paris but there is one he does not suspect, one who was able to warn me of the plan to exile me. In order to protect that person's identity I allowed you to believe that I was unaware of your intention to abduct me. It is arranged that I will be collected from Santa Maria. By the time you return to England, France will have invaded and the Admiralty and everything else in the stinking country will be French.'

North, completely composed but inwardly very interested in Marshall's boastful revelation, said, 'you place a great deal of faith in Bonaparte's ability to invade. One would have thought that working inside the Admiralty might have made in clear to you that the Royal Navy would need to be neutralised before an invasion could be made. If you really think the French have that ability perhaps they should have confined you to Bedlam instead of burdening me with you. "Moral insanity" might serve the purpose. Still, now that you have been so candid with me I will return the compliment.

'Your life and liberty are of no concern to me since, clearly, you are an admitted traitor to the country of your birth and your betrayals may well have cost the lives of some of your fellow countryman. You should be thankful that I do not simply have you hung from the main-yard arm as a confessed traitor. You are also under the impression that the options open to me are limited to marooning you at Punta Delgado. Well, we shall see if a more elegant solution is possible. For your information I have no intention of calling into any port in the Azores.'

Marshall's eyes opened wide in astonishment. 'But I was told ...'

'You were told that I intend to take on water and wood and meet two Company ships at Punta Delgado? Do you think me stupid? I have no written orders concerning you. Having been given a great deal of discretion in the matter I made my own plans. I doubt that the French navy would have presented any great risk of them intercepting us in the Azores but I decided before I left England that the convoy would send in boats to Sao Jorge Island further north of Punta Delgado for water and wood and it is there that the Company ships will join me.'

'Then where will I be landed?'

'Tell me the name of the other traitor?'

'That I cannot but you can be sure that Paris knows exactly where you are going. You are in for a warm reception.'

'Rubbish! You can't possibly know our destination; only two people in England besides me and the First Lord know that. You are an idiot.' North goaded.

Marshall leaned forward, 'Idiot, am I? You were supplied you with charts for Cape Horn and the South Pacific by Joseph Mudge at the Admiralty? Mr Mudge's midshipman son is in the prison at Verdun and I can assure you it was very easy to persuade him to let me know where you are going.'

North shook his head, 'You will have to do better than that. All Mr Mudge knows is that our first landfall in the Pacific is Hawaii beyond that I did not draw charts.'

Marshall sneered, 'But a glance at Mr Nepean's file was all that was needed to reveal your true mission. You are to make your way to Manilla in the Philippines to cover the landings of Company troops and secure the islands as a base to facilitate passage from China to India as a safer route for their ships.'

'Well, thank you for that. I was completely unaware that I was going there,' said North sarcastically. At least the Admiralty had not been thoroughly penetrated and North now had valuable information as to other traitors.

Marshall now did not look so certain. 'So what so you intend to do with me, Captain?'

'Ah, that is for me to know and for you to worry about, Marshall. Now, if you don't mind I have despatches to write and put on board the Mail packet that will call at Punta

Delgado in a few days. I expect Mr Mudge, not being as well protected as you by noble rank, will be dealt with on the basis that his life may be spared if he gives up the rest of your filthy gang.'

The stop in the Azores was practically touch and run. The Company's ships, having been warned by North's letter, carried on the outbound Plymouth packet *Westmoreland* a few days earlier, had slipped their moorings at Punta Delgado and were waiting in the lee of Sao Jorge Island together with *Rose Harcourt* and the schooners. The senior captain had used his initiative and had a dozen rafts of firewood floating nearby and as many spare barrels of water as the two ships had been able to fill. It remained only for extra barrels to be filled by the boat's crews of the flotilla and nets of fresh cabbages and oranges to be transferred together with other stores from the Company ships.

The convoy was on its way less than twelve hours after reaching the channel between Sao Jorge and Pico, heading due west for half a day and then south again and over the equator, after *Juniper* had rejoined them following her trip into Punta Delgado with despatches and mail.

King Neptune and his court dealt summarily with those pollywogs that had not crossed the equator before and three days later St Helena was in sight.

Again it was touch and run as *Juniper* was again sent in with a copy of the despatches to be carried home by the first HEIC ship to call in case those already sent did not reach London.

The third landfall 23 days after the Azores was at the island of Tristan da Cunha where they watered.

Chapter 21

Monday 10th August, 1800

'I have never been here before, sir,' said Lieutenant Goddington, as he and the captain looked out over the oddly named Busiharbour Bay on the West side of Tristan da Cunha. The small settlement was slightly to the north with a good anchorage. Being around 1,500 miles from St Helena, its remoteness meant that the person who had named the harbour clearly had a sense of irony.

North replied, 'nor I, but Mr Bishop was here about ten years ago on board *Grampus* bound for the Indies. He tells me that it is not an unpleasant place, warm enough in the summer though there is an excessive amount of rain all year round brought in by the westerly winds. Not a bad place to be marooned. There is a small community here and a platoon of Company marines. It is a port of call for Company ships to take on fresh water. You may send on shore some of our sharp shooters to bring back a few feral goats to supplement the meat. I am going on shore with our passenger for an hour or two. Have his baggage put into the launch, please.'

The huts of the settlement were mainly of mud and straw with one or two larger buildings to accommodate the marines. The officer in command was a lieutenant who, despite the few contacts he made with the outside world, was smartly turned out, as were his marines, and clearly making the best of his twelve-month posting.

North accepted a dish of tea. 'So, you see, Lieutenant, it is the wish of the Admiralty that Mr Marshall remain here as your guest until further notice or until I collect him. I hand you 60 guineas to cover his rations and accommodation. You will not allow him to have contact with the crew of any ship that visits, please, and under no circumstances must he be allowed to leave the island without a direct order from their lordships or until I collect him. I must impress upon you that this man is a traitor to his country and if he is able to take passage for France he could continue to do untold damage to our country's security.' He handed a written authority to the lieutenant.

'Rely on me, Captain. As far as the rest of the world is concerned he has never been here and we have no knowledge of his existence.'

....

As Tristan da Cunha was about 4° south of the Cape of Good Hope, the flotilla could take a course following the 37th parallel for around 100 miles before turning north east to make for Diego Garcia, staying out of sight of Africa.

During that part of the voyage North briefed his captains and the captains of the two 1200 ton HEIC ships, the *Ganges* and the *Hindostan*, and the *Rose Harcourt* as to his plans for the landing on Diego Garcia. The Company troops on *Ganges* would be increased by 300 more when the flotilla met up with the other three Company ships at the atoll group of Egmont Islands, to the north west of Diego Garcia at that part that the French called Île Sudest.

The weather was kinder than usual and the journey safely made.

Chapter 22

Thursday 4th to Monday 8th September, 1800

Approaching through the north-western passage into the lagoon which formed most of Île Sudest, North could see that the remaining three Company ships were already at anchor. He picked out their names on the transoms: *Rockingham* and *Prince William Henry,* which were both of about 800 tons, and *Preston* which was smaller at 670 tons.

The meeting between the Royal Navy, the army officers and the Company captains took place on the atoll away from the heat and noise of the ships for although it was still very hot here, awnings had been erected the previous evening by the Captain Kenning of the *Rockingham.*

There was a moment of confusion before the main party of senior army officers arrived since they were led by Colonel Arthur Braddock who was unsure who was senior, him or North, the two ranks of Captain RN and Colonel by convention being given equal status. After a whispered conference between Captain Kenning and Major MacLeod of the 3rd Extra Battalion Madras Native Infantry, this was judiciously solved by introducing North as *Commodore* North, thereby allowing Colonel Braddock the graceful excuse that North was probably the equivalent of a brigadier.

The orders of the respective parties had in fact made it clear that North was in command at sea and that Braddock would be in command on land, subject to North's overall command.

At Braddock's disposal were two Sepoy companies of the 2nd Battalion 16th Bengal Native Infantry, a company of the

European Battalion of the Madras Regiment and three companies of *Macleod ki Palan* (MacLeod's Battalion). There was also one Engineer's company.

Supported by the navy's marines if necessary, the Company soldiers would go on shore the following morning at 8 o'clock. The current information was that there were no French soldiers on the island but no chances would be taken. With *Prince Rupert* half a mile offshore, guns ready, the main force would land on the west of the island at Eclipse Bay. The Madras Regiment's company would be carried by *Sarabande* into the lagoon which formed the main area inside the island landing those soldiers further south.

The flotilla was off the west coast of Diego Garcia as dawn broke. North looked through his spy-glass at the long white beach which comprised most of the land-mass of the island. There were many coconut trees along the 12-mile length. Much of the island, a great circle around the lagoon, was less than a quarter mile wide – the total dry land being about 13 square miles. At the northern end where the landings were to take place was the main settlement with a number of man-made cisterns for storing rain water and the rudiments of an enclosed area around a few dozen sheds, some single-storey houses and two barracks like longhouses for the French settlers' slaves.

North nodded to Lieutenant Lang, 'Make to all ships, commence landings, Mr Lang.'

At first there was a sparse rattle of musketry from the settlement which quickly died down. A midshipman sent in with Braddock's soldiers ran up a signal hoist on the flagpole in the enclosure – 'prize secured' – and it was all over. An

264

anticlimax after the planning and discussions of the previous day but thankfully without loss of life with the exception of Princess, the European Battalion mascot, an overweight white goat that had fallen overboard from one of *Ganges's* boats.

North decided that the larger vessels would stay at anchor off the western shore and only allow the smaller ships through the treacherous Barton Pass into the lagoon. The broken remnants of the British merchantman *Hampshire* that had sunk trying to negotiate the gap seven years earlier was a stark reminder that caution was the watchword.

North came on shore shortly before noon and congratulated Colonel Braddock, wishing him joy of his command. Work was already underway to transform the settlement into a strong point. The Indiamen were sending off their hold cargo in the boats and patrols were making their way around the island collecting up stray settlers. It took but a few hours to convince the white islanders that their best option was quiet co-operation with their conquerors; after all, France was a long way away and all they wanted was to carry on their pleasant way of life. Nobody bothered to ask the slaves what they thought.

The 'fort', which took a week to construct, was a nine-foot stockade made from coconut tree trunks gathered in from this and other islands of the archipelago, which enclosed three more huge cisterns blasted out of the coral and filled from barrels carried on the Indiamen. Due to the population now being increased by some 550 people replenishment would need to be made regularly by sea. Also inside the fort were extra quarters built of coconut leaves and coral blocks cut from the new cisterns. These were allocated to the Company's officers, some of whom had brought their womenfolk with them perhaps unaware of the Admiralty's intention to occupy the island for six months only.

Satisfied that Colonel Braddock was completely at ease with his role and leaving him only Lieutenant David Crosby as liaison officer, North left the island under the eyes of two of the armed Indiamen to watch over things and a pinnace and crew to act as courier for Crosby.

Having discharged cargoes of various stores, *Rose Harcourt* and the three smaller Indiamen set off northwards for Bombay. *Prince Rupert* made a short trip back to the group of six small islands to the North West called the Egmonts. The most southerly island, Île Sudest, had a small settlement where another copra factory was located. Here there were about two dozen slaves with a white French overseer. The small group of settlers had already been visited and persuaded that it was in their best interests to behave themselves. Apart from Diego Garcia and Boddam Island in the Salomans, this was the only other permanently occupied island in the archipelago, though coconuts were harvested from other uninhabited islands such as Danger Island further north.

North had decided to make Île Sudest the base for his raiders rather than Diego Garcia, being still unsure as to exactly how far the Admiralty's secrets had been penetrated. Diego Garcia could serve as a useful port of call for Indiamen. Captured privateers and their crews could be held there under guard of the garrison awaiting convoy to Bombay but here a more secret presence could be maintained.

He gave *Sarabande* and the other three ships their orders and they set off westwards to seek out privateers.

Chapter 23

Sunday 28th September to Friday 24th October, 1800

Three weeks had passed since *Prince Rupert* had anchored in the lagoon north-east of Île Sudest and only *Heron* had returned, bringing three prizes, the largest of which was a ten-gun French privateer schooner taken by *Sarabande* twenty miles west of Reunion. The two smaller ships were another schooner and a lugger both taken by *Heron.* North had retained *Sarabande's* prize, the *Franklin,* sending on board her Midshipman Henry Adams, a master's mate, a gunner's mate and sixty men given a cruise to see what they could pick up to the north between the Chagos and Rodriguez.

The morning had begun with a fresh breeze blowing from the east but as the day wore on it became oppressively damp and still; even the numerous birds seemed to droop languorously as they lined the bare spars of the ship. Tempers became short and petty quarrels more noisy than usual. North had an awning set up on the quarter deck but the moist heat was still tiresome. There was little relief below decks with no breeze to enter through the open hatches.

Sniffing the air North quickly turned to Lieutenant Lang, who had the watch. 'Batten down the hatches immediately, Mr Lang, and secure the guns more strongly. I believe we are in for a blow.'

Lang was unaware of the slight change in the atmosphere but did as he was bid, calling up the watch below.

North called to the master, 'Mr Bishop, have the stream anchor set astern. I believe a storm is approaching.'

Bishop had divined something similar and sure enough within fifteen minutes the sky had darkened and the wind was already building to a wild crescendo. Crewmen ran barefoot to lash down the guns with extra tackles and the captain's steward in his snug pantry carefully stowed the best plates in an oak chest, each wrapped in a fold of blanket.

Soon visibility had dropped so much that the shoreline of the lagoon had vanished. There was a smell like sun-baking seaweed carried on the wind which blasted and ebbed in no discernible pattern as it rocked the ship at its doubled anchors in what had been the sure shelter of the lagoon. Then with a mighty howling wind and biting rain, the full force of the hurricane struck. The ship heeled under the weight of wind but fought back. The bosun called for man-lines to be rigged and the only creatures lost over the side were three frigate birds, their clawed feet frantically scrabbling on the sodden deck as they were flushed through the scuppers.

It was only as eight bells were barely heard above the storm that North realised that the ship had been enveloped in the darkness and cacophony of the storm for almost four hours. The ship was battered from all directions but managed to shrug off the tempest. Head aching with the noise, he stayed near the wheel, his tarpaulin coat streaming water down on to the deck; his neck sore from constantly shaking his head to clear his eyes that filled relentlessly with the endless lashing of the torrents of water. Then silence and calm and a blessed relief from driving rain.

Lang looked across at him. His throat was hoarse with long hours of shouting. Now he said nothing but the puzzled expression on his face was enough.

'The eye of the storm, Mr Lang. The hurricane is moving all the time. Soon the wind and rain will return but I know not when.'

Midshipman Poole, who had the forecastle deck, called back, 'Sir, I see another ship in the lagoon, it is too big to be one of our flotilla, perhaps an Indiaman?'

'Where away?' barked Lang.

'Fine on the starboard quarter, sir; less than two cables distant. Now the rain conceals her – I can't see her.'

North and Lang, joined by the master, had their glasses trained forward of the ship as the storm blasted them again.

North asked, 'What do you think? There, I believe I saw her too, damn this rain. Mr Lang, don't beat to quarters but have the crew stand ready to man the guns in case she is an enemy.'

Another hour dragged past. The temperature had risen again and the rain slackened. Then like a silent thunderclap the sun burst out through the clouds and the storm was gone as if a massive door had suddenly been closed behind the retreating winds and rain. The sea which had been thrown up in angry swirling disorder even in the shelter of the lagoon became a gentle shadow of its former self as if it were a sleepy child worn out after a day's play.

Floating in the now placid waters less than three hundred yards from *Prince Rupert* were not one but three ships, the largest one of the three listing dangerously and bare of all her sticks.

The next smaller ship is size was a frigate, to North's practised eye French-built and carrying 42 guns but not under colours.

To carry 42 guns was unusual and the ship was not in any class he recognised but the French often built one-off frigates as experiments. The third ship was a graceful brig with clean lines and although her sails were furled he could see by their golden-hue that that they were made from Bombay canvas. He called to Lang to beat to quarters. The gun crews, augmented by many more hands, having been ready below, had the guns loaded and run out in less than three minutes.

The strange frigate could be manned by either British or French sailors – her construction was meaningless in a war where the Royal Navy had been able to sweep up scores of the Gallic nation's ships of all sizes in a remarkable affirmation of British professionalism and superior abilities. As North watched, the tricolour was run aloft and immediately struck. On the larger ship there was no mast beyond a stump that would serve so a tall, very thin man was waving a white sheet at *Prince Rupert*. The brig, which North had recognised as a country ship, followed suit.

Ordering Lieutenant Goddington to take possession of the frigate and Midshipmen Boswell and Grimmond to lead prize crews in the cutters for the other ships, which appeared to be prizes of the frigate, North went below to his cabin to change his clothes.

On his return Lieutenant Lang pointed at the red cutter being rowed back said, 'Sir, Mr Goddington is sending over the captain of the frigate. She is the *Arc en Ciel* of 42 guns. I must say, sir, this is a stroke of luck; three prizes with not a shot fired.'

'Indeed,' North replied, 'not even the face-saving gesture of firing one shot *pour le pavillon*. What a shock it must have been for the captain to find himself accidentally under the guns of a British 74.'

The captain of the *Arc en Ciel* was a short red-faced man with sparse ginger hair, revealed as he removed his hat to the ensign. His name was Armand Didier and he was clearly very upset.

'What cursed luck brought you here, Captain?' he asked in faultless English. 'I recognised your ship as our *Aquilon* taken at the Nile but I did not realise your navy had it in commission.'

North grinned and handed him a glass of wine, dissembling. 'We are merely passers-by, M'sieur le Capitaine; what of your own presence? I see you have one of our Indiamen and a country ship with you which of course I now have the pleasure of having recaptured *without a shot.'*

'You can mock if you like, sir, but when Admiral De Pleville finds out you at large in his ocean I would not give much for your chances. The *Campbelltown* was taken by me on the 13th August south of the Maldives, the *Lady Derwent* the following day. I was making my way to Mauritius when I realised that a hurricane was about to blow up. Unfortunately for me *Campbelltown* was already badly damaged and dismasted and I doubt she would have survived the storm. My sailing master knew of this anchorage so we made our way here with *Campbelltown* in tow. In fact it was a stroke of blind luck that I found the damned place in the gathering storm. If we had not made it here we might have just reached Diego Garcia.'

North refilled his glass which had been very quickly emptied. 'Well, Captain, you and your officers will be my guests for a while. In fact I intend to take your ship to Diego Garcia, *where we have now reasserted our sovereignty,* and the crew will be transferred to a ship to carry them to Bombay. Your frigate is an excellent vessel; I must compliment you on that. It will make a useful addition to my squadron, particularly if M'sieur De Pleville comes my way.'

That evening North caught up with his journal and paperwork and added another two pages to his serial-letter to Isobel. He spent several minutes simply staring from the stern-lights thinking about her, as he did every day. He was still experiencing that same delight he felt when they had declared their love for each other in her house in Dulwich. If anything all these months away had strengthened his feelings and he felt that he should start thinking of leaving this ocean and returning home. It was only in moments alone like this and with no pressing matter to deal with that he had the chance to really fill his mind with the happiness he felt.

The following day, leaving *Juniper* at Île Sudest, North took *Prince Rupert* and *Arc en Ciel*, towing *Campbelltown* to Diego Garcia, where the 300 crew of the frigate was sent on shore to await the next Indiaman carrying supplies from Bombay. The fact that he carried extra men on his ship to man prizes meant that by using them and 70 of his own regular crew, he could put 170 men on board *Arc en Ciel* under Lieutenant Lang with Midshipmen Poole and Dawson and two master's-mates to assist.

Commander Butt in *Fly* had followed him down from Île Sudest escorting no fewer than four prizes, captured near the Comoros; three French privateer schooners and a Dutch brig.

He had found out that the *Lady Derwent* was the property of a syndicate led by Francis Latour, the Madras banker. She had been built in India for the Country Trade, was much larger than the traditional brig and showed in her appearance why the methods of the Indian shipbuilders were often thought much better than those at home. Her timbers were of Malabar teak and her planks were rabbeted rather than butted together which made it a very dry sailor and caulking unnecessary. Her rope-work was of rot-resistant rope made from coconut fibre and many of the lighter spars were made from bamboo. The hull was painted with a mixture of lime and fish-oil that was particularly efficacious against the teredo worm. The hull itself had no tumble-home, was wider below the water and flatter on the bottom – allowing her greater freedom to enter shallow waters.

Looking at her beautifully carved ornamentation and elegance, North was entranced by her and wished for a moment he owned her.

The *Campbelltown* was something of a surprise. It turned out the 900-ton ship was another owned by North's friend James Farquharson and captained by his brother-in-law Angus Shaw. She was not only loaded with spices, timber and tea but carried a large number of passengers amongst them being Major General Connors of the British army with his wife and staff as well as Hector Darke, MP for Ipswich, and the Bishop of Calcutta, the Right Reverend Roger Bulstrode. Just as interesting were a prisoner and escort.

Callum Arkwright was a major of the marines who was being carried to England to face trial for piracy, having deserted His Majesty's service and set himself up with the dregs of Penang – French, Dutch and Lascar – to prey upon friend and foe alike. He had been engaged in a murderous campaign which had only ended after three years when he had been captured by Admiral De Pleville and handed over under a flag of truce to the Governor of Calcutta.

He was immediately recognised by *Prince Rupert's* marine captain Jolyon Bracewell, who restrained himself with difficulty. It transpired that Bracewell had lost a cousin when Arkwright had captured a merchantman carrying him. Arkwright had murdered dozens of ship's officers and passengers, sparing only those he could ransom.

Captain Didier confided to North that he was glad to see the back of the pirate whom he had been very tempted to hang out of hand.

General Connors spoke for the passengers when he asked what North intended to do with them.

'*Campbelltown* cannot be refitted in these islands, sir, 'said North, 'and I doubt she will reach India in this condition; in particular we do not have adequate mast timber. As you can see all that the islands can provide is trunks from the coconut trees which are unsuitable. Her fate must remain unsolved until I have found a solution. Her cargo will be sent into Bombay on one of my flotilla's prizes in due course and the ship herself will remain in the lagoon.

'As far as the passengers are concerned there is a strong possibility that we will see a suitable Indiaman here within a week or so that can take you back to Bombay or possibly an out-bound ship for England – I am afraid that is the best I can do, General.'

'Damned nuisance all this, North, I am under orders to go to Lisbon with Mr Darke. Things are moving fast there towards a French invasion if the Portuguese don't abandon our ancient alliance and I have been appointed to assist Hookham Frere who will be sent to Portugal as a plenipotentiary and is expected to be there by the time I arrive.'

North folded his arms and sat in thought for a few moments. 'If you feel you really need to make the journey, General, I can retain the Dutch brig brought in by *Fly* and give you use of it to get to Lisbon albeit with a small crew and leave you while continuing to England. It will be taking a chance on evading the enemy, of course.'

'Well that is most accommodating of you, Captain. I have with me a corporal and a dozen privates of the 33rd due to be discharged in London; they can help man the brig?'

North said, 'I will impress some of the English and Lascar crew of the *Campbelltown* for the rest of the crew and the 2nd lieutenant of *Fly*, Mr Wragg, shall command. Once we have provisioned the brig you can get underway.'

General Connors was extremely grateful. Apart from his family and staff, he took with him Mr Darke, Bishop Bulstrode and a couple called Kenning who decided to brave the journey.

The remaining passengers elected to stay on *Campbelltown* to await passage, except for the pirate Major Arkwright and his escort, consisting of Commander Geary late of the sloop *Justinian* that had foundered on the coast of Malabar, and Lieutenant Topping-Higgs who had been carried on *Justinian* as a supernumerary. With them were six seamen, also part of *Justinian's* crew. North accommodated this party on *Prince Rupert* and used the opportunity of keeping Arkwright in irons to have Commander Geary and Lieutenant Topping-Higgs each stand a watch to augment his one remaining

Lieutenant.

Before *Prince Rupert* sailed for Île Sudest the Indiaman *Ganges* arrived with supplies and carried the remaining passengers back to Bombay.

Callum Arkwright, his vicious spirit undiminished by his imprisonment, sat on the deck inside the manger waiting for the armourer to fix a bolt to the deck to secure his leg-irons. He had spotted James Lang as he had been hustled aboard with sharp digs and blows from the escorting marines. Arkwright had been a pupil at Eton College and James Lang was four years his junior

Lang, in the black gown of a King's Scholar lived in College House. Arkwright, was an Oppidan and lived in the town in Jourdelay's. He was thoroughly spoilt by the Dame of the house. In fact Arkwright had been expelled for cheating and knew Lang for just one term. During that few months he had terrorized any smaller boy within kicking distance.

Lang had been a particular object for his anger since, despite the age difference and physical size, Lang stood out for his fearlessness. Arkwright was even more enraged by Lang's quick tongue, having made him look foolish on more than one occasion. Arkwright's rage had finally boiled over when having incurred the customary punishment for being persistently tardy in attending a class he had been awarded a hundred hexameters and Lang had refused to write them for him.

Lang being accommodated within the college itself and Arkwright being a "townie", returning to Jourdelay's each evening, their paths seldom crossed after dark. One evening Lang had been sent by the Lower Master to deliver a letter to the Dame at Godolphin House and was walking along the Long Walk. Arkwright, lounging on the wall had seen him approaching. He had crouched down behind the wall and when Lang passed by, he had jumped on him and beat him to the ground. Lang had moved quickly, rolling away as Arkwright had tried to boot him. Arkwright rushed forward but Lang, now on his back on the cobbled path, had managed to brace himself against the curbstones and thrust out a foot into Arkwright's knee.

It had been purely by luck that the force of foot against knee was enough to rip into the cartilage around Arkwright's kneecap. Without a word Lang had got to his feet, dusted himself down and walked away. Unfortunately for Arkwright, the incident had been witnessed by one of the praeposters who hauled the pain-wracked bully before the headmaster and he had been rusticated. His expulsion had occurred the following term and he had not seen Lang since the incident in the Long Walk.

Seeing his enemy after all these years only served to make Arkwright's imprisonment a deeper humiliation. He knew that Lang had recognised him and had pointedly ignored him. He may be attached now to a length of chain and forced to shit in a cracked leather bucket but he would find a way to revenge himself for the grumbling pain that rarely left his kneecap.

Chapter 24

Friday 5th December, 1800 to Thursday 3rd January, 1801

James Lang stood on the weather side of the deck of *Arc en Ciel* watching the crew as they settled down to working the new ship. Of course he was excited by this his first command but determined to conduct himself as befit the captain of a rated ship, he exhibited an outwardly calm appearance. Apart from two lieutenants, Henry Jones, late of *Sarabande* and David Nye, who had been the senior mid on *Fly*, he had three midshipmen. All of his warrant officers held temporary appointments but they were seasoned petty offices and soon had the men working well.

Making his way south-westwards, Lang hoped to find some trade in the sea east of Rodrigues. However with strong winds against him, he allowed the course to be more westerly and after three days *Arc en Ciel* sighted the two tiny islands of Agaléga. The sun had set but in the after-glow the low-lying verdant islands spread to left and right.

Approaching the shallow channel of La Passe, between the two islands, Lang was checking his chart, spread on one of the two quarterdeck carronades. To the south was Hawkins Point – to the north a promontory called La Far-Far. He tapped the chart and turned to say something to the quartermaster, Derek Dove. He was interrupted by a hail from the foremast lookout. There was a ship an anchor in the Petit Mapou bay off the east coast of the south island.

Arc en Ciel had very little water under her keel in La Passe but the chart was marked with a note that it was navigable with

278

care. Therefore Lang had her moving slowly under fore stays'l and jib. This probably reduced her shape to any watchers on Hawkin's Point and visibility would have been further reduced as darkness fell.

Calling for silence, Lang quickly ordered all sails to be taken in and the best bower anchor set. He called his officers to the cabin.

'Gentlemen, it is yet to be determined if the strange ship is friend or enemy. What we shall do is to send on shore a small party, led by Lieutenant Nye with cox'n Ryan. You will cross the point and see what you make of the ship. I appreciate it will be dark and you may need to get quite close. The islands are practically uninhabited apart from a few stray souls who no doubt will be hiding themselves. So anybody you see on the shore in the bay will probably come from the ship.'

Ten minutes later Lieutenant Nye went down into the waiting gig and Cluney Ryan gave the order to shove-off. Under muffled oars it took less than twelve more minutes before the two men in the prow of the boat stepped down into knee-depth warm water and eased the boat forward on to the sandy beach. The moon had cleared the horizon and the sand was silver by its light. A nesting bird grumbled a bit and shrank lower in her scooped nest as the shore-party crossed the high-water mark and struck out towards the small bay to the west.

The land here was low-lying, at its highest it was less than thirty feet above sea-level. The party of sixteen spread out and crouching, moved forward together as quietly as they could.

Their goal was less than a hundred yards away. As they reached a point about twenty paces from a ridge separating the beach from the area of short grass they were crossing, voices could be heard.

Gesturing to the men to remain where they were, Nye crept forward with Ryan by his side. A dozen men were dragging brushwood into a pile and one of their number was striking flint to start a fire. From the blackened stones around the timber it was clear that this fire place had been used regularly.

Nye nudged Ryan and whispered. 'If they are not speaking French I will eat my hat, Ryan. What do you think?'

'Frogs for sure, your honour. It looks like they are settling down for supper.' His stomach agreed noisily with this observation.

The ship was a corvette pierced for 18 guns but there were two smaller ships, a schooner and a two masted ketch inshore of the corvette. The schooner had her jib struck down.

'We have seen all we need, Ryan. Let's get back to the ship.'

Half an hour later Lang had listened to Nye and gave his orders. There was only time for a tot of neat rum for every man by way of supper.

....

In the near darkness, the officer of the watch on board the French navy corvette *La Néarque* recognised *Arc en Ciel* by her unusual number of guns, what he was not ready for was her colours floating down to her deck as a different hoist was run up. To his horror he saw the red ensign of the British navy at the peak just as the first of a rolling broadside of guns thundered from her side.

If that was not enough of a surprise, the barrage was matched by the rattle of musketry from the dunes as a strong shore party took the French sailors on the beach by surprise. Some of the mostly unarmed Frenchmen managed to scatter inland, some were killed or wounded and the eight survivors threw up their hands in surrender. They were held under the muskets of four marines and the rest of the shore party rushed into the two boats that had been drawn up on the beach. Pulling for all they were worth, a dozen men made for each of the two smaller ships.

The 10 gun privateer schooner, *La Gracieuse,* would normally have had at least forty men to crew her but with almost half her number away in Mauritius with a prize, she was overrun within a few minutes. The ketch had just an anchor watch. Most of her crew were those in the party on the beach.

To take her undamaged, Lang was determined to move as close as possible and board the corvette. He had the larboard battery run-in forty feet from the side of the smaller ship. *Arc en Ciel's* crew were already clinging to shrouds and pushing forward from behind, eager to get on board the enemy. A few were cut down by a panicky defence but as they reached the French deck it was clear that the surprise attack had succeeded beyond Lang's hopes. *La Néarque's* officers had rushed to her quarterdeck with as much determination as they could muster and the fight there was intense.

With the captain and two of his lieutenants badly wounded, the resistance faltered and died after less than fifteen minutes.

The tension and wild energy in Lang began to recede and he found himself breathing easier as he looked around. All three enemy ships had been captured and if was not for the stink of burnt gunpowder and the groans and cried of the wounded it almost seemed there had been no battle.

....

The surprise arrival of the British squadron had produced a good harvest.

At Île Sudest, North was pleased to find that Henry Adams had a successful cruise with two fat Dutch trading brigs captured south of Rodriguez. *Sarabande* and *Heron* had also rendezvoused with a bevy of prizes. These were two armed cutters, an Arab dhow used by privateers, two small merchantmen and a French mast-ship which carried enough masts and spars to refit *Campbelltown* ten times over. If they could make good her timbers from the wreckages of ships scattered around the archipelago, there was just a chance she could be made seaworthy enough to reach India under escort. There was also the ship's company of the scuppered gun-brig *Fury*, taken by the French, to augment his manpower, and more controversially an American trading brig, the *Ulysses*, carrying powder and shot which Commander Cartwright of *Sarabande* had boarded.

The captain of the *Ulysses*, Benjamin Larcom of Beverley, Massachusetts, was furious as he stood in North's cabin. 'This is outrageous, Captain! Your Commander Cartwright stopped and searched me unlawfully!'

'There are only two relevant questions, Captain Larcom: what were you carrying as cargo and to whom were you delivering it?'

'You know it was powder and shot bound for Madras, you can see from my papers.'

He waved an impatient hand at the desk.

North folded his arms and leaned back. 'It seems that you were careless, Captain. Indeed these papers bear out your story but unfortunately for you Commander Cartwright found the papers you hid in case you were boarded by the French, stating in some detail your rendezvous with Rear Admiral de Sercey in Mauritius. Having lost all his ships he would seem to have little use for your cargo, though I doubt you were aware of this when you left Boston. These papers state that your cargo is required for the use of Lieutenant Jean-Marthe-Adrien L'Hermite, Commander of the 44-gun frigate *Preneuse.* You may not be aware that *Preneuse* was driven ashore months ago and wrecked by HMS *Jupiter.* L'Hermite was taken prisoner. De Sercey has given his parole and therefore can have no trading intercourse concerning weapons.'

'Well, as you say those papers were only to be used if I was boarded by the French.'

'I might have believed that if you had not been within half a league of Mauritius when Cartwright boarded you. If you were bound for Madras, you would never have sailed that close to Mauritius. Furthermore the sheer detail of the French papers gives a clear indication that you must be in collusion. It will not do, Captain Larcom. I am sending in your ship and cargo to the prize court in Bombay to decide the matter. I am confident they will condemn the cargo if not the ship.'

In the following three weeks a further eight privateers, twelve merchantmen, two luggers, four cutters and the French sloop *Constant 14* were brought in along with a privateer which was *Garnet's* first and only prize.

Arc en Ciel's cruise had proved spectacularly successful.

Apart from the prizes secured in the cutting-out action at Agaléga she had secured four merchantmen that were in the hands of privateers, and hidden amongst the atolls around the island of Johanna under the protection of the Sultan - Alawi bin Husain.

North rapped his glass with a fork to gain attention and the company fell silent. 'Gentlemen, if my mathematics is correct, we have captured a frigate, a corvette, four sloops, fourteen schooners, three luggers, eighteen merchantmen – including six Indiamen recaptured– six cutters, one mast-ship and a French flagged dhow. Together with cargoes and head money, quite a satisfying haul in prize money. However with the privateers back in Mauritius and also probably wagging tongues in Bombay the cat may well be out of the bag.

'My original instructions were not to remain here for more than six months or to withdraw at my discretion without risking losses to a superior French force. I believe that it is now time to move our flotilla and the remaining prizes to Bombay where we will settle with the Vice Admiralty court before making our way back to England.

'Colonel Braddock will maintain the garrison here for the time being and withdraw at his discretion if the French decide to bring in a larger force of ships to replace those of Admiral De Sercey. I am leaving the sloop *Constant* here for his use and he has the Company's transports.'

....

Bombay was huge, crowded and stank but none of *Prince Rupert's* crew and the crews of the other ships that were allowed shore leave were concerned with anything but pleasure. Seven men deserted but the majority, still stunned by the size of their share of prize money, returned with some measure of contentment after their run ashore.

Captain North and his senior officers were fêted day and night by the merchants of the Company and its officials. Rich food and strong wine had their effect on most of them and it took some men time to shake off the effects of over-indulgence. It was something of a relief when it was time to weigh anchor and set sail for home. Apart from his original flotilla North retained *Franklin* and *Arc en Ciel*; the remainder of the prizes being condemned as lawful by the court and sold with cargoes except for the American brig, which lost her cargo but was allowed to go free. The Company also took the opportunity to ask North to allow four large Indiamen to convoy under his protection. There was also a heavy chest containing £12,000 in gold and silver which by custom meant that North would be entitled to £600 in 'passage money.'

On 3rd January the chance occurred for which Callum Arkwright had been waiting. Lang and *Prince Rupert's* carpenter were inspecting some wormy planks in the forepeak. This necessitated standing in the manger where Arkwright was in chains, sitting on the sill that prevented seawater from flooding onto the gundeck.

Lang had continued to ignore Arkwright's presence. He knew perfectly well who he was but considered him to be so worthless as to be completely beneath contempt.

As Lang bent beside the carpenter to examine a strake that showed signs of particular weakness, Arkwright rose from his perch, rushed over and raised his manacled hands to throw the chain over Lang's head and strangle him.

Hearing the noise of chains being dragged on the deck, Lang turned swiftly and threw himself to one side. The carpenter was not so lucky. As the ship heeled under a particularly heavy wave, Arkwright staggered to one side and the extended manacles struck the carpenter to the deck.

Half a dozen seamen leapt upon Arkwright and restrained him. The carpenter was unconscious. He was carried to the orlop where the surgeon treated him for concussion and lacerations. Arkwright, screaming rage and defiance was unchained and carried to the deck where it had been the intention of the crew to throw him into the filthy waters of Back Bay. There were stopped by Lang who had him dragged to the cabin to be dealt with by Captain North.

The following morning hands were piped up to witness punishment as the marine at the binnacle turned the glass at 11 o'clock and rang the bell.

Arkwright was swearing and kicking which only made his hefty escort handle him more roughly.

The officers were dressed in their best uniforms and white gloves and all had sheathed swords as they stood at the head of their divisions or behind North. They listened to Lieutenant Goddington read out the charge of assaulting the carpenter and the punishment of a dozen lashes. As Goddington ordered him seized-up Arkwright shouted, 'North, you fucker, you can't have me flogged, I'm an officer!'

North raised a hand to still the upsurge of anger from the assembled crew.

'Your activities as a pirate rendered your commission null and void, Arkwright. Consider yourself lucky that I have not exercised my prerogative to award more lashes than the regulations stipulate. Bosun! Do your duty.'

The bosun opened the red baize bag. He had detailed his most muscular mate to swing the cat. The nine-tailed cat itself was of soaked and dried leather, larded with pitch and would cut deeper than a softer whip made from fresh hemp. It had been made by one of the bosun's mates who was a particular friend of the carpenter.

That the punishment was administered with serious strength was obvious. The second blow, landed 15 seconds after the first - timed by the bosun's quarter-minute glass – fell directly on the stripe of the first blow. The flesh on Arkwright's back opened and he howled with the pain. By the time the last swing was made three and a half minutes later, Arkwright was sagging in his restraints and the deck at his feet was liberally spattered with blood and tiny scraps of cut flesh. He had opened his bowels and the stink tainted the air around him.

His screams had been stifled when a rolled piece of dirty leather had been thrust between his teeth and tied off around his head. He was whimpering as they cut him down and dragged to the orlop deck where he received scant treatment by the surgeon.

Despite the justice of the punishment James Lang felt no satisfaction in witnessing Arkwright's pain. At day's end, when he had completed his log entry, he continued a letter he had been writing to his father. Arkwright's reputation at Eton had been well known to the high level of society that Lang's father frequented and Lang had no doubt that Arkwright's capture and his conduct on *Prince Rupert* would be widely reported in the salons and clubs of London.

Three hours before dark, on the evening tide, the flotilla stood out to sea, with the frigate *Arc en Ciel* leading the main column and *Prince Rupert* next in line followed by *Sarabande* and *Fly* with the four Indiamen to lee. The two schooners *Heron* and *Garnet* sailed before and after the main flotilla as scouts and *Franklin* and *Juniper* stood to windward

Once well away from land sea life settled down again to a routine which was only broken seven days out by a hail from *Prince Rupert's* mainmast lookout that *Juniper* was signalling that there were ships to windward. Glasses trained, the officers could see that there was a line of three large ships and several brigs and schooners. It seemed possible that this was the new squadron of Admiral de Pléville, of whom intelligence had been received in Bombay but they were distant and with the wind set against them, North considered them to be a small threat since they appeared to be turning away even as the lookouts reported them. He ordered the men to action stations as a precaution but did not anticipate a battle.

Georges-René Le Pelley de Pléville was 74 years old and had been sent to the Indian Ocean to relieve Rear Admiral de Sercey a few months before. Until now he had cruised with his three 74s and had had little effect on either the trade of the Honourable Company or any threat to British interests.

His lookouts reported the large group of ships and erroneously identified the four Indiamen as 74s. This mistake was compounded by Captain Cotentin of the privateer

Lucienne. Having been picked up by de Pleville some six weeks previously, he had been stranded after his ship was driven on to the rocks of a small island by *Sarabande.* It was his firm opinion that the ship (whose name he did not know) that had destroyed his privateer was at least a 74 and accompanied by several other large ships – probably also 74s. Perhaps in younger years de Pleville would have thrown caution to the winds but on this occasion he decided to exercise restraint.

As darkness fell the distant ships faded into the night. North would be vigilant over the next few days but the French squadron was never seen again.

Perhaps the absent enemy was a sign. It seemed that the good fortune North's ships had enjoyed when based in the Chagos Islands had deserted them in the matter of prizes. All the way to Capetown and beyond they saw few ships. Two Danish merchantmen, an American brig and a Swedish brig were boarded and a total of six deserters secured from the American ship.

Three weeks out of Bombay they had dropped anchor for a few hours at Tristan Da Cunha to pick up Winslow Marshall. Marshall was silent and apparently chastened by his sojourn with the extremely unfriendly Company soldiers.

The following days spent were looking into the ports along the West African coast and two weeks later, having parted company with the Indiamen in mid-Atlantic, North led his ships west to the Dutch colony of Suriname, now in British hands, for wood and water. As they set out to sea again they passed close to the three volcanic islands, named by the unfortunate colonists the Isles of Salvation, just off the coast of the French colony of Cayenne. Here in the lee of Devil's Island they collected their only new prize.

The encounter had fallen to one of North's smallest vessels, the 8-gun schooner *Juniper* scouting inshore of the squadron.

Juniper was originally the property of the American navy in 1793 and had been captured in Chesapeake Bay. She carried fore and aft sails on her two masts, as well as a square headsail on the foremast. She was a fast sailor with a shallow draft – just nine feet in the hold.

It was in the sweltering tropical and richly smelling dawn as she rounded a rocky point and entered peaceful bay on the east side of the island that she saw an anchored ship.

The ship she found there was ready for her, her French captain had set up an observation post on the point and had plenty of time to prepare a reception.

Lieutenant Fowler had his crew at action stations but was aware as soon as he sighted the French sloop that he was outgunned by at least four 6-pounders. On the other hand *Juniper* had four of her guns replaced with 12-pound carronades. If he could close with the enemy without being seriously damaged, he had a good chance of crippling her. He also had a slight advantage in the fact that his opponent was anchored and less manoeuvrable.

He maximised his sail-handlers by leaving his long-guns unmanned and having just four men to each carronade. In consequence the schooner, swift and sure in her motions was within a quarter-mile of the sloop before the French opened the engagement. Instead of a full broadside only three guns were fired.

Two balls struck *Juniper*. The guns were aimed high on the up-roll and though one smacked a great hole in a jib-sail, it caused no harm and the other ball glanced off the mainmast truck. Before they could reload, Fowler had his helm put up and his two larboard carronades bellowing a response.

There were chaotic moments on both ships but for some reason there was no further gunfire from the French except a half-hearted fusillade of musket fire. The size of each crew was similar; around 65 men, but as *Juniper* came closer, her rail lined with bloodthirsty British tars, it was the French captain that flinched first. He gave the order to cut his cables and let fall his sails but the order was far too late in coming.

With a screech of clashing timber, *Juniper* struck the side of the sloop, which rode higher in the water. Yelling with all their might, the Junipers came on to the French deck with cutlasses, pistols and boarding pikes sweeping the deck in front of them.

It was over in less than ten minutes and the captain was found cowering on the orlop deck among the French wounded. His flight from the quarterdeck had been a major cause of the crew's willingness to throw down their arms.

The prize had been captured with just four British wounded, two dead Frenchmen and nine of their number wounded.

The reason for the weak resistance was quickly discovered. Her crew had been reduced by almost half by yellow-jack and many of those still alive were still fighting the disease. Fowler made a draconian decision. Every Frenchman, wounded or whole was set on shore. *Juniper's* crew scrubbed and cleaned every surface of the prize with vinegar, set bowls of burning sulphur in each part of the ship and then, with her helm tied off and her sails brailed up, she was towed behind *Juniper*.

Three men who had previously survived the fever volunteered as boat-keepers but the rest of the *Junipers* stayed resolutely on their own ship.

Each man was drenched under the pumps and his clothing scrubbed vigorously. The hammocks were hung from the shrouds for all of the day and presented a bizarre sight when *Juniper* rejoined the flotilla.

The captain of the prize, although a naval vessel, had loaded goods into every space he could find. This had hampered the movement of his guns and accounted for the poor quality of the barrage. She was carrying cocoa beans and several tons of extremely hard wood called lignum vitae that the Spanish called palo santo – the holy wood. This timber and some other exotic woods were carried in lengths of no more than six or seven feet on account of the low growing habit of the lignum vitae but packed between the guns, and with a weak crew, they had ensured the ship's downfall.

Chapter 25

Wednesday 20th to Tuesday 26th May, 1801

It seemed an age before Portland Bill was in sight again. *Prince Rupert* had left Buckler's Hard on the 3rd day of July, 1800 and returned on 20th of May, 1801, an absence of ten months during which they had sailed halfway round the world and back and had accumulated enough prize money for those hands trusted ashore to buy up the whole of Portsmouth, which they proceeded to do starting with tickets for their back pay of around £30 to £40 each.

The big shock was the news buzzing around the dockyard that Earl Spencer and most of their lordships had been replaced at the Admiralty the previous day. Now the First Lord was the Earl St Vincent – known irreverently as Old Jervie, since he had been Admiral Jervis before being elevated. Lord Arden, Admiral 'Dismal Jimmy' Gambier and the other naval lords were out and only Sir Philip Stephens and the Hon. William Eliot remained. In came James Adams and William Garthshore and the two Sea Lords, Sir Thomas Troubridge and Captain John Markham.

Orders waiting for North had arrived by courier in response to a message from the telegraph system that the flotilla had been reported as 'off the Needles'. He was to keep the ship in commission allowing leave only to warrant officers and officers, apart from any he felt he could trust not to desert. The rest of the ships would be sent separate orders with the exception of *Heron* and *Juniper*, which he was to keep in company. North had mixed feelings. This could be a sign of further employment. Two years ago he would have relished that prospect but with Isobel and his estate so near he would hope for time to rest and be there for a while. His orders were to attend the Admiralty the following Thursday at two o'clock in the afternoon but he had permission to sleep out of the ship in the meantime. At least he had three days once he was able to leave the ship on the day after he arrived.

His heart's joy was waiting eagerly for him as he rode up to the front door of his house, his hard-pressed hired horse flecked with foam. A groom that he had never seen before took the horse and Con Riley, smiling widely, hurried down the steps a few paces behind Isobel, who was laughing and crying as she ran to his arms. Cluney Ryan, a good horseman though a little more cautious than his master, trotted his mare up a few minutes later.

North was at first lost for words. He dearly loved his wife and was still amazed by his good fortune in marrying her and in a strange way he was nervously guilty that he had been apart from her for so long, though never far from his thoughts. Now he had to tell her that he was only here for a few days before returning to London.

He need not have concerned himself. Isobel, holding him at arm's length to look at him frankly and appraisingly, simply said, 'I had almost forgotten how you delight me just by looking at you, Michael. Please kiss me, my dear.'

Arm in arm they went into the house. There had been changes under Isobel's hand; changes that had transformed the house that had been merely functional when owned by the Crown. It was now a home, though Isobel told him how empty it had seemed without him.

Holding both her hands so that he could look straight into her eyes, he said, 'Isobel, one of the very worst things a married captain has to endure is the separation war causes. I am so happy to be home but unhappy that I fear it cannot be a long stay. I am not the master of my own time. I have to report to the Admiralty in three days.'

She smiled as she responded. 'I trust our marriage is strong enough to stand such absences, darling but I feel it very much too. The war inflicts this sadness on all the navy's wives and sweethearts and it is difficult to bear. Your letters to me have been read over so many times the very paper is wearing thin and on rising in the morning and on lying down to sleep I pray for your safety and miss you so very much.

'I am sure you don't think me some quiet mouse content to sit snug in my nest while you are away but believe me it is enough to have thoughts of your love in my head and in my heart. Besides running the estate is a way of losing myself and the days pass more swiftly.

'Now, why should we not travel up to Town together? I can see our man of business and we can stay at a hotel or simply return to Dulwich each evening.'

Before he had left England North had arranged things so that Isobel would have the managing of his affairs, assisted by Riley and with Jeremiah Wolfson to advise if needed. After the disaster of her first marriage she had become a competent manager of financial matters. With North's personal fortune now expanded by another £16,500 from prizes in the Chagos campaign and a very useful income from the estate, the couple were becoming very comfortable in finances indeed.

As evidence that Isobel could spend well but wisely she later conducted him on a tour of the refurbished stable block, now set up to house three carriage pairs and three riding horses of excellent quality including a heavy hunter she had chosen as his birthday present. There was a trap and several other equipages as well as two carriages, one of them the one she had bought prior to their marriage.

Most of the touring and visiting only took place after she had enjoyed being with him in the privacy of their bedroom for most of the afternoon. They had set out after breakfast the following day for North to be introduced to his tenants and to the notables of the village. Invitations having been extended by the richer people, North had to ask for their forbearance until he was spared by the Admiralty, pleading the requirements of the service and the war. In many places he detected tiredness and discontent with the war, a sentiment he shared.

The journey to London was a pleasant one in the summer sun; the carriage was comfortable and there was a hamper of food garnered from the estate along with a bottle or two of excellent French wine. The wine was shrewdly bought by Isobel from stock which the vintner had assured her was laid down prior to the present unpleasantness with France. It is doubtful that the Revenue officers would have been convinced but Isobel decided she would appear gullible if ever challenged.

On the box of the coach was Con Riley, with Cluney Ryan beside him regaling him with a more than lurid account of his latest adventures.

They reached Guildford by 2pm and after taking a meal and resting the horses for two hours, continued northwards at a leisurely pace. It was near ten in the evening when they arrived in Dulwich and the house was in darkness but the housekeeper was up and about in minutes organising the maid and the cook. North and Isobel shared the table with Con and Cluney. Isobel was afterwards treated to a few sweet songs from Ireland in which North joined his baritone voice.

Settling down with her beloved husband a little after midnight Isobel stroked his hair and drowsily whispered her delight and contentment. He had been away from her side for many long months and perhaps soon destined to leave again. If he was bound to leave her in a short time then that was the nature of things being married to a sea officer and she had no regrets since every one of the short moments she was with him was so perfect. She had never had such kindness, gentleness and passion in her life before she met him and her smile was now constantly on her lips as she enjoyed his love.

The following day they set out from Dulwich in the mid-morning sunlight, having spent an hour or so in the garden where he had proposed to her, leaving Cluney Ryan to assist Riley in some necessary repairs to the rose arbour.

As they crossed the Thames at Southwark, London crowded in on them once more. The sheer scale of the noise and tumult even made the horses shy a few times as their driver steered the carriage past an overturned cart, turnips and cabbages strewn amongst helpful bystanders who were relieving the carter of the need to carry them further.

Isobel pointed out a turbaned gypsy with bare legs and ancient sandals who was goading his sad, moth-eaten bear into a dance, causing a couple of early-rising 'ladies of the town' to scuttle with shrill squeals into the safety of the alleyway leading to the door of the Cheshire Cheese. North noticed that more new tall buildings were being squeezed into narrow gaps of recently demolished houses that had witnessed the passing along Fleet Street of the likes of William Shakespeare. Fleet Street had also rung to the sound of Richard II' s horses hooves as he cantering towards the city to meet and murder Wat Tyler and dupe his rebels into surrender.

At the front of St Martin's in the Fields, they were held up for nearly twenty minutes in the press of traffic until they could take the final quarter mile to his brother's house in Panton Street. Sir James was at home despite the summer heat which would normally have kept him at the country house in Blackheath. He was in London to attend to parliamentary business, having taken his seat for the Ancient and Honourable Borough of Frensham after being elected by the thirteen burgesses who comprised the electorate, at a cost of a mere ten guineas apiece and a promise to present a private member's bill enclosing a few dozen acres of common land.

Sir James was reckoned one of the most handsome men in London, constantly accompanied by his wife Alice and scornful of dalliances, much to the regret of the ladies at the soirées and salons of the haut-ton. Thanks to his excellent marriage and his brother's generosity in sharing his good fortune, James was solvent and applying his money with care and success, while building his own wealth.

He and Alice greeted their sister-in-law with particularly affection. There had been two or three reciprocal visits while North was away and a strong bond had been forged between the two women. Alice was in her late thirties and was the daughter of Lord Conway. She was tall and slim and habitually wore blue dresses though on this occasion she was in a white, full skirted dress clearly showing that her next child was near to being born.

Alice was an accomplished cook in her own right but had brought to her marriage two of her own family servants, her lady's maid and her father's cook. The result was a steady increase in Sir James' waistline.

Chapter 26

<u>Wednesday 27th May to Saturday 13th June, 1801</u>

At the Admiralty, with the changes at the top, there was naturally an element of confusion and uncertainty as to the future but the war was still being fought and therefore life went on.

On his way into the building a clerk had ushered North into a small ground-floor office where Evan Nepean, the secretary, was waiting. He smiled as he shook hands. 'Politics, Captain! Now, with all the changes and Lord Arden and Earl Spencer having left, the secret missions you have carried out for the Admiralty are known in detail only by me. However, Lord Arden – who is a close friend of Captain Markham – had seen fit to entrust him with all the necessary information to allow him to carry on with the special role Arden had in respect of such secret operations. Therefore it is he who you will be seeing today. Do you know him?'

North replied, 'I have never met him, though I believe him to be an excellent officer.'

'Just so. But now he is Member of Parliament for Portsmouth, and having been given the Admiralty seat, in my opinion is the ideal man for the job. I think you will get on well with him; he is your sort of fighting sailor. You may speak freely with him concerning secret matters and indeed the new First Lord has a high opinion of you.'

In the boardroom John Markham leaned back in his chair. North looked across at him. The 39-year-old Markham, the son of the Archbishop of York, was a tall, well-built man with

300

grey receding hair, deep brown eyes and a ruddy complexion. He rubbed his brow before continuing.

'When we confronted Mudge about leaking information he told us that his son, who is a prisoner at Verdun, would be executed if he did not co-operate. As a result of his confession we have now, I trust, identified and dealt with the traitors inside the Admiralty but of course we must still be on our guard against complacency. Mudge is being sent to the Isle of Man where he will be employed as a clerk to the Trinity House superintendent of works until the new lighthouse has been completed. We have sent a clear message to the authorities at Verdun that Mudge junior is to be exchanged for two French officers we are holding in Gibraltar or failure to do so will result in unpleasantness to some of their agents in this country. I would like to thank you for the way you extracted that information from Marshall.'

'May I ask what has happened to Marshall after I sent him on to London?'

Markham paused for a moment. 'Having raved about some curious nonsense that he had been kidnapped and marooned on an island deep in the South Atlantic it is the opinion of the surgeons that his mind is gone. For his own safety he has been sent to Moorfields to stay in Bethlem Hospital until he recovers. He will be kept in some luxury in solitary confinement, thanks to the generosity of the Board, at least until this war is over and he might be returned to the bosom of his family.'

North remembered speaking to Marshall concerning Bedlam and had a strange feeling that this had been preordained.

Markham carefully rearranged the line of quills on a pewter

dish in front of him and looked up. With a smile, he said, 'Now, Captain North, as far as you are concerned their lordships are very pleased with the results of your mission in the Chagos Islands. There may still be privateers coming out of Mauritius but our information is that sixteen of them including Robert Surcouf are returning or have returned to St Malo, counting the risks too high. It also gives us ammunition to persuade the new government to fund similar missions in the future. I believe Addington is a firm supporter of this office though he is stronger for peace than Mr Pitt was.

'There is still much to do in this war, North, and I believe the more successes we gain, the more likely we can shorten the war if only by demoralising the French. In a way your next voyage will build on those successes.

'As you are aware the Americans also have a change of administration; Mr Thomas Jefferson started his presidential duties on the 4th of March but a few weeks ago the American Ambassador in London made it clear that Jefferson wanted to keep America out of the war. From our information it seems, however, that he has another problem. Yusuf Karamanli, the Bashaw of Tripoli, has sent Jefferson a demand for $225,000 as an inducement to refrain from setting his pirates on American shipping. Until now the United States have been spending huge amounts in these bribes but Jefferson, being the honourable man he is, will refuse point blank to give in to blackmail. We believe there is another problem sitting on his desk right now concerning Morocco, which by not paying off the Bashaw is going to give him an even bigger headache.'

North had a fair idea of the situation along the Barbary Coast. For centuries there had been an unhealthy trade in piracy; as well as from preying on the sea traffic in the Western

Mediterranean it also victimised the inhabitants of the European side of the sea and seized many thousands of Christians as slaves. The pirates' ships were based in Tunis, Tripoli and Algiers. For more than 150 years the Americans had been sending emissaries to the Barbary Coast to buy back Christian slaves. British shipping was fairy immune from attack by these states, subject as they were to Ottoman rule. Even a hyena gives a lion a wide berth, he thought. He was less familiar with the corsairs who sailed from Moroccan ports such as Bou Regreg and Salé on the Atlantic Coast and as Morocco was not a part of the Ottoman Empire, any tribute demanded by them would be a different one from that demanded by the Bashaw.

It seemed to him a great pity that the body of the Bashaw could not be hanging in chains beside that of the late pirate Major Arkwright whose eyes at this moment were being picked out by the crows as he swung on the gibbet in Wapping dockyard.

Markham continued. 'It is with Morocco that the Americans have a separate problem, that of ransom for some important American prisoners. If Jefferson pays them off, his stance against Karamanli is greatly weakened. Now, while we have enough problems of our own to worry about, it suits us to lend moral and even practical support to the Americans while at the same time using this as an opportunity to weaken any feelings of friendship between the new American administration and Napoleon.

'We understand that Napoleon is less likely now to want to use New Orleans as a way into America. He had plans to persuade Spain to hand over the Floridas to him but that plan has also fallen away in the light of reality. Thanks in some measure to your efforts in Canada, he knows now, if he did not do so before, that invasion there is impractical.'

He went on to explain how the Moroccan pirates came to be in possession of the hostages. The people concerned were George and Katherine Johnston, who were relatives of the new vice-president, Aaron Burr. Harold Pond and Hector Kingsley, who were prominent New England merchants, were also being held. All four had been travelling with their servants on an American ship which stopped to water in the Canaries on the way to Buenos Aires. In early January as they were leaving El Hierro behind them their ship was attacked by a pirate galley and they were carried into the Atlantic port of Salé.

Markham continued, 'We have friends amongst the large Jewish population in Salé who tell us that the hostages have been moved down the coast to the town of Essaouria, that the Portuguese call Mogador.

'We want you to retrieve the hostages and convey them to New York. There is no question of a ransom, of course. How you do it is a matter for you but you will have the assistance of Mr Jeremiah Wolfson, whom you know well. He has first-hand knowledge of our agent in Mogador and being fluent in Arabic can go on shore to meet with him.

'At your disposal will be *Prince Rupert, Juniper* and the frigate *Arethusa* of 38 guns. To preserve secrecy *Arethusa* will be shown as on convoy duty with *Endymion* and *Champion* whereas in fact she will be with you. You will also have a strange little ship recently captured by *Boadicea* in January. Her name is *Bombarde* and she was taken in the Channel. The ship is more like a raft and only draws 3 feet and 6 inches. She is lugger-rigged and armed with one 24-pounder at the prow, four swivel guns and a 13-inch mortar. She has unusually wide gangways which are fortified and built over ammunition cases. She has a crew of 30 under Lieutenant John Lackey, who had the armed cutter *St Vincent* last year. More importantly she can carry up to 150 men having originally been one of Bonaparte's invasion barges.

'Some of our best ship designers have looked at her and caused her to be fitted with an experimental device, a retractable blade-like keel which will make her more stable in heavy seas. Frankly, I would not be surprised if she sinks on you, but that is just my opinion. I have been asked to provide a secret voyage to test her so it might as well be yours; if she is lost there will be no blame attached to anybody but if she survives the Bay of Biscay, she may be of use to you.

'I have arranged for an extra company of marines to join *Prince Rupert* from Dover. Your own marine captain, Jolyon Bracewell, is being promoted to major and will command the marine force when on land, of course.'

They spent another half an hour going through details and North left with mixed feelings. He would be away at sea again for several months and this was hardly fair to Isobel, though there was some slight consolation that it would not be nearly as long this time. While it had been left unsaid, his chances of finding the hostages let alone securing their release were by no means foolproof. He would need to have first-class information as to the place they were being held for one thing and for another, a plan would have to be formulated that would not result in them being spirited away before he could reach them. On the other hand the difficulty of the operation would make its success an even bigger feather in his cap.

305

Henry Adams thanked North for looking after his grandson though North told him that he had no special treatment and that the young midshipman's own abilities had proved him to be an invaluable member of the crew.

Adams and North sat side by side on a settle outside the master shipwright's cottage looking out over the Beaulieu River, pewter tankards of cider in hand, with Adams smoking a long-stemmed clay pipe. In the shipyard there was a 74 on the stocks, the *Swiftsure,* the keel of which had just been laid and a few bare ribs attached like the skeleton of a beached whale. Close by it was the 36-gun frigate *Aigle* which would likely be afloat by September and in the two nearer stocks from *Prince Rupert* were two gun-brigs, the *Snipe* and the *Starling,* like twin birds resting before flight. They would be on the water and ready to be towed round to Portsmouth dockyard to be fitted out in a few weeks.

'Busy time, sir,' remarked North.

Adams took his pipe from his mouth, exhaled contentedly and used the pipe as a pointer. 'Over there is where I built my first ship for the Navy, the *Mermaid* – 6th rate. It took me two years and I finished it on the 22nd of May, 1749. Before that I had only built a few small brigs and some repairs on my own account. I was 34 when I took over the yard from John Darley who went bankrupt building the *Woolwich* 44 – old Moody Janverin had to finish the ship and we launched it a few months before I started up here on my own account. The old duke charged me £5 a year rent for the Hard – those were the days!

It was hard to think that the war would ever end, so long had it been fought; no sooner was there peace with the seemingly eternal enemy – France – than war came back like the inevitable march of the seasons. Whether it be a long or a short peace when it did come there were no doubt too many shipbuilders in the country to carry on earning a living. The East and West Indies trade would need ships but even that was a limited pool in which to fish. Another factor that weighed viability in the balance was the soaring price of timber.

He had balanced some of the rising costs of shipbuilding by a profitable trade in timber to HM Dockyards and other places.

At present shipbuilding was a fine balance between making a small profit and going under and if peace broke out business could easily fade away. There was no doubt that the yard would have to be tightly managed if it was to survive.

....

Prince Rupert's third departure from Buckler's Hard was at night with North's flotilla of ships preceding him and waiting off Weymouth to form up into line. *Juniper* ranged out ahead to scout, followed by *Prince Rupert* with *Bombarde* immediately behind her so that she could be kept in sight and *Arethusa* bringing up the rear.

North woke the following morning and left his bed-place to sit at his desk, write a letter to Isobel and bring his journal up to date.

There were new members of the crew of whom he had but a brief knowledge and he would need to get to know them quickly to assess their various capabilities; their strengths and weaknesses. His officers had impressed him so far –

particularly the fairly new 1st and 2nd lieutenants. Six new midshipmen had come on board this voyage with ages ranging from 14 to 27. When a midshipmen reached 15 years he was termed an oldster and was berthed on the orlop, while the youngsters stayed in the gun-room.

The two newcomers that concerned North the most were 24 and 27 but it seemed that their more mature years gave little assurance of ability. Unless they were late joiners or had come up through the hawse hole it was usually the case that such older men lacked the necessary skills to pass for lieutenant.

North also had several new junior petty officers, two of whom had so far not pleased him. Of the senior warrants he was unsure of his new carpenter, David Lord. He was a transfer from *Cumberland.* So far he had annoyed every lieutenant and the master by his truculence and bigotry towards those who were not from his native Ulster. North had cause to speak firmly to him twice about oppressing the seamen.

There were several dozen seamen from the south of Ireland, most of them Catholics and under no illusion that though the captain might show favour to them on occasion through being born amongst them, there were some members of the crew who would victimise them through sectarian tendencies. Despite his misgivings about the size of the David Lord's mouth, North did not want to find that he had disappeared over the rail one dark night.

Another man that he felt needed watching was his new purser. Having lost Mark Lewis whose eyesight had deteriorated badly in the past six months and perforce had gone on shore to swallow the anchor, North had received George Constable on board along with his wife Henrietta, a small, sullen, woman who appeared never to be fully sober but not drunk enough to subject herself to disapprobation.

It was likely, in North's view, that Constable was a little too gregarious – especially with some of the other seven women on board, particularly the younger ones. North had deliberately failed to overhear Bosun Giles offer Constable the back of his hand if he didn't lay off his wife.

As far as venality was concerned although this was rampant in the navy it had been almost unknown on North's ship and he was determined to discourage obvious abuses, as he had explained in a forthright manner to Constable. He made it clear that the line would be crossed if he found the purser taking advantage of the lack of financial acuity of any of the seamen.

There was also a draft of 27 replacements, all of them rated able, being survivors of the wreck of the sloop *Havick*. He noted that there were six Jerseymen and two Guernseymen amongst them, together with several French Royalists who were volunteers. Normally he would have no prejudice but he called for Georges Lascaux, his French cooper, who he had found to be eminently trustworthy.

He asked Lascaux to quietly assess both the Channel Islanders and the Royalists as to their loyalty. He did not expect him to spy on them but like any other crew member he had a duty to report any unlawful association or seditious talk.

There were a few minutes of quiet after Lascaux had left the cabin, carrying a borrowed copy of a collected edition of Shakespeare plays. He sat for a while thinking about Isobel and their parting. She had been positive and firmly suppressed her tears but it was with heavy heart that he climbed into the carriage. This voyage would be shorter than the last, with any luck, but he could not expect to be away for less than three to four months.

He took his second cup of tea to the quarterdeck, nodding to the helmsman and the uncovered midshipman – a new arrival, Charles Calhoun, 24 years old and unlikely to progress further unless he made a sterling effort. The sky was overcast and the sea grey as the four ships sighted Ushant on the port bow. In sight of the coast was a scurrying merchantman, Danish flag at the peak, probably carrying contraband but North had decided that there should be as little delay as possible. The only diversion had been to send *Juniper* in to Plymouth to bring Jeremiah Wolfson on board, his face wreathed in smiles at being once more on *Prince Rupert*.

North turned to look down the spar deck and frowned. 'Mr Calhoun, the red cutter appears to be loose in her gripes, get somebody to attend to it immediately, please.'

The master, who had just reached the quarterdeck, looked around at the red cutter, the stern end of which was certainly shifting as the ship rolled in the light swell. His face reflected annoyance and puzzlement. The boat should have been made secure at the beginning of the watch.

Instead of calling out to one of the crewman to deal with it, Calhoun made his way to the cutter itself. He raised a hand to wave to Bosun's Mate Harwell but as he did so the ropes tying down the cutter parted, the weight of the boat causing them to flail outwards and strike the midshipman full in the face, sending him tumbling backwards.

North shouted, 'Harwell! Look to Mr Calhoun! Halsey, Cogswell, secure that boat! You men on the fo'c'sl look lively, lend a hand!'

The cutter slid wildly and struck Seaman Halsey squarely on the chest. North and the master ran quickly and were joined by other men as they heaved the cutter clear of Halsey. He was coughing blood and moaning in agony. North shouted for the surgeon to be called. The cutter was wrestled back into its place and securely tied down. Midshipman Calhoun had a red welt diagonally across his face and having struck his head as he fell was unconscious. It had all happened in less than a minute.

Lieutenant Lang arrived from the lower gun deck. 'Sir, a word, please.'

North stood up and walked over to him, 'What is it, James?'

'It's the surgeon, sir, indisposed,' he said softly.

'Do you mean drunk?'

'Aye, sir, I believe so. His assistant is coming up from the orlop.'

Surgeon's Mate Walter Dryden arrived a few seconds later and went to look at the midshipman who was now groggily conscious and holding his face in his hands.

North snapped, 'look to Halsey first, if you please, I believe his to be the more serious injury.'

The master approached him from the other side, 'Sir, this rope was cut, as were the gripes securing the green cutter. This is deliberate.'

'Make sure all is secure here, check the lashings on the

311

pinnaces and gig and come to my cabin in fifteen minutes please, Mr Bishop, and bring with you the bosun and the master-at-arms. Mr Lang, we shall visit the surgeon.'

The surgeon cabin's was rank with the smell of vomit and spilt gin. Richard Horrigan was on his knees spewing into a leather fire-bucket.

North said angrily, 'Stand up, sir, what do you mean by this?'

Horrigan tried standing, fell sideways on to his bed and struggled upright again, gripping tightly on to a nearby bookshelf. 'I'm not drunk, if that's what you think, it's this wretched seasickness.' His words were far too slurred to admit any chance that he was being truthful.

North looked at him contemptuously. 'You are a disgrace, Mr Horrigan, a *disgrace*, do you hear me! This is not the first time I have seen you beastly drunk! Mr Lang, you will have a corporal search this cabin for alcohol and dispose of it. The surgeon will be confined under guard until he is sober and you will then have him brought in front of me to be dealt with.' His voice rose in anger as he looked down at Horrigan who had collapsed on to the deck. 'Damn me, I should have set you on shore the moment I saw you. I have two men injured and you incapable of doing your duty. You will answer for this, sir, believe me you will!'

In his cabin the 1st lieutenant was waiting with the master, the bosun and the master-at-arms.

Still in a foul mood, North stared at Hengist Giles. 'Well, Bosun, the boats have been deliberately loosed, when did you last check them?'

Giles straightened himself, his head a bare inch below the ceiling. 'This morning watch, sir. The boats were well secured at just after three bells. I checked them personally.'

The master agreed, 'I am sure the boats were secure at that time, sir. I watched Mr Giles tug at the ropes.'

'I see, it is now 7.45 so whoever cut those gripes must have done so between 5.30 and 7.30 or thereabouts. Master-at-arms, you will exercise your best endeavours and resources to identify this villain. I need not tell any of you that the safety of the ship itself is in danger. This time it was the cutters; next time, who knows? Bosun, have Major Bracewell join me here; I will have extra marine guards on the magazines and the tiller ropes until this maniac is found. Then you will get together your mates and crew and make a thorough inspection of the entirety of the standing rigging. You will carry my compliments to the gunner and the carpenter who must also check on their areas of responsibility.

'Now, Mr Goddington, how are Mr Calhoun and Seaman Halsey?'

'Halsey has several broken ribs and lost three teeth and the surgeon's mate says his face and throat were badly bruised and cut about but other than that no permanent damage. I handed Dryden the keys to the surgeon's chest for him to hold until further notice and he has drawn laudanum to administer to Halsey who is in some pain. Mr Calhoun is fit for duty, he complains of a severe headache, but nothing worse than that, sir.'

'Then we have been lucky this time, have Mr Calhoun's duties covered for this and the next watch and have him rest. Headaches have a way of developing into something worse.

Likewise Halsey will not resume his duties until fully fit. Stay here for a few minutes, Mr Goddington, while I see Major Bracewell; you too Mr Bishop.'

Jolyon Bracewell arrived shortly afterwards, his face red with hurrying from the lower deck where he had already posted guards on all companionways and the magazine door.

'Major, please emphasise to the sentry that he must ensure we are not overheard.' Bracewell nodded and went to the door for a moment.

North waved the officers to seats. 'Gentlemen, I do not wish to sound alarmed but this incident must be taken as a serious indication that we have somebody on board determined on destruction. Even if he confined himself to cutting ropes serious injury can occur, as we have seen, and if it were a vital part of the ship, such as the rudder-lines, the whole ship could be in danger. We must all be alert for signs that damage is being caused. Mr Goddington, please advise the other lieutenants and older midshipmen accordingly and Mr Bishop, your mates but none of the rest of the crew – please emphasise that we do not wish to drive this person underground by a highly visible hunt. Therefore we proceed quietly. Major, the guards you have placed must be vigilant at all times.'

Bracewell said, 'indeed, sir, I intend to have the guards doubled and changed every hour to keep them alert. May I suggest we include the gunner in this matter?'

'Yes, but none other for the time being unless I approve it. I hate having to point this out but we have four dozen or so new faces on board that we have not had time to acquaint ourselves. *Aude, vide, tace,* must be our watch-words – hear all, see all and say nothing, gentlemen. Thank you; that will be all. Mr Goddington please stay for a moment.'

North called his steward for fresh tea for both of them. He looked at the slightly-built lieutenant who had been with *Prince Rupert* for almost ten months now. In that time they had not forged a close friendship but great mutual respect. North had a high opinion of his senior lieutenant who had carried out his duties in an exemplary manner; being in every way an excellent successor to Erskine Rockwell. North had little doubt that he was fit to command his own ship at any time and was determined he would do everything he could to see that this happened. However, there was a slight doubt in his mind about the level of ambition hinted by Goddington.

Breaking the somewhat protracted silence, North asked what Goddington made of the incident.

Goddington replied, 'I believe we cannot be too cautious, sir. A fanatic might take us to the bottom of the sea and in doing so sacrifice himself. One wonders if it had not happened before in this war. Though the cutting of the securing lines was not a trivial matter, perhaps it was just a first step, if you will, a practice exercise before something more deadly is attempted.'

'Quite so, Alan. Now strictly between ourselves I have some misgivings – perhaps ill-conceived – that the person or persons behind this are recently joined. I believe in all the events of the past year or so I have got the measure of our crew as we were when we arrived home from Bombay but the newcomers, particularly the new warrant officers and the *Havicks,* are an unknown quantity. I believe we should not discount other possibilities but we should watch them

315

carefully. I hope I am not doing them a disservice and of course, I hope they are completely innocent.'

Goddington set down his teacup and stood up. 'We are *ad idem*, sir. With your permission I will entrust Mr Lang and Mr Hodges the marine lieutenant with the particular task of keeping an eye on the warrant officers. I only hope that this was an isolated incident but I fear more could happen.'

After he had left, North sat drumming a teaspoon on the palm of his hand for a few minutes while he sat in thought. Then he rose and walked to the quarter gallery and stood with his fingers reaching into his waistcoat pocket to finger Isobel's brooch while he looked out at the waves and the odd little bomb vessel thudding through the sea behind *Prince Rupert*.

He decided to go back on deck for some fresh air to clear his troubled thoughts. He emerged on to the quarter deck, his eyes swiftly and automatically checking the ship from stem to stern as he walked to the weather-side and began pacing, his hands behind his back, head bowed in thought. The officer of the watch, Lieutenant Lang, lifted his hat and moved to the opposite side of the deck. Midshipman Hector Wise, at 14 years of age, newly joined and still green, was necessarily yanked over to the lee side by master's mate Philips, who handed him his hat as he whipped it off his head. The two helmsmen nodded to each other at the captain's obvious elsewhere-ness.

Like most captains, Michael North left the day-to-day running of the ship to his officers as much as possible and likewise did not disturb the crew too much by wandering about the barky poking and prying – though it did seem to the more perceptive that the ship was so much part of the captain

316

that he could feel every creak and sigh of her movements and see every nail and hempen strand of her in his mind.

He looked up from his reverie and said quietly, 'Mr Lang, have Mr Philips check the heel-lashing on the flying jib, please. It seems to be overstretched and the jib-sail is making a distinct thumping noise. It would be as well if you ask the bosun to double-check the wear on the lashings when he has a moment.' He lowered his head and kept pacing.

Philips raised his eyebrows and grinned as he whispered to Lang, 'How does he do that, sir?'

Lang smiled back, 'You heard the captain, Mr Philips, please attend to it now and ask the bosun to come aft.'

Michael North was an intuitive sailor and consciously tried to feel the ship as much as watch it. Even in the confines of the cabin he would sometimes close his eyes and listen to the movement of the ship. Each groan and creak meant something; each turn, twist and dip, however slight, could tell him the interaction of ship and sea and weather. Sounds and sights belonging to the ship were communicated to ear and eye but it needed a receptive mind to interpret the messages the ship was sending.

It was said that a captain in tune with his ship could be awakened in the night by a bump or jerk out of place like a musician who hears a discordant note in a symphony. Anticipation and expectation that went hand-in-hand with experience and empathy made Michael North feel happy to be in a sense part of his ship.

The captain's isolation in the sanctity of command affected men in different ways. In some it expressed itself in self-indulgence and even drunkenness; in others it caused unconscious resentment which expressed itself in harsh and brutal conduct. In others, perhaps more balanced as human beings, it evinced itself as being at one with the ship and the satisfaction of a well-run, finely-tuned ship, the reward.

After a few more minutes watching the ship and the sea, as if he had made a decision, North turned abruptly and went to his cabin where he asked Naylor to send for Mr Wolfson. It lacked a few minutes before noon but North poured his friend a glass of wine while taking a glass of sugared limejuice himself.

'No doubt you have heard what happened this morning, Jeremiah. Your thoughts would be appreciated. It is possible that this wilful damage is simply being caused by a disaffected seaman but I must be cautious that I don't dismiss the possibility that a more sinister presence has arrived on the ship. I believe firmly that the traitors in the Admiralty that were identified could have no knowledge of our mission but is it possible that there were others; could it be that spies were operating independently of each other and with no knowledge of their compatriots presence, or am I being too fanciful? Do we have somebody on board determined to thwart our mission or is it perhaps a larger scheme aimed specifically at this ship itself?'

Wolfson gathered his thoughts as he held the sturdy glass up to the light and swirled the blood-red wine.

'I believe that it matters little the depth of the infamy or the direction in which it is focused, Michael. The thing is to seek out this person or more than one person before he or they can cause serious problems. I would also respectfully remind you that as captain of this ship and leader of this endeavour you are almost if not quite indispensable and that you must take care for your own safety. Apart from which if anything happened to you I fear the moment I have to face Isobel and break the news. So be careful for yourself, as well as for the success of the mission and the safety of your ship. I will do my best to lift the various corners and crannies as I walk about the ship and it may be that those who have recently come on board do not know of our friendship, so may not be so careful in their talk and actions.'

'Thank you, Jeremiah. By the way, I am pleased that you have made a friend of Georges Lascaux who I believe can be trusted. He is something of an oddity on the lower deck, even amongst the warrant officers, and I believe there are some who think he is a little too studious for his own good, apart from being French, of course. I have asked him to keep his ears open anent the Channel Islanders and the Royalists, so I would appreciate it if you would watch his back for me.'

Chapter 27

Sunday 14th June, 1801

There were two unpleasant matters North had to deal with after Wolfson had left the cabin. The first person to enter the cabin, escorted by the master-at-arms, was Mrs Constable. She was barely capable of standing.

'For goodness sake, sit down, Mrs Constable,' said North.

The master-at-arms knuckled his forehead. 'I regret I had to bring Mrs Constable aft due to the state of her, sir. She was on deck and likely to come to some harm. I can't find her husband but I wanted this sorted out as quietly as possible.'

North groaned; it seemed this was the day for drunks. He called out to his steward, 'Naylor! Find the purser and tell him I want to see him immediately! Now, Mrs Constable, you really cannot wander about the ship in this state. Are you ill?'

'Just sick and tired of that pig chasing every skirt he stumbles across, sir. I wish I never agreed to come to sea with him.' She leaned heavily sideways before righting herself with some effort.

North was saddened. 'Mrs Constable, your husband is a warrant officer in the Royal Navy and apart from the fact that he has bonded thousands of pounds for his warrant, should be respectable in every way. His wife, like that of Julius Caesar, should be above reproach, reflecting the responsible nature of his position.'

'But Caesar cast out Pompeia even though there was no evidence she encouraged Publius Clodius, so I think the boot is on the other foot, sir.'

Taken aback by Mrs Constable's erudition, North said, 'You have a point, madam.'

There was a knock on the cabin door and Constable was admitted. He looked down at his wife in amazement.

North said, 'Mr Constable, you will please take your wife back to your quarters and see that she is comfortable and care for her. I would also suggest that you are with her more frequently from now on to see that loneliness and disappointment don't tempt her to overindulge, do I make myself clear?'

Constable stammered, 'I am sorry, sir, I don't know what to say!'

As he had a sudden thought, North said, 'Mrs Constable, we have several new midshipmen on board, youngsters. Perhaps you could occupy yourself by assisting the parson in his schoolmaster duties. You are clearly a well-educated woman and I am sure it would be an interesting diversion for you.'

For the first time she had come on board her face lit up in a genuine and transforming smile. She straightened herself and drew away from her husband. 'That's very kind of you, sir. Will the chaplain approve, do you think?'

'Leave it to me. I don't think he will need much convincing.'

After he had eaten his midday meal North sent for the surgeon. This was a more difficult matter but he was determined to solve it.

Horrigan was at least a little cleaner though his clothing was wet, having been thoroughly drenched under the pumps by Lieutenant Lang. He was mumbling to himself and clearly so far gone in drink as to be teetering on the edge of delirium. North folded his arms and sighed inwardly. Normally he would have had two surgeon's mates on board but had sailed with only one. It was even more imperative therefore that the surgeon himself was fit for duty. Looking at the man, he could see how desperately drunk he was. It seemed to him that whatever he said would have little effect – the man was so addicted that curing him would be most unlikely. However he decided to try a different tack.

'Mr Horrigan, let us suppose that you are in your consulting rooms in Dublin when a patient is brought to you in the hopeless grip of alcoholism. What courses of treatment would be open to you?'

Horrigan peered at him through bloodshot eyes and there were visible signs on his face of a man struggling to bring his mind in focus. 'Well, I suppose that the only sure treatment is confining him and depriving him of alcohol until his body is so cleansed of the effects of long-term drinking that he would be dry, so as to speak.'

'This would be a difficult course for the patient, would it not?'

Horrigan struggled into a more upright position. 'Horrendously difficult in some cases, I believe. Men have been known to be driven temporarily mad with the delirium, conjuring up demons of the mind and in terror and agony from the illusion of the pains of hell being upon them. However deprivation and purging seems to be the only sure remedy. The bigger problem is often ignored by doctors since it requires much more work.'

North asked, 'what is that?'

Seemingly mildly annoyed by the interruption Horrigan continued as if lecturing to a student.

'The patient can be dried out but the mental attitude also needs to be attended to and this can take much longer and in some ways is the most difficult part. The body can be put to rights, though the process be incredibly painful to the mind but the mind will not accept the loss of the drug. In truth, there is no true cure, though few of my colleagues accept that. The patient has to want never again to allow his mouth to taste alcohol for once it does, he is lost! You would not believe the many times I have seen this happen! A man, fully *compos mentis* in his normal being, will need to fight his own demon for the rest of his life.'

'But it could be done?'

'It could.'

'Doctor, you will dictate to your assistant a complete programme of treatment and subject yourself to this course. If you fail in this I will have no alternative but to have you turned out of the ship. Of course I will do everything in my power to assist in this process but as you are fully aware, "the physician must heal himself." You will go with Mr Lang to your quarters and take pen to paper immediately. You will also eat regular meals and drink only water and watered lime juice in sufficient amounts to assist the treatment. Is that clear?'

Horrigan stood unaided for the first time in days. 'Yes, sir, clear indeed. I cannot promise success but it won't be for the want of trying.'

323

North's interview with the chaplain followed Horrigan's departure. North had tried to like the man but found him to be narrow and bigoted in his views. He had been downright rude to Jeremiah Wolfson making remarks in his hearing that were anti-Semitic. His wife was to be more pitied than disliked, often sitting outside her cabin staring blankly for hours on end with never a smile. It would appear that like many middle-class women she had not been blessed with formal education and could barely read or write. With little to occupy her and a dry stick of a husband who was a stranger to affection, she had simply retreated into a world in her mind which kept her mildly happy and distant from the real world.

Chaplains were often entrusted with the additional task of schoolmaster in the absence of such a person though why it should be assumed that clergymen would have deep knowledge of mathematics was unclear. The position did carry an extra salary, so North would have to make it clear that if the purser's wife was to be his assistant, it would not affect his income. Rumbold sat primly on the edge of his chair, fingers steepled together looking over his half spectacles as North spoke.

'You are aware of course that Mrs Constable is not a happy person and this has expressed itself in heavy drinking. I felt it right to help her as much as possible by finding something useful for her to do. Assisting you in schooling the youngsters, without pay of course, seems to me a good idea. I have long thought that extending the same idea to the ship's boys in basic literacy would be a benefit in life to them. With an assistant, perhaps it could be made to work? These projects would be completely under your guidance, of course. How do you feel about that?'

Luke Rumbold sucked in his cheeks and shook his head. 'It is difficult, sir. The young men need a sober example to follow and …'

North held up his hand, 'Forgive me, Mr Rumbold but I believe she is intelligent enough to have worked that out for herself and will do her best to remain sober. Of course it she cannot be trusted we can cancel the arrangement. At least give her a chance.'

Rumbold remained silent. North reached into his desk drawer for a bible – not something he would normally turn to, being lukewarm towards organised religion and believing the good book to be more abused than respected by many preachers of Rumbold's type. He opened the book at 1 Corinthians Chapter 13, beginning at verse 1, and read it aloud. "Though I speak with the tongues of men and of angels, and have not Charity, I am become as sounding brass or a tinkling symbol – though I have all Faith so that I could remove mountains and have not Charity, I am nothing."'

Rumbold nodded. 'You are in the right, Captain, we must do our best for the poor woman. I would be pleased to have her help me.'

The business of running the ship proceeded apace and North habitually made his full inspection on Friday afternoon, today being no exception. The men had been exercised at the guns. Since the weather was dry the bosun and the sailmaker had the spare suit of sails spread on the spar deck to dispel chances of mildew and check the soundness of the stitching. There was some minor rat damage but all was well enough and repairs were completed quickly by the sailmaker's mate, his crew of four and half a dozen seamen.

The gunner's stores were in order but North had noticed that almost a dozen of the salt-boxes used to cover the powder-bags as they were passed to the powder-monkeys were in need of repair. Hans Schumann, the gunner, was a stolid Austrian with an eye for detail and North was surprised he had not noticed the deficiency. The yeoman of the powder room was another matter. John Gosling was a work-shy, loud-mouthed ship's lawyer who was due a good hiding if Schumann had been anything but the placid man he was.

Schumann frowned in annoyance. 'I am sorry, sir. I thought I had asked the carpenter to repair these, perhaps he has not had time. I will attend to it immediately.'

North waved a hand in dismissal, 'I leave that to you. I am minded to switch around the standing officers' yeomen, Mr Schumann. It is always a good idea to keep them from becoming too complacent.' He was also aware that the huge boatswain would not stand for Gosling's nonsense and the carpenter's yeoman was another man he was less than pleased with.

As he moved on to the bread room with Lieutenant Goddington, North noticed a scurrying crowd of flour-dusted rats coming from a hole near the door and pointed it out. He snapped, 'Have the carpenter see to that, please.' There were split sacks within the wooden chests in the storeroom.

North said testily, 'this is not good enough, Lieutenant, get a grip of the carpenter, please. He has two mates and can call on the cooper, the caulker and his two mates. There is no excuse.'

A least there was nothing to concern North on either gun deck or the quarterdeck but as North climbed aloft the mainmast he noticed that the rope supporting the starboard pendant yard tackle was frayed. The bosun, who was immediately behind him, made a mental note in response to the captain's comment. All in all, North was satisfied that there were minor problems only and that in most respects the ship was in good order. Bearing down on his warrant officers could be counterproductive though there was a limit to the allowances he was prepared to make.

The gunner's wife, Eleanor, bobbed a knee to the captain as he passed her. She was a middle-aged, somewhat ungainly woman, who spoke poor English but was good-hearted and adored by the youngest midshipmen; North thought she mothered them a little too much but perhaps that was no bad thing. He stopped for a moment.

'Good afternoon, Mrs Schumann, are you well?'

'I am good and well, Herr Captain, thank you for asking me. Sir, can I ask Cook for some ... thing that is in top of cooking-pot ... I don't know word given to this? I vant to make strudel for boys with apples I have from you Missus Captain.'

North remembered that Isobel had cleared the apple-store ready for the new crop and had sent over some barrels with the last two and a half-hundredweight of the best of the apples for the crew. They were edible as they were but no doubt would be good cooked.

'Ah, you want some slush? Yes, of course, tell the cook I said you could have what you need. If he asks you for money, you have my permission to kick his backside. Why don't you use some butter too, some of it is still reasonably fresh, and if you need cane sugar or molasses, use some of that too.'

North's steward, who was a close friend of the gunner, had improved his own cooking on advice by Mrs Schumann and the gift of spices from the small cedar chest she refilled every time they touched land. North was tempted to ask for some strudel himself but resisted the temptation, knowing that if he did so it would probably mean less for the midshipmen.

He loosened his neck-cloth when he returned to his cabin and drew out the half-completed letter he had been writing to Isobel. As he lifted his pen he heard a noise outside his door and frowned. It sounded as if somebody had fallen over. The ship was leaning into the wind but not excessively. He bent to his task again as the wind rose and beat upon the stern lights rattling them and causing the timbers to creak and groan as the ship picked up speed. His officers were more than competent to deal with the situation and he would not interfere.

There was an alien noise, the scrape of metal on the outside of the door. North frowned and opened the drawer of his desk, slipping a dirk out and on to the top of the desk. He started to push back the chair just as the door opened and two men rushed in. They were two of the *Havicks* – an Irishman called Keeley and a Jerseyman whose name he did not know. Both were armed with pistols.

'Now then, Captain Michael North!' growled Keeley, 'we've a favour to ask you. Well, since you won't have any choice in the matter, perhaps I should call it an *order*. You will send for the 1st lieutenant and have him close with the French coast where we will be leaving the ship taking you with us. Just in case you feel like trying to stop us, we know what happens to mutineers so don't think we will hesitate to shoot you.'

North folded his arms and leaned back. 'You stupid idiot. You can't possibly think I will co-operate with you.'

'You will or you die, pig!'

'Do your worse, you treacherous scum!' He thrust the chair backwards and snatched the dirk as he rolled on to the chequered deck.

There was a sharp explosion followed by the sound of a falling body. The Jerseyman had fired his pistol at the same moment as Georges Lascaux had beat Keeley over the head with the butt of the marine's cutlass. He swung the weapon to the right, burying it deep into the screaming Jerseyman's chest just as North hurled the dirk at the same man. It struck him on the left side of his head as he fell.

Lascaux ran to help North to his feet. The ball from the pistol had shattered a lantern and burning oil was streaming down on to the deck. North pointed. 'Attend to that, Lascaux, quickly.'

Lascaux was beating out the flames with his pea-jacket as men rushed into the cabin. James Lang called out, '*Sir!* Are you all right? What happened?'

'I am unhurt, James, have Keeley restrained immediately and look to this other man. Lascaux, have you burnt yourself?'

The cooper shook his head, '*Non, capitaine,* but my jacket is destroyed.'

Lang said, 'the sentry sir, Private Coombes, I am afraid he is dead, stabbed in the back.'

Keeley was awake and struggling with the handcuffs that the

bosun had thrust on to his wrists.

North brushed himself down. 'Mr Lang, have this dead man carried out and take care of Private Coombes' body. Major, have two marines outside with loaded pistols for the time being. Mr Goddington, have all hands mustered in ten minutes. Mr Goddington, Mr Wolfson, stay here for a moment, please. Bosun, keep an eye on the prisoner; the rest of you, to your duties. Lascaux, my compliments to the purser; he is to supply you with a new jacket against my name.'

He walked over to Keeley who was standing with the bosun and one of his mates who were ready to strike him down if he moved. 'Now, Keeley, as you said yourself you know the penalty for mutiny and for assaulting an officer. Have you anything to say as to why I should not have you strung up on a yard this instant?'

Keeley glared at him. 'We are sick and tired of your damned war. Defarge has relatives in Bordeaux and we reckoned if we handed you over to the French they would pay us well.'

'Who else is in this? Don't lie now, I will have all the *Havicks* in irons and without food or water until they talk!'

'Nothing to do with them clueless bastards. We could see that the *Havicks* would get the blame for the sabotage and we wasn't going to stand for it. We didn't do nothing wrong and we weren't going to stay around to get the blame.'

North said angrily, 'You fool! If you knew me better you would know that I would never blame a group of men without evidence. You have killed Private Coombes and if it had not been for Lascaux you would have killed me too. You will pay with your life, Keeley; as soon as we reach Gibraltar you will face the court martial for murder and mutiny.'

After he had been taken away Wolfson said, 'Was he telling the truth, do you think? Are there others involved?'

'Unfortunately we may not know unless the sabotage starts again.'

Chapter 28

Monday 15th to Tuesday 23rd June, 1801

There had been a strong squall in the night but North was pleased to see that the converted *chaloupe cannonière, Bombarde,* was still valiantly waddling along like a seriously overweight duckling in *Prince Rupert's* wake. He had left orders that if she got into difficulties she was to fire off a gun kept loaded and ready for the purpose so that he or the frigate could pick up the crew. He had also assured himself that every member of her crew was a swimmer – being well aware of the singular fact that fewer than one in three sailors could swim. There was a certain strange logic in the rationale which dwelt in a sailor's mind. If you were unlucky enough to be cast into the sea miles from land and you could swim the chances were still heavily against you surviving – nobody could swim an ocean. Therefore it might be better if you drowned as quickly as possible through not being able to swim. With the thought of *Bombarde's* vulnerability in mind North turned to the lieutenant, who had the watch.

'In future I want a midshipman and four men in one of the cutters or the launch sailing to windward of *Bombarde* at all times, it will be good practice for the men and in the event she capsizes we can reach her quickly. I will have a message sent over to *Arethusa* to ask Captain Wolley to alternate his boats with ours – watches of three hours by day and two by night.'

'Very well, sir, I'll see to it straight away.'

Jeremiah Wolfson joined him a few moments later and wished him a good day. North was about to point out the grey line of the Spanish coast to the east when a hail came from the lookout. 'Deck there, sail to lee, maybe a league on the larboard beam, looks like a brig!'

North snapped open his glass and watched the stranger; she was an odd little vessel with a noticeably short mizzen. He lowered the glass and turned to Goddington, who had hurried to his side. 'She's no threat, Mr Goddington, just keep a careful eye on her.'

Wolfson said, 'Pray tell me, Michael, what manner of ship is that? I don't think I have ever seen the like.'

'She is a snow, Jeremiah. There are few of them afloat nowadays, very old-fashioned. You see the stubby mast abaft the mainmast; it bears a trysail though the rest of the rigging is brig-like. This one is carrying just two guns a side, so I expect she is a small trader. She carries a Ragusan flag but she could be owned and crewed from any country from the Levant to Morocco. She is not worth bringing to; we'll leave her to go about her business.'

North walked to the forecastle and used his glass to seek out *Juniper* who was ranging ahead near the horizon. As he did so a signal was run up on her mizzen. He read, 'Strange ships in sight. Four sail. Stand by.' A few seconds later Midshipman Adams called out the same information to Lieutenant Crosby.

North having returned to the quarterdeck, Adams reported, 'Sir, signals from *Juniper*, stranger is French. One two-decker and three smaller ships. Two ships laden with timber. Compass signal no. 26 – ships are to the south west. Ships are one league from me.'

'Very well. To *Juniper* and repeat to *Arethusa*, form line ahead on *Juniper* and attack enemy when within range. To *Bombarde* move inshore, cutter to keep company. Mr Crosby, have the men called to their stations.'

The marine drummer was already standing by and with bosun's calls shrilling below the crew came to action stations in less than 14 minutes – a respectable time but one which could be improved upon. The lookout now had the enemy in sight. There were in fact six vessels. There was a 74 and a large frigate with two merchantmen and further to the south west two more large frigates. The more distant frigates were carrying Spanish flags.

At that moment Capitaine de Vaisseau Pierre Gourrège was freeing himself from the clutches of his mistress as Aspirant Felix Jacon hammered on the cabin door to tell him that the whole of the British fleet was about to arrive.

Gourrège, a Breton built like a bull, stormed out on to the quarterdeck of the *Minerve,* pulled up his breeches and shouting for his 1st lieutenant, *Lieutenant en pied,* Paul Hubert to ask him what the fuck was going on? If this was his idea of a fucking joke, he would be cleaning the heads for a week!

Hubert drew himself up to his full 5 feet and 1½ inches and looked up at the giant above him completely without fear. 'Captain, you pig's-arse, did you not hear your crew stumbling about like drunken donkeys in a henhouse as they went to what we laughingly call actions stations on this so-called warship? There is an English 74 and a frigate about three miles to the north east and in my naive ignorance I thought you might like to be involved in the coming battle.'

Gourrège burst into laughter. 'One of these days, you fucking pygmy, I am going to pick you up and throw you into the sea.

All right, I was out of order; now let us ready ourselves for the fight. I assume the guns are all manned?'

'Provided those soldiers can work out which end of the guns to put the balls in, yes sir.'

Gourrège took in the line of three English ships heading towards him on a converging course. 'Signal to the prizes and to *Derwent* to make for the coast. *San Antonio* and *Brigada* to engage the frigate. I suppose even the Dagoes can't fuck up when it's two to one, can they?'

The signal aspirant called over to him, 'Excuse me, sir, but the Spaniards seem to be withdrawing.'

'What! Those damned cowards! Signal *Derwent* to engage the English frigate, unless Captain St Jean has buggered off too!'

74 against 74 and frigate against frigate. The English frigate appeared to be of 38 guns – 30 of which were probably 24-pound carronades – and *Derwent*, which had been captured in from the British in 1797 was about as bad a sailing ship as only the English could build. At least *Derwent* had the advantage of 44 guns and her crew, which was a damned sight better than the bunch of morons that Gourrège had the misfortune to lead, should be more than a match. Louis St Jean, despite being a Parisian, had Gourrège's grudging approval. He was a remnant of the Royalist navy and probably knew his trade even better than Gourrège.

The two 74s were now in range of each other and despite an overexcited idiot firing off his cannon without orders, the rest of *Minerve's* gun crews held their fire.

Gourrège growled at Hubert, 'Remind me to keelhaul that

335

prick when this is over.'

Since Gourrège had hardly punished one man in past three months, except to give offenders a beating with his blacksmith-sized fists rather than waste time on a lashing, Hubert knew that he would have forgotten he said that in a few minutes. In any case keel-hauling in the French navy had been banned fifty years ago.

Prince Rupert drew closer. Hubert said, 'I believe that is the *Aquilon* that the British took at the Nile.'

'Yes but now she is called the *Prince Rupert* and is commanded by that Captain North. I have heard all about him. He is one of their best captains – the Tiger of the St Lawrence, they call him. He has captured at least two of our 74s and wrecked another one apart from sending Surcouf and his pirates scuttling out of Mauritius. This should be interesting.'

'*Interesting*, Pierre, that's hardly how I would describe it. With this bunch of halfwits we have as a crew the battle will be over in ten minutes. Perhaps we should make a run for it?'

'*Roustons!* We will fight them to the last soldier! Load the upper deck cannon with grape after the first broadside and tear up his sails. If we can get alongside him the soldiers can board him. The British never carry the size of crew we do.'

Gourrège folded his arms and looking down noticed he had not put his boots on. 'Deladier! Fetch my boots and you had better bring my sword and hat too!'

Seaman Deladier's rather insulting single-fingered salute apparently went unnoticed as *Prince Rupert's* first broadside struck the side of the ship with a mighty deafening punch that sent every man on the quarterdeck tumbling, except Captain Gourrège. The fact that he was standing was in a way unfortunate as a long splinter of oak smacked into his left shoulder. He grunted more in indignation than pain and, grasping the shard, snatched it from his shoulder and threw it to the deck. His blood was soaking his shirt. 'Oh yes, and I had better have my best uniform coat, Deladier, preferably without you giving me the fucking finger again!'

The upper deck was chaotic. Three guns were overturned and another had rolled backwards, killing six men and smashing into its opposite number on the larboard side.

The gunner – Dufresne – was smoking a scruffy pipe as he wandered unconcerned supervising the rest of the guns on the starboard side rather than keeping his place in the magazine. He shouted to the captain, 'Any chance of you giving the order to fire, old boy?'

'What's happened to Lieutenant Gaspard?'

'His head is at one end of the deck and the rest of him at the other end, my dear.'

'In that case, you are in charge, so fire the guns and let's have a little bit of FUCKING RESPECT!'

At last a ragged broadside was hurled at the English ship which had an immediate effect. More by luck than judgement, the forward half of *Prince Rupert's* bowsprit was smashed, though that was not where the shot was aimed. The debris swung upwards and backwards tearing into the rest of the jib sails and the foremast main sail. *Prince Rupert* swung to leeward just as her guns fired again. Consequently the majority of the shot struck forward of the Frenchman's mainmast. At least five yards of the rail disappeared completely and the ships boats were all wrecked where they sat. This was also the moment when most of the casualties occurred.

Gourrège shouted for the helm to be put over hard to starboard. With luck he could use the advantage to cross *Prince Rupert's* stern. It was not to be.

Not only were his helmsmen so transfixed by the sight of the captain's clerk carrying his uniform jacket and boots being reducing to a ragged heap of bloody flesh all over the wheel but the same stray shot smashed the wheel to pieces. The two helmsmen miraculously escaped with a few cuts and bruises.

Gourrège ordered men below to steer from the orlop using the tiller itself with more men stationed to repeat his orders on each deck. He was beginning to think that a strategic withdrawal was a good plan, bearing in mind *Prince Rupert's* forecastle being mobbed by men gamely hacking away the wreckage which would mean that pursuit was unlikely.

'All right, Paul, enough is enough, let's get out of here.'

Hubert nodded. He knew his friend well enough to know that he was no coward but the game was not worth the candle.

On *Prince Rupert* North was sitting on a tub on the quarterdeck having his left shoulder dressed. One of the enemy sharpshooters had hit him with a lucky shot. The ball had ploughed a deep, bloody furrow and although he could not move his left arm, he was thankful that it was not worse. 'Report, please, Mr Goddington.'

'Three dead and seventeen wounded. Two of the dead are

marines and also most of the wounded. The two shot that struck the forepeak ploughed straight into them on the lower gun deck. As to damage we have but nine shot between wind and water and nothing below. The jib will take about half an hour to jury rig and the sails are already up and about to be hung. It could have been much worse.'

'True, Alan, we had but barely started. It would seem Brother Frenchman suffered much more than we did and has gone off with his tail between his legs. How fares the *Arethusa?*'

Goddington grinned, 'I have the honour to advise that she re-took the *Derwent* with a single exchange of broadsides when *Derwent* struck her colours. Likewise *Juniper* assisted by Lieutenant Lackey on *Bombarde*, who seems not to have received your signal, has secured two of our mast-ships that had been prizes to the 74.'

'Thank you. Did you notice, incidentally, that our fight was auspiciously within sight of Cape St Vincent? Being this close to the Med, we will send prize crews to the captives and all proceed to Gibraltar. I shall be in my cabin if needed.' He nodded his thanks to the surgeon's mate after he had adjusted the sling to make him more comfortable.

Later that day North was dozing uncomfortably on the stern seat when the marine announced the 1st lieutenant. He brought news that Surgeon Horrigan was gravely ill. North hurried to the surgeon's cabin to find Horrigan pallid and sweating. His assistant told North that the surgeon had had a heart attack. As he spoke Horrigan moaned and reached up a hand feebly to cover his chest as it was wracked by a massive spasm. 'My wife, please ... tell her ... I ... tried to ...' His head jerked forward, eyes opened wide and he tried to speak again but nothing came. As he fell backwards North knew he was dead. He reached over and closed the man's eyes as the chaplain, who had entered behind him started to say softly, 'I am the resurrection ...'

North left the room saddened by the man's death. He had not been a likeable man and his addiction to alcohol had caused problems for the ship as well as to North but his willingness to try to stop drinking was at least something of which he could have been proud. North returned to his cabin without a word. Lifting a pen he wrote a letter to the surgeon's wife. Neither in the letter nor in his journal did he make any mention of the part the alcohol had undoubtedly played in ruining the man's constitution.

Half an hour later Lieutenant Goddington came aft with a white-faced Midshipman Holmes, one of the older middies, to tell North that Holmes had found Keeley dead in the hold, his throat sliced open and nobody nearby. Presumably whoever had killed him had taken advantage of the noise and mayhem of the battle. North was not sure if he was annoyed or relieved. There would be no court martial now but he would still have to go through the motions of trying to discover the man's killer.

Their arrival in Gibraltar was preceded by *Juniper* with reports for the resident commissioner, the master intendant of the dockyard and the governor, conveying North's respects and an account of the action with a request that space be found for 369 prisoners and that artificers be made available to assist with repairs. As a consequence, when *Prince Rupert* arrived, her damage being still very obvious, she received a spontaneous five-gun salute from the three anchored 74s and a similar salute from the shore batteries.

The governor, General Charles O'Hara, walked over to his window and said over his shoulder to his secretary, 'it seems that this Captain North is something of a warrior, Mr Gleeson. We have it on good authority that he follows Nelson's strategy of going straight at the enemy on every occasion. Have somebody carry an invitation to him and his senior to take dinner with us tomorrow evening, please. Also invite the admiral, of course.'

For the sailors of the flotilla the next three days were a welcome distraction from the war. It was the universal view of the inhabitants, who were almost entirely soldiers and sailors, that even perpetual drunkenness was preferable to boredom together with bad food brought over from the African coast and scarcity of water. Despite this the Rock was a pleasant change for the Ruperts, who were almost all allowed a run on shore. Although Gibraltar was technically under siege, the port itself was more or less open to British and to neutral shipping. The siege was ineffectual and even the enemy Spanish were realistic enough to realise that life had to go on.

· ·

Shortly before sailing Jeremiah Wolfson approached North as he inspected the upper deck guns. 'Sir, I have a suggestion regarding the late surgeon. Yesterday I went into the town where I have a number of friends. I chanced to meet Saul Levy, a highly qualified physician and surgeon. I took the liberty of asking if he would be willing to come on board to discuss the possibility that he could act as surgeon until we return to England. I realise that he does not have a warrant but I would be willing to pay him a salary from my own purse and cover his expenses. I have asked him to come to see you if you are interested.'

'Well, Jeremiah, there is no doubt that we have urgent need of a qualified doctor and there is none to be had from the navy in Gibraltar. Since you vouch for him I would be most happy to see him and the matter of payment could be covered from the ship's exchequer I am sure; I can sign him on as volunteer first class or captain's servant for form's sake. Ask him to come on board as soon as possible, please.'

'You don't think the crew might object to a Jewish doctor?'

'My friend, if a man is in pain and in fear of death, the last thing he will want to discuss is the doctor's pedigree. Frankly it matters little to me a man's religion; though having a belief in the Almighty seems an appropriate minimum. As long as he can do his job well, I don't care if he came from the mountains of the moon and I will make sure that the crew don't either.'

Thus it was that Saul Levy came on board *Prince Rupert* with his curious monkey on his shoulder, looking like a tiny golden lion, and with a young black servant loaded down with boxes and books. Levy's appearance was at odds with most of the sailors' preconceived ideas. He was less than 30 years old and very tall, possibly the tallest man on the ship. He had a muscular physique but his hands were slim and long-fingered. His face was as long as that of a Norseman. His hair was the colour of old gold and his eyes were blue.

He set about his duties with immediate effect, having some effective cures and potions that impressed the crew with their efficacy. Amongst the grateful were several jacks who had

342

returned with diseases only acquired through indulging those passions which were so readily catered for in Serruya's Lane and other seedier parts of the seedy town.

Chapter 29

Wednesday 24th to Thursday 25th June, 1801

Leaving the prizes behind, *Prince Rupert* led the other ships out of Gibraltar for the journey out into the Atlantic, past the Canary Islands and along the Moroccan coast. Three days of good sailing weather brought them within sight of land about 30 miles north of Mogador.

The previous evening North had entertained the captains of the *Arethusa* and *Bombarde*, together with Wolfson, his 1st lieutenant, Major Bracewell and Captain Hugo Lockwood, second-in-command of the Marines. After an enjoyable meal, North had the table cleared and proceeded to discuss his plans to rescue the American hostages. The first plan assumed that contact with the British secret agent could bring about a rescue without serious force of arms. The alternative plan consisted of a party sent ashore under Major Bracewell comprising two marine companies of *Prince Rupert*, with fifty of *Arethusa's* marines.

Bracewell would have with him most of *Arethusa's* marines as well as Marine Lieutenant Archibald Flood and Lieutenant Crosby of *Prince Rupert*. In support would be Patrick Neesom, the 3rd lieutenant of *Arethusa*, Henry Gibson, the 4th lieutenant of *Prince Rupert* and 40 seamen. The total shore party would consist of 218 marines and 40 seamen.

A second party would be standing by to reinforce if necessary, commanded by Marine Lieutenant Hodges, with 30 marines from *Arethusa* and 100 seamen from *Prince Rupert*.

Before either plan was put in place, North sent off Jeremiah

Wolfson with Cluney Ryan and two seamen who could speak Arabic, having both been slaves on a Barbary galley. The party was landed from the six-oar gig in a small bay eight miles north of the town.

It was an anxious wait for North but for Cluney Ryan, it was an adventure. All four were clothed in coarse white woollen Arab sbemas or burnooses, the head covered with the hood. This was Ryan's first time ashore in North Africa and the town that he could see as they approached it after walking for nearly two and a half hours was far less exotic than he had imagined. The day was very hot and the air still. Wolfson pointed out shapes and buildings called minarets, a golden domed mosque, tall white towers where waiting men were stationed, apparently calling to the faithful. Ryan noticed that much of the architecture was decidedly European. In the centre of the town the streets were as broad as those he remembered in Lisbon, even if those in the port area were more typical of the Arab disdain for symmetrical order.

Wolfson led them to a small apothecary shop in the Jewish quarter.

Leaving the two seamen sitting on the ground outside, Wolfson and Ryan opened the shop door. Entering the semi-darkness of the shop from the burning sunlight of the street was like plunging into a cool bath. Once Ryan's eyes were more used to the gloom he could see that this shop was little different from those he had seen elsewhere. There were shelves packed with small labelled boxes in a language completely indecipherable and on the wall behind the scarred mahogany counter was a full-length diagram of the internal organs of the body. A mandrake root, sinister in its pseudo-humanity, hung from a rafter. On one end of the counter was a pyramid of three monkey skulls and on the other end a glass case in which several dozen black and smaller brown scorpions seemed like toys on the sandy floor, so still was their posture.

The man who emerged from the rear of the shop was thin and bent-backed, dressed in a long black caftan with a hood which was drawn up over his head. As he saw Wolfson, the man threw back the hood to reveal a scarred face in which his eyes seemed to burn like black fire.

'Jeremiah! It has been more than six years since I last saw you but from your appearance it would seem that you were here but a few hours past. Life must be well with you; you look very healthy and well-fed. I am not going to make any profit from you or your companion, an Irishman if ever I saw one. He looks like he has been fed on the finest beef and butter from the beautiful fields of Kerry.'

This might have been a slight exaggeration since although Ryan was certainly healthy, he was slender, compact in size.

Jeremiah made no immediate reply but crossed the room and hugged the man to him. 'Too long Isaiah, far too long. If there is time we will talk together of our lives later but now I must know. Are the American hostages still being held in the town?'

'Assuredly, brother. The woman Mrs Johnston has been ill for some three weeks and I have been called in to provide medicines for Doctor Tascher, a Frenchman in the service of the Bey. I was there this very morning. You should also know that with the four Americans is an Englishwoman, Mrs Patricia Moncrieff, her young son Peter, a French noblewoman, Eugénie de Pierres and also three servants. The

Bey is not a barbarian but he is trusted by the corsairs and the hostages are in his care. He will not release them willingly unless the corsairs agree but they are in no danger at present. They could be in a much worse state.'

'If they are rescued, Isaiah, will they all be fit to travel?'

The apothecary frowned and stroked his beard. 'It will not be comfortable for Mrs Johnson but, yes, it could be done. They are guarded by the Bey's household, though the corsairs' man visits the palace daily. If it is intended that a party break in to release them the best time would be in the afternoon when the men of the palace go to the Salat al Asr.'

'When would that be?' asked Ryan.

'The local people follow the Hanafy school, which believes that the prayers of Asr must begin when the length of any object's shadow is twice the length of the object plus the length of that object's shadow at noon.'

Ryan looked at him blankly.

Isaiah relented. 'Well the time at *this* time of the year should be around three in the afternoon but like you and me, the locals can't get their heads round the fine detail so they usually prepare for prayer at around 2.45 and prayer finishes between 3.30 and four o'clock. This is often a longer period than the later sunset prayer so there would be more time to get the hostages moving. I can go up in the morning and let them know so that they will be ready to leave.'

Wolfson said, 'No, it is better they do not know. For one thing it could affect their behaviour in the meantime and lead to suspicion and secondly, since we cannot be certain when we can move, I don't want their hopes to be raised only to be dashed.'

'Of course, of course, I should have thought of that but surely there is something I can do to help?'

'Your help so far has been crucial, my old friend. Two more things would be of enormous help. A diagram or map of the palace and the prisoner's quarters?'

Isaiah tapped the side of his nose. 'Already done, Jeremiah – here, it is hidden beneath my lovely scorpions where no right-minded Arab would look.'

He drew on to his hand a long leather glove and reached into the sand at the bottom of the glass cage to retrieve a tightly rolled parchment covered in canvas.

'What was the other thing?'

'If you could arrange for say four or five donkeys or horses to be left near the bay where we landed in the early afternoon? Here is some silver to pay the owners.'

They took tea together and exchanged news of their lives. Then after hugging him again, Wolfson hid the parchment under his sbema and he and Ryan left the shop. Without wishing to embarrass his friend he had surreptitiously hidden a leather bag containing 100 gold Spanish dollars in a drawer of the cabinet which appeared by its rubbed brass handle to be regularly used.

....

Final instructions given, all three ships stood well away from the shore that night without showing lights. In the light of

348

Isaiah's information North had modified the plan.

A smaller party consisting of Lieutenant Lang with Wolfson, Ryan and 15 seamen, all disguised, were landed in the small bay where Wolfson had gone ashore the previous day. A second party led by Marine Captain Lockwood with 40 marines went on to the same shore 20 minutes later. Lang's party was the spear-point. They would enter the palace at precisely 3pm. Lockwood's party would take up positions a hundred yards away in a small public park. They were dressed in the sort of clothing worn by the Barbary pirates and carrying only pistols and cutlasses.

At exactly 3.15pm, *Prince Rupert* would enter the harbour and commence a bombardment of the anchored pirate ships while *Bombarde* would drop anchor on the other side of the promontory to the north of the harbour and fire its mortar on the fort. The action would be kept up for no more than 30 minutes.

Lang's party, having secured the hostages, would make their way escorted by marines back to the small bay to the north, where *Prince Rupert's* launch and both cutters were waiting to take them off. There was no assumption that everything would go completely to plan but North had made other arrangements to cover emergencies including sending *Arethusa* to take up position south of the town and send the original 280-man landing party ashore under Major Bracewell with most of the available boats to make a noisy feint towards the town.

That nothing could be guaranteed to go smoothly was proved as soon as Lang's party landed. North had decided to go with the party to get a better idea of the land approaches to the bay and see if it was necessary to have marines posted there. Lang tripped awkwardly over a half-hidden anchor that had probably lain beneath the sand for many generations. As he got to his feet, he gasped and fell again. His ankle was badly sprained and there was little chance he could walk the eight miles into the town.

North toyed with the idea of Lang riding one of the two horses or four donkeys which was tethered to some driftwood logs nearby, but realised the impracticability of this. Instead he ordered him into the waiting cutter and led the party himself. Before setting off, he discarded the sling he had been wearing and flexed his arm.

Leading the animals, they walked to the town. The weather was very hot and North, who had removed his jacket and donned Lang's robe over his shirt, was bathed in sweat after a hundred yards. He pulled the hood lower over his eyes to deflect the glare of the sun. The land around here was parched but away from the shore it appeared fertile enough. A sad donkey walked an interminable circle to pump water from a well into shallow channels to water the fields. Nearby stood several shadoufs, primitive but effective manual pumps that tired boys dipped and lifted with no enthusiasm to send muddy water gushing into the greedy crops.

After about an hour they passed a grove of date palms and passed handfuls of the sticky golden-brown fruit around. Washed down with water from a nearby tiny spring, the small repast was very welcome.

It lacked just nine minutes before three o'clock when North and his men reached the piazza outside the palace, which in style appeared to North uncannily similar to that of the

Spanish town of Oliva. A few hundred yards away on the edge of the Kasbah was the French consulate and North, who had no previous indication of a Frenchwoman's presence among the hostages, was at a loss as to why the consul had not intervened for her release. There was no occupant of either the British or Dutch consulates at this time, although there were representatives of the Portuguese further away towards the Northern Scala, or fort.

As the muezzin called the faithful to prayer from his minaret, one of North's seamen, approaching from a shaded corner, looked quickly in all directions before hurling a grapnel at the crenulations surmounting the palace wall. Three men scaled the wall in less than thirty seconds and a few minutes later an ornate door was opened and a beckoning hand caused the remainder of the party to move forward. Just before entering North looked over his shoulder to see that four shabbily dressed men, the first of the marines, were wandering casually into the park and settling down on the ground beneath the trees. If anybody was wondering why they weren't hurrying to prayer, they did not show concern.

Without Isaiah's diagram the palace would have been a maze but like Ariadne's thread, the line on the plan led them around the deserted ground floor to the left and right until they reached an open courtyard. There were three men in the courtyard lounging on the edge of a stone fountain their muskets in a stack nearby. They reacted too slowly and were beaten to the ground, bound and gagged.

Using the key hanging outside the widest of the doors North opened it and went in. There were three European men in their shirtsleeves sitting on cushions around a low table smoking and talking quietly amongst themselves. North flung aside his robe. One of them, seeing North, sprang to his feet. 'Good Lord! Who are you?'

'My name is Captain Michael North of the Royal Navy, I have been sent to take you from this place.'

As he spoke the first muffled roar of guns could be heard from the direction of the harbour.

The man rushed over to him excitedly, followed by the other two. He stretched out both hands and grasped North's right hand in his. 'I am Harold Pond. My God, sir, my God!'

'There is no time to lose, gentlemen. Please fetch the ladies and the rest of the hostages, we must leave here immediately.'

The next five minutes were a rushing cacophony of tears and laughter and a mêlée of anxious women and excited men but the party was on the move within seven minutes and led by Cluney Ryan with five men making their way swiftly through the corridors and courtyards. Mrs Johnson had to be carried between her husband and a servant called Mowbray.

The rearguard of eight men disturbed a crowd of screaming women but rushed on after the others with no more than a few nasty scratches and half a dozen bruised shins.

Ryan encountered two armed men as he neared the gateway. One fired his musket, hitting a seaman in the neck and causing a wound which bled copiously but was not over-serious; the other man's weapon misfired and both were literally trampled down as the leading group charged over them.

Lockwood and his men rushed forward to surround the hostages and lifting the women and the young boy on to horses and donkeys, they moved off quickly.

In the harbour there were several dozen ships. Two of them were flying French flags and most of the others, by their condition, were easily identifiable as belonging to pirates. The Harbour Scala had been built by Genoese architects together with the Northern Scala and although it bore six heavy cannon had been much neglected. Its garrison, many of whom had been at prayers as the British 74 opened fire, were only now struggling to get their guns into action. Matters were made more difficult by nine mortar shells from *Bombarde* that exploded over the fortifications within eleven minutes. As several more mortar shells burst over the hitherto impressive walls began to disintegrate.

More than half the pirate vessels were heavily damaged and six so severely that they sank. One of the French merchant ships cut her anchor cable but fell against a burning galley and was consumed. The other French ships escaped almost unscathed.

As *Prince Rupert* withdrew she signalled to *Juniper* who was acting as a repeater, to let *Arethusa* know it was time for their troops to re-embark.

Arethusa's party had created an impact which had caused the Bey to rouse out his troops to move southwards as their outposts came under sustained fire from the lines of red-coated marines as they moved towards the town. He was confident that his harbour guns would see that the attack would not succeed at that point and that the main attack was from the south. It was not until screaming wives and battered retainers had managed to get the message across that the hostages had been released that His Highness belatedly sent off his household guards to pursue them.

North's group were moving quickly. The seamen were hardy and even on land more than capable of running several miles at a steady pace so that it was less than an hour before they came in sight of the beach. The hounds were at their heels or at least those fifty or so that had mounted horses and overtaken their comrades trotting along the coast road.

Half a mile from the landing place North sent 20 men on with the hostages in their midst while he called to the marine sergeant who had met them to form up the marines and seamen in a double line across the road. Armed mainly with pistols and cutlasses it took nerve for them to wait until the screaming Arabs were almost upon them, their horses' breath almost close enough to be smelled. Loosing three volleys was enough to cut down about one in three of the cavalrymen and the rest wheeled and thundered back the way they came. The British then continued their retreat.

As they reached the beach more marines met them and took post to cover their embarkation. The local troops had reformed; those on foot hanging on to the stirrups of the riders as they ran alongside but before a shot could be fired they lost heart and withdrew.

Within the hour North and the hostages were on board *Prince Rupert* and North had received reports that nobody had been killed and apart from minor injuries to his crews and superficial damage his ships were intact and now formed up in the lee of the 74. The hostages, still wearing nothing more than they had at the moment the British soldiers had entered their quarters, and carrying little by way of personal possessions, were in a stunned but happy group in the captain's dining cabin. The steward kept them supplied with watered lime juice and fresh baked sweet biscuits which he had prepared with the help of the gunner's wife. As soon as North entered the room still without his coat that somehow had been lost on the shore they burst into applause. As he held up a hand in protest Mrs Moncrieff gasped and pointed. North's shoulder wound had re-opened in the race from the palace and his shirt was wet with spreading blood.

He looked down. 'Please do not concern yourself, Madam, it is not a fresh wound and it looks much worse than it is.'

His steward handed him a folded cloth which he pressed to his shoulder.

'We have not had time to make proper introductions but I should explain to you that we were sent by the British government to rescue you and take you back to America, but we were not aware than Mrs Moncrieff and her son and Madame la Baronne de Pierres were also being held. I assume that Mrs Moncrieff is happy to be carried to England but I am not sure how you feel, my lady?'

Eugénie de Pierres was a beautiful woman in her late thirties. Despite the haste and clamour of the past two hours she was composed and intrinsically elegant in every respect. North had addressed her in her own language but she had an excellent command of English.

'Captain North, I probably owe you my life. The French consul had sent a message making it clear that because I have so deeply offended that little Corsican upstart there was no possibility that I would be ransomed even if my worthless husband could be persuaded to open his tightly clenched purse. Without the consul as an intermediary the money would not be paid even if it reached Mogador. I believe that it was only the Bey himself who was preventing me from being sold as a slave, with all the horrors that would have undoubtedly followed. So with all my heart I thank you and your men for rescuing me. If I would not be too much of a burden I too would like to be taken to London where I have émigré relatives upon whom I can rely.'

George Johnson, who had been sitting on a chair beside a sofa upon which Katherine was lying, said, 'words cannot express how deeply we all are in your debt. My dear wife had been treated well enough by the Bey's physician but she has made little progress. Although it may be some time until we reach home I am sure we can get more expert help there.'

North groaned. 'Forgive me Mr Johnson; I don't know what I was thinking. Please take your wife to my bed-place through that door and I will have our surgeon join you. He is not a naval surgeon but is highly skilled and I am sure he will be able to help somewhat.'

Baroness de Pierres said, 'perhaps I could sit with Katherine while the doctor sees her, George?'

'Thank you, my dear. I will not be far away if needed.'

Saul Levy arrived a few minutes later with Surgeon's Mate Dryden, whose tactlessness was well known to North. His hands on his hips, in his heavy Irish brogue he said, 'Now look here, Captain, I told you to be careful of that wound. With all those flies and God knows what dreadful diseases on land I would not be surprised if you haven't caught some horrible plague, at all.'

North did not know whether to berate the man or laugh, so he

356

just grinned and responded in Gaelic. 'Now, now, Walter Dryden, a little respect would not go amiss.' He went into his day cabin so that Dryden could re-dress the wound.

As he cut away the sticky shirt Dryden muttered, '*Respect*, it's you that should respect yourself, Captain North. This ship may not fall apart without you but life would be far less interesting.'

North ignored him. He was thinking about his dispositions for the voyage to New York. He thought it best to release *Arethusa* and *Bombarde*, the latter ship because an Atlantic crossing even at this the milder season would be hazardous and *Arethusa* since the best reward he could offer Captain Wolley was a written order to cruise along the coast and up through the Bay of Biscay on his way home to see what prizes he could pick up. The two ships would need to be sent off in company since *Bombarde* on her own was an easy target for a privateer or almost any small enemy ship.

Harold Pond and Hector Kingsley knocked on the intervening door and asked to speak to him. North had a fresh shirt over his bandaged shoulder and since he had lost his second-best uniform jacket, he was stiffly pulling on his best one.

'Well, gentleman, how can I be of assistance?'

Kingsley was a short man who was probably considerably heavier before his captivity but now wearing a green jacket borrowed from the master who was a well-built eighteen-stoner, he looked as if he had shrunk inside it.

'Actually, we think you might be interested in something we found out that could be very useful to you. Harold, perhaps you would like to explain?'

357

The taller Harold Pond was a forthright Bostonian with a shrewd business mind and the owner of a fleet of eight merchantmen as well as several coal mines in Pennsylvania.

'It's like this, Captain. Our friend the Bey was not a bad fella but had one weakness which was not typical of his religion. The old boy liked strong liquor. Finding that this tendency was one which it was difficult to indulge in with his own people he would often visit and sit up at night with Hector and me, sipping a few whiskies and improving his English, as it were. Well, like the Romans said, *in vino veritas*, the Bey may have let fall a few secrets he should have kept to himself.

'As you may know he is trusted by the pirates and it suits him to keep up a reasonably friendly concordance with them. On their part they give him respect and cause no trouble in his town. They also pass on information to him that he finds useful such as the state of affairs along the Barbary Coast and what is going on nearer home.

'Anyway, a few nights back he told us about two Spanish frigates that were due to reach the island of San Sebastián de le Gomera in the Canaries in a few days from now to meet with a ship from the Spanish Main carrying gold and silver to Spain. The pirates thought the escort was too powerful to tackle and there was no certain date as to the arrival of the treasure ship. Now it seems to me that this ship may not be under escort at present or why would Madrid send out two frigates to meet her?'

North nodded, 'And presumably if she is headed in towards the Canaries it is possible that a ship such as ours, travelling west, might come across her?'

'Exactly. Of course, this could just be idle gossip but since we are going that way anyhow, maybe you should do a little fishing?'

North reached for the brandy bottle and poured three large glasses. 'Gentlemen, I salute you. We have nothing to lose by following this rumour for a few days and I will keep *Arethusa* and *Bombarde* with me so that we can proceed in line abreast, the better to cover the ship's possible route. If this is successful I will of course expect you to share in the prize.'

Pond replied, 'Not at all necessary, Captain. If this works out, let us just say it is a gift in gratitude for our rescue. It may not be too obvious to you but Hector and I will have much to gain by being returned to our business. We made important contacts in London and Lisbon and intend to trade more or less exclusively with England and Portugal from now on.'

The passengers were accommodated as best they could be with North taking the 1st lieutenant's cabin at night and using his dining cabin as a day cabin while the Johnsons had his bed-place. The Baroness and her maid, with Mrs Moncrieff and her child had the day cabin and Pond and Kingsley, a spare lieutenant's cabin and the master's cabin.

Doctor Levy spent twenty minutes with Mrs Johnson and came to her husband with the news that he believed she had a gastric infection from eating contaminated fish. 'It is called Ciguatera. It was first described by William Anderson, one of the surgeon's mates on HMS *Resolution* in 1774. Unfortunately there is no instant cure and she will need to get as much rest as possible until it works itself out of the system. I will induce vomiting several times over the next few days by getting her to drink heavily salted water and there is some indication that drinking the juice of the guava and pomegranate helps – the latter to my certain knowledge being cultivated in the Canaries. Perhaps if we touch land there I can have some brought on board.

'As far as you are concerned you could help by getting her to drink as much liquid as possible and making sure she rests. This will pass but I cannot say how long it will be.'

Chapter 30

Friday 26th June to Tuesday 28th July, 1801

North had decided to sail west-south-west so that they could land briefly at one of the Canary Islands to pick up supplies including fresh fruit and vegetables, so Dr Levy was able to bring pomegranates to Mrs Johnson.

Four days after leaving the coast of Morocco, the four ships were in line abreast some 40 miles to the west of the Canaries.

The two Boston merchants stood with North on the quarterdeck as the noon sighting was taken. Both men owned ships and were keenly aware that the efficiency of the Royal Navy was unsurpassed. The 1st lieutenant with his chronometer in hand and the master with his sextant shot the sun, and noon was pronounced and longitude fixed. At the end of a line of snotties, the smallest but clean-scrubbed midshipman piped out 'minus 22 degrees and 29 minutes, from Greenwich, sir!'

'Do you all have that, gentlemen?' from the master and nine aye-ayes squeaked and growled in response.

'We take the longitude as 22 degrees and 29 minutes for your journals and you are dismissed,' confirmed the lieutenant.

Despite keen lookouts it seemed that the Spanish treasure ship had either failed thus far to reach that point or had unknowingly avoided them by sailing further south or north in her eastward journey. Just as North was prepared to shrug his shoulders and give *Arethusa* and *Bombarde* leave to part company, three strange sails were seen on the western

361

horizon, black silhouettes against the setting sun. Whether they had seen the English ships or mistaken them for their escort was still not clear as night fell and they maintained their converging course.

North called a quick conference of his captains. He realigned his ships so that *Arethusa* made off slightly to the north and *Juniper* to the south. *Bombarde* would follow *Prince Rupert* headed straight towards the three ships, the second of which seemed to be a smaller three-master. The third was a large merchantman.

As the distant ships took in sail and moved more slowly forward on foretopsails alone, the British ships, having had to tack in order to close the distance, simply followed suit and took in all sails to wait for their prey to arrive.

So it was that the *Nostra Señora de Atocha* which was an 80-gun ship *en flute* with half her guns removed and the frigate *El Burlando* 44 came in range of the English ships at just past one o'clock in the morning. The third ship, the *Sorpresa* of 800 tons, was carrying sugar which had been the cargo of a captured pair of British traders carried into Cartagena as well as 50 tons of sugar from Vera Cruz and a quantity of other luxury goods.

The broadside of *Prince Rupert* being considerably bigger than that of her opponent, most of whose guns were struck down into her hold, was to make the battle that followed much shorter than it would otherwise have been. Taken by surprise having anticipated a meeting with his promised escort, Capitán de Navío Indalecio Zamora had not sent his men to action stations.

Zamora was no coward and the exchange of shot was just as determined as he could make it. The damage done to his ship was severe though not crippling and there was a chance he could escape but *Prince Rupert* was too formidable. Almost alongside, Zamora could see his crew were heavily outnumbered. Reduced by more than 40 percent by fever, many men buried now in the sand at low water mark off Cartagena on the Main, he lost all hope of victory and his flag tumbled to the deck.

The captain of the *El Burlando* was killed in the first clash between his ship and *Arethusa* but for a while the fighting was hot and determined. His senior lieutenant would probably have lowered his flag and waited for the inevitable but seeing how the under-manned and lightly armed *Nostra Señora* was resisting, he was shamed into fighting on. *Arethusa* was able to stand off and since her guns were heavier and had a longer reach she could inflict damage and stay practically intact.

The end came when the smaller ship, the *Sorpresa,* badly handled, fell onto the side of *El Burlando* as her captain tried to hide his ship from the line of fire behind her larger companion. He misjudged the distance in the darkness of night and the swirling clouds of gunpowder smoke. The resulting chaos ended as *El Burlando's* colours were struck.

North had himself rowed over to the larger ship and met her captain in his cabin. Conversing in French he asked the nature of his cargo.

Zamora shrugged his shoulders. 'We are carrying cocoa, cochineal and Jesuit's bark but the valuable part is in the trunks you see before you, Captain. To save you the trouble of counting it, there is gold and silver to the value of some one and a half million dollars. What do you intend to do with my ships?'

'You have over 900 men including those on the frigate and I will be seriously incommoded by having to guard them. I propose to send most of them in the *Sorpresa* under a cartel to Cueta. You may select two of your lieutenants to go with them. You and the other captains will be carried on *Prince Rupert* as my guests and if you give your parole, will enjoy a certain degree of freedom. Your other officers will be carried to England on *Arethusa*.

'*Nostra Señora de Atocha* and *El Burlando* will accompany us to the Leeward Islands where I will have them handed over to Rear Admiral Duckworth, for decision in the prize court. The bullion chests will be accommodated on *Prince Rupert*, of course.'

There would be an astonishing amount of prize money to be shared amongst the flotilla rivalling that enjoyed by the crews of *Triton*, *Alcmene*, *Ethalion* and *Naiad* when they captured the Spanish ships *Santa Brigida* and *Thetis* five years ago. The specie in *Nostra Señora* alone was worth around £150,000 in prize money. It also took half a day to carry over the cargoes of the three ships which together would fetch £30,000 without the hulls of the ships.

Conditions being favourable, the 4,800 miles distance to the Leeward Islands was covered in 31 days during which *Prince Rupert's* passengers enjoyed a quiet time though her crew were kept up to the mark by her officers who had it impressed upon them from above that this was not a pleasure cruise.

North entertained his guests as well as he could and on one evening towards the end of the voyage to the Leeward Islands had all of them to supper in his dining cabin, together with Lieutenant Lang and Midshipman Adams. As the last of the food was cleared from the table Harold Pond asked North about a theory he had heard from a sea captain in London whose opinion it was that ships built from timber cut in the winter months were much drier than those built of summer-felled timber. It was a widely held belief in some quarters but North was sceptical.

'In my opinion the main factor that makes a difference is whether the timber is well seasoned. Green timber expands and contracts in a different way than mature timber, wouldn't you say, Mr Adams?'

'So my uncles and grandfather believe, sir. Grandfather Adams swears that he has never knowingly put a scrap of green timber in a ship and I believe it is well accepted that his ships are amongst the best in England.'

Hector Kingsley was curious about the ship's galley. 'I notice that this ship has its galley between decks and also has an oven, which I believe is uncommon on English ships.'

'That is because she is a French ship, sir,' replied North. 'The French prefer to have the galley there and it certainly does provide a warm area around which the men off duty can congregate in cold or wet weather. The oven is also French and I wish the Royal Navy too would adopt the idea. I can provide my men with fresh bread made from the flour we carry in tight casks rather than just issue wormy biscuit. Our cook does have more skill than most of his ilk and when challenged can cook more than just boiled meat and peas.'

The company joined in the conversation with favourable comments on the food that had been served up to them by Naylor, the captain's steward and the two seamen who had been allocated to assist him in looking after the civilians.

Dropping anchor in the beautiful serenity of English Harbour, *Prince Rupert* and her prizes received a visit almost immediately from the governor, Ralph Payne, Lord Lavington. It appeared that Rear Admiral John Duckworth was away from the island at present and had undertaken the seizure of Danish, Swedish and Dutch Islands in the Caribbean, the last of which was the Dutch Island of St Eusabius from which the French garrison had evacuated on the 16th April. The senior captain presently with the small number of British ships in the harbour was Captain David Milne of the 42-gun frigate *La Seine* who in fact should have been in Jamaica but was here still undergoing repairs after her titanic fight with the French frigate *Vengeance*.

In the circumstances Captain David Milne was the next visitor and between them, he and North decided that the matter of the prizes would be taken up when Rear Admiral Duckworth returned and that North could leave Milne with despatches which would explain the situation.

After wooding and watering and bringing on board fresh supplies of fresh food, *Prince Rupert* set off northwards with *Juniper* ranging ahead like a hound seeking a scent.

Chapter 31

<u>Thursday 30th July to Friday 21st August, 1801</u>

Prince Rupert had passed to the East of Santo Domingo on the 4th May and was making good progress along the eastern side of the Bahamas when she found a pair of English 74s, *Carnatic* and *Thunderer*, off Great Abaco Island. North was in the rare situation of meeting a post captain with less seniority than he had. In fact King was awaiting his transfer to another ship as his first full command.

Both men were of similar age, being a year or so older than North, causing Mrs Moncrieff to remark to her companions how young the captains of such great ships seemed to be.

The three captains dined together on *Carnatic* and exchanged news before going their separate ways, Brisbane and King to continue south to take over the blockade of Santo Domingo and North to continue his journey to mainland America.

The next landfall after hailing the coast of Georgia was on the small island of St Simon near Brunswick to take on fresh water. From there to New York, it was eight days' sailing with weather conditions warm but slow progress pushed by predominantly light winds.

Finally, to the joy of the American passengers, as they sighted the highlands of New Jersey to the west they came near Sandy Hook lighthouse to port and the East Bank Shoals to starboard. As *Prince Rupert* negotiated the tip of the Hook, North fired off a gun and gratefully took on board a pilot who had been rowed out to him across the bay. Many a ship had come to a disastrous end on the shoals and sandbars hereabouts and North was not going to make the same mistake.

The pilot guided them 21 miles north by north-east between the banks, through the Lower Bay and into the narrows between Bluff point on Statten Island and New Utrecht on Long Island then a slight course alteration to north by north-west into the Upper Bay. With *Juniper* behind her *Prince Rupert* saluted Fort Columbus on Governor's Island, came to anchor about a quarter of a mile from the shore and sent Lieutenant Crosby on shore in the pilot boat to announce his arrival to the authorities.

Looking out at the city from his quarterdeck, North was struck by the great number of commercial ships and the sunlit neat roofs, cupolas and spires of the city as it hustled and rushed through the business of industrious merchants and artisans.

Crosby being accompanied by George Johnston turned a lukewarm welcome into a more friendly one. Crosby then went on to deliver his captain's respects to the British consul. Rather than rush ashore the Americans on *Prince Rupert*, with Katherine Johnston very much better in health, seemed reluctant to leave. In the end they persuaded North at least to come ashore with them for a few hours.

There were around 30,000 people living in the city of New York and the area around it and most of them seemed to be in the port area which was a bustling, noisy place, filled with the smell of fish and tar. There were great piles of grain sacks, white pine masts, pitch barrels and hemp bales constantly growing and waning as sweating men carried them to waiting trading ships. A few stared openly at the tall English captain, but many ignored him. There was always some fearfulness amongst the mariners, wary of impressment and more than a few deserters scuttled inside hostelries and down dark alleyways at the sight of a British captain and boat's crew.

The Johnstons hired two carriages to take the party to the house of Johnston's cousin Aaron Burr. The vice-president was in Philadelphia but his daughter, Theodosia, was in residence having just returned from Niagara Falls after her honeymoon with her husband, Joseph Alston. North was charmed by the graceful, black-haired Theodosia and her husband. They were both very young but Alston was already a successful plantation owner in South Carolina. Since they were about to leave for Murrell's Inlet the following day they were more than happy for the Johnsons to stay for a few days to rest after their voyage.

That evening they threw a dinner party for the Johnstons and North. On his return to the ship he found the 1st Lieutenant with the master-at-arms and a platoon of marines searching the ship.

'What is amiss, Mr Goddington?'

'Sir, I believe we have discovered the culprit of the recent sabotage and possibly Keeley's murder.'

He went on to explain that he had been checking the sail room with the master. As they entered the room a man rushed past them, his lower face covered by a kerchief. The master had chased after him but by the time he reached the deck the miscreant had lost himself amongst the watch which was changing at that moment. When the inspection was resumed, Goddington turned over a bundle of canvas to check the wooden tag which identified it when to his dismay he found that this and a dozen other sails had been liberally strewn with lamp-oil. A pistol and tinderbox lay nearby; the flint from the pistol loose on the deck.

Immediately he called for all hands to be mustered on deck and a roll-call taken. Two men were found to be missing. They were Joseph Brand and George Coogan who had joined the ship as volunteers at Buckler's Hard. Coogan was found hiding in the cable tier but of Joseph Brand no trace was found.

Standing in the cabin in front of his captain, Coogan trembled.

'Well, man, what have you to say for yourself?'

Coogan steeled himself for what was to come. 'I say Free Ireland and long live the Revolution!'

'You stupid man! What example would you take from France? Would you have guillotines in Dublin? Have you not seen for yourself the miseries of your own people? Would you have it that the government sends in German mercenaries to once more beat the people into submission? If Ireland is to be free it will be through the likes of William Pitt pushing Catholic emancipation through parliament. It will not be by through destroying His Majesty's ships by fire. Where is Joseph Brand?'

Truculently, Coogan shook his head. 'I don't know. Gone over the side if he has any sense.'

North turned to Goddington. 'Take the fool away and have him held on the orlop in irons.'

The following day George Johnston had himself rowed out to *Prince Rupert* with Pond and Kingsley to say goodbye. With repeated speeches of thanks and good wishes they shook hands with North and his officers and went back to land, rather the worse for the amount of wine they had consumed.

After the three Americans had left the ship North made his regular Friday inspection. He was about to descend to the hold when the 4th lieutenant, Henry Gibson, came upwards, his face strangely calm. 'Sir, the master informs me that water barrels have been contaminated! I don't know how to tell you this ... there are *body parts* in them!'

North watched appalled as one after another a dozen barrels yielded grey portions of human flesh. The master was standing pale-faced watching the bosun, who had been assisting him in the inspection. The bosun, a man who had seen most horrors that a long life at sea could produce, was visibly shaken as he held up a head by the hair. It was that of the missing Joseph Brand.

North cursed softly. He beckoned the men closer and spoke quietly. 'Open every barrel, bosun and mark all those that are defiled. Mr Gibson, stay here and keep this area clear. Not a word to anybody.'

North had Coogan dragged before him again.

'So, now we know what happened to your friend Brand! You killed him!'

Before he could continue, Coogan burst out, 'He's no friend of ours! He would have betrayed us – eavesdropping ...'

Suddenly realising what he was saying, Coogan's face twisted with genuine horror, 'No, no, I didn't kill him. I hid myself as soon as the officers chased me out of the sail room. I never saw him!'

North looked at him thoughtfully. 'You said "friend of *ours*." Who else is in this with you?'

Coogan shut his mouth firmly and stared defiantly in front of him.

'Very well. Take him back to the orlop, master-at-arms.'

Goddington looked North. '*Another* conspirator, perhaps more than one? How do we proceed, sir? I have no idea how to find these people.'

'Nor I, at this moment, Alan, but find them we must. The ship is in danger but we must try not to alarm the crew or we could have a riot on our hands. All officers to be armed and in the cabin in five minutes; we need to make sure every one of them is alert. Now the contaminated water barrels need to be emptied, dried and sulphured before we can fill them again. You will have the rumour spread through the ship that none of the contaminated barrels were used. It may or not be true but panic will not help the situation. One thing is for sure, it would have taken time for the body to be dismembered so whoever did it is not one to panic. Did you notice that the wounds were clean, not hacked? Have the surgeon check that his instruments are all in place.'

Saul Levy reported that his longest bone-saw and two razor-sharp knives were indeed missing. He had also inspected the hold and the body parts and gave his conclusion that the body was probably cut up on the spot. All parts had been identified and had been recovered from fifteen different barrels, which had now been emptied into the scuppers and were drying on deck before being sulphured.

No person was allowed away from the ship except the crews of the launch and pinnaces with four armed marines and two officers on each boat watching them closely. They had to fetch and carry and have the refilled water barrels brought to the ship. There were no desertions.

No progress had been made with the search for the traitor but ten days before they were due to sail Coogan was found with his throat cut in the hold in a manner virtually the same as the late Keeley.

North was livid. The master-at-arms had found the marine corporal, who had been one of those constantly guarding the prisoner, beaten over the head and near to death. By now the whole ship was in a state of high tension. Messmates who had known each other for years looked askance at each other as they messed together, wondering if one of their friends had betrayed the ship. All of the two score Irishmen on the ship came under suspicion of the shipmates, adding to the tension. Fights broke out and the cat was used a dozen times in five days, contrasting greatly with the normal situation.

During the forenoon watch on the day following discovery of Brand's body something snapped. North was called from his cabin by Lieutenant Lang to attend the wardroom urgently. There he found Major Bracewell lying on the deck being attended by the surgeon. He had been stabbed in the chest with one of the surgeon's knives but by sheer luck the blade of the knife had snapped and the broken tip was lodged against a rib. He struggled to speak.

North touched his shoulder. 'Easy, Jolyon, take your time.'

He gasped. 'I can't believe it, sir! It was Lieutenant Gibson! I was talking to him about the traitor when I noticed his

373

attention seemed elsewhere.'

Haltingly Bracewell explained that he had remarked that it was fortunate that it had been the Master who had happened to inspect a barrel with a body part in it. He asked if Gibson had any suspicions of the two dead Irishmen, both of whom had been in his division. Then he noticed an angry look spread over the man's face. Before Bracewell could grasp what was happening Gibson had a knife to his chest.

Gibson's anger had turned into rage. 'What do you know of this, Bracewell?' He had muttered fiercely, his eyes blazing. 'What does the captain know? You are trying to trick me. Is he nearby waiting for me to drop my guard?'

'Before I could say a word, sir, he lunged at me. I ducked and the knife struck my gorget.' He feebly pointed to the dented crescent of metal that hung below his throat – a remnant of armour of ages long past that had at this moment saved his life. 'Then he stabbed me in the chest. I can only believe the knife was weakened by the contact with the steel.'

'Thank God for that, Jolyon. Pray continue.'

'There is nothing more to say. Having stabbed me he ran from the room. I was too shocked and weakened by the force of the attack to follow him.'

North turned to Goddington and Lang. 'Find him, he must not be allowed to leave the ship.' Lang left the room and Goddington told North that he had already sent Lieutenant Crosby with a dozen marines to search.

Gibson was found clinging to the mainmast tops, a pistol at the throat of the lookout.

North looked up at him. 'Mr Gibson, I am coming aloft. This madness must cease now! Release that man and I will take his place as your hostage.'

Lang and Goddington remonstrated with him, telling him that he must not put himself in such danger. North replied that this was his ship and his responsibility and climbed the shrouds until he reached the tops, climbing outwards to avoid the lubbers-hole where Gibson had a second pistol trained.

North looked at him calmly. 'Let Richards go now, Gibson. It will be one less person for you to watch.' Gibson nodded but as the man started to rise Gibson shot him. North leapt forward to catch Richards who started to topple from the platform, his ankles tangling in the rat-lines. He heard a click as the hammer of the second pistol fell on to the powder pan but there was no explosion. The gun had misfired.

One arm around Richards under his shoulders and his other arm hooked around a stay, North looked up at Gibson who raised the pistol to smash it over his head. As the lieutenant stretched to put more force into the blow another shot rang out and Gibson fell to one side, blood streaming from his chest. He gasped, 'The Devil take you, Michael North, for Ireland and for my father Malcolm Kennedy, I would that I had destroyed you and your ship ...'

He screamed as he toppled to the deck below, his dead body falling at the feet of the cooper, Georges Lascaux, who had snatched a musket from a marine and shot him with unerringly accuracy.

Willing hands were already relieving North of the weight of Richards' body. The seaman was deathly pale but awake, blood spreading from a wound in his side. 'Thank you, sir, you saved my life!'

'Gently now, lads, lower him down carefully,' said North.

Searching Gibson's belongings, letters and papers were found to show that his mother was a cousin of the traitor Kennedy who had died on the orlop deck of the frigate *Epée d'Or* those many months ago when she had been taken by *Phoenix*. There was also a letter written to Gibson by his mother on her death-bed confessing that it was Kennedy not Robert Gibson who was Henry Gibson's father. Gibson had always been close to his 'uncle' and had shared his secret Fenian obsession. He was not on *Prince Rupert* by chance. A friend at the Admiralty had innocently made sure he was posted to her.

It took a few days for the ship to calm down and North delayed departing until he was satisfied that things had returned to at least a reasonable degree of normality. North had spent hours writing his despatches to place on board the Liverpool Post Office packet-ship *Chesterfield*, which left four days before *Prince Rupert* and would no doubt arrive nine or ten days before her.

There was another visitor before *Prince Rupert* sailed; Phineas Bond who was the British consul in Philadelphia, where the Congress was now sitting. He was acting as British envoy after the previous ambassador, Robert Liston, had returned to London the previous autumn.

Bond was about 50 years old and a confirmed Anglophile. In North's day cabin he came to the point of his visit. 'Captain, I have a letter here to be delivered to you personally from Vice-President Burr and two further letters for you to carry to London, one from Mr Burr to the First Lord of the Admiralty and the other from the president to your Mr Addington, the

King's First Lord of the Treasury. Mr Burr would like me to emphasise the deep gratitude he has for your restoring his cousin and the other Americans to their native land. I am sure you are aware of the delicate diplomatic situation the kidnapping provoked and thanks to your government and to you, a most satisfactory solution was found.

'Mr Jefferson and Mr Burr are aware, of course, that a financial reward would not be appropriate to your good self but a special but unofficial gesture was to have these medals cast for you and your officers. I trust also that you will allow the President to show his appreciation to your crews by a gift of 20 United States dollars apiece.'

He opened a velvet-lined rosewood case in which, suspended on a red, white and blue neck ribbon, was a two-inch wide heavy gold medal with two crossed staves supporting a Union Flag and a United States Flag; on the obverse were the words 'Mogador Expedition 1801.' In the box were 16 silver medals of the same design.

Lifting the gold medal from the box North smiled. 'Well, I must say, Mr Bond, this is a very pleasant reminder of our mission and although, as you say, it is unofficial, I shall be honoured to keep it as a very special reminder of friendship.'

Chapter 32

Friday 2nd October, 1801

The voyage home from New York was in some respects an anticlimax but their welcome at Spithead was completely unexpected. It appeared that Phineas Bond had seen fit to send an urgent despatch to London on the New York packet which arrived two weeks before *Prince Rupert* and even before the Liverpool packet. As a result Lord St Vincent himself had travelled down from London and gone on board his old flagship *Ville de Paris.*

The signal to *Prince Rupert* from the flagship was 'Captain to repair on board Flag,' to which order North struggled into his best uniform and Canadian presentation sword and climbed down into his launch as quickly as he could.

He was welcomed on board by five bosun's calls, removed his hat to the ensign and was about to walk aft when he was surprised by the completely unexpected sight of the First Lord alongside Captain John Markham. Both men were smiling broadly.

As soon as North had saluted the earl grabbed his hand and shook it firmly. 'Welcome home, North. A despatch from the Philadelphia consul reached us to say you would be here about now and we had Plymouth send a messenger to Portsmouth and telegraph to the Admiralty as soon as you made your number. Splendid result in Mogador, could not be better, but what about those treasure ships, hey! My God, sir, if only I had been your admiral but under Admiralty orders you won't have to share your "eighths". I have read your

378

despatch a dozen times and if it were not for the secrecy attached I would have made sure you had a Gazette to yourself for Mogador, though the treasure ships Gazette is the talk of England! Now come along, I don't know about you but I am parched.'

Captain Gordon, temporarily in command of the ship, led them to the great cabin of the huge 110-gun ship, the largest in the navy. On the starboard side a long oak table was spread with a selection of food and bottles of wine. North stood transfixed for a moment, his eyes wide as he beheld his wife. Isobel came to him, her hands outstretched. The earl walked to the table to personally bring back two glasses but waited patiently while the couple embraced.

North looked at her with some puzzlement, she looked ... different. 'My dear ...'

'Yes, my darling, you will be a father! Did you not receive my letters?'

North had been able to send several letters home but there was no opportunity for any of Isobel's letters to have reached him. A *baby*! He was thunderstruck with the realisation of fatherhood and the joy of it swept over him.

North had to gain enough composure to nod his thanks to St Vincent, a man known more for bad temper than kindness who said, 'Nice surprise, North? John Markham's idea, actually. Of course we took great care bringing your wife to the ship.' St Vincent's attitude towards marriage for sea-officers was well known but he had a well-hidden romantic streak.

Markham rapped on a nearby table and it was only then that

North realised there was a large gathering of people, many of whom he knew very well, including the Duke of Bridgwater with Evan Nepean. There was Isaac Wolley and John Mills of the *Arethusa* with John Lackey of *Bombarde*, Captains Rockwell and Spicker, who had been lieutenants on *Prince Rupert*, with Lewis Shepheard who had also received his step. He was also delighted to see his old friend Lord Arden who was standing to one side with three men who, did he but know it, were to have a significant part to play in his life: Magistrate Patrick Colquhoun, the art dealer Michael Bryan and his friend, the West Indies planter George Hibbert. But the best surprise was his elder brother James and his wife together with his younger brother, Commander Peter North, who were standing with Lewis Shepheard.

After repeating the table-rap, Markham continued, 'Your graces, ladies and gentlemen. I give you Michael North, a splendid officer and a credit to the Service!'

Spontaneous applause was halted by St Vincent's raised hand. 'I have one pleasant duty before I allow you all to enjoy yourselves. Captain North, it gives me great satisfaction and honour to acquaint you with the pleasure of His Majesty the King in appointing you Knight Companion of the Most Honourable Order of the Bath. It being customary for His Majesty to install the knights in the Henry VII chapel in Westminster Abbey each 17th of June, of course you were still at sea. You were therefore installed *in absentia* but the ceremony was witnessed on your behalf by your good friend the Duke of Bridgwater who now has a duty to perform.'

His hand releasing Isobel's and still completely unable to take it in, North looked round as Bridgwater approached him carrying a velvet cushion. He grinned at North. St Vincent and

Markham took up position either side of him, Markham receiving the cushion in his hands. Taking a red sash from the cushion Bridgwater draped it over North's right shoulder and then with the words, 'On behalf of His Majesty I invest you with the Order of the Bath, please hand me your sword and kneel on one knee.'

North complied and felt the touch of the sword on each shoulder as Bridgwater said loudly, 'rise, Sir Michael North, Knight Companion of the Bath!' There was now loud applause as Bridgwater pinned the Star of the Order on North's left breast. He returned the sword, stood back and taking North's hand in his own shook it firmly.

'My dear Michael, never was such an honour so richly deserved.'

From various quarters came the cry, 'Speech!'

Taking Isobel's hand, North cleared his throat and in the silence said, 'If I had known this was going to happen I would have had some words ready but as Cato the Elder is alleged to have said, "*Rem tene, verba sequentur.* Grasp the subject and the words will follow."' He paused for a few moments while the silent company waited. 'I believe I will simply steal more of Cato's words. "I think the first virtue is to restrain the tongue; he approaches nearest to gods who knows how to be silent." Thank you, your grace.' In the laughter that followed, Isobel squeezed his hand.

Bridgwater shook his head, 'No thanks necessary, *Sir* Michael, my reward is in seeing merit justly honoured. Now *Lady* Isobel, can I fetch a chair for you?'

Isobel replied, 'Kind of you, your grace, but I am happy to

stand for a while longer.' She turned to Captain Markham. 'Sir, may I make a request? I believe my husband should be here to enjoy the company but would it be possible for me to be taken over the *Prince Rupert* where I can wait for him in comfort?'

'But of course, my dear. One moment, please.' He turned, beckoned to a lieutenant and instructed him.

Isobel kissed her husband's cheek, 'I insist you enjoy your afternoon, my darling. I am not a fragile flower. With the convenience of the bosun's chair I can move from ship to ship in comfort. In any case I am anxious to meet your guests. I believe I am acquainted with Madame la Baronne's sister who lives in Lower Norwood near Beckenham. Please take your time.'

With that she left with her in-laws James and Alice with whom she could not have been better cared for than the Queen herself.

It was several hours later that Captain Sir Michael North rejoined his ship, having been seen off the flagship with three rousing cheers and receiving three more as he came on board *Prince Rupert*. His crew were delighted by the honour to their captain as well as grateful for the order the 1st lieutenant had given as soon as Lady Isobel had stepped on to the deck, which was to issue a double measure of rum.

North was accompanied by Bridgwater, who greeted Jeremiah Wolfson with obvious pleasure. He also carried a letter for Lieutenant Goddington advising him that he had been made post and was to repair immediately on board the frigate *Janus* of 32 guns which was moored a few hundred yards away nearer to Ryde on the Isle of Wight. He was to read himself in from the enclosed commission.

In the day cabin Isobel was seated in a deep cushion-filled armchair, in animated conversation with her sister-in-law and Mrs Moncrieff and the baroness. When North entered both rescued women rose and kissed him on the cheek as they congratulated him on his well-merited knighthood, then left the cabin with the duke.

Chapter 33

Saturday 4th to Sunday 5th October, 1801

Having allowed North the privacy of the evening and the night, Bridgwater sat down with him at around ten in the morning, tea in hand.

He said that in North's absence the weariness with the war had increased but another element had crept in. There was much talk of invasion. Nelson had been charged with instilling some of his bravery and patriotism into the recruitment of the Sea Fencibles but many of the more than 2,500 men recruited with some experience of the sea were wary of going on board ship due to apprehension that this was just another ploy which would lead to impressments. According to Nelson they had protested that they were employed only to leave their homes for a day or two but said they were willing to 'fly on board' when the enemy were known to be come upon the sea. Plans were being drawn up by Nelson to attack the assembled invasion craft in the harbour at Boulogne and many were the small craft lying off Deal ready for that work.

In Boulogne Latouche-Tréville, that most competent of France's admirals, watched as Nelson sailed by in his frigate *Medusa* and knowing his intentions had a line of 24 brigs across the entrance to the harbour, well anchored and linked by chains to prevent them being cut out.

Addington had received approaches from the French for peace and terms were being passed back and forth between the two capitals.

Like most of his contemporaries Bridgwater was extremely sceptical and cynical of Bonaparte's motives but Addington was a pale shadow of determination compared to Pitt and there was little doubt peace would come – at a price.

'The country wants it and Bonaparte needs it. To my mind the invasion threat is bluff written large but there is no way the population can be shaken out of their fears. There will be some bitterness in various quarters that the bellicose stance taken by those in power has cost many lives, for example by not allowing the excellent accord made by Sir Sidney Smith to allow the French army to leave Egypt under a truce rather than continuing to wage a pointless war against these already defeated troops. Peace will be seen as a great victory by our people even if we have gained nothing by it. Mark my words, we will be at war again within a year or so and Napoleon will have readied scores more ships to fight us.'

North was inclined to agree. 'It seems to me that Bonaparte's appetite for conquest is insatiable. It would be completely out of character for him to sue for a *lasting* peace. Unlike Alexander the Great I cannot see him weeping because there are no more worlds to conquer.'

'I would spare you this if I could, Michael, but it is more than likely that you will be called upon yet again to perform extraordinary services for your country in the coming months. Many would think these exertions pointless if peace is already a certainty but we must think ahead to that time when darkness once again covers the land. St Vincent and many of those in power agree with that analysis while having to keep it unexpressed. So you see clandestine operations may well grow in number and scope even as overt activities decline and vanish.'

'So what will they need from me now, John? I have just been blessed with the prospect of fatherhood and desire a respite so that I can be with Isobel, at least for a while?' North realised he must have sounded plaintive but Isobel's news had only reinforced a desire for some peace and quiet at Tarring.

'I am sorry, Michael, but all I can do is buy you a week or two. Later this morning you will receive a note from the First Lord allowing you to sleep out of your ship for a week so you can repair to Tarring and be with Isobel. I regret to say that certain matters are afoot which may interrupt your rest but I will try to give you as much time as possible. When you receive a letter from me I have to ask you to return to London. I also regret that it is likely you will be temporarily without a command since *Prince Rupert* will soon be captained by another officer but I feel sure that this will be only until another ship is given to you.'

....

North did have the option to refuse a command but despite his wish to give priority to Isobel he was hampered by a sense of duty to his country.

With much on his mind to talk over with Isobel, North barely noticed time passing that morning until she reminded him that the Baroness and Mrs Moncrieff were about to go on shore. Cecil Moncrieff had arrived the previous evening to a tearful reunion with his wife and as North and Isobel came on deck he came forward with hands outstretched and words of deepest gratitude.

'I am not without friends and influence, Sir Michael,' he said, 'and though I trust my support may never be called upon, if ever you need a friend, I will be there for you. My wife and son restored to me are gifts I can never repay you.'

Madame la Baronne, having with some difficulty restrained her feelings of passion for North over the past weeks, also came to them and kissed both of them in a very Gallic display of happiness. Extracting promises to visit her in Lower Norwood whenever they were in Dulwich, she left the ship with a mountain of baggage she had acquired in New York despite apparently having not a sou to her name. North had charged his clerk to discreetly tuck a purse with 200 guineas into her grace's luggage.

Now there was the question for North of himself departing the ship that had been a home to him for so many adventure filled months. He had decided he would allow himself the privilege of taking some people with him. If he had been merely exchanging to another ship he would have had the benefit of many more of his people. Cluney Ryan and his steward George Naylor would probably have deserted and followed him anyway. The cooper, Georges Lascaux, had saved his life twice and in fact was something of a square peg in a round hole aboard ship. These would leave along with the gunner and his wife. The gunner had decided to use the prize money due to him to buy a hostelry had happily fallen in with a plan by Isobel to take up the tenancy of an inn at Tarring. They renamed the inn the North Star.

At two in the afternoon another surprise awaited North. To the shrill of bosun's pipes a freshly turned out captain appeared at the gangway, looking just as much surprised by the spanking new single epaulette on his shoulder as by the rolled commission in his hand. It was North's younger brother Peter who had been given his step on impulse by St Vincent with the added signatures of Markham and Nepean and was to command *Prince Rupert* – another North to take the quarterdeck of the ghost ship.

North sent Isobel and most of his people into Portsmouth with Sir James and Lady Alice, while he had the crew mustered to speak to them.

'Officers and men of His Majesty's ship *Prince Rupert*. I leave you with a heavy heart. Together we have seen many wonderful sights from the freezing seas off Canada to the baking heat of Diego Garcia and Morocco and have shared many dangers and joys. Our reward has been significant prize money which, I trust will bring us all some security in the years to come. Some of you are being discharged on shore and will take with you memories which I am sure will last a lifetime, as indeed will be mine to treasure for always.

'Your loyalty and comradeship have made me proud and happy. This is not the end of our voyage of life, merely a continuation of something which can never be taken away from us. I wish you safe seas and a happy return and I entrust to your care your new captain, who, while I know he is not as soft and amiable as I am, will lead you with a firm but just hand.'

He turned to his brother and for a moment looked at him as perhaps other people might. Richard Peter North, known as Peter in the family to distinguish him from his father, the late Sir Richard, was of the same height as his brother and two years younger. He had inherited his mother's thick red Irish hair and his father's deep green eyes. North was pleased for his brother and happy to trust him with his treasured command and crew.

'Captain North. I will now leave you to your ship, wishing

you as much satisfaction as I have been privileged to receive from the officers and crew.'

As he shook hands with his older brother, Peter said, 'I thank you, Sir Michael, for the excellent state of the ship you hand over to me.' He turned towards the forecastle.

'Men! Three cheers and a huzzah for Captain Sir Michael North!'

The cheers still ringing in his ears, Michael North descended into his launch for the last time. As he did so Peter North unrolled his parchment and began to read himself in.

North felt strangely conflicted. He had been given a title way beyond his expectations but he had lost his ship; he was returning to an estate he could never had expected to own and to a wonderful wife whom two years ago he could never have envisaged in his dreams and a child not yet born. As a prospective father he was filled with happiness. He was extremely rich due to his good fortune in the matter of prize money but unsure as to what would become of his career. Although now that he was on the list of post captains it was just a matter of living long enough to be given his flag; he was addicted to action and wanted nothing more than to be able at least for a few years to stand feet braced against a driving wind at his back on the deck of a ship – any ship!

Isobel, her senses finely attuned to her husband's feelings, was acutely aware of the cause for silence as he sat alone with her hand in his in the leading carriage as they approached their house along the paved driveway. Half a dozen of the farm labourers, hats in hand, paused as they worked in the afternoon sun and watched the master pass by.

At the house Con Riley welcomed him and then his old friends George Naylor and Cluney Ryan. Georges Lascaux looked around him even more heron-like than usual at his new home. His role in the North household had not been fully defined but North had suggested that his literary skills and organisational abilities would make him a fine secretary. Lascaux joined the other three sailors in unloading the carriages as Sir James and Lady Alice arrived. The duke of Bridgwater and Jeremiah Wolfson were in a third carriage. There was also a fourth carriage in which the diminutive person of Midshipman Poole was retrieved from under a pile of baggage and North's personal effects from the cabin of *Prince Rupert*. The Honourable Francis Poole was going on leave to stay with his parents in nearby Worthing but had been invited to stay to dinner that evening.

Chapter 34

<u>Sunday 4th to Thursday 8th October, 1801</u>

A few hours later North stood with his hands linked behind his back looking out of his bedroom window at the golden fields of wheat in the distance. There had been three bad years of harvests in the country but it was to be hoped that this year would be different. He turned and smiled as he looked at his wife, propped up against pillows in the bed and still, like him, happily recovering from those exertions to be expected from a couple who had been so long apart. He walked over and touched her stomach, still wondering at the separate life within.

'Who would have thought it, Isobel North? A man as lucky as I am to have such a beautiful wife and soon a precious child, for which I am eternally grateful. I love you dearly, my darling, and I wish that I never had to leave your side again.'

Isobel touched his cheek then lifted her hand to stroke his hair. 'My dearest wish is your happiness, Michael. Of course you will go to sea again and I will have to cope with the anxiety while you are away. Like most wives I will shed tears and no doubt you will be sad too. But when I can have you with me like this on your return, it makes it much easier. There's no point in regretting the way things are. Even if peace doesn't come, we will be together one day and I promise you, I won't ever want to let you out of my sight.'

As she dressed she turned to him again.

'Michael, while you were away Lord Bridgwater took me fully into his confidence. Momentous things are happening and there may be peace on the horizon. I believe these will be interesting times.'

'Indeed, my dear. He made an intriguing remark to me this morning. He asked if I had a particular view of politics. I told him I favoured no party but those which truly served the king and the people though since the Whigs would seem to do anything to pacify Bonaparte, I tend towards the Tories. I suspect he has something in mind that he will wish to discuss before dinner. '

In the library the duke, together with Wolfson and Captain Markham, who had arrived for dinner a half hour before with George Hibbert, sat with North, glasses in hand in comfortable armchairs and settee.

Markham said, 'Michael, we are all friends in this room. It is true that you don't know Mr Hibbert well but you can take it that his views coincide closely with ours as far as the well-being of the country is concerned. I want to put an idea to you which I hope will appeal.

'It is not for any sinister reason that you have been relieved of command of the *Prince Rupert* – more on that later. You may not be aware but the borough of Steyning to the north-east of here returns two Members to Parliament. Currently one seat is held by Sir James Lloyd and the other by John Henniker, who will stand down for family reasons. Both of those men are strong supporters of William Pitt. Now, there are at present 118 registered voters in Steyning, about 40 of whom are tenants of the Sussex Member Mad Jack Fuller.

'All of John Fuller's people will follow his directions and about half of the remainder will heed John Henniker, both of whom have promised to back you as the next Member if you agree to stand.

'I know you will protest that you are a career naval officer and besides which have no interest in or deep knowledge of politics but I do not see any conflict in you continuing your career while being a Member of Parliament, as indeed many of your fellow captains have done. The advantage to us, by which I mean your friends and your colleagues, would be to have a naval man in the House who has no obvious connections. Furthermore by virtue of not wanting a political career he cannot be persuaded to hold his tongue if he believes that government policy is wrong. There is also the opportunity of serving your country in a different way.'

North asked, 'In what way do you see this to be useful? I assume that there is going to be a peace – however shaky that structure may be – and that as war recedes in the mind of parliament there will no doubt be changes of emphasis. Ships may be laid up or even broken up, the number of seamen reduced but there will still be a navy.'

Markham said, 'It is precisely those issues that concern us, Michael. While we cannot resist such an inevitable and logical reduction it must not mean that the country's main bulwark of defence is weakened to the point that we cannot adequately defend ourselves or our interests. That was the mistake that the administration of your distant relative Lord North made following the Seven Years War and it took us years to catch up with the French and Spanish. George, I think you have something to add?'

George Hibbert was an interesting man. North was aware that he held large business interests in the Caribbean with sugar plantations and a year ago had placed a bill before parliament to formally establish the West India Company. An avowed believer in the benevolent ownership of slaves for economic reasons and a strident opponent of the Abolitionists, he was also a renowned botanist and with his extensive gardens in Clapham, the importer of many new and rare specimens from distant parts of the world particularly hostas and proteas.

He rose from his seat and stood in front of the empty marble fireplace.

'One of the demands of the French is the restoration of those islands taken from them by us during the war and they will probably get them since Addington is depressingly eager to lick Napoleon's boots. Personally this does not affect me greatly but commensurate with the regaining of Martinique and other places will be an influx of ships and soldiers for the French to reaffirm their control over the populations. When they have achieved that it is my fear that those forces will stay in the Caribbean afterwards and make a damned nuisance of themselves, particularly if, as we suspect, Napoleon will keep on acting aggressively even if there is a notional peace. This is only one of our concerns and applies just as much to other parts of the world.

'Since the time of Queen Elizabeth our island nation has spread its colonies and conquests further and deeper around the world and with this expansion has become a greater and greater need for a strong navy to defend our interests. Spain, our nearest rival, particularly in the New World, has enough of a navy to need balancing. The Dutch, while their empire may be smaller and their navy designed more for protecting their colonies, is as significant a threat as the Spanish. This is so particularly since the Netherlands navy is far better in quality than the Spanish even with fewer ships. Our allies the

Portuguese also have important African and South American possessions and would pose no threat to us if it were not for the possibility of invasion and assimilation by the Spanish.

North nodded. He was well aware that the Portuguese navy was equipped with few good quality ships and her army much smaller than that of her neighbour.

'As you well know the situation with the Americans is finely balanced but constantly their eyes turn north even as they plough their furrows further westward. Jefferson may have a soft spot for you personally but he is a shrewd and clever man and has no love for England.

'I believe, on the face of things, we would need most if not all of our ships and men even without war with France, just to insure our ability to protect our colonies and possessions around the world.'

Bridgwater added, 'I believe our concern is that any reductions in the navy should be controlled primarily by the Admiralty. Parliament should be convinced that while "dead wood" needs to be culled, our fleet and our men should only be reduced to the level where we retain the best. Further ship building needs to take place even though the cash would have to be wrung like water from a rock.'

North replied, 'So far there is nothing I can argue with. There are other naval officers in parliament, including you, John. Why do you think I should make a difference?'

Markham said, 'Sparing your blushes, Michael, you are a hero of the first order. Parliament is aware of this, if not of all the details, and you will receive positive attention for that reason. Some had wished Nelson to come to the House but, frankly, while he is a brilliant admiral and the nation's darling, we believe he would not be at his best in such an environment, although in the Other Place he might make a difference. Besides which he has other duties that are of great importance to our defence at present. No doubt if called upon he will take up his seat, being a viscount but, between us, though he has enormous talent with the written word, he lacks eloquence when speaking in public. Furthermore he is not as popular in the House as he thinks he is.

'On the other hand you are a man who has excellent tactical skills and a wide knowledge of recent affairs in places like North America and the Indian Ocean where, to say the least, far less focus has been directed than should be the case. You also have the added distinction of being one who does not seek public adulation. That means that you are not perceived to a threat to other peoples' *amour propre*, for, to paraphrase Rochefoucald, "everything in the end comes down to self-interest." You would not come to the House with preconceived ideas about commerce and industry but a deep knowledge of naval matters and the real world of foreign affairs. Any other arrows to your quiver can by supplied by us and others with specialised knowledge.'

Bridgwater nodded. 'We believe politics needs to move in a different direction to reflect the changing times. To date Members have been selected with exceeding little control from above on the basis of self-interest and mainly a background of privilege. We believe the time is coming when expertise rather than tribalism must influence government decisions and indeed it is interesting that within the labels Whig and Tory there are often different emphases of attitude.

'We need to make sure parliament does not abrogate powers

to itself in areas where it lacks superior expertise. If, for example like the French, we handed command of our ships to political appointees and subordinated our navy to the army it would be an exercise in madness, yet many of the Members could be persuaded to allow such nonsense in the spirit of their own self-perpetuation and self-interest.

'Our army is officered by many men who are only given rank in response to the depth of their purse – though there are notable exceptions. Thankfully even the dimmest light amongst these cannot entirely negate the professionalism of many of those of lower rank. At least there are more officers in the navy whose rise has been by merit rather than entirely by influence. As far as you are concerned there can be no doubt that you are gifted with real talent and professionalism. To hold up the hand of experience and good sense would be the object of having people like you in the House.'

'There must be more suitable men than me?'

Hibbert shook his head. 'Adequate, perhaps, but not with the same flare of ability that can grasp the realities of a changing situation on the ground, such as in North America and the Indian Ocean. A mind that displays the energy and skill that captured or destroyed several 3rd rate ships apart from the *Nostra Senora* and many smaller ones besides. Your fund of prize money alone reflects that genius and it was not merely in gratitude that this estate was given to you by a grateful parliament, it was an acknowledgement of your value to your country.'

After a few moments' thought, North said, 'I will accept the nomination and the task implied though I wish it to be known that I still want to go to sea whenever an opportunity arises.'

Also, without wishing to offend, I am my own man and I will vote in parliament only within the limits of my conscience and speak honestly, whomever that might offend.'

Hibbert groaned, 'Oh my God! We have created a monster! An *honest* man in parliament; whatever next!'

The rest of the men in the room joined in his laughter.

Turning to Hibbert, North said, 'There may be one issue between us that could cause friction. I am instinctively against the slave trade and while I am aware that your own attitude is far less stringent than some slave-owners, I would have to express my views if asked.'

Hibbert rested his hands on his comfortable stomach. 'Sir Michael, you may not be aware that Wilberforce and I worship in the same church in Clapham. My views and his are completely opposed and I will take issue with him at every opportunity but I trust that there is mutual respect and politeness even if not friendship. Please do not think that I sleep peacefully each night and never think of the basic immorality of owning another human being. I command my agents to act benevolently and I require a less than maximum level of production in order to ease the burden of labour. My slaves are given adequate food and enjoy much better housing and education than most. On the other hand I regard the free labour of slaves as an economic resource without which the commerce of this country would be fatally wounded – though it is impossible for me to get Wilberforce and his friends to see it from that point of view.

'Without wishing to give offence I am bound to say from personal experience that the treatment of my slaves may be in some ways better than the way the navy treats its seamen; for what, pray, is the difference in impressing an unwilling man? In taking him from the bosom of his family it is sometimes the case that his wife and children starve for want of a breadwinner or suffer the indignities of Poor Relief. His life on one of your ships is stark and grinding to say the least. On some ships he is fed worse food than a pig, kept in damp and disease-breeding conditions and stands in fear of being flogged by a tyrannical captain. Then comes war and he will be lucky to return home, sometimes after many years forbidden to leave the ship, with limbs and sanity intact. Should he be crippled his life on shore will be miserable beyond belief.

'I hasten to say that I believe that in many cases such as on *Prince Rupert* the men are treated better than on some ships but are they free? No, sir, they are slaves with their burden lightened merely by a few paltry shillings in wages, which, when on land are swindled from them or wasted on a brief adventure of riotous living to forget the misery of their service.

'In your case I accept that you are more humane and decent than many of your fellow captains and pray that you will not take my remarks personally. I would say that if we differ in our principles I hope it would be openly and without rancour; such as to perhaps allow a friendship despite our differing views.'

North extended his hand and said, 'Well said, sir.'

Later with Isobel he found he had mixed feelings which she shared. It was an opportunity to be with her more often, which was most welcome, but parliament was like a new uncharted ocean to him and he was far from sure that he would enjoy the voyage.

Chapter 35

Monday 12th October to Thursday 5th November, 1801

After a few days with the company of all except Markham and Hibbert to enjoy, since they had returned to London earlier, North was making arrangements for to travel with Isobel up to Dulwich.

A messenger arrived from the First Lord with a letter appointing him Deputy Adjutant General of the Fleet vice Sir George Grey, who had been St Vincent's flag captain in *Ville de Paris* in the Mediterranean. Perhaps it would add authority to his voice should he succeed in the coming by-election. It was a sinecure, an almost meaningless title which bore the useful salary of £1,000 a year but it ensured his name was known in the corridors of power. Paradoxically his captain's pay of around £350 a year had been halved since he was not actively employed at sea.

He had visited Steyning and made himself known to the voters, having gone through the formality of buying a newly built row of small houses in the village to establish qualification as a landowner. They had originally been built by a local farmer for his workers but he had gone bankrupt. North immediately donated them for five years on a repairing lease at a peppercorn rent to the vicar of Steyning to provide homes for poor and indigent parishioners at as low as possible a rent.

He learned in Dulwich a few days later that he had been elected second Member of Parliament by the voters of Steyning.

Five days later he was walked into the Chamber of Westminster Hall by John Markham on one side and Thomas Erskine, the other Member for Portsmouth, on the other. A man of many parts, the 51-year-old Erskine had served as a midshipman in the navy for four years and then as a lieutenant in the army before taking up the life of a lawyer; he was well known for gifted but controversial defences of men like Thomas Payne.

North was presented to the speaker Sir John Mitford, the relative of another old naval friend, Jack Mitford, as he took his place. He was fascinated by the activity in St Stephen's Chapel where the members were overcrowded and the situation made worse by an extra 100 members representing Irish constituencies who had just been added, increasing the number of Members of the Commons to around 650, roughly the same number as the crew of a 74.

It took less than two weeks before North was on his feet making his maiden speech. He spoke eloquently for almost twenty minutes to the subject of the neglect of the North American Station and consequences that could follow from a lack of ships and soldiers if the United States decided to join the French against Britain. He gave way to an Honourable Member who asked whether he believed that the United States would invade Canada if peace were agreed between Britain and France. To which he replied that there might be a reluctance amongst ordinary people in America but that he believed that ambition to extend the United States westwards would at the same time have them looking northwards.

This did not involve any feelings of revolutionary zeal for fellowship with the French but rather the practical notion that Canada curtailed would leave the United States with a free hand to exploit the entire North American land area right up through Canada to the Arctic sea and south-west to the Pacific Ocean. A proposed expedition under Lewis and Clark up the Mississippi and along the waterways to the west could make feasible a route to the western coast.

Jefferson's plan seemed to include creeping colonisation of Louisiana, which vast state comprised most of the hinterland. North also said that he believed the stopping of American merchant ships to weed out deserters and curtail the carrying of war materials to the French was like a running sore to those surrounding President Jefferson but he believed that they would avoid war or armed neutrality.

His speech was well received and gained some four column inches in *The Morning Chronicle.* Truth was that while he was happy spending time with Isobel in Dulwich he was still having problems coming to terms with the fact that he had no ship to sail.

He also had time to deal with some prosaic matters such as making a new will to accommodate fatherhood and sifting through months of paperwork in relation to his estate and his professional affairs. Prize money, a never-ending story of delay and uncertainty, was less difficult to finalise due to his reputation in the country.

In the world at large peace was increasingly in the air.

Peace might be growing like a welcome flower in the minds of the people but the streets of London still felt the feet of a few determined agents of the French, one of the most able of them being Thomas Davoust. The son of a Lyons mayor, Davoust was a man entirely without scruples in the cause of France and his meeting with Napoleon's emissary, Gerard Constant, had provided him with a mission entirely to his liking. Peace was a fiction – for Davoust the war continued.

The French minister of police, Joseph Fouché, had charged Davoust with the task of assassinating the hated English sea captain, Sir Michael North. Strangely it had been the toss of a coin to decide between North and Nelson. Although Nelson was seen to be the greater threat to France, it was the less flamboyant and equally gifted North that had the dubious honour of winning the toss.

Over a period of six weeks, Davoust studied his target to the point of obsession but not in such a way as to attract attention. A germ of a plan was in his mind but he wanted to see more of the man before finalising the details. He had half a dozen rogues at his bidding who would do anything for a handful of gold but he wanted to see with his own eyes this monster who vexed and frustrated the admirals and generals in Paris. Now he could see him striding through the park near the Admiralty. The tree-lined path beside the waters of the lake was lined with leafy trees, their branches stirring a little in the evening breeze. The young man was taller than he had imagined and walked quietly and with long strides. There were other people in the park and many of them turned their heads in recognition as North passed by.

Davoust moved stealthily further around the trunk of the oak tree as North drew level with him. Davoust could see that the hilt of North's sheathed sword was free of his cloak – a wise enough precaution even in this part of London.

He waited until North had reached the middle of the Horseguards Parade Ground before moving after him. He knew that he would not be allowed through past the guards and into Whitehall without an ivory token, whereas as a Member of Parliament, North would at this moment be drawing one out of a waistcoat pocket. He left North to finish his walk. How feasible as an ambush area was the park? He decided to look for other places but the park was a possibility.

The following afternoon, chance brought Davoust an unexpected opportunity. He was with two of his minions following North along Piccadilly when he saw him enter a tailor's shop. Opposite the shop was a gloomy, narrow alleyway between two buildings. Davoust took up a watching position. It was nearly an hour before North emerged. He turned towards St James Street and walked down to a building on the right at number 64 called the Cocoa Tree Club with Davoust and his men on the opposite side of the street. North having entered the club, Davoust cast about trying to find an inconspicuous way of following him. In Blue Ball Yard he found a hostelry near the rear a hundred yards or less from the park boundary. Opposite was a row of stables and coach houses and alongside of it was a narrow opening which led into an alleyway.

The alleyway wall separated the premises from the rear yard of the Club and could be scaled quite easily. Sending one man back into St James Street to watch the street door of the Cocoa Club, he and the man with him, a Londoner called Cutter, climbed the wall and dropped down into a yard wherein boxes, barrels and crates were stacked.

Leaving Cutter hidden amongst the boxes, Davoust sneaked in through the back door of the club. It took a few moments for his eyes to become accustomed to the dim interior of the room he entered. There was a noisy kitchen off to one side and a man walked quickly past him carrying a tray of steaming vegetables. He took no notice of Davoust, assuming he had the right to be there.

It took Davoust ten minutes to find that North was not in the lower two floors of the Club and a mild enquiry to a broad-shouldered waiter elicited the response that he believed the captain was in the select member's loft and pointed to the yard. Davoust had no idea what this meant but dare not show his ignorance. Frustrated he moved back through the club and into the yard to instruct Cutter. This exposed him to the view from the windows of the select members' room above the stables.

Michael Bryan, art dealer, spymaster and friend of George Hibbert, was looking down into the yard at that moment, listening with one ear to the conversation behind him between North and George Hibbert.

He turned and beckoned. 'George, Michael, come over here. There is something strange going on below.'

The three men could see two men crouching behind a large barrel, engaged in heated conversation. As they watched, the less well-dressed man took two pistols from under his coat and handed one to the other man. They moved stealthily towards the stables, clearly unaware they were observed.

North said to Hibbert, 'George, stand back, please. If these men attack us I want you to throw that chair through the window to attract attention. Michael, do you have your pistol?'

'I do indeed,' said Bryan, taking his own pistol from his tailcoat. North drew his sword and the two men moved to the top of the flight of stairs. By now the intruders were inside the stable and at the foot of the stairs. North called down.

'Lay down the weapons! We will not hesitate to shoot our own pistols!' He drew Bryan back quickly away from the open area at the top of the stairs as a shot rang out.

There was a loud curse from the stables and the coarser of the men started to run up the stairs, a pistol in each hand held out in front of him. Bryan did not hesitate. He fired his own pistol into the man's face. Cutter fell back with a scream and tumbled down the stairs. At that moment George Hibbert threw the chair through the window with a crash of breaking glass. Davoust turned and ran, unaware that his quarry did not have a pistol.

North leapt down the stairs. Cutter's unused pistol was lying beside him. North scooped it up and hurriedly checked the priming as he ran. Davoust was scrabbling to reach the top of the back wall. North shouted for him to stop. Davoust turned and with a shaking hand aimed his pistol at North. Both pistols exploded at the same instant. North felt a numbing pain in his leg, staggered against a nearby box and fell into a pile of straw. Davoust gasped in agony and sank to the ground on his knees clutching his side. Bryan and Hibbert ran to North who was looking down at blood running from his right thigh. He pointed to his dropped sword, calling out to Bryan. 'Secure that man, Michael.'

Other people were rushing from the back door of the club into the yard, shouting enquiries and throwing hands up in confusion. One of the waiters reached North and Hibbert and gasped as he saw the spreading blood on North's white breeches.

Hibbert took charge. Swathing North's leg in a silk tablecloth he had two of the servants carry North to his carriage which was in the street near the entrance to the club. Bryan stayed to deal with the situation at the club and to send a man to the nearby St James' Palace to fetch some guardsmen to seize the wounded Davoust.

Hibbert had his driver take him and North to the Admiralty where he was confident a surgeon could be quickly found. Luckily a navy surgeon was in the eating house opposite the Admiralty gates waiting for his captain, who was in the Admiralty. Two hours later North was sore but more comfortable lying on a settee in a room in the private residences next to the main building. Davoust was sore and chastened in the guard-room at St James' Palace.

Two naval captains assigned by the First Lord had interrogated him. They had discovered his name and intentions but Davoust had refused to disclose from whence came his instructions. It was of little importance; the hand behind the assassination attempt was obvious and great anger spread like a wave of heat from Westminster to each part of the kingdom at the perfidy of the French who were professing peace. Addington himself was loathe to make a protest to the French emissaries in London but some angry citizens took matters into their own hands and set fire to the building in which the French were in occupation though mercifully not in residence at that moment.

Strident headlines were emblazoned across all national and local newspapers and there were unheeded demands in parliament for Addington to insist that Bonaparte arrest and imprison the minister of police in Paris as the very obvious *eminence grise* behind this dastardly act. In music halls and theatres patriotic songs were interspersed with re-enactments of the dreadful drama – many of them being considerably more dramatic than the original event. Pamphlets purporting to be written by 'patriots' urged parliament to ignore the French overtures of peace and send the navy up the Seine to avenge their hero.

In her home in Dulwich, Isobel paced anxiously but was repeatedly reassured by Hibbert and Bryan, as well as the local doctor, that her husband's wound, though serious, was not judged critical. He had been brought to her in a closed carriage escorted by twenty mounted cavalrymen and a major of the Hussars.

Two weeks later Davoust was brought to the Old Bailey where, after a short, and it must be said, somewhat arbitrary trial he was sentenced to 25 years in prison with hard labour for malicious wounding despite the jury urging the judge to hang the swine.

Despite the dreadful incident Michael and Isobel North went on to enjoy almost three months of quiet but purposeful happiness. The early winter had brought with it coal fires and warm blankets but the weather was bright and although the air was sharp it was a pleasure to sit on the terrace and look out over the bare-branched trees to the sea in the distance. North's leg healed well and although there was still some soreness when he walked some distance, it discommoded him little. The baby was growing fast it seemed and there was a warm contentment between them arising from this precious time of being together.

They had spent just three weeks in London where in the House of Commons North had begun to coalesce around him a number of Members who were actively following his lead in pressing for a maintenance of the best of the navy and opposition to breaking up ships unless absolutely necessary.

North tended towards support and admiration for Nelson's achievements but had a less vainglorious attitude to war. He believed the war was in a just cause and his profession was to fight it to the utmost of his ability for his country but could not see the sense in war for its own sake. He had become much more informed about politics and the recent history of battles such as the siege of Acre and the regrettable battle for Copenhagen. This had shaken his belief in some of the measures taken in the name of war.

There was a final resolution to the meandering machinations of the peace process. In October a *de facto* peace existed which would be ratified in due course. In the meantime hostilities had practically ceased.

It was unlikely that his services as a sailor would be needed, though he would be pleased to be called to go to sea again; but for the moment he was making the most of his freedom to manage and enjoy his estate. He had a fortune of more than £170,000 and had decided to put aside one tenth of it to do something for indigent seamen. In this he and Isobel had found a kindred spirit in Lawrence Dundas and with him and several other like-minded people set up a charity to provide housing and support for poor and distressed sailors.

Isobel was nearing her confinement and North smilingly likened her to a mother hen, clucking around and checking that her nest was suitable. The nursery was bright with soft green and blue paint and freshly hung with floral wallpaper.

On the 3rd November he had been present in the House when Nelson had made a speech to the Lords concerning the importance or otherwise of the retention of the Cape of Good Hope, Malta and Minorca as well as the other possessions that Grenville would hand back to the French. North had squirmed in his seat with embarrassment. Nelson had made a complete fool of himself in the opinion of many of the Members.

With phrases such as 'Malta is no sort of consequence to this country' and that the Capetown was merely a 'tavern on the passage (from India)' he had either shown his ignorance of the true importance of such places or was wilfully and painfully twisting the facts to support Grenville's shoddy acceptance of Bonaparte's demands. As Earl Spencer had remarked in North's hearing, 'anybody would think we had lost the damned war!'

St Vincent had sided with Grenville and remarked that the retaining of Trinidad and Ceylon more than compensated England for giving up the other conquests – an attitude that greatly surprised North.

His view of politicians before joining them had been that the majority were pretty worthless and now he felt that same opinion even more strongly. He wryly remarked to Wolfson that he hoped that if he was to be remembered at all he hoped it would be as a salt-sea sailor than a politician. It seemed to him that the House was infected with far too much self-importance and a false superiority on almost all matters of importance. *Amour propre,* as Rousseau had so tellingly pointed out, was much inferior to *amour de soi.* A man who was comfortable in his own self-confidence had no need of the adulation of others and therefore was a happier and more useful member of society.

As he chatted with Isobel he looked over her shoulder at a carriage being driven up the drive towards the house. He walked over to the front of the house and greeted the Duke of Bridgwater and George Hibbert who were accompanied by Michael Bryan. He smiled, 'I take it this is not a social visit, your grace?'

'I hope we can make it as pleasant today as possible for Isobel's sake but we do need to speak.'

They adjourned to the library. It was Michael Bryan who spoke to North.

'You are probably aware that his grace and a few of us do our best to further the country's interests while at the same time using our business affairs as a cover for seeking out information and assistance from the many French people who are opposed to the Revolution and more recently Bonaparte's ambitions.

'We have been receiving excellent information from Laborde's son Alexandre but now that things are about to become peaceful between France and England he wishes to concentrate on his private life. Of course we have no confidence that the so-called peace will amount to more than an interlude between wars and we would want to keep our sources of information flowing without interruption. To this end I have been meeting Alexandre's brother François, the Marquis de Méréville, who served in the French navy and who now lives in London.'

North had heard of de Méréville, a sailor who was as admired by his enemies and his was by his countrymen.

'While he was unwilling to involve himself deeply, being in

412

poor health, he agreed to act as a post-box for his brother's letters. Alexandre believes that there is strong evidence that Bonaparte is planning to reform a Grand Army of 100,000 men and make a drive northwards through Poland to seize St Petersburg as soon as the peace with us is concluded.'

North asked, 'How does he hope to hide this scheme from us? As soon as 100,000 men are on the march it will be clearly an act of aggression that we cannot ignore.'

'Poland yearns for freedom and Napoleon has been promising for years that he will drive northwards to free her. He has his Polish legions who serve under him hoping that he will keep his promise. He only has to convince them that he will invade for them to follow him there – twenty or thirty thousand men to which he can add many of the men withdrawn from the Channel coast. Sixty or seventy thousand would not be an unreasonable army and more reinforcements could follow, without any suspicion that the true target is Russia.

'Although we could have an alliance with Russia, we believe it is not one that our government would seek at present; therefore Britain would not intervene. Experience leads to caution where Russia is concerned, of course. Our long-term interests in the Balkans rely on a free Russia but for our government to see that as a compelling reason to go to war again is unlikely.

'We need to know the full extent of Bonaparte's plans. To do so we have brought together three of our best agents and sent them to Paris to gather information. The plan requires that we have fast means of getting reports back to England. Now, on the French side of the Channel we have a well-organised system in place but the weakness is in getting that material

413

across the channel speedily. To this end we have availed ourselves of an unorthodox facility we have enjoyed in the past few years. I speak of Captain Tom Johnstone, do you know of him?'

North replied, 'Not personally but I hear he is little better than a convicted smuggler using the war to keep in with the authorities by passing information on. On the other hand I believe he also piloted Admiral Mitchell's convoy to Den Helder in '99?'

'I share your scepticism, Michael. However, it seems that Captain Johnstone has been thinking ahead as to ways to profit illegally from the peace. He has designed a vessel that is considerably faster and more manoeuvrable than any we have at present – a type of cutter, a cross between a schooner and a galley, crewed with between 25 and 40 men, 40 foot long and seven feet across. It is based on the Deal galleys, fitted with sails and 14 or 18 pairs of oars. If he cannot out-sail a pursuer he believes he can use the oars to row against the wind and lose him that way.

'The Admiralty is very interested in this idea and as a consequence have given a contract to Balthazar Adams and to Peter and George Handley at Gosport to each produce three of these boats as quickly as possible. The Handleys have two ready and they are being taken round to Shoreham as we speak.'

North sat forward in his chair. Shoreham was not far distant from Tarring. He was curious to see these cutter-galleys.

'You will receive orders from the Admiralty that in the cause of secrecy will appear benign enough. You will be seconded to the Revenue Service as officer in command of special measures to counteract smuggling in the area of the Channel between Hastings and Weymouth, though most of that duty will devolve on to the existing customs officers. You will have a duty of oversight in respect of their operations which we believe will be mutually beneficial while providing plausible cover for other activities.

'It seems you will have the frigate *Fisgard* 38 now under Captain Gustavus Spicker as well as *Juniper* and her crew together with seven extra lieutenants, 250 sailors and a company of marines. It would be advisable to make as deep inroads as possible into genuine suppression of the smuggling trade, of course, but the underlying aim is to have two boats lying off the French coast at all times ready to bring off couriers. From time to time you could also carry some of our people in the opposite direction. Of course none of what I have said will be confirmed except at the Admiralty but we thought it useful to prime you with as much information as possible.'

North said, 'It seems like an interesting plan and I suppose there would be no objection to me using Tarring Manor as my base, with a forward post on the coast at Shoreham?'

'That seemed to us to be a good idea, too. We would also appreciate the use of some of your stable space to accommodate fast horses as the first and last point of a relay system we are setting up between here and London.'

North said, 'All the same, I am surprised that Lord Nelson was not entrusted with this enterprise, it has all the earmarks of his trade.'

Bridgwater said, 'John Markham and I agree, all our experience of Nelson is of genius and courage – reckless courage in some cases – but his spontaneous dashing against the enemy does not always produce the best results. His valour and enthusiasm have a crucial place in the scheme of things but there are times when a more subtle and controlled hand on the tiller can produce even better outcomes. If we are to win this peace which comes before renewed war, it will not be by charging full tilt at the problem. A cool but brilliant and incisive mind controlled by a personality that has no use for the trappings of public worship will serve the country better in this phoney peace.'

The phoney peace was to last for exactly 420 days but for Michael North that time was spent just as actively in service to his country as if it was a war.

FIN ......for now.

Author's Note

In telling the fictional story of Michael North I wanted to attempt to weave into the fabric as much factual and historical truth as possible. That particular period of English history is fascinating because the stimuli of war and trade continued and expanded the impetus that created what became the greatest empire the world had ever seen even after losing the United States. In all this the Royal Navy stands as an exceptionally important factor.

The politics of Britain at the time were a continuation of the practices and beliefs of the 18th century and built on a strong foundation of self-interest and privilege and unlike the French system did not fail. As far as the French were concerned, despite the man for the hour – the genius Bonaparte – the Revolution fatally wounded any chance of a successful invasion and subjugation of their island neighbour.

I have tried to treat the real-life personalities in this story fairly and where it has been necessary to speculate on actions and words they *might* have taken the results have been in accordance with what history tells us about them. Entire campaigns such as the Canada expedition and the Chagos Islands project are of course wholly fictional but they would have been feasible.

I am sure that experienced historians would baulk at the way I have made North uniquely advanced in his promotions and there is little doubt that, as in the case of Edward Pellew, promotion into a ship of the line would inevitably have put a crimp into this young captain's career, robbing him of independence. However having through expediency created the situation where he was in effect an acting commodore as soon as he was made post, I justify this on the basis that it would hardly have been seemly for such a capable officer to be reined in so strongly.

Finally a word about the ships themselves. The natives of the British Isles have had the great privilege of being protected for many hundreds of years by what has been the finest navy in the world. Without the Royal Navy and its ships there is little doubt that the chances of losing our freedom would have been very great. I have taken some liberties with certain ships, particularly those that seemingly did not serve again after being captured from the enemy. It is possible that clandestine use of some ships may well have taken place and not recorded, such is the nature of the secret elements of war. Many of the captains and officers are drawn from real life and are as accurately placed in the timeline as possible.

So as the crew of *Prince Rupert* are piped to supper and the sun sets in the west, we will leave her to sail on, for now.

Michael North's story continues in **North to the Baltic Sea.**

Visit us at www.sailingshipsatwar.com

419

Made in the USA
Charleston, SC
20 January 2015

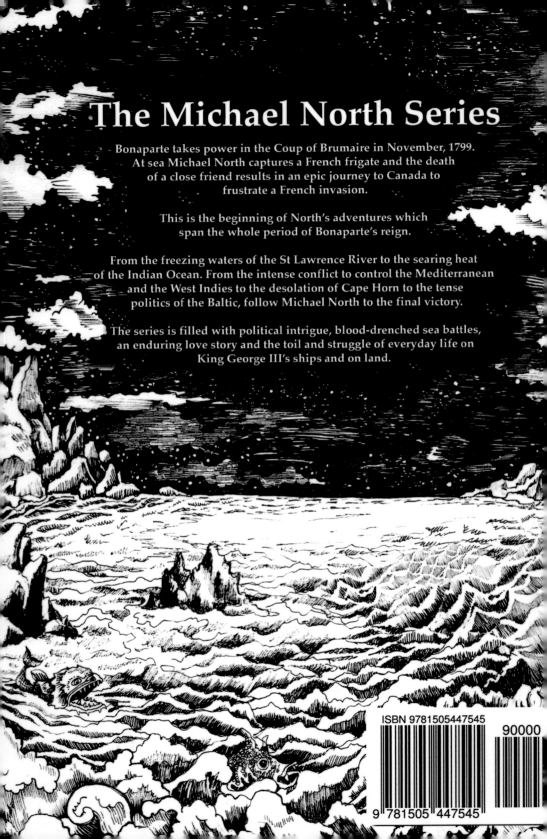

The Michael North Series

Bonaparte takes power in the Coup of Brumaire in November, 1799. At sea Michael North captures a French frigate and the death of a close friend results in an epic journey to Canada to frustrate a French invasion.

This is the beginning of North's adventures which span the whole period of Bonaparte's reign.

From the freezing waters of the St Lawrence River to the searing heat of the Indian Ocean. From the intense conflict to control the Mediterranean and the West Indies to the desolation of Cape Horn to the tense politics of the Baltic, follow Michael North to the final victory.

The series is filled with political intrigue, blood-drenched sea battles, an enduring love story and the toil and struggle of everyday life on King George III's ships and on land.

ISBN 9781505447545

90000

9 781505 447545